SHADOWS
FALL

SHADOWS
FALL

Simon R. Green

BENBELLA BOOKS, INC.

DALLAS, TEXAS

First BenBella Books Edition May 2005

BenBella Books
6440 N. Central Expressway
Suite 617
Dallas, TX 75206
Send feedback to feedback@benbellabooks.com
www.benbellabooks.com

Publisher: Glenn Yeffeth
Editor: Shanna Caughey
Associate Editor: Leah Wilson
Director of Marketing/PR: Laura Watkins

Printed in the United States of America

10 9 8 7 6 5 4 3 2

Library of Congress Cataloging-in-Publication Data

Green, Simon R., 1955–
   Shadows fall / Simon R. Green.-- 1st BenBella Books ed.
      p. cm.
   I. Title.
   PR6107.R44S53 2005
   823'.914--dc22

                                                      2004017167

Cover art copyright © Donato Giancola
Cover design by Laura Watkins

Distributed by Independent Publishers Group
To order call (800) 888-4741
www.ipgbook.com

For special sales, contact Laura Watkins at laura@benbellabooks.com.

List of Characters

LEONARD ASH: He came back from the dead.

RHEA FRAZIER: Mayor of Shadows Fall. A politician.

RICHARD ERIKSON: Sheriff of Shadows Fall. Not known for diplomacy.

SUZANNE DUBOIS: A friend in need.

JAMES HART: After twenty-five years, he's back in Shadows Fall.

DOCTOR NATHANIEL MIRREN: He wanted answers about Life and Death.

SEAN MORRISON: He used to be a great rock and roller.

LESTER GOLD: The Mystery Avenger.

MADELEINE KRESH: A punk with HATE tattooed on both sets of knuckles.

OLD FATHER TIME: Symbol of the Seasons, and of Years. Immortal, sort of.

FATHER IGNATIUS CALLAHAN: A man of great faith.

DEREK and CLIVE MANDERVILLE: Cemetery technicians (gravediggers).

BRUIN BEAR: Every boy's hero and friend.

THE SEA GOAT: Bruin's friend. Nobody's hero.

OBERON: King of the Faerie.

TITANIA: Queen of the Faerie.

PUCK: The only elf who was not perfect.

POLLY COUSINS: Out of her minds.

WILLIAM ROYCE: Imperial Leader of the Warriors of the Cross.

PETER CAULDER: A Warrior who saw the light.

JACK FETCH: Scarecrow.

There's a town where dreams go to die. A place where nightmares end, and hope itself can rest. Where all stories find their ending, all quests are concluded, and every lost soul finds its way home at last. There have always been such places, scattered here and there in the dark corners of the world, but down the years, as science grew and magic waned, much of the wonder went out of the world, and the hidden places grew few and far between. Now there is only the small town of Shadows Fall, tucked away in the back of beyond and overlooked by the everyday world. Few roads lead there, and fewer still lead out again. You won't find Shadows Fall on any map, but it'll be there for you, if you need it badly enough.

You can find all sorts of things at Shadows Fall. There are doors that can take you anywhere, to lands that no longer exist and worlds that some day might. Strange people and stranger creatures walk the sprawling streets, along with everyone you ever knew or hoped you'd never have to meet again. In this far away town, mothers and fathers can find lost children, and children grown old can find their parents once again, to unsay harsh words and angry silences, and heal old wounds that have never been forgotten. In Shadows Fall you can find judgement or forgiveness, old friends and childhood enemies, love or hope or a second chance. It's that kind of place.

Mostly, though, it's a town where people go to die. People, and other things. Shadows Fall is the elephants' graveyard of the supernatural, where people, creatures,

7

concepts and stories go to die when no one believes in them any more. Everything that is believed in strongly enough takes on a kind of presence, a kind of life that persists even after the belief has gone. But there is no room for such as that in the real world. And so they go, travelling through city shadows and back streets no one uses any more, until at last they come to Shadows Fall, step through the Forever Door and pass out of the awareness of the world, for ever. Or they can stay in Shadows Fall, become real, grow old and die a natural death.

At least, that's the idea. The reality, as usual, is much more complicated.

1

Carnival

It was Carnival in Shadows Fall once again. A time of feasting and revelry, parades and fairs, conjurors and costumes and marvels. At the edge of town, tents and stalls had appeared all over Lumpkin Hill as though by magic, springing up overnight like the kind of mushroom that gives unquiet dreams when eaten. Bands played and couples danced, and children ran shrieking through the good-natured crowds, so full of happiness and excitement they felt as if they might explode at any moment, and sprinkle all the people with wild delight and *joie de vivre*.

It was early in the evening in the middle of November, the darkening sky just dark enough to set off the glowing paper lanterns and the occasional spontaneous burst of fireworks. A brisk wind stirred the flags and pennants and the ladies' dresses, and spread the smell of barbecues and roasting chestnuts across the cool evening air, already sharp with the promise of winter. A dozen songs rose and fell, somehow never clashing but always finding some harmony they could agree on.

It was a time of celebration, of life and living; a final farewell for those passing through the Forever Door, and a time of comfort for those who stayed behind, or who had not yet worked up the courage to approach the Door. Even those who are only partly alive can still fear the final darkness, the final mystery. But there was never any pressure or impatience; the Door had always been there, and always would be. In the meantime, it was Carnival, so eat, drink and be merry, for tomorrow is another day in Shadows Fall.

Leonard Ash stood alone by a brightly-coloured tent offering mulled wine, the steaming cup forgotten in his hand. He looked out over the Carnival, watching the people come and go, and wished he could be like them, happy in their everyday lives, full of hope and purpose and meaning. Ash no longer had a future, and though he tried hard not to get too depressed about it, there were times when he missed the simple pleasures of planning things to do, places to go, people to meet. As it was, he went on from day to day, and tried to be content with that.

Ash had been dead almost three years now, but he didn't like to complain. Like everyone else who was no longer entirely real, he could feel the constant call of the Forever Door, but he couldn't leave Shadows Fall. Not yet. He looked out over the crowds at the town below, spread out in the growing gloom, its street lights glowing proudly against the coming night. No one knew how old the town was; it was older even than its own records. Ash used to find its sense of permanence comforting, knowing that one thing at least was constant in an ever-changing world. But since his death he'd discovered a growing sense of resentment at the knowledge that the town would go on quite happily without him, not needing or missing him in the least. He felt his leaving, as and when it finally happened, ought to leave a distinct gap; a space defined by his absence. He could accept the thought that his life hadn't mattered, but he liked to think he'd at least been noticed. He smiled sourly. He'd always been a loner, by choice and temperament, and it was a bit late now to be having second thoughts. But though he would have liked just to plunge into the Carnival crowd and forget his problems in casual revelry, it wasn't in him. He'd always chosen his own path, gone his own way, and the comfort of crowds was denied him.

A stilt-walker lurched past, ducking his head now and again to avoid the strings of lamps criss-crossing above the tents and stalls. He doffed his battered top hat to Ash, who nodded back politely. He'd never liked heights. He looked deliberately in a different direction, and smiled as he spotted an Aunt Sally standing patiently before a dozen small children, her straw-filled stomach acting as a lucky dip for their eager hands. They all found toys or candy, and none of them were disappointed. The female scarecrow looked across at Ash, a contented smile on her cloth face. She raised a ragged arm in greeting, and Ash smiled back stiffly. Even a scarecrow was more alive than he was. He realized he was feeling sorry for himself again, but couldn't bring himself to give a damn. It was a dirty job, but someone had to do it.

He looked around, searching for something to distract him. That was why he'd come out, after all. At the base of the hill, a Yeti and a Bigfoot were giving kids rides on their shoulders. A cartoon mouse with a giant mallet was chasing a cartoon cat. And six different versions of Robin Hood were holding an impromptu archery competition, and arguing more or less good-naturedly as to which of them was the realer. All the usual faces, in other words. Just another evening in Shadows Fall.

Leonard Ash was a tall, gangling sort, with an amiable face and hair that always looked as though it could use a good combing. Even at his best he tended to look as if he'd left the house in a hurry. He had calm, thoughtful eyes that were sometimes grey and sometimes blue, and missed very little. He lived, if that was the right word, with his parents, and had few friends, though that was no one's fault but his own. He'd never been particularly gregarious, even before he died. He was thirty-two, and had been for almost three years now. Nothing special to look at; just another face in the crowd. If you'd asked him, he'd have said he was happy enough, mostly, but he would have had to think about it for a moment first. He looked out over the tents and the stalls and all the people, an ordinary-looking man whose greatest sorrow was that he had no one to dance with. That was about to change, dramatically. He

11

had no right to be surprised. Nothing ever stays the same for long in Shadows Fall.

Not far away, Mayor Rhea Frazier shared a smile and a joke with an elderly couple whose faces were familiar even if their names weren't, and wondered how best to rid herself of the confused-looking man who'd attached himself to her. He'd only just arrived in Shadows Fall, and didn't seem entirely sure what had brought him there. In the meantime, Rhea had made the mistake of showing him a sympathetic face, and he'd latched on to her like a long-lost friend. Rhea didn't mind, except that he was distracting her from her Mayoral duties of shaking hands and exchanging pleasantries with as many voters as possible, while simultaneously reminding them of the upcoming election for Mayor, and her excellent record in that position. Voters tended to forget all the good things you did for them, if you weren't careful to remind them now and again.

Rhea Frazier was a brisk, good-looking black woman in her mid-thirties, with short cropped hair, a direct gaze and a professional smile. She wore fashionable clothes with style and dignity, and had a mind like a rat-trap; solid, reliable and unforgiving. Together with Sheriff Erikson, Rhea Frazier was what passed for authority in Shadows Fall. The town had a way of sorting out its own problems, that was part of its nature, but still there were times when things threatened to get out of hand, and then either Rhea or the Sheriff would step in. She tended to play the voice of reason, and present a sympathetic and impartial ear, while the Sheriff tended to glare at everyone menacingly.

There was a town Court and a town jail, but neither of them saw a lot of use. Few people wanted to cross the Sheriff, so Rhea spent a lot of her time listening to people's troubles, and then directing them to those people in the community who could best help them. She enjoyed her work, and had every intention of continuing it for as long as possible. On the whole, the town seemed happy enough with her work, which was just as well. Shadows Fall had some efficient but not terribly nice ways of dealing with Mayors who couldn't cut the mustard.

Rhea glanced unobtrusively at the man at her side, and thought it was time she did something about him. Adrian Stone was a short, middle-aged man with thinning hair and sad eyes. He kept looking about him in a vague, hopeful way, but was quite unable to tell Rhea what he was looking for, or what had called him to Shadows Fall. It wasn't an uncommon situation. The elderly couple said their goodbyes and moved off into the crowd, and Rhea decided she'd better give her new friend a nudge in the right direction. Like most visitors, he'd lost something or someone precious, and had come to Shadows Fall in search of it. All she had to do was help him remember what it was.

'Tell me, Adrian; are you married?'

Stone smiled, and shook his head almost apologetically. 'No; I never found the right woman. Or she never found me. Anyway, there's only ever been me.'

'How about your parents? Were you very close?'

Stone shrugged, embarrassed, and looked away. 'My father was always away. And my mother was not a . . . demonstrative woman. I never had a brother or a sister, and since we were moving all the time, there were never any friends, really. I never wanted for anything money could buy, but then, money isn't everything, is it?'

'You must have been close to someone,' said Rhea patiently. 'What about the people you work with?'

'You couldn't really call them friends,' said Stone. 'They were just people in the office; someone to smile at and chat with, and wave vague goodbyes to at the end of the day. We kept to ourselves, and concentrated on getting the job done. The management didn't believe in wasted time or idle hands. I didn't mind. I've always been . . . awkward in company, and it was interesting work, mostly.'

Rhea looked at him exasperatedly. 'There must have been someone; some time in your life when you were happy! Think, Adrian! If you could relive any part of your life, any part at all, what would you choose?'

Stone stood silently for a long moment, his gaze turned inwards. And then the clouds lifted from his brow, and he smiled suddenly, looking somehow younger, and more at peace with himself.

'I had a dog called Prince, when I was a boy. A great big boxer dog with an ugly face and a heart as big as he was. I was six years old, and we went everywhere together. I could talk to him, tell him things I couldn't tell anyone else. I loved my dog, and he loved me.'

Stone smiled shyly at Rhea, and she noticed without surprise that he was now less than half his previous age; a slight young man in his mid-twenties. He had all his hair and he stood a little straighter, but his eyes were still sad.

'I suppose everyone thinks their dog is special, but Prince really was. I taught him tricks, and I was never scared or uncertain or alone when he was there. He died just before my seventh birthday. He had a growth, a cancer in his stomach. Apparently boxers are prone to such things, though of course I didn't know that at the time.' He frowned, remembering. He was a teenager now, growing steadily younger as he talked.

'I came home from school one day, and Prince wasn't there. My father told me that he'd taken Prince to the vet, and had him put to sleep. Prince had been ill for some time, growing weaker and thinner, but I'd just assumed he'd get better. I was only six, after all. My father explained to me that Prince wasn't going to get better, ever, that he'd been in a lot of pain, and it really wasn't fair to let him go on suffering. He told me that Prince had been very well-behaved, right to the end. The vet gave him an overdose of anaesthetic, and Prince closed his eyes, and went to sleep for ever. I don't know what the vet did with the body. My father never brought it home. Perhaps he thought it would upset me.'

Adrian Stone looked up at Rhea, his mouth quivering, a six-year-old boy with eyes full of tears he would not shed.

'I loved my dog and he loved me. The only one who ever did.'

Rhea knelt down beside him. 'What did Prince look like? Did he have any special markings?'

'Yes. He had a white mark on his forehead, like a star.'

Rhea took him by the shoulders and turned him gently round. The crowd parted before them to reveal a large boxer dog with a white mark on its forehead. 'Is that him, Adrian?'

'Prince!' The dog's ears pricked up as the boy called his name, and he came bounding forward to leap around the boy like a great overgrown puppy. Adrian Stone, six years old, happy at last, ran off with his dog and vanished into the crowd.

Rhea got to her feet again, and shook her head, smiling slightly. If only all of her problems could be solved that easily. Someone waved to her at the corner of her eye, and she looked round to see Sheriff Richard Erikson making his way towards her. The crowd parted before him, giving him plenty of room. Rhea groaned silently, and wondered what had gone wrong this time. More and more these days, it seemed to her that Richard only sought her out when he had a problem he couldn't solve, so he could dump it in her lap and turn his back on it with a clear conscience. It hadn't always been that way. They'd been friends once, and probably still were, if you stretched the term a bit. She kept all that out of her face, and nodded coolly to Erikson as he came up to her.

The Sheriff was a tall, broad-shouldered man in his mid-thirties with dark hair and darker eyes. He was handsome enough, in an overpowering sort of way, and his great muscular frame gave him a sense of presence that was almost intimidating. Not that Rhea ever allowed herself to be intimidated, by Erikson or anyone else. She smiled briefly at him, and he nodded calmly in return, as though he'd just happened to cross her path.

'Hello, Rhea. You're looking very smart, as always.'

'Thank you, Richard. You're looking very yourself.'

15

He didn't smile. Instead, he looked out over the crowds with a thoughtful, proprietary air. 'A good turn-out, Rhea. Most of the town's here tonight.'

'I should hope so,' said Rhea. 'This is Carnival, after all. One of the few times in the year we all get to let our hair down, and allow our neuroses to run free. A night like this does more to help people than a dozen sessions on a psychiatrist's couch. But then, you don't believe in frivolous things like having a good time, do you?'

'Not when I'm the one who has to keep the peace and clean up the mess afterwards. I'm the one who has to keep an eye on the drunks and the creeps and the troublemakers, and keep the paranormals from settling old scores. Hell, half the community are still carrying hurts and grudges from before they came here, and with the town's magic running loose and wild tonight, that's like throwing fireworks into an open fire. Carnival's a dangerous time to be walking around with an open mind. You never know who might walk in.'

Rhea shrugged. 'We've had this conversation before, Richard, and no doubt will again. We're both right, and we're both wrong, but then, that's Shadows Fall for you. But whatever we say or think, celebrations like Carnival are necessary. They're a safety valve, a mostly harmless way of letting off steam before the pressure gets too great. You worry too much, Richard. The town is quite capable of looking after itself.'

'Yes,' said Erikson. 'It probably is. But the town does what's best for the town, not for the people who live in it. We stand between them and the town, and that's all that makes living here bearable. People weren't meant to live this close to magic; it brings out the worst as well as the best in us.'

Rhea looked at him thoughtfully. 'I can't believe we're actually just standing here chatting, for a change. Are you sure there isn't some dire emergency you want to drop on me from a great height and a safe distance?'

Erikson smiled slightly, but it didn't reach his eyes.

16

'Everything seems to be in order. Or as close as it ever gets in Shadows Fall. But I've a bad feeling about this evening, and it won't go away. If anything, it's getting worse. Have you noticed how many of the paranormals are out tonight, even those who wouldn't normally put in an appearance for anything less than divine intervention? I've seen faces tonight I thought I'd never see, and some I thought were just rumours.'

'What are they doing?' said Rhea, frowning. She tried to look about her without giving the impression of doing so.

'They're not doing anything,' said Erikson. 'They're just . . . waiting. Waiting for something that's going to happen. You can feel the expectancy almost crackling on the air when you get near them. Something's coming to Carnival, Rhea. Something bad.'

Rhea scowled, and glared openly at the crowds around her. Reluctant though she was to admit it, the Sheriff had a point. There was something in the air. There were too many nervous eyes and forced smiles, and laughter that rang too loudly and too long. Nothing special, nothing you could put your finger on, just . . . something. Rhea shuddered suddenly, and had to fight down a growing urge to peer back over her shoulder in case something was creeping up on her. She breathed deeply and pushed the thought firmly aside. There was nothing wrong. It was all in the mind. She'd been perfectly happy with the Carnival until Richard turned up to infect her with his paranoia, and she was damned if she was going to let him spoil her evening.

She searched the surrounding crowd for an excuse that would let her change the subject, and she smiled wryly as her gaze fell on Leonard Ash, talking animatedly with a bronze head on a pedestal. Of course; if everyone else was out and about, it stood to reason he would be too. There was a time when she and Ash and Erikson had been close friends, so close they were practically family. But things changed, as they do, whether people want them to or not.

Erikson became Sheriff, she became Mayor, and Ash died. She remembered standing with Richard at the funeral, wearing a formal black dress that didn't suit her, and throwing a handful of earth down into the grave. She remembered crying. But then he came back from the dead, and she didn't know what to say to him. The man she'd known was dead, and this stranger with a familiar face had no right to Leonard's place in her affections. So she and Ash and Erikson drifted apart, separated by their shared past, until they each had their own lives, and barely nodded to each other in the street.

Rhea shook her head. You'd think living in a place like Shadows Fall would inure you to things like ghosts and revenants, but it was different when it happened to you, or someone you knew. Had it really been three years? Where did the time go . . . Ash always used to be one of the Carnival's main organizers, but he lost interest in a lot of things after he died. She felt a sudden need to talk to him again; him, Leonard Ash, whatever he was now. She squared her shoulders and gave the Sheriff her best business-like look.

'You're making a mountain out of a molehill, Richard. There's nothing wrong here; just people enjoying themselves. Now, if you'll excuse me, there's someone I need to talk to.'

Erikson looked across at Ash, and then back at her. 'Do you really think that's a good idea, Rhea?'

'Yes,' Rhea said flatly.

The Sheriff looked at her for a long moment, until she grew uncomfortable under his gaze, and then he looked away. He sighed quietly. 'Sometimes I wish he'd just go through the Door and get it over with. It's not fair on you.'

He turned and walked away before she could say anything, and she was grateful to him for that, at least. She wouldn't have known what to say anyway. Perhaps that was a sign of how far apart their lives had drifted. There was a time when they could have said anything to each other; anything at all. She looked back at where Ash had been standing, and was immediately relieved when she saw he was no longer there. She didn't know what she would have said to him, either. She shook her head sourly, amused despite herself. She wasn't usually at a loss for words. That was after all one of the reasons why she'd been elected Mayor; she'd talked her opponents into the ground.

She sighed and shrugged and looked around for something to distract her. This was supposed to be one of the few nights of the year when her office became redundant; when she could put her duties and obligations behind her, and just relax for a change. A conga line streamed past her, an endless line of flushed and laughing faces, and Rhea felt a sudden desperate desire to join the line, and laugh and sing and kick with the others. It seemed years since she'd done anything simple and spontaneous, just for the hell of it. But still she hesitated, held back by the dignity of her office, and by the time she'd brushed that aside, the conga line had moved on, leaving her behind, standing alone.

Someone cleared their throat politely behind her, and she spun round, startled at being caught off guard. Leonard Ash smiled at her, and the familiar sight caught at her heart for a moment before she clamped down hard on her memories, and showed him a polite, noncommittal smile.

'Hello, Leonard. Are you enjoying the Carnival?'

'It's very colourful. How are you, Rhea? It's been a while.'

'Being Mayor is a full time job, especially in a town like this.'

'You never came to see me,' said Ash, his gaze direct and unwavering. 'I waited a long time, but you never came.'

'I went to your funeral,' said Rhea, forcing the words out despite a tightening in her throat. 'I said all my goodbyes then.'

'But I'm still here; still me.'

'No, you're not. My friend died, and we buried him, and that's an end to it!'

'Not here, not in Shadows Fall, Rhea. Anything can happen here, if you want it badly enough.'

'No,' said Rhea. 'Not everything. Or you wouldn't be standing here with my dead friend's face and voice, pretending to be him.'

'Rhea; how can I convince you this is me? Really me?'

'You can't.'

They stood there for a long moment, neither wanting to be the first to look away. In the end, Rhea pulled a handkerchief from her sleeve, and pretended to blow her nose.

'So,' said Ash after a while. 'How's life treating you these days?'

'Oh, the usual,' said Rhea, concentrating on tucking the handkerchief back into her sleeve. 'Good days and bad days. The job keeps me busy.'

'Yes. I heard about the trouble with Lucas.'

They shared a grim smile, brought together for a moment by a problem that made their own seem almost trivial. Everyone in Shadows Fall knew about Lucas DeFrenz. When he'd been alive, he'd been nothing special. Ran the local drugstore and liked to second guess doctors' diagnoses. Then he died in a stupid street accident, the kind that could have been avoided if everyone had been paying attention. But Lucas looked the wrong way as he stepped off the kerb, and the driver of the car was daydreaming, and Lucas died in the ambulance taking him to the hospital.

One week later, he came back from the dead. Nobody paid much attention, at first; this was Shadows Fall, after all. Dead men walking were rare, admittedly, but not unheard of. But it didn't take the town long to discover that when Lucas returned from the dead, he'd brought something back with him. Lucas was possessed, by an angel called Michael. The angel was unthinkably powerful, able to work miracles, and could unnerve a whole room just by

20

entering it. He called himself God's Assassin, come to judge the unworthy. He hadn't actually killed anyone yet, but everyone was ready for the other shoe to drop at any time.

'Have you met Michael?' asked Rhea. 'I would have thought the two of you had a lot in common.'

'Hardly,' said Ash. 'I'm just a revenant, a memory of a man made flesh and blood. I don't know what Michael is. Or Lucas, come to that. I take it you've met him?'

'Once. Scared the shit out of me. He walked into my office one morning, and all my potted plants died. The temperature dropped to freezing, and he glowed so brightly I could hardly look at him. But I didn't have to see him; his presence filled the whole office. A deaf and blind man would have known who it was. While he was there I literally couldn't think of anyone or anything but him. He announced he'd come to sit in judgement on the town, told me to go to church more often, smiled, and then left. I always thought angels were supposed to be warm, kindly beings with wings and a halo and a harp fixation. No one ever warned me about things like Michael.'

'You should read your Bible more often,' said Ash. 'The angel Michael is supposed to have slain a dragon with a spear and wrestled with Satan himself. Hard to imagine someone like that lolling about on a cloud in a long nightie. He's here, you know; at the Carnival.'

'Oh great,' said Rhea. 'Just what I needed. What was he doing?'

'Nothing too worrying. Just walking about, glaring at people. Like he was looking for someone. Everyone's been giving him plenty of room.'

'I'm not surprised.' Rhea hesitated for a moment, and Ash winced inwardly. He recognized the look on her face. It was the one people always wore when they were about to ask the Question. The Question everyone asked him sooner or later.

'Leonard; what's it like, being dead?'

'Restful,' said Ash simply. 'It takes a lot of pressure off,

21

knowing nothing's expected of you any more. Of course, sometimes it's frustrating, knowing that my life is over in every way that matters, but I'm still here. There's not much for me to do. I don't eat or drink, unless I choose to, and mostly I don't see the point. Hunger and thirst are things of the past for me, like sleep. I miss sleep, being able to escape from everything for a time. I miss dreaming too. Mostly, I miss having a sense of purpose. Nothing really matters to me, any more. I can't be hurt, but I don't grow old. I can never be more than what I am now. I'm just marking time, waiting to be released, so I can go through the Forever Door, to whatever lies beyond.'

'How long do you think it'll be before your parents release you?'

'I don't know,' said Ash. 'It's my mother, mainly. She needed me so badly she brought me back, and it's her will, her love, her denial that holds me here.' He paused, and held Rhea's eyes with his own. 'It really is me, in every way that matters. I remember everything that happened while I was alive. I remember you, and Richard. The things we did, or were going to do.'

'But that's the point, isn't it?' said Rhea. 'You're not going to do those things any more. You can't. You went away and left me, Leonard. And you couldn't even do that right.'

Her mouth twisted as she fought back sudden tears. Leonard put out his arms as though to hold her, and then lowered them again as she looked at him angrily. She sniffed a few times, and then was back in control, as though it had never happened.

'I'm sorry,' she said brusquely. 'This can't be any easier for you than it is for me, whoever you are.'

'It's something you learn to live with,' said Ash, solemnly.

Rhea smiled reluctantly.

'I walked right into that one, didn't I?'

They smiled at each other. It was a moment that could go either way, and they both knew it. Rhea opened her

22

mouth to say something polite, that would let her walk away, and was honestly surprised when she found herself asking something else entirely.

'Does it frighten you, Leonard, knowing you'll die again, permanently, when you finally go through the Door?'

'Damn right it scares me,' said Ash. 'I'm dead, not crazy. But it's not like I have a choice in the matter. I can't go on like this, and wouldn't if I could. I don't belong here. You know, it never ceases to amaze me that in a town as crammed full of strange and wonderful people as this, I can't find anyone who can give me any clear idea of what lies beyond the Forever Door. There are lots of theories, and any number of religions claiming to know, but there's no real evidence. The only person who might be able to tell me is Lucas, and so far I haven't been able to work up the courage to ask him. Maybe because I'm frightened of what his answer might be. I'd hate to think Heaven was full of people like Michael.

'But this is worse. This . . . limbo. I'm getting fuzzy at the edges. I've started forgetting things; memories, personality traits, all the little things that made up who and what I was. If I don't go through the Door soon, I have a horrible suspicion that I'll just fade away, bit by bit, day by day, till there's nothing left at all. That really does frighten me.'

He stopped abruptly, and smiled briefly at Rhea. 'Sorry. I'm rambling. I've waited for so long for a chance to talk to you. There are so many things I want to say . . .'

He stopped again as he saw her face change. The warmth was gone from her smile, and shutters had come down in her eyes, until there was nothing left before him but the polite and friendly mask she used for strangers.

'You still don't believe I'm me,' said Ash. 'Or maybe you can't afford to believe it. Because then you'd have to open up your heart again, and risk being hurt when I have to leave.'

'I really don't think about it that much,' said Rhea. 'Leonard Ash was a part of my past, and that's where he belongs, with my other memories. Now, if you'll excuse me . . . '

Ash nodded tiredly, and started to offer her his hand to shake before realizing he was still holding his cup of mulled wine. He offered it to her.

'Would you like this? I haven't drunk any; I couldn't taste it anyway. I bought it for the bouquet. I always enjoyed the smell of spiced wine.'

Rhea started to say no, and then took the cup anyway. She was thirsty. She sipped cautiously, and then swallowed hard as the wine seared her tongue. A pleasant warmth filled her head, and seeped slowly down her chest. She smiled at Ash, and then turned away from him. The spiced wine was bringing tears to her eyes. Ash took a step after her, and then they both stopped as a running figure burst out of the crowd and headed right for them.

Suzanne Dubois skidded to a halt before Rhea, and then had to stand and breathe heavily for a moment before she could talk. She looked dishevelled and anxious, but then, she often did. Suzanne was a tall, leggy blonde in her mid-thirties who dressed in accumulated rags and tatters that looked as though they'd come from the Salvation Army's reject box. She was pretty in a Nordic sort of way, all washed-out eyes and prominent cheekbones. She wore her long hair in braids that looked as though she'd run out of patience half-way through. She read tarot cards for a living, and was an unofficial mother figure for anyone who needed one. She looked . . . A sudden tension pulled at Rhea's stomach as she realized Suzanne didn't just look frightened. She looked terrified. Rhea quickly handed her cup to Ash, took Suzanne by the arms and smiled at her reassuringly.

'Take it easy, dear. Get your breath back; I'm not going anywhere. Now what's happened?'

'The Sheriff sent me to find you,' Suzanne said finally, forcing the words out. 'You're to come at once. I can't explain here. Too many ears.'

Rhea and Ash looked about them automatically, but no

one in the surrounding crowds seemed to be paying them any undue attention.

'All right,' said Rhea soothingly. 'I'll come. Lead the way.'

'I'll come too,' said Ash.

'This sounds like official business,' said Rhea. 'There's no need for you to be involved.'

'Stop arguing and come with me!' Suzanne snapped, and then plunged back into the crowd, without looking back to see whether they were following. Rhea glared at Ash exasperatedly, and hurried after Suzanne. Ash threw the cup of wine aside, and followed Rhea. They caught up with Suzanne easily enough. She was too winded to keep up her pace for long. They moved in on either side of her, trying to reassure her with their presence. She smiled briefly at them both, to show she appreciated the intention, but the fear never left her face for a moment.

'Just how bad is this?' said Rhea, beginning to feel worried herself.

'Bad,' said Suzanne. 'Very bad.'

She led them down the side of the hill, past the brightly-coloured tents and awnings, and people gave way automatically before them, reacting as much to Suzanne's urgency as Rhea's authority. A few people called after them curiously, but Rhea just flashed them a quick smile and kept going. It was only a short distance to Suzanne's home, standing alone surrounded by weeds at the edge of the river Tawn. It wasn't much of a place, just a one-room wooden shack held together with tarpaper and rusty nails. Ash shook his head slowly as they approached the shack. Suzanne's friends had been trying to get her to move somewhere more civilized for years, but in this as in so many other things, Suzanne was quietly stubborn, and would not be moved.

There was only one door and one window. A light burned behind the drawn-together curtains, and the door was closed. Suzanne knocked twice, waited a moment, and then knocked again. Rhea and Ash exchanged a glance

25

behind her back. There was the sound of a key turning in the lock, and bolts being pulled back, and then the door swung open, spilling bright lamplight out into the evening gloom. Suzanne darted into the shack, and Rhea and Ash followed her in. They both jumped as someone shut the door behind them.

They spun round to see Sheriff Erikson lock the door and slam home the bolts again. He nodded to Suzanne and Rhea, raised an eyebrow at Ash, and then gestured at the body lying on the floor, the upper half covered by a blanket. Blood had soaked through the blanket by the head, and there was more on the floor. Suzanne dropped into a chair, clearly exhausted, while Rhea knelt by the body. Ash took the opportunity to look around him. It had been some time since he'd visited Suzanne's home, but nothing had changed. The place was still a mess. There was an unmade bed, pushed up against the far wall, with a battered dresser next to it. The broad mirror on the dresser was covered with lipsticked messages from Suzanne to herself, and a motley collection of curling photographs. There were three chairs of varying designs and comfort, mostly buried under old clothes and general junk. Empty fast-food cartons lay scattered across the bare wooden floor. The walls were covered with fading posters from films and shows that never were. The place was a tip, but it was a homely tip, and most of the many people who came to visit Suzanne found it cosy. Ash had always felt at home there.

And then, finally, because he couldn't put it off any longer, Ash looked at the corpse. Rhea had pulled back the blanket to reveal the dead man's head. The skull was crushed and misshapen from what looked like repeated blows. There was blood and brains in the hair, and one side of the face was a bloody ruin, but even so Ash recognized who it was immediately. It was Lucas DeFrenz, the man who claimed to be possessed by the angel Michael.

Suzanne rocked back and forth in her chair, hugging herself tightly to keep from shaking, and carefully not looking at the body. Rhea looked up at the Sheriff, her face professionally calm and unmoved.

'Do we have any witnesses as to when and how he died?'

'No,' said Erikson quietly. 'Suzanne came home half an hour ago and found him lying there. He hasn't been dead long. The blood is still tacky in places. Whatever happened here, it wasn't a robbery gone wrong. He still has his wallet. The money and credit cards haven't been touched.'

'Are you saying this was murder?' Rhea stood up and stared at Erikson, actually shocked. 'There hasn't been a murder in Shadows Fall for centuries. That's part of the nature of the town. Such things can't happen here!'

'Looks a pretty painful way to commit suicide,' commented Ash. Rhea glared at him.

'I've sent for Doctor Mirren,' said the Sheriff quickly. 'He should be here soon. He won't be able to do much, though. We don't have the facilities for a proper forensic examination. We'd have to go outside the town for that.'

'No,' said Rhea immediately. 'If word of this were to get out, the whole town would soon be overrun with outsiders. We can't allow that. There are other ways of getting information from the dead. We'll use those.'

There was a long pause, as they all stared at the dead man.

'Who the hell would be crazy enough to kill an angel?' said Ash.

'Good point,' said Erikson. 'Michael always scared the shit out of me.'

'So our killer couldn't have been just an ordinary man,' said Rhea. 'Whoever did this had to be pretty damned powerful in his own right, just to get near Lucas. Someone so powerful that even God's Assassin couldn't stop him . . .'

Suzanne shivered suddenly. 'And right now, that killer is walking around loose in Shadows Fall, probably already looking for his next victim. We have to warn people.'

'If word gets out too soon there'll be a panic,' said Erikson.

27

'The Sheriff's right,' said Rhea. 'We have to keep a lid on this for as long as we can. If the town's nature has changed so fundamentally, we have to find out what caused the change. And what else is now possible in Shadows Fall.'

'Lucas came back from the dead once,' said Suzanne quietly. 'Perhaps he'll do it again.'

'That's a possibility,' said Erikson. 'But I don't think we should count on it. There are records of quite a few revenants in the town's history, but I never heard of anyone coming back twice. Unless you know better, Leonard?'

Ash shook his head. 'Just because I'm dead, that doesn't make me an expert. Your guess is as good as mine. But there's one question no one's asked yet. Why was Lucas killed *here*?'

'Someone must have told him to come here,' said the Sheriff slowly. 'Someone who knew Suzanne would be out.'

'Which would imply it was someone Lucas trusted,' said Rhea.

'You mean he knew his killer?' said Ash.

Rhea shrugged. Erikson looked thoughtfully at Suzanne. 'Was Lucas a close friend of yours, Suzanne?'

'Not really. I knew him fairly well before he died, but when he came back with Michael he was changed, cold. I didn't even like being in the same room as him. No one did.'

'Or to put it another way,' said Ash, 'there's no shortage of suspects. Michael said he'd come to judge the unworthy, and there's never been any shortage of those in Shadows Fall. Presumably one of them beat Michael to the punch.'

2

Unexpected Answers

It was past midday, and well past the time for a midday meal, when the bus dropped James Hart at the crossroads and roared off in a cloud of exhaust. Hart looked round hopefully for some sign of civilization, preferably a café that served hot food and cold drinks, but all around him the land lay wide and open and empty, for as far as he could see. There were no landmarks, only the two crossing roads heading off into the horizon, both of which had the dusty, faded look of routes that saw little traffic from dawn to dusk and liked it that way. Hart felt a strong temptation to run after the bus and shout for it to stop, but he didn't. His determination and his grandfather's map had got him this far, and he was damned if he'd give up now. He wasn't going to let a little thing like being stranded alone miles from anywhere bother him. Or the fact that he'd had nothing to eat or drink since a very early breakfast, and his stomach was getting restive. Hart's mouth tightened into a straight line. Being hungry didn't matter. Being tired didn't matter. He'd spent four days of hard travelling to get here, and he wouldn't give up now.

He took out his wallet, removed his grandfather's letter and carefully unfolded it. He didn't need to look at it. He'd read and reread the letter so often he could have practically recited it word for word by now, but looking at the map helped. Helped him remember why he'd left everything he'd had or hoped to have behind him, to go chasing off into the middle of nowhere in search of a dream. A dream called Shadows Fall. He studied the single sheet of paper

29

carefully, as though looking for some clue or sign he might somehow have overlooked.

The paper was browned with age, and cracked where it had been folded and unfolded many times. It was a letter from his grandfather to his father, written in that immaculate copperplate hand that no one can be bothered to learn any more. It was the only thing of value Hart had inherited after his mother and father died in the car crash. His mind stumbled over the last part of that thought, as it often did. They'd been dead six months now, and he still found it hard to believe they were really gone. That they weren't there any more to nag him about his clothes or complain about his haircut, or criticize his lack of ambition. He'd gone to the funeral, stared down at the single grave they shared, by their instruction, and said goodbye, but even so sometimes he caught himself listening for the sound of their voices, or a familiar footstep.

The reading of the will hadn't helped much. What money there was went to paying off the burial arrangements and other debts, and the only thing that was left was an envelope, bearing a short inscription in his father's handwriting; *To be opened only in the event of my death, by my son James and no other.* Inside the envelope he'd found his grandfather's letter, giving clear concise directions on how to find the small, out-of-the-way town of Shadows Fall. The town where James Hart had been born thirty-five years ago, and which he had left when he was ten years old. A town he had no memory of at all.

He couldn't remember anything of his early life. His childhood was lost to him, surfacing only rarely in troubled dreams he could barely remember on awakening. His parents had never talked about it, and refused to answer any of his questions, though sometimes he'd overhear brief muttered conversations when they thought he was out of earshot. He heard enough to know they'd fled Shadows Fall in a panic, pursued by someone or something so terrible they wouldn't even hint at it, even with each other. Whatever their secret was, they'd taken it to their grave.

Now he was on his way back to Shadows Fall. And one way or another, he was going to get some answers.

James Hart was an average-height, average-looking man, carrying a little more weight round his middle than he could really afford, but not so much that it worried him. He had more important things to worry about, and it showed in his pinched face and haunted eyes. He wore sloppy, comfortable clothes, and had his long dark hair pulled back in a thin pigtail. It was only midday but already he looked as though he could do with a shave. He also looked very much like someone prepared to stand where he was for one hell of a long time, if that was what it took.

Though if truth be told, it wasn't just stubbornness. He stood there, a man alone in the middle of nowhere, and wondered uneasily if he really wanted to take this last, final step of his journey. Whatever it was that had scared his parents into leaving Shadows Fall twenty-five years earlier, it had been so bad it kept them silent for the rest of their lives. It was only sensible that he should have strong reservations about walking blindly into possible enemy territory. But the bottom line was, there was a great gaping hole in his life, and he needed to know what he'd lost. Part of what made him tick, a central formative period of his life, was a mystery, and he had to try and solve it if he was ever to be at peace with himself. Anything would be better than the endless horror of not knowing who and what he really was. Anything.

He sighed and shrugged and scuffed his shoes on the ground, and wondered what to do next. The map had brought him this far, but it ended at the crossroads. And the final instructions in the letter made no sense at all. According to his grandfather, all he had to do now was call to the town, and it would do the rest. He looked carefully about him, but the world stretched away alone and empty for as far as he could see.

This is crazy. Grandfather was crazy. There's no town here.

He shrugged again. What the hell. He'd come this far,

31

he might as well go the whole hog. Arise ye prisoners of reality; you have nothing to lose but your marbles. He carefully refolded the letter, tucked it back into his wallet, and put it away. He cleared his throat uneasily.

'Shadows Fall? Hello, Shadows Fall! Can you hear me? Can anybody hear me?'

Nothing. No response. The wind murmured to itself.

'Dammit, I've come a long way to be here, so show yourself! My name is James Hart, and I have a right to be here!'

The town was all around him. There was no fanfare of trumpets, no sudden rush of vertigo or swimming senses. Just one minute there was nothing, and then Shadows Fall was there, looking real and concrete and inflexible, as though it had always been there. He was standing in the outskirts of the town, and the streets and houses spread out before him, open and pleasant and indisputably real. There was even a charming little sign, saying *Welcome to Shadows Fall. Please drive carefully.* He wasn't sure exactly what he'd been expecting, but this ordinary every-day location wasn't it. He looked behind him, and wasn't at all surprised to find the crossroads had vanished, replaced by rolling grassy fields and low hills.

He smiled briefly. Whatever happened now, he'd finally come home. And he didn't intend to leave without some hard answers. He looked slowly about him, but none of it looked familiar. He supposed he shouldn't be surprised; a town can change a lot in twenty-five years. And yet even as he thought that, something that might have been memories danced at the edge of his thoughts; dim and out of focus for the moment, but still full of hints and implications and meaning. He didn't try to force them. They would come out into the light when they were ready. He realized suddenly that all his doubts and uncertainties had vanished. There were answers here; he could feel it. Answers for all the questions he'd ever had. Somewhere in this small town his lost childhood was waiting for him to come and find it, and with it the early lives of his parents.

And perhaps he'd also find what he really came to look for; some kind of meaning or purpose in his life.

He walked unhurriedly down the street and into the town. It looked open, warm, even friendly. Nice houses, neat lawns, clean streets. There weren't many people about, but they nodded pleasantly enough to him as he passed. A few even smiled. To look at, Shadows Fall could have been any town, anywhere; but Hart didn't think so. A feeling, then a certainty grew in him as he made his way through the town, heading for the centre as though by instinct. This was a place of possibilities. He could sense it, feel it in his bones and in his water. He had a sudden strong feeling of *déjà vu*, of having walked this street before. Perhaps he had, when he'd been younger. He tried to hang on to the memory, but it slipped away and was gone in a moment. It didn't bother him. It was a good sign, and he had no doubt the memory would return when it was ready. Perhaps it would bring a few friends back with it. Probably felt lonely out on its own.

He smiled, feeling pleasantly light-headed. His confidence was growing all the time. A feeling of simple peace suffused him, together with a sense of belonging, of coming home, he'd never felt before. Certainly not in any of the faceless houses and schools he'd attended down the years as he followed his father from posting to posting. The Company didn't like its people having roots or preoccupations outside the Company. It wanted to be thought of as home, family and loved one, first and foremost. It didn't like the idea of conflicting loyalties. And as long as the Company kept its people in a constant state of flux, unable to form outside attachments, it worked quite well. Hart smiled, nodding to himself. He'd never thought of it that way before. Just being in the town had cleared his mind like a whiff of oxygen. He was thinking more clearly, understanding things that had puzzled him for years. It was only too clear to him now why he'd turned his back on the Company and its kind, and become a journalist, a seeker after secrets and hidden truths. Even then, he'd really been searching for his own secret truths. Sublimation is a wonderful thing.

A steady putt-putting sound nagged at his attention, and he looked round vaguely, trying to place it. It sounded like one of those old-fashioned lawnmowers that produce far more noise than its work can ever justify. He finally noticed a handful of people looking up at the sky, and he tilted his head back to see what they were looking at. And there, hanging high above them, was the source of the noise; a First World War biplane, puttering through the cloudless sky. The plane was bright crimson in colour, and it moved lazily, effortlessly along, its short stubby wings held together by thin metal struts and good faith. Hart grinned up at the plane. He wanted to wave at it, but was worried the others would look at him, so he didn't.

And then another biplane appeared out of nowhere, a faded khaki colour with British markings. It plummeted down towards the red plane like a striking bird of prey, and Hart's jaw dropped as he heard the unmistakable sound of automatic gunfire. The red plane banked suddenly to one side, sweeping out from under the other plane's attack. The British plane plunged on, unable to stop, and the red biplane swung round in a viciously tight curve that put it right on the tail of its enemy. Once again there was the harsh chatter of gunfire, and Hart winced as the British plane shuddered under the impact, dodging desperately from side to side to try and escape the hail of bullets.

The two planes swooped and dived around each other like squabbling hawks, neither able to gain the advantage for long, both pilots pushing their planes and their skills to the limit and beyond. The fight could only have lasted a few minutes, but to Hart it seemed like hours, both planes escaping death and destruction by inches again and again. They flew at each other like Japanese fighting fish, all fury and aggression, attacking and retaliating, swooping together and roaring apart while Hart watched, entranced. And then suddenly smoke billowed from the British plane, thick and black and shot with flying sparks. The nose dropped and the plane fell like a stone, flames leaping up around the engine casing.

Hart watched the plane fall, his hands clenched into fists, silently willing the pilot to bail out while there was still time. But there was no sign of the pilot anywhere. Hart looked at the small crowd of people watching with him.

'Why doesn't he jump? If he doesn't jump soon there won't be time for his parachute to open!'

An old man looked at him sympathetically, and when he spoke his voice was calm and kind and utterly resigned. 'He can't jump, son. That's a First World War plane. Pilots didn't have parachutes then. Wasn't enough room in the cockpit for a pilot and a parachute.'

Hart gaped at him. 'You mean he's . . .'

'Yes, son. He's going to die.'

The plane smashed into a low hill some distance outside the town, and exploded in a rush of flames. Hart watched numbly as shrapnel from the explosion pattered down like hailstones. Black smoke rose up in billowing clouds, and high above the red biplane soared on, alone and supreme and unchallenged. The old man patted Hart reassuringly on the shoulder.

'Don't take it so hard. This time tomorrow they'll be up there fighting again, and maybe then the British plane will win. He does sometimes.'

Hart looked at him. 'You mean that wasn't real?'

'Oh, it was real enough. But life and death aren't that simple in Shadows Fall. They've been fighting that duel for as long as I can remember. God knows why.' He smiled at Hart, not unkindly. 'You're a newcomer, aren't you?'

'Yes,' said Hart, making himself look away from the crashed plane and concentrate on the old man. 'Yes. I've only just arrived.'

'Thought so. You'll see stranger than this after you've been here a while. Don't let any of it worry you. Things happen here. That's the way it is, in Shadows Fall.'

He nodded a goodbye, and then continued on his way. The rest of the small crowd was already dispersing. They went on about their business, chatting quietly as though this was just another day. Hart looked up at the cloudless sky, but there was no sign of the red biplane anywhere. He moved slowly away, his racing heart only now beginning to slow.

He turned a sudden corner, and found himself walking down a Paris street. He recognized the style and the language and the sidewalk cafés. No one paid him any attention, though he gawked shamelessly like the most obvious tourist. He turned another corner and found himself in what appeared to be Europe in the Dark Ages. The road was a dirt track, and people and animals milled this way and that, all talking at once so that the air was full of sound. He didn't recognize any of the languages. A few people glared suspiciously at Hart as he passed, but most just nodded politely. He trudged on through the thick mud and soon left the past behind him.

He passed through a dozen moments of history, different places with different styles and languages, from day to night and back again, and everywhere he went people smiled at him as though to say, *Isn't this fun? Isn't this marvellous?* And Hart smiled and nodded back, *Yes, it is marvellous. Yes, it is.* And just as suddenly he was back where he belonged, in the familiar world of cars and traffic lights and rock-and-roll blasting from a teenager's ghetto blaster. He walked on, and the street stayed the same, and he didn't know whether to feel relieved or disappointed.

He came to a park and sat down on a wooden bench, to rest his mind as much as his feet. Two children in Ninja Turtles T-shirts were throwing a ball for their dog, a great shaggy beast of indeterminate breed, which seemed to be having some difficulty following the rules of the game. Sometimes it would chase after the ball, and other times it would just sit there and look at the boys, as if to say, *You threw the ball, you go and fetch it.* The dog looked across at Hart with bright, laughing eyes, its tongue lolling out of the side of its mouth. Hart decided he identified with the dog. Shadows Fall was playing a game with him, and he wasn't sure if he wanted to play or not.

He looked unhurriedly about him, studying the park. It seemed tantalizingly familiar, like a word on the tip of your tongue that continues to elude you. His gaze stumbled over a great stone cenotaph in the middle of the park, and he felt a sudden thrill of almost recognition. The tomb looked harsh and uncompromising; a great solid block of stone on a raised dais, with letters etched into its side. Hart got up from the bench and walked over to get a better look at it. The words turned out to be Latin, a language he had only a vague familiarity with, but he recognized the word Tempus, set over a stylized bas-relief carving of Old Father Time, complete with long beard, scythe and hourglass.

'You look lost,' said a voice behind him, and Hart spun round, startled, to find himself facing a man about his own age, tall and dark-haired with a friendly smile and vague eyes. 'I'm Leonard Ash. Can I help you in any way?'

'I don't know,' said Hart carefully. 'Maybe you can. I'm James Hart. I was born here, but I left town when I was still a child. This is my first time back. I don't remember any of this at all.'

'You wouldn't,' said Ash. 'The town adjusts your memory when you leave. Nothing personal. It's just a defence mechanism, to protect the town. After you've been here a while, all your old memories will come back to you. Better hold on to your hat, James. It's likely to be a bumpy ride.'

'Thanks,' said Hart. 'That's very reassuring. Look; what the hell kind of place is this? I've been seeing all kinds of strange stuff . . .'

'And you'll see more. Shadows Fall is a magnet for the strange and unusual. Not to mention unnatural. Just by being what it is, the town attracts people and places from all over. This is a place of magic and destiny, James. The beginning and end of all stories. You can find anyone or anything here. If they want to be found.'

'Listen,' said Hart, just a little desperately, 'It's a hot

day, and I've come a long way. Before you destroy my sanity completely, is there any place around here where I can get a cold drink and something to eat?'

'Oh sure,' said Ash. 'I don't notice things like the heat any more. Come with me. There's a decent little bar just around the corner; if it hasn't moved itself again.'

He strode away, without looking back to see if Hart was following. Hart shook his head slowly, and hurried after him. If nothing else, Ash seemed willing to provide answers, even if they didn't make much sense.

'That cenotaph,' he said, drawing alongside Ash. 'Whose tomb is it? Who does it commemorate?'

'The Sarcophagus, you mean? That's the tomb for Old Father Time, celebrating his death and rebirth at the end of each year.'

'Old Father Time,' said Hart.

'That's right. If anyone could be said to be in charge around here, it's him. He symbolizes the passing of time and the changing of the seasons, death and rebirth. Which makes him the most powerful being in Shadows Fall, though he prefers not to get involved unless he absolutely has to. Think of him as a kind of umpire, making sure everyone sticks to the rules. Shadows Fall tends to the chaotic as a matter of course, but you can always depend on Time to put things right. He's a nice old fellow; I'll take you to see him later on, if you like.'

Hart looked at him. 'Would you mind running all that past me again; I think I fell off at the corner.'

Ash laughed, not unkindly. 'Sorry; it's just that you've come to a rather complicated place, and it plays hell with explanations. It's best on the whole just to take things as they come. Keep your eyes and ears open, and your guard up. Things will become clearer after you've been here for a while. Or as clear as they're ever likely to get. This is Shadows Fall. We do things differently here.'

They left the park behind them and walked down a street that looked reassuringly normal, until Hart happened to notice a gargoyle high up on a building casually buffing its claws with an emery file. A few people nodded to Ash, and he smiled vaguely at them in return.

'Why does the period keep changing?' Hart said finally, checking an approaching intersection cautiously. 'Half the time I cross a street I end up in a different century.'

'Time is relative here,' said Ash casually. 'Only don't ask me relative to what. Basically, things, people and places end up here because they belong here, and naturally those of a particular period prefer to stick together. Which is why one area has electricity and sewers, and another has medieval squalor with hot and cold running plagues. And by the way, stay well clear of the park after it gets dark. It tends towards dinosaurs. Is any of this starting to seem familiar to you?'

'No,' said Hart. 'I can't honestly say that it is. Are we far from this bar, only a stiff drink is seeming more and more necessary by the minute.'

'Almost there,' said Ash. 'You'll like it, it's very restful. James Hart . . . you know, the more I think about it, the more familiar that sounds. Wouldn't it be fun if it turned out we were actually old friends, and didn't know it? It's quite possible. This town is lousy with coincidences. Ah, here we are . . .'

Hart studied the exterior of the bar suspiciously, but it seemed normal enough. Even so, he gestured for Ash to lead the way in. Inside it was pleasantly cool, the light just dim enough to be easy on the eye without being gloomy. Ash found them a table at the rear, and Hart settled himself comfortably while Ash went in search of liquid refreshment. There were half a dozen people scattered across the room, all of them reassuringly ordinary to the eye. It seemed pleasant enough, especially when compared to the grubby watering holes he usually did his drinking in. The kind of place where there's no sawdust on the floor because the cockroaches have eaten it, and the glasses get dirtier when you wash them. Ash came back with two beers in frosted glasses, and Hart downed almost half of his in quick, desperate gulps. He sat back and sighed

39

quietly, relishing the delicious chill as it moved slowly down his chest. He noticed Ash wasn't drinking with him, and raised an eyebrow.

'Something wrong with your beer?'

'No,' said Ash. 'Something wrong with me. I don't drink any more, but I still like the smell, and the feel of a cold glass in my hand. Please don't let me stop you. Drink up.'

Hart gave him a long, thoughtful look, then shrugged mentally and drank some more of his beer. Ash seemed harmless enough, and he'd seen a lot stranger things in Shadows Fall than a man ordering a beer and not drinking it.

'So,' he said finally. 'You think you remember me as a kid? What was I like?'

'I don't really know,' said Ash, frowning. 'It was a long time ago, after all. You were probably a bit of a toad, like most kids that age. I think back on some of the things I got away with, and it amazes me I ever survived to reach puberty. If you are the one I'm thinking of, you were very good at football, and even better at faking an illness whenever a teacher threatened a test. Ring any bells?' Hart shook his head, and Ash shrugged. 'Don't push it, James. You'll remember everything, eventually. Whether you want to or not. What brings you back here, after all these years?'

'My parents died suddenly,' said Hart, staring into his glass. 'That started me thinking about my past. Then I was made redundant, almost literally overnight, and I needed something to do. Something to keep me occupied. So here I am.'

Ash looked at him thoughtfully. 'I have to warn you, James; you've chosen a bad time to return. Shadows Fall isn't at its best right now. There's a lot of anger and suspicion in the air, and it's manifesting in rather unpleasant ways. To some extent, the town reflects the mood of those who live here, and the current climate is stirring up images and memories that would have been better left undisturbed.'

'Why?' said Hart. 'What's happened?'

Ash met his gaze steadily. 'Seven people have been murdered, all in the space of a few weeks. Beaten to death with a blunt instrument. We've no clues, no suspects; nothing to point us in the right direction. There doesn't seem to be any connection between the victims, so we have no way of predicting who the next victim might be. The whole town's in a panic. Because of the town's special nature we can't call in outsiders to help, so we're forced to rely on our own resources. Which are strained, to say the least. Our Sheriff is doing his best, but . . . ah, speak of the Devil and up he pops. The large gentleman heading in our direction is Sheriff Richard Erikson. Not a bad sort. For a Sheriff.'

He waved languidly at a dim figure by the door. Hart was impressed. Whatever else you could say about Ash, it seemed he had excellent eyesight. The Sheriff arrived at their table, looming ominously over them with an unsmiling countenance. Ash nodded to him, blatantly unimpressed, and gestured at an empty chair. The Sheriff sat down, sighing heavily as he stretched out his long legs. Ash made the introductions, and Hart nodded politely to Erikson. The Sheriff was a big man, not entirely overpowering, but definitely a powerful presence. Erikson looked at Hart thoughtfully.

'We would have been contemporaries,' he said slowly, 'But I can't say I remember you. You should look by the old school, check out their records. But I do remember your parents, Mr Hart. So should you, Leonard. There was quite an upset at the time.'

Ash sat up straight, and looked at Hart with new interest. 'That Hart? You're *their* son?'

'Apparently,' said Hart stiffly, not sure he liked the Sheriff's tone or Ash's reaction. 'I'd be interested in anything you could tell me about my parents, or my time here. Do you know why they left?'

'I remember,' said the Sheriff. There was something that might have been sympathy in his stern face, but Hart

41

didn't relax. There was something bad coming in his direction. He could feel it, like the tremor of an approaching train in the steel tracks. The Sheriff leaned forward, lowering his voice. 'I don't know all the details. I don't think anybody does, except possibly Old Father Time, but twenty-five years ago there was a prophecy concerning your parents. Something to do with them and the destruction of the Forever Door. Whatever the prophecy was, your parents sold off everything they had, took you and left town, all in less than twenty-four hours.'

'That's it?' said Hart, as the Sheriff paused. 'They just upped and left because of a damned fortune-teller?'

Erikson met his gaze steadily. 'We take prophecies seriously here, Mr Hart. There are quite a few residents in Shadows Fall with some form of access to the future. When they talk, we listen.'

'Wait a minute,' said Ash, frowning. 'With a prophecy of that importance, involving the Forever Door itself, why were they allowed to leave?'

'Good question,' said the Sheriff.

'All right,' said Ash, when it was clear the Sheriff had nothing more to say. 'What about the town records? There should be some kind of record of the prophecy.'

'That's right,' said Erikson. 'There should. But there isn't. It's one of the great unsolved mysteries of the last twenty-five years. Which is why I find it rather strange that you should choose to return just now, Mr Hart, when the town is tearing itself apart. Are you sure you don't know anything about this prophecy?'

'Not a damned thing,' said Hart steadily. 'I have no memories of my time here, and my parents never talked of it. But now I'm here, I want to know more about it. Is there anyone I could talk to who might know something?'

'Old Father Time,' said Ash. 'He's your man. He knows everything. Mostly.'

'Would he see me?' said Hart. Ash looked at Erikson, who shrugged.

'He might. But don't expect too much from him. He's

42

in the last part of his cycle, and his memory isn't what it was. I have to go and see him myself later today. You can come along if you like, Mr Hart.'

'Thanks,' said Hart. 'I'd like that.'

'I'm coming too,' said Ash. 'I'm not missing this.'

Erikson gave him a hard look, and then shrugged. 'Why not? The way things are at the moment, I can use all the friends I can get.'

Ash nodded understandingly. 'Pressure still coming down from Above?'

'From everywhere. I'm doing all I can, but I don't have the training for this. Never thought I'd need it. Murder is supposed to be impossible here. That's part of the town's nature; the only thing that makes it possible for so many conflicting parties to co-exist here peacefully. If that's changed, for whatever reason, we're in serious trouble. Right now, it's taking everything I've got just to keep the peace. Are you going to drink that beer, Leonard? If not, pass it over here.'

Ash handed him the glass. 'I seem to recall something about officers of the law not drinking when they're on duty.'

'I think you have me confused with someone who gives a shit.' Erikson drank deeply, and then sighed wistfully. 'What do you say; let's take the afternoon off and really tie one on. I need a break. Come on; let's get drunk and chase women.'

'I don't think . . .' said Hart.

'All right; let's get women and chase drunks. I don't care.'

Ash looked at Hart. 'The trouble is, I think he means it.'

There was a sudden commotion over by the bar, and they all turned to look. Half a dozen six-foot pixies with Technicolor hair and a weight problem were pushing and shoving an equal number of grizzly bears wearing biker's jackets and chains. The bears had started shoving back, and the language was appalling. Erikson sighed heavily, and got to his feet.

43

'No rest for the wicked. Or those who might be wicked, given half a chance. I'd better do something before they wreck the place. See you again, Leonard, Mr Hart. Hope it all works out.'

He strode purposefully towards the disturbance at the bar. Ash shook his head dolefully. 'The neighbourhood is going to hell, James. Either that, or hell is coming to the neighbourhood. One or the other. The town is not what it was.'

Hart looked at Ash steadily. 'Excuse me if I'm getting too personal, Leonard, but is there something about yourself you're not telling me? I mean; you don't drink, you don't feel the heat . . . and why are you dressed all in black?'

Ash smiled. 'I'm in mourning for my sex life. And yes; there is something I haven't been meaning to tell you. I'm a revenant, James. I died, and came back.'

Hart sat up straight. The air seemed suddenly colder. He could feel his gut muscles tightening and the hair on the back of his neck rising as he realized Ash was quite serious. He cleared his throat carefully, not wanting his voice to be unsteady when he spoke. 'You're a ghost?'

'No,' said Ash patiently. 'I'm a revenant. I have a body just as you do. Only yours is real and mine isn't. It's all very complicated. I don't understand it all myself. The condition doesn't exactly come with a user's manual, you know.'

Hart looked at him thoughtfully, and Ash winced internally. He knew that expression. It meant the Question was coming.

'So,' said Hart casually. 'What's it like, being dead?'

'I don't know. I wasn't really dead long enough to get the hang of it. What I do remember is pretty hazy. I had all the usual near-death and out-of-the-body experiences: hurtling down a long tunnel towards a brilliant light, hearing loud and mysterious voices. But maybe I only saw those things because I expected to. For all I know, they could have been just the last echoes of birth trauma. I'll say this much for being dead; it means you're never at a loss for something to talk about. It's a great ice-breaker at parties. No matter how messed up your life is, it's got to be better than mine.'

'At least you can remember your life,' said Hart. 'Ten years of mine are missing. Leonard; are ghosts . . . commonplace here? Do all ghosts come to Shadows Fall?'

'Not without good reason. Why do you ask?'

'I just thought . . . my parents might . . .'

'I'm sorry,' said Ash. 'It's really not very likely. Look, let's go and see Old Father Time. He understands more about these things than I do. And he should definitely know something about your prophecy and missing childhood. Assuming he can remember who he is today.'

Hart frowned. 'Is he senile, or something?'

'Something,' said Ash. 'Definitely something.'

He got to his feet and waited patiently while Hart drank the last of his beer. Hart put the empty glass down, and looked over at the bar. The bears and the pixies had left, and so had the Sheriff. The only person at the bar now was a large day-glo pony with its head buried in a bucket of champagne. It was wearing stockings and suspenders and heavy eye makeup. Hart decided he wasn't going to ask. He didn't think he really wanted to know. He got to his feet and nodded to Ash, who led the way out on to the street.

'We'll try the Gallery of Bone first,' said Ash. 'And let us hope and pray he's in a good mood.'

'And if he isn't?'

'Then we run like hell. That scythe of his isn't just for show, you know.'

The Morgue was bitter cold, but Rhea had expected that. What she hadn't expected was to be kept waiting in the cold for almost twenty minutes. What was the point in being Mayor if you couldn't make people jump when you snapped your fingers? Of course, Mirren had always been

45

a law unto himself, like most doctors. Rhea hugged herself, and wished she'd worn a heavier coat.

The Morgue wasn't very large, as Morgues go, barely twenty feet square, but the snow and ice caking the tiled walls and ceiling made it look even smaller. Icicles hung from every surface, and a faint hint of fog pearled the air. Whoever had set up the freezing spell to save relying on a generator's electricity had done their work perhaps a little too well. If it had been any colder, the Morgue would have been full of polar bears doing . . . well, whatever it is polar bears do. Rhea realized she'd lost track of the thought, and let it go.

A single body lay on the examination table, respectfully covered with a sheet, for which Rhea was grateful. She'd seen the state of the other corpses, and was in no hurry to see the damage done to this one. His name was Oliver Lando. Used to be a detective in a series of stories written in the sixties. His brief star soon faded, and by the seventies no one remembered him save a few collectors. He came to Shadows Fall in 1987. And that was the last anyone had heard of him till now. Rhea had never heard of him at all, till she read Erikson's file on him.

She jumped despite herself when the door slammed open behind her. She took her time turning to glare at Doctor Mirren as he slammed the door shut again, but he only had eyes for the body on the table and the clipboard in his hand. Doctor Nathaniel Mirren was a short, squat man in his early forties, with an unhappy face and a receding hairline. He was brusque, sarcastic, and didn't suffer fools gladly. His bedside manner was just short of distressing. But he was an expert at diagnosis and puzzle-solving, so everyone made allowances, and bit their lip a lot when they had to have dealings with him. Rhea knew him of old. They'd crossed swords more than once on the town Council over town funding for his various researches. Every time she had to meet him, she swore she wouldn't let him get under her skin. And every time he did it to her again. He could put her teeth on edge just by the way he entered a room and pretended not to see her. She glared at his unresponsive back as he stalked over to glare at the body on the table, then took a deep breath and moved over to join him.

'Well, Doctor? Did the autopsy reveal anything useful this time?'

'Not really,' said Mirren. He scowled at his clipboard, sniffed once as though in disgust, and dropped it carelessly on to the corpse's chest. Rhea winced in sympathy. Mirren pulled back the sheet to reveal what was left of the victim's head, and Rhea fought to keep her face calm. The skull was a mess of torn skin and broken bone, held together by dried blood. One side of the head had collapsed inwards, and the features were indistinguishable. The teeth were broken and shattered, the jaw hanging loosely, barely attached to the head. Mirren touched the head here and there with surprisingly gentle fingers, then covered the bloody mess with the sheet and picked up his clipboard again.

'As with the previous six victims, death resulted from extensive damage to the head. A frenzied attack. From close examination of the various injuries, I was able to determine that the damage was caused by a blunt instrument of some weight, probably metal, approximately one inch in width. I counted no less than seventy-three separate injuries, undoubtedly delivered in swift succession.

'I can determine the time of death fairly accurately. The victim's watch was smashed, presumably when he lifted the arm to protect his head, and the watch face shows ten minutes past five. This would agree with the state of the partially digested meal in his stomach. And that is as far as my examination has taken me. Anything more would be guesswork.'

He dropped the clipboard back on to the corpse's chest and glowered at Rhea, as though daring her to disagree with anything he'd said. Rhea pursed her lips thoughtfully, and let him wait a moment or two before speaking.

47

'Seventy-three blows in swift succession. A frenzied attack. Could our murderer be . . . more than human?'

Mirren sniffed and frowned, as though considering the question, but Rhea had no doubt the thought had already occurred to him.

'This could be the result of an inhuman or paranormal attack, but I would have to say it could also have been accomplished by a normal human, if sufficiently strongly motivated. You'd be surprised how much damage a man can do, while in the grip of rage or terror.'

'What about forensic evidence? Have you found anything that might help us identify the attacker?'

Mirren looked away for a moment, his scowl deepening. He always hated having to admit anything that might seem a failure on his part. 'Forensic medicine is not my field. You need an expert for that, and we don't have one in Shadows Fall. I have performed as thorough an inspection of the body as I could with my limited equipment, and found nothing of any use. Which is only what I expected. If we are to proceed any further in this investigation, you must allow me to use my own methods.'

'I don't believe in necromancy,' said Rhea flatly. 'The dead should be left to rest in peace.'

'Your prejudice arises mostly from ignorance,' said Mirren, barely bothering to hide the contempt in his voice. 'We don't have the time for such squeamishness any more. All the previous victims were brought to me too late, but I can do something with this one. Provided you don't interfere.'

'Have you contacted the next of kin?'

'Doesn't appear to be any. This is your decision, Ms Mayor.'

'What precisely did you have in mind?' said Rhea reluctantly, and Mirren smiled.

'First a sample scrying; see what can be seen through his blood. Then I'll call his spirit back, bind it with Words of Power and ask it questions. We're near enough to the Forever Door that I can tap some of its power and break through the Veil, enabling us to have a nice little chat with the dear departed. But you'd better make up your mind quickly. The silver cord that links the spirit to this body is growing weaker by the minute. It'll break soon, and then even I won't be able to call him back.'

'Do it,' said Rhea. 'Do whatever you have to.'

Mirren had enough sense to smile only briefly before turning away to rummage through the instruments in his bag. Rhea looked away, and folded her arms tightly across her chest. There was a chill in her bones that had nothing to do with the coldness of the Morgue. They were treading dangerous ground now, and Mirren wasn't anywhere near as skilled in the Art as he liked to believe. If there'd been anyone else . . . but there was no one else she could trust, and he knew it. And she was, after all, desperate for any kind of lead. Four men and three women were dead, and the Sheriff hadn't been able to provide her with a single suspect. So now she had no choice but to put aside her misgivings and her scruples and turn to Mirren, in the hope his dark magics might help where science had failed her. She had to put her faith in someone.

The trouble was that as Mayor, everyone turned to her for answers and decisions. But there was never anyone she could turn to. Her family didn't understand the pressures, Erikson was always busy, and Ash was dead. She was alone, forced to be the solid rock to which everyone else clung. Only some days she didn't feel like a rock at all. She smiled briefly. She'd known what she was getting into when she campaigned for the job of Mayor. Only the dedicated, the obsessive and the more than slightly crazy could handle all the things the job entailed. You couldn't deal with the casual insanity of Shadows Fall day after day without some of it rubbing off on you. Rhea didn't give a damn. Mostly. She'd wanted the job because she'd known she could do it. She was proud of her record. Or had been, till the murders started. Now every new death was like a slap in the face, a reminder not just of her continuing failure to stop the murders, but also, on a deeper level, of her failure to understand and control the nature of the town itself.

There was a time she'd thought she understood the town, but it had grown and changed dramatically even in the four years she'd been in office. Shadows Fall had only ever been intended as a resting place for those the Forever Door called. A place to stop and say goodbye, before going on to death or destiny. But over the years more and more people had turned away from the call of the Door, and settled for the strange reality of Shadows Fall rather than face the unknown. The town's population had more than doubled in the last twenty years, and while its enchantments kept the town safe and protected from the outside world, the growing mass of people stretched and tested the magic's limits more and more every day. Something would have to be done, and soon, but for the moment she was forced to spend all her waking hours trying to solve the mystery of the murders. There just weren't enough hours in the day to worry about both.

She pushed the thought to one side, and made herself concentrate on Doctor Mirren. He took a test-tube full of blood from a rack on the table and poured it out on to a silver platter, muttering under his breath as he did so. The crimson pool swirled and heaved on the platter, rising suddenly now and again before falling back, as though disturbed by something just below the surface, though the liquid could only have been a fraction of an inch deep.

'I took this sample directly from the brain,' said Mirren casually. 'It should provide acceptable images of everything the victim saw prior to his death. Ideally, I would have liked to use the vitreous fluid from the eyeballs, but both eyes were severely damaged during the attack. Which suggests, if nothing else, that the killer may have had a reason to be fearful of what a scrying might reveal.'

Rhea nodded non-committally, and watched interestedly as Mirren stirred the pool of blood with the tip of an ivory wand. The blood steamed where the wand touched it. Mirren chanted something rhythmic in Gaelic, moving the wand through a series of patterns. The surface of the blood bulged suddenly upwards, forming a demonic face. Mirren fell back a step, startled, and yanked the wand out of the blood. Horns sprouted from the crimson forehead, and the leering mouth gaped wide with soundless mockery. The air was thick with the stench of blood and the buzzing of flies. Mirren shouted two Words in quick succession and stabbed at the bloody face with his wand. The face exploded, spattering both Mirren and Rhea with blood. For a moment they just stood there, breathing heavily. Without quite knowing why, Rhea had no doubt they'd just had a narrow escape from something very dangerous. She glared at Mirren as he wiped blood from his face with his sleeve.

'What the hell was that, Doctor?'

'I must admit, I'm not entirely sure.' Mirren reached cautiously forward and prodded the few drops of blood remaining on the silver platter with his wand, but there was no response. 'Most interesting, though. Most interesting. It would appear our killer has enough magic to cover his tracks quite efficiently. Certainly we can forget any further attempts at scrying. Which leaves us with only one option. Questioning the victim directly.'

'Are you sure about this?' said Rhea. 'If the body was warded against scrying, it's probably warded against necromancy too. There could be all kinds of magical booby-traps, just waiting for us to activate them.'

Mirren looked at her and smiled superciliously. 'I know what I'm doing. I'm not an amateur. I have done this before, you know. The victim has only been dead a matter of hours, so the spirit will still be within reach. Called in the correct manner, with the proper terms and commands, he will answer. He'll have no choice.'

'You'd better be right about this,' said Rhea.

Mirren took that as permission to go ahead, and began the ritual. It was simple and vulgar, and not nearly as repellent as Rhea had expected. Mirren ran through the ritual with a speed and ease that suggested he'd done it many times before. Rhea made a mental note to look into

51

that. Even the dead were entitled to privacy. Mirren began a long, involved incantation studded with words from a dozen dead languages. Sweat beaded on his face despite the cold. Rhea could feel a growing tension in the Morgue, a feeling of pressure, of something struggling to break into, or perhaps out of, reality. Mirren broke off, and stared at the corpse eagerly, almost greedily.

'Oliver Lando; hear my words. By the power of this ritual, by agreements entered into with the Powers and Dominations, I command you to rise and speak with me.'

For a long moment nothing happened. Then shadows swayed disturbingly across the Morgue's walls, though there was nothing present to cast them, and the buzzing of flies returned, louder than ever. Rhea looked at Mirren questioningly, and then jumped back, as the corpse sat up. It slowly turned its destroyed head and looked at Mirren with its blind eyes.

'Who calls me? Who disturbs my rest?'

'I called,' said Mirren firmly. 'I conjure and command you, speak only truth in my presence. Do you remember your name?'

'I remember. Send me back. I should not be here.'

'Answer my questions, and I shall release you. Did you see the face of your murderer?'

There was a pause, and then something changed. There was a new presence in the room, something old and sickening. Rhea backed away another step. The corpse ignored her, its attention fixed on Mirren. The jaw settled comfortably into place, and a slow smile spread across the dead man's face, cracking and splitting the dead lips. Pinpoints of light glowed where the eyes had been, and two thin plumes of smoke curled up from the ruined eyesockets.

'Little man,' said the corpse, 'you should not have called me here. I am old and powerful, potent far beyond your feeble magic's control. I shall tell you secrets, dark and awful truths that will destroy your reason and sear your soul.'

'You're not Oliver Lando,' said Mirren, struggling to keep his voice calm. 'Who are you? Speak, I command you.'

'You have no power over such as I,' said the corpse. 'Don't you want to ask me questions? Isn't that what you did with all the others? You wanted knowledge of what lies beyond the Veil. I can tell you that, but you won't like my answers.' It turned its head suddenly, and looked at Rhea. It giggled happily. 'Welcome to Hell, girlie. We're going to have a great time.'

The corpse swung its legs over the edge of the examination table. Mirren stuttered out an incantation, but the words had no effect. The dead man rose to his feet. Mirren shouted a Word of Power, and the corpse shivered a moment, but was not stopped. It took a step towards Rhea, its hands reaching out eagerly. Mirren shouted another Word, lunged forward and thrust his ivory wand into one of the corpse's empty eyesockets. A horrid screaming filled the Morgue, harsh and primal and deafening, and then there was silence, and the body collapsed to the floor and did not move again. Rhea realized her hands were shaking, and not from the cold. She thrust them into her pockets and glared at Mirren.

'What the hell was *that*?'

Mirren tried for a casual shrug, but couldn't quite bring it off. 'Whoever our murderer is, he has powerful allies. Powerful enough to override my summoning, and send that . . . thing in place of the true soul. The implications of that are . . . disturbing.'

'You always did have a gift for understatement,' said Rhea. 'Make the proper arrangements for the body, and then write up a full report of what just happened here. One copy to me, one to the Sheriff. Apart from that, you don't talk to anyone about this. Understand, Doctor?'

Mirren nodded, just a little shakily, and Rhea stalked out of the Morgue, while she could still trust her legs to support her.

*

It was comfortably past midday, in the lazy part of the afternoon, and Suzanne Dubois and Sean Morrison were sitting together on a battered old sofa on the front porch of Suzanne's shack. They passed a hand-rolled back and forth, and looked out over the river Tawn. The sun poured down like honey, thick and slow and golden, and butterflies flickered by like pastel leaves tossed by the breeze. They'd been sitting there for the best part of an hour, talking of this and that and nothing in particular, and Morrison still hadn't said why he'd come to see Suzanne. She didn't feel any need to hurry him. He'd get around to what was troubling him eventually, and until then she was content just to enjoy the moment and the sunshine.

Suzanne looked down at the river's edge and smiled as she watched the cartoons playing with the animals. The real and unreal creatures found each other endlessly fascinating, and there were always a few of one kind or the other playing their simple games near Suzanne's shack. She seemed to attract them in some way, like all the other walking wounded who came to her for comfort. She sometimes thought they came because they felt safe with her. She wished there was somewhere she could go to feel safe, and protected. She didn't feel safe anywhere any more. Finding Lucas's dead body had been bad enough, but to discover it in her house, the one place where she'd believed the world couldn't touch her . . . Her mouth firmed into a flat line. She should have known. She should have known there was nowhere really safe, not even in Shadows Fall. A hot flush of anger swept through her, as much at the spoiling of her mood as anything else. The shack was her home, and she was damned if she'd be driven out of it by anyone or anything. But at night she locked the door and checked the single window and slept with the light on.

She smiled down at the animals, the real and the cartoon, the innocent ones who knew nothing of what had happened and still saw her place as sanctuary. All the cats and dogs and birds came to her eventually, stopping for a few moments or a few days, before continuing on. It would have been nice if one of them could have stayed, but they never did. Any more than the men or women who came to her for love or comfort or an understanding ear.

She looked at Sean Morrison beside her, a slender, brooding figure with a mass of black curls and an intensity that anyone else would have found intimidating. He looked, as he always did, as though he was about to leap up from where he was sitting and take on the whole world single-handed. And it would have been a brave individual indeed who would have bet on the world. Morrison was in his late twenties, though his eyes were older, and he looked like he carried grudges. He was Shadows Fall's resident bard, drunkard and trouble-maker. He had few friends and many enemies, and it was sometimes difficult to be sure which he treasured the most. He was fascinated by the Sidhe, the wee folk, the denizens of Faerie, and spent as much time as they'd allow talking with them in their land beneath the hill.

'I need your advice, Suzanne,' he said suddenly. His voice was a pleasant tenor, slightly roughened by years of drinking and cheap cigarettes. He didn't look at her, his eyes fixed on the slow moving river.

'I'll help if I can, Sean. You know that. Shall I fetch the Cards?'

'No. I don't know. I have a decision to make, and I'm not sure if I came here looking for support, or to be talked out of it. It's about the murders. I've had an idea.'

'Is that wise?' said Suzanne dryly. 'As a rule, your ideas get you into more trouble than even I can get you out of.'

'You're never going to let me forget about those elementals, are you?'

'Considering the damage they caused after you let them loose, no.'

'It was an accident. We got them all back again, didn't we?'

'After they'd caused an earthquake, a flash flood, a major fire and a tornado simultaneously, yes.'

'I said I was sorry. Look, do you want to hear my idea, or not?'

'Of course, Sean. Go right ahead.'

'Erikson's not getting anywhere with the murders. And he's not going to. He's in over his head and he knows it. The killer has power. Which means we're going to need someone of power to find him. Someone who can look at the problem and the town with a fresh, outsider's eyes. I'm going to visit the Faerie and petition the Unseeli Court for help.'

'I'll say this for you,' said Suzanne after a moment, when she'd got her breath back, 'You don't think small. Aren't we in enough trouble as it is, without inviting the Faerie folk to meddle with the situation? They embody Chaos, Sean, and they have little love for most of us at the best of times. Which these aren't.'

'They'll come if I ask them,' said Morrison stubbornly. 'They have magics and sciences we only dream of. Maybe they'll see something we've missed.'

'Do this much at least,' said Suzanne. 'Let's talk about this with a few people first; see what they think about it.'

'No. If you tell anyone, they'll just try to stop me. I only told you because I thought I could trust you to keep it to yourself.'

'Of course you can trust me, Sean. Give me a minute to think about this. After all, what you're proposing is a major change in the town's politics. Shadows Fall and the Faerie have gone their separate ways for centuries, bound to peace by oaths almost as old as the town. There's a delicate balance in everything that happens here, between magic and science, real and unreal, and if that gets upset . . .'

'Seven people are dead, Suzanne! How much more upset can things get?'

'I don't know,' said Suzanne levelly. 'Do you want to find out the hard way?'

Morrison scowled, but looked away, and Suzanne knew

she'd made a point. He sighed heavily, and looked out over the river.

'All right; let's talk to a few people. But not Erikson. He'd shoot it down anyway, just because it was my idea. He's never liked me.'

'Very well,' said Suzanne. 'Not Erikson. Give me twenty-four hours to come up with some names.'

'Twenty-four hours. And let's hope no one else gets murdered in that time.'

He broke off as the sound of approaching footsteps broke the afternoon quiet. The two of them looked round and saw a large figure coming along the riverbank towards them, the sun at his back. He looked broad and powerful, with a weight-lifter's muscles. Suzanne recognized him as he drew nearer, and relaxed a little. Lester Gold could be trusted. She smiled warmly at him, and Morrison grunted an acknowledgement as Gold stopped before them.

Gold was in his seventies, but had a physique that a man in his twenties might have envied. His face was heavily lined, and his hair was grey shot with silver, but his back was still straight as a rod and his eyes were as sharp as they'd ever been. He wore a suit that hadn't been fashionable for years, and wore it with quiet style. He smiled at Suzanne, and nodded politely to Morrison.

'I hope I'm not intruding,' he said mildly, 'But I did want to talk to you, Suzanne, if it's convenient.'

'Of course it is. It's good to see you again, Lester. Do you know Sean Morrison?'

Gold looked at Morrison with renewed interest. 'The one who let loose the elementals?'

Morrison groaned. 'Am I ever going to live that down?'

'Probably not,' said Suzanne.

'Sorry to have brought it up,' said Gold. He put out a hand for Morrison to shake. It was large and muscular and freckled with liver spots. Morrison shook hands carefully, aware that Gold could crush his hand easily if the mood took him. Gold smiled at him, as though reading his thoughts, let go of his hand and looked at Suzanne.

'I really do need to talk to you, my dear.'

'Then please do. There's a spare chair inside you can bring out.'

'I'll leave if you like,' said Morrison.

'Thanks,' said Gold, 'but that won't be necessary. I'd value your opinion. I'll just fetch that chair. Won't be a moment.'

He headed for Suzanne's shack, stepping carefully to avoid treading on the small animals and cartoons that were playing a raucous game of tag under and around the sofa. Morrison waited until Gold had disappeared into the shack, and then leaned over to Suzanne. 'I know the name, but I can't place him. Should I know him?'

'Not necessarily,' said Suzanne, her voice carefully low. 'He used to be a pulp hero in the thirties, and a super-hero in the forties, like the Shadow and Doc Savage, though he was never that popular. His comic was cancelled in the fifties, and he turned up here not long afterwards. He's been here ever since, running a florist's in the Old Market, growing older and more real with every year. For a while collectors used to track him down, to get him to autograph old copies of his magazine, but no one's asked after him for years. Every now and again he remembers who he was, and wants to get involved in town affairs, but it never lasts. His memory isn't what it was.'

'He still remembers you,' said Morrison dryly, looking back at the shack.

'Of course,' said Suzanne. 'Everyone knows me. Now be nice to him, Sean. He's a perfect gentleman, and I don't want him upset.'

She broke off as Gold emerged from her shack, carrying a large and heavy chair with effortless grace. He dumped it down beside Suzanne, and sank into it with a happy sigh. Morrison eyed him respectfully. He'd moved that chair himself on occasion, and almost ruined his back doing it. Gold looked at Suzanne, and then away again, clearly unsure where to start or what to say. He looked down at the cartoons and the animals playing together, and smiled like a child.

'That's more like it. That's how things ought to be. You look at some of the characters they've got in comics today, and it makes you want to weep. Costumed thugs and killer vigilantes. What kind of example is that to be setting children? In my day we understood the value of honour and fair play. Even the villains. Everything's different now. I don't understand the comics and I don't understand the world, as often as not. I suppose all old people feel that way, though I never really thought of myself as old before. The murders changed that. I can't just sit around and do nothing, while people are being killed. It's time for me to make a comeback, Suzanne. I'm needed now. Erikson's never even investigated a murder before, but I solved hundreds in my day. I'm an expert at this sort of thing.

'And yet, I can't just walk up to the Sheriff and say I'm taking over. He'd just look at me and see an old man, who should be safe at home in his slippers, by his fire. He's probably never even heard of Lester Gold, the Mystery Avenger. So what should I do, Suzanne? You tell me.'

Suzanne smiled at him, and reached out to pat his hand briskly. 'Sean here has been feeling much the same as you. I think you two should talk. You'd make good partners, if you'll just listen to each other. Sean, you can start by telling Lester your idea, while I go fetch some beer I've got cooling in the river.'

She got up and went down to the river's edge. She pulled at the string attached to the six-pack sitting on the bottom of the river, and all the animals and cartoons came to watch what she was doing. Behind her, Lester Gold's voice rose in outrage.

'You want to ask *what* for help?'

3

Galleries of Frost and Bone

It was late afternoon shading into evening by the time James Hart and Leonard Ash returned to the park, and most of the day's visitors had already left, heading for the comfort of home and the security of locked doors and windows. So far the murders had all taken place at night, and few felt at ease any more once the sun had gone down. Street lamps were already blazing at every street corner, though the shadows had barely started to lengthen. There was a tension on the air from the constant pressure of assessing eyes as people hurried down the emptying streets. Even those who preferred the dark and blossomed in the moonlight walked warily in the narrow streets, and sought the company of their own kind whenever possible. But even so, there are always some with pleasures or business that can only be satisfied after dark, in the privacy of shadows. They walked alone, in dignified haste, with carefully averted eyes, and ignored Ash and Hart as they passed. Ash watched them all with thoughtful eyes, but no one came close, even when he nodded politely.

The park turned out to be empty, apart from half a dozen kids playing some complicated game with two frisbees. They didn't acknowledge Ash's or Hart's presence, but allowed the course of their game to move them away from the Sarcophagus as the two men approached. A faint mist had sprung up, pleasantly cool on the skin, but the air had all the tension of an approaching thunderstorm. The temperature dropped sharply as they neared the Sarcophagus, and Hart was surprised to find his breath steaming on the air before him. Sudden chills shook him, and he plunged his hands into his jacket pockets. He looked back at the T-shirted kids who'd been playing in the last of the sunlight, but they were gone with the rest of the park, swallowed up by the thickening fog.

He looked reluctantly back at the Sarcophagus, a great block of solid stone standing fixed and immutable on its raised dais. The stone showed no signs of age or weathering, but still there was a definite air of permanence to the Sarcophagus, as though it had been designed with constancy in mind. It looked bigger than Hart remembered, and seen up close again it seemed somehow more solid too. More . . . real. He stood with Ash before the stone, and shivered from something more than just the growing cold. The underlying tension of the evening was more centred now, more focused, and Hart shifted uneasily from foot to foot as Ash just stood there, looking at the Sarcophagus, apparently lost in thought. As though he was . . . waiting for something. Hart spun round sharply as he glimpsed something moving in the mists from the corner of his right eye, and then froze where he was as two dark figures stepped out of the mists to confront him. He knew their faces. He recognized their clothes, and the way they held themselves. Standing before him were another James Hart and another Leonard Ash, wearing casual, easy smiles. The Ash at his side nodded amiably to the two doppelgängers, and his double nodded amiably in return.

'Time has been known to act strangely around the Sarcophagus,' said Ash calmly. 'Not really surprising, given the stone's many functions and responsibilities, and the fact that many of us suspect it of having a really devious sense of humour. One of the more common manifestations is time doubling back upon itself, so that the future ends up in the past. Or vice versa. Or something. I'm trying to sound like I know what I'm talking about, but like most people who live here, mostly I'm flying by the seat of my pants. Or had you already guessed that?'

The other Ash looked at the other Hart. 'You're right. I do talk too much.'

'Nobody move,' said Hart. 'I think I've got it. We're looking at ourselves, leaving the Sarcophagus *after* having visited Old Father Time. Right?'

'Got it in one,' said the future Hart. 'Time knows you're coming, so you'd better get a move on. He really hates to be kept waiting.'

Both the Ashes nodded. 'Is he in a good mood?' said Ash.

'Is he ever?' said his double.

'Good point,' said Ash. 'Let's go, James.'

'Wait just a minute,' said Hart. 'If you've already been through the meeting, can't you just tell us what happened? Then we wouldn't have to bother Time at all.'

The two Ashes looked at each other knowingly. 'Time doesn't work that way,' said Ash. 'Trust me. This is not something you want to think about too much. If you push it I'll have to explain about differing time-lines, probability maths and fractal theory. Which would not be a good idea because I don't really understand them either.' He sighed wistfully. 'I always thought things would seem so much clearer after I died.'

Hart looked at his future self, who was looking sympathetic. 'Can't you at least give us some advice on what to do when we meet Old Father Time?'

The other Ash and the other Hart looked at each other. 'Don't touch the saki,' said the future Hart, and the future Ash nodded firmly.

They both smiled at their earlier selves, and then turned and walked unhurriedly away, disappearing into the mists. Hart looked at Ash.

'Is this kind of thing going to happen often while I'm in Shadows Fall?'

'Probably,' said Ash. 'It's that kind of place. It helps if you remember that not everything is necessarily what it seems. Take the Sarcophagus, for example. It looks like a great big slab of stone, but it isn't. It's a moment of Time

63

itself, given shape and form. It's as solid as matter, but more permanent, unchanging and unaffected by the tides and stresses of the material world. You're looking at a single, rather special moment in Time; the exact moment when the town of Shadows Fall was created, back when the world was young. At this point people usually ask why that moment should have taken on physical form, and my usual answer is, beats the hell out of me. Common belief has it that the moment became solid to protect itself, but no, I don't know what from.'

'Do you know anything useful?' said Hart, just a little more sharply than he'd meant.

Ash raised an eyebrow, and his gaze was briefly cold and thoughtful. 'I know how to get into the Sarcophagus, and how to get you an audience with Old Father Time. That is what you wanted, isn't it?'

'Yes, it is,' said Hart. He took a deep breath and let it out again. 'I'm sorry. This is all . . . very new to me.'

'Oh sure, I understand,' said Ash. 'I'm dead and buried, and this place still disturbs the hell out of me.' Ash fished around in his jacket pocket and finally produced a small plastic snowscene, the kind of cheap junk kids lust after for no good reason, and tourists pick up for souvenirs of places they quickly forget. Ash held it up for Hart to look at, but drew back his hand when Hart went to take it. 'Don't touch, James. Just look.' Hart shrugged, and leaned forward to study the snowscene closely. It filled Ash's hand; a smooth dome of clear but hazy plastic holding within itself a single dark building. Ash shook the snowscene gently, and thick snowflakes whirled around the indistinct building.

'Not everybody gets in to see Old Father Time,' said Ash. 'He's always busy, and he doesn't like to be interrupted. But some people, such as myself, cannot be denied access, so he gives us each a key. This is mine. I don't know what anyone else's looks like, but this is my invitation to the Galleries of Frost and Bone. Time lives in the Gallery of Bone.'

'Who lives in the Gallery of Frost?' said Hart, when Ash hesitated.

'No one lives there,' said Ash quietly. 'That's where the Forever Door is. The final destination of everyone who comes to Shadows Fall. I came back through the Door because I was needed here, but I can still hear it calling. I always will. That's why I have this key. Because the Door is waiting for me to go back.' Ash smiled briefly. 'It's got a long wait ahead of it. Now then, we can't just stand around here all day. Time waits for no man. Particularly when he's coming to ask a favour. Let's get going, shall we?'

'Do we have to?' said Hart. 'I'm beginning to get a very bad feeling about all this.'

'You're probably right,' said Ash. 'The Gallery of Bone is a dangerous and disturbing place, even to visit. But we have to go, because we did. You saw your future self. I can practically see the words Free Will forming in your mind, but forget it. I've argued every side of the question there is, and a few I made up specially, and I'm still no wiser. Basically, it's easier just to go with the flow and not make waves. Try not to think about it. It'll just make your head ache.'

'Too late,' said Hart.

Ash grinned unsympathetically, and held the snowscene up before his eyes. The snowflakes were still whirling, even though it had been some time since Ash had shaken it. Hart studied the snowscene almost in spite of himself. It became somehow more impressive the more he looked at it. The drifting flakes seemed more real, and the building in the centre of the storm began to take on depth and focus. Details formed, and lights glowed at tiny windows. Only they didn't seem so small any more. The snowscene leapt up to fill his eyes, rushing out to fill the world, and then Hart was falling headlong into the howling blizzard. His stomach lurched as he flailed helplessly about him for something solid to hang on to, but there was nothing

65

there, only the hammering wind and the bitter cold that seared his lungs with every breath.

Hard-packed snow leapt up below him and slammed into his feet. He fell sprawling and lay stretched out, trembling violently in reaction to the fall. The snow was wet and crunchy under his bare hands, but the solidness of it was a comfort, and the tremors left him as his breathing slowed. He got his feet under him and stood up, raising an arm to keep the flying snow out of his face. It was night, and the moon above him was a perfect silver circle, its bright shimmering light punching through the storm. The hard-packed snow supported his weight, but he had no idea how much snow there was between his feet and the ground below. The thought gave him a kind of vertigo, and he decided very firmly not to think about it again. He hugged himself tightly, trying to hold in what warmth he had left, but the bitter cold leached all the strength out of him. The frozen waste stretched away in all directions, disappearing into the swirling snow. Each way looked as futile as any other, and he might have stood there for ever, frozen in indecision, if Ash hadn't appeared suddenly out of the storm to take him firmly by the arm.

'First step's a bastard, isn't it?' said Ash, shouting to be heard over the roar of the storm. 'Sorry about that. Stick with me. It isn't far now.'

He set off into the swirling snow, half leading and half pulling Hart with him. The cold didn't seem to be bothering Ash at all, but then, Hart thought crazily, it wouldn't. They trudged on, slipping and sliding on the uneven snow and battered by the howling wind, but a dark shape soon formed in the white glare ahead. The storm seemed to deepen, as though to deny them this new sanctuary, but Ash and Hart plunged on, fighting the wind for every step. Ash tried to shield Hart with his own body, but the knife-edged wind seemed to blow right through him. Hart hunched his shoulders, narrowed his eyes to slits, and fought on. He hadn't come this far to be beaten by the weather. Ash had promised him there were answers to be found here, and he was going to have them, no matter what it took.

The building suddenly loomed up before him, vast and overpowering, a great black shape with few details and bright lights shining out of high windows. Ash pulled Hart in close beside the nearest wall, and the battering wind died away, unable to bring its full strength to bear on them any more. Hart panted for breath, wincing as the cold stabbed his lungs. He'd never felt cold like it, and the thought slowly surfaced that they'd better find a way in soon, very soon, or frostbite would start gnawing on his extremities. He'd already lost all feeling in his hands and feet. Ash pulled him along the side of the wall a way, and then stopped and hammered on the wall with his fist. A door swung suddenly inwards, almost as though it had been waiting for them, and a warm golden glow spilled out into the night. Ash hauled Hart inside, and the door slammed shut behind them.

Hart sank to his knees on the bare wooden floor, and groaned aloud as warmth flooded into him, forcing out the cold and bringing feeling back to his frozen extremities. Ash knelt down beside him and rubbed briskly at Hart's hands, to get the blood moving again. Hart slowly straightened up, grimacing at the agony of returning circulation, and looked around him through watering eyes. He and Ash were kneeling in a huge, old-fashioned Hall, with tall wood-panelled walls, and a raftered ceiling high overhead. So high that Hart wouldn't have been surprised to find owls nesting up there. Or bats. The Hall itself stretched away into the distance, but Hart's attention fastened on to the stacked log fire crackling brightly in a great stone fireplace, only a dozen steps from the door. He staggered to his feet with Ash's help, and moved over to stand directly before it. The warmth sank into him like cup after cup of the very finest coffee, filling him with a wonderful glow that forced out the last chill from his bones. Hart smiled beatifically, quite content to stay where he was indefinitely. Or even longer. But thoughts of the world

67

and its pains returned, and he turned an accusing glare on Ash.

'*The first step's a bastard?*'

'Ah,' said Ash. 'Sorry about that. I would have warned you, but it isn't usually that bad.'

Hart looked at him sharply. 'You mean that blizzard was . . . arranged, deliberately, to discourage us from coming here?'

'It's possible,' said Ash. 'Time really doesn't like visitors.' He shrugged and smiled vaguely, and looked around him. 'The Hall changes sometimes too, though I've never worked out why. Time's a whimsical sort, and his sense of humour often escapes me. Take a moment and get your breath back, James. There's no need for any hurry here. In here, there's all the time in the world.'

Hart turned his back to the fire so that his backside could get the full benefit of the warmth. 'This . . . Hall. Is it really the same building we saw in your snowscene?'

'Oh yes. Perhaps it's the same house inside all snowscenes, if only people knew how to get inside them. This is All Hallows' Hall, James, the house at the heart of the world. Take the left-hand path, and you'll come to the Gallery of Frost. The right-hand path leads to the Gallery of Bone, and Old Father Time himself.'

Hart looked at him thoughtfully. 'The Gallery of Frost. The Forever Door.'

'That's right,' said Ash. 'I can hear it calling me. It's very clear here. Don't ask me to take you there, James. I can't. It's too dangerous.'

'To me, or to you?'

'Very good, James,' said Ash approvingly. 'That combination of common sense and naked paranoia will serve you well in Shadows Fall. And no, I'm not going to answer your question. I only met you today, and already you know far too much about me. You must allow me to keep a few little surprises in reserve. But I'm feeling generous, so I'll allow you one more question. If you're quick.'

'All right,' said Hart, determined to get some information out of him at least. 'Why is it called the Gallery of Bone?'

'Now that is a good question,' said Ash. 'I wish I had more of an answer for you. Essentially, the Gallery of Bone is constructed from ancient fossilized bones, from a creature so ancient no one now knows what it was. Legend has it the bones came from a creature set to guard the Forever Door, in the days before Shadows Fall existed, and the world was a hell of a lot younger. No one knows how or why this creature came to die. Time might know, but if he does, he isn't talking. Speaking of which, we'd do well to get a move on. Time knows we're here, and the longer we keep him waiting the less likely it is he'll feel like answering your questions.'

Ash set off down the Hall at a determined pace. Hart glanced wistfully at the crackling fire, sighed once, and then set off after Ash. They walked together for a while in silence, the only sound in that vast Hall the quiet murmuring echoes of their footsteps. Light appeared around them from no readily detectable source, and moved along with them, so that they were always walking in a wide pool of golden light. The panelled walls slid smoothly past, innocent of any decoration or embellishment. Hart had been expecting a fair selection of old and valuable paintings and portraits; it seemed that kind of place. But the walls were bare and characterless, and there weren't even any other doors or corridors leading off in other directions. There was only the Hall, and the light they moved in. Hart looked back over his shoulder once, but only once. Behind them there was nothing but an impenetrable darkness.

They walked for a long time, or at least it seemed that way. There were no landmarks, and Hart wasn't really surprised to find his watch no longer worked. He'd actually started to get a bit bored when a tall slim figure stepped suddenly into the light ahead of them. He stopped immediately, and the figure before him stopped too. Ash stood at his side and looked from one figure to the other with a calm knowing smile.

The newcomer was a human form composed almost entirely of clockwork. Wheels turned and ratchets clicked, and there was a general whirring of working machinery and moving parts. The whole figure was a complex structure of interconnecting parts, fashioned in minute and intricate detail. Every bone and muscle and joint had its steel or brass counterpart, but there was no layer of skin to hide the mechanisms from view. The face was a delicate porcelain mask, with exquisite painted features. But the eyes were flat and blank, and the smile never wavered, and the overall effect was more inhuman than any steel mask could have been. The figure stood patiently before them, whirring quietly, as though waiting for some question or command.

'Is this . . . Time?' said Hart finally.

'No,' said Ash. 'Just one of his servants. Step aside, and it'll be on its way.'

Hart did so, and the figure moved gracefully forward, walking with a style and efficiency no human form could ever equal. It quickly stepped out of the light and disappeared back into the gloom. Hart could hear it for a while, walking serenely in the dark, with no need for light or warmth or any other human weakness.

'Automaton,' said Ash briskly. 'Time makes them, piece by piece. Partly as a hobby, partly so he can have agents to walk abroad in the world and do his bidding. You'll see more of them as we get closer to Time's lair. Don't let them worry you. They're harmless; nothing more than glorified errand boys really.'

'Are they . . . alive, in any way?' said Hart, as he and Ash continued on down the Hall.

'Not really. They're Time's eyes and ears outside the Gallery. He rarely enters the real world any more, save for those occasions and ceremonies where it's expected of him. He gets more and more insular and broody as he gets older, but he's never been keen on company at the best of times. Still, he'll want to see you. I think. Come on.'

They continued on their way in their pool of light and

70

more automatons came and went, their sightless eyes staring straight ahead, in the service of some unknown mission or command. And finally, Ash and Hart came to a door at the end of the Hall. It was huge, easily fifteen feet tall, fashioned of polished wood patterned with black iron studs. It towered above them, and Hart felt like a small child unexpectedly summoned to his headmaster's office. He tried to stand a little taller, and deliberately crushed the feeling within him. He was a supplicant, not a child. Not any more. There was no handle or knob, so he reached out to knock, but the huge door swung smoothly open before he could touch it. Ash smiled briefly, and led Hart into the Gallery of Bone.

The Gallery stretched away before them, with more floors above and below, falling away and rising above for as far as they could see into the warm honeyed light. Hart moved slowly forward after Ash, numbed and awed by the sheer scale of the place. He couldn't see the end of the corridor he was walking down, and just trying to calculate the overall size of the Gallery made his head ache. Portraits lined both walls, an endless series of scenes and faces captured in delicate filigreed silver frames some six feet tall and three feet wide. He recognized one of the scenes, a slowly changing view of the Sarcophagus in the park. The mists had gone, but masses of crawling ivy covered the stone, as though centuries had passed since Hart last saw it. He looked at the next portrait, and saw people walking unconcernedly down a market street. There was nothing in their attitude to suggest they knew they were being watched. Ash coughed politely, and Hart looked round, startled. He realized he'd come to a complete halt, and hurried on to catch up with Ash, while trying to look as though he'd really meant to stop all the time.

There were portraits without end, and Hart shook his head dazedly as he tried to grasp the scale of the Gallery. The endless prospects flowed past him like scenery viewed from a slow-moving train, and there were always new sights and wonders, places and people seen from far away

71

or in such close-up detail that Hart felt as though he could just reach out and touch them. The scenes in the portraits were silent until he stood before them, and then sounds and voices would whisper in the Gallery, tantalizingly faint, as though they'd had to travel unimaginable distances to reach him.

'Time doesn't get out much,' said Ash easily, 'But with the Gallery to keep him informed, he doesn't have to. Every place and every person in Shadows Fall can be seen somewhere in the Gallery of Bone. You'd have to be crazy to keep track of it all, but then, that's Time for you. If it was an easy job, anybody could do it.'

Hart frowned. 'Wait a minute. I don't think I like the sound of that. What about people's privacy?'

'What about it?' said Ash. 'Given that there are an almost infinite number of places, people and things that Time has to keep track of, what are the odds that he's going to be watching you? And even if he was, that you'd be doing anything that was (1) interesting, and (2) something he hadn't seen before? Mostly we all just assume he's watching someone else, and mostly we're right. Don't worry about it.'

'You keep saying that, but it doesn't help. This place worries the hell out of me; it's Big Brother with a vengeance.'

'I prefer to think of him more as Big Uncle; well-meaning but preoccupied. Let me show you something that'll take your mind off it. The portraits have other functions too. Take a look at this. You'll like this.'

Ash stopped before a particular portrait, and Hart stopped with him. The scene was a high-tech latticework of steel corridors jammed together like a honeycomb, with shadowy figures scuttling back and forth, too quickly and too briefly seen to be identified. The lights were painfully bright, too intense to be meant for human eyes, and there were no shadows anywhere. Here and there, intricate machines like living sculptures performed silent, unguessable tasks.

'What is that place?' said Hart, his voice low, as though afraid he'd be overheard.

'The future,' said Ash. 'Or possibly the past. It doesn't matter. Keep watching.'

One of Time's automatons came striding confidently down the harshly-lit corridor, its steel feet clapping loudly against the steel floor. It walked towards the portrait, already so close its painted eyes and smile could easily be seen. It soon filled the view, and Ash backed away. Hart realized suddenly what was about to happen, and stumbled backwards, his eyes still fixed on the portrait. A slow tension formed on the air, pressure building remorselessly until an uncomfortably warm breeze gusted out of the portrait and into the Gallery. It smelt of ozone and machine oil. The automaton stepped gracefully out of the portrait and down into the Gallery, and walked away without even bothering to glance at Hart and Ash. The warm breeze broke off abruptly, and all that was left was the disappearing automaton, and the last few traces of ozone and machine oil on the air.

'How's that for timing?' said Ash. 'What were the odds we'd be in just the right place at the right moment to witness that?'

'Yeah,' said Hart slowly. 'What were the odds? They'd have to be astronomical. Much more likely that Time's watching us, and has been for quite some while.'

He looked quickly about him, as though expecting to see Old Father Time right there in the Gallery with them, but Ash just shrugged and shook his head. 'Not necessarily,' he said easily. 'Coincidence is one of Time's favourite tools. Come on; we don't want to keep him waiting.'

'Will you stop saying that! It took me twenty-five years to get back here; it won't hurt him to wait a few minutes longer. You'd think he was a King or something, the way you all jump at his name.'

'You don't understand,' said Ash. 'You will, when you've had a chance to meet him. He really is rather special.'

Hart sniffed, and looked after the disappearing automaton. 'How many of those . . . things, does Time have?'

'I don't think anyone knows for sure, except Time himself. It takes him years to make one, but by all accounts his various selves have been making them for centuries. They're his thoughts and his hands in the outside world, and in a sense they're his children too. The only children he'll ever have.'

'Why's that?'

Ash looked at him expressionlessly. 'Think about it, James. Time is immortal, or as near as makes no damn difference. How many children would a man have after a few thousand years? How many children would they have? No, James; there've never been any children and there never will be.'

'Doesn't he mind?'

Ash shrugged. 'He's had a lot of time to get used to the idea. But yes, of course he minds. Why do you think he keeps making automatons?'

Hart looked at the portraits on the walls and then at the Gallery around him. He knew what he wanted to say, but he didn't know how to say it without sounding naïve. So he said it anyway. 'Leonard; is Time human?'

'A fair question,' said Ash, 'And one that has been troubling the minds of people in Shadows Fall for a good many centuries. He looks human enough, and he has enough human frailties to more than qualify, but he was never born and death can't hold him. He appears as a baby, lives a man's lifetime in one year and dies an old man, only to appear again from his own ashes. Some say he's the ancient phoenix of legend, others that he is the very concept of Time itself, given shape and form and blood and bone. Everyone has an opinion, but no one knows, and Time isn't talking. There's only one thing that everyone agrees on where Old Father Time's concerned.'

'What's that?'

'He hates to be kept waiting. You walked right into that one, James.'

74

'No I didn't; it mounted the pavement and ran me down.'

'Whatever,' said Ash. 'Let's go.'

They walked along in silence for a way, their footsteps echoing hollowly in the empty Gallery. Scenes and faces came and went on the walls they passed, and occasionally a quietly whirring automaton would stride gracefully past on its master's bidding. Hart began to wonder how much further he'd have to walk; it seemed like he'd spent most of the day travelling from one place to another, and his feet were killing him. He'd been walking for some time now, but like the Hall earlier, the Gallery seemed to go on for ever. He looked back the way they'd come, but there was no longer any sign of the door they'd entered through. The Gallery stretched away for as far as he could see in each direction, as though it had no beginning and no ending. The thought disturbed him, and he searched for something else to say that would distract him. He didn't have to search far.

'Leonard; you keep saying Old Father Time is important to Shadows Fall, but what does he actually do, apart from spy on people and fiddle with clockwork?'

'It's complicated,' said Ash, in a tone that clearly suggested he didn't want to talk about it.

'Then simplify it,' said Hart remorselessly.

Ash sighed. 'Basically, you have to understand that Shadows Fall is by its very nature essentially unstable. New time zones are always appearing and disappearing, for a whole variety of reasons. People and creatures of all kinds come and go, some of them extremely powerful and potentially destabilizing. Someone has to hold the reins, or the whole town would fall apart overnight. Time keeps things stable by balancing one zone against another, settling disputes before they can get out of hand, and generally practising preventive maintenance. It helps that he's so powerful that absolutely no one wants to mess with him, but he generally leaves the dirty work to his agents.'

'You mean the automatons?'

'Them. And others.'

Hart frowned. 'I'm missing something here. What makes him so powerful? How does he deal with things that are too tough for his agents?'

'Trust me,' said Ash, 'You really don't want to know. Mostly he just sends a message via an automaton, and that's usually all it takes. No one wants Time mad at them. On the few occasions when someone refuses to follow his advice, Time sends Jack Fetch after them. If you're lucky, you won't ever have to meet him. He's . . . rather disturbing.'

'What does the Sheriff think about all this?' said Hart slowly. 'I mean, he's supposed to enforce the law here, isn't he?'

'Time is more important than the law. The law can't cope with a situation like Shadows Fall; it's too inflexible. Everyone accepts that, even though some, like our good Sheriff, don't agree with it. But most people have enough sense not to rock the boat too roughly. Time is conscientious and hard-working, and doesn't give a damn what people think of him. Or how many toes he has to tread on to get the job done. Mostly the Sheriff and Time are terribly polite to each other, and try very hard to have as little to do with each other as possible.'

He broke off, and they both stopped as an automaton came striding down the corridor and stopped immediately before them. Its painted porcelain face looked first at Ash and then at Hart. The face had a painted moustache and a monocle. It took Hart only a moment to decide that this made the face look even more unreal than usual. He met the painted gaze steadily with his own, and had no doubt that someone else was watching him through the automaton's flat eyes. It whirred and clicked as though thinking about something, and then words sounded in Hart's head like the tolling of a leaden bell. The words were clear and distinct and so loud they made him wince with each new syllable. God probably sounded similar when he wanted some Old Testament prophet to pay particular attention.

Leonard Ash. Have you come seeking the Forever Door at last?

'No,' said Ash calmly. 'I'm just taking advantage of your good nature again. I've brought someone to meet you. A newcomer called James Hart. Except he's not really new; he left Shadows Fall with his parents when he was ten. You remember; there was a prophecy . . .'

Yes. I remember. Bring him to me. The puppet will show you the way. Stick to the path. For your own safety.

The voice broke off sharply and Hart shook his head gingerly. His ears were ringing, and his head felt as though he'd been standing too close to the speakers at a rock concert. He looked at Ash, who was smiling understandingly. The voice didn't seem to have bothered him at all.

'Don't let the burning bush act throw you. He's always this way with strangers. All part of the image, you see. Time's always been very concerned about projecting the right image. Besides, he likes to be rude to people. It's one of the few advantages of his job.'

The automaton ticked loudly twice, turned smoothly on its heel and started off down the corridor. Hart and Ash hurried after it. They walked along in silence for a while, and then Hart sighed resignedly.

'All right, Ash; what are you looking so worried about? This puppet's taking us where we wanted to go, isn't it?'

'Well, yes,' said Ash. 'That's what's bothering me. I was expecting more of an argument. Time really hates visitors. In fact, the only thing he hates more are strangers. And you're both. I think we have to assume he knew you were coming.'

'Wait a minute,' said Hart. 'Even if he'd seen me in one of his portraits, he couldn't really know who I am, and who my parents were. Could he?'

Ash sighed, looking thoughtfully at the automaton's back. 'Time knows a lot of things he shouldn't. It's one of his more disturbing qualities. I'm beginning to wonder if I did the right thing in bringing you here. The prophecy about your family's connection with the town's destruction is quite specific, according to everything I've heard. He might have decided you're too dangerous to be left running loose in Shadows Fall. And Time has some very unpleasant ways of dealing with dangerous people.'

Hart glared at him. 'Now you tell me! Well, don't just stop there; what does he do to people he thinks are dangerous? Lock them up? Send them back to the Stone Age to play tag with the dinosaurs? What?'

'Look to your left,' said Ash.

Hart looked, and came to a sudden stop. Ash stopped with him, and a few steps ahead of them the automaton came to a graceful halt. It didn't turn round to see what they were doing, but waited patiently for them to continue on their way. It gave the impression of being prepared to wait indefinitely, if necessary. Hart didn't notice either of them. His gaze was fixed on the portrait before him. At first glance he'd thought it was just another face on the wall, but the moment he met the glaring haunted eyes, staring madly out at the world, he knew that something horrible had happened here. The mouth was twisted in an endless snarl, and the hands at the figure's sides were clenched into white-knuckled fists, but the figure didn't move at all, standing very still. Impossibly still, as though caught between one movement and the next, between one moment and the next.

'He's been taken out of Time,' said Ash, his voice carefully level. 'Trapped in a stolen moment like an insect caught in amber. While he stands here in the Gallery, Time moves on without him. Everyone he ever knew is dead. All his friends, all his family, everyone who ever knew him is gone. Gone to dust and less than dust. And still he stands here in Time's Gallery, an object lesson to anyone who might think they can stand against Time.'

'How long will Time keep him here like this?' said Hart finally.

'No one knows,' said Ash. 'He hasn't released anyone yet. Let's go, James. We don't want to keep Time waiting.'

Hart tore his eyes away from the still figure's mad gaze,

and nodded curtly to Ash. The automaton set off again, without once looking back to see if they were following. Hart strode after it, scowling at its unresponsive back. He didn't look at Ash, who walked quietly at his side, keeping his own counsel. Hart scowled. He'd trusted Ash. Liked him and trusted him. He'd wanted to believe he had one friend at least in this unnatural town, and who better than someone who'd known him as a child. He'd also wanted to believe that Old Father Time would have answers for his questions, would know the who and why and what he was. But now it seemed the friend had betrayed him, and Time had nothing for him but a frozen eternity in his private Gallery of horrors. He thought briefly about running, but where would he run to? He didn't even know how to get back to Shadows Fall without Ash's help. He'd come so far, fought so hard, hoped so much, and all for nothing. He smiled suddenly, and there was little humour in it. He wasn't beaten yet, and if Time thought he was, he was in for a nasty surprise. Hart didn't believe in giving up. Ever.

'How many people does Time have frozen?' he said finally, still not looking at Ash.

'No one knows. Well, I assume Time knows, but he's never felt inclined to discuss the subject.'

'In other words, he's judge, jury and executioner, and everyone lets him get away with it.'

'Who's going to stop him? This is his reason for existence, to serve and protect Shadows Fall from harm.'

'But he decides who's guilty and who's dangerous. Or potentially dangerous.'

'Who's better equipped to know than him? The portraits in his Gallery provide him with all the information there is. At any given moment he knows more about what's going on in Shadows Fall than anyone else.'

'And you trust him with that kind of power?'

'I trust him to do what he thinks is right and best for Shadows Fall,' Ash said carefully. 'Please believe me, James; I didn't bring you here to throw you to the wolves. If anyone can answer your questions, it's Time. And it's much better that you should come to him, than that he should send someone to fetch you. Trust me, James; it's better this way. If he decides to help you, he has access to people and information that no one else has. He's not a bad sort. Considering he's not really human.'

Some of Hart's anger began to die away. It was hard to stay mad at Ash. He had all the open vulnerable honesty of a puppy that keeps falling over himself because his feet are too big. 'So,' he said finally, allowing his tone to soften a little, 'Time just freezes people who annoy him, is that it?'

'It's not quite that arbitrary. A lot of the people stored here are those who were supposed to go through the Forever Door, but couldn't work up the courage. People who were no longer believed in, who no longer served any function in the real world, but refused to admit it. So they hung around Shadows Fall, growing realer and crazier all the time as the world moved on and left them behind, but still unable to face the Door. Eventually they just fell apart and lashed out at who or whatever happened to be handy, and Time brought them here and froze them, for everyone's safety. It's a compromise no one's really happy with, least of all Time, because there are always more of them.' Ash broke off to stare thoughtfully at a face in a portrait. 'I could end up here myself, some day. It's not a comforting thought.'

They turned a corner and came to a sudden halt as the Gallery ended in a closed door. The automaton stood completely still before the door, as though awaiting further instructions. Hart peered over its shoulder. The door looked ordinary, unassuming and everyday, of entirely normal size and proportions. Hart looked at Ash, who was looking expectantly at the door. Hart was about to ask acidly if they could at least try knocking when the door swung suddenly open, smoothly and silently, without anybody touching it. The automaton stepped gracefully to one side and gestured for them to go in. Ash did so, and Hart followed him in, giving the automaton plenty of room. The automaton stepped gracefully to one side and gestured for them to go in. Ash did so, and Hart followed him in, giving the automaton plenty of room. The painted porcelain face seemed more alien and enigmatic than ever. Hart felt even more unhappy when he got inside, and found there was no one there who could have opened the door. It could have been something as simple as an automatic switch, but somehow he didn't think so. The door closed itself behind him with quiet finality, but Hart refused to give it the satisfaction of looking. He squared his shoulders and looked casually about him as though this sort of thing happened to him all the time.

He didn't know exactly what he'd been expecting of Time's private domain, but this definitely wasn't it. The room might have started out as large and airy, but now it was crammed from wall to wall with clanking, shuddering machinery that looked like something out of Victorian England. There were pipes and gaskets and turning wheels, with more than a hint of building steam pressure. Clock faces and dials sprouted up everywhere there was a space, most of them contradicting each other. Over in a corner a huge counterweight rose and fell with calm, unhurried motions, though what it was connected to was anybody's guess. From all around came a low continuous murmur of moving parts, and the occasional hiss of vented steam. Oil dripped slowly from the odd seam, but there was always a carefully placed container to catch it. The air was pleasantly warm, and just a little hazy.

A narrow passage led through the bulk of the machinery, and Hart moved slowly along it, Ash drifting along behind him. There was a strong sense of purpose to the room, as though all the clumsily interlocked machinery was busy doing something important and vital. It felt suddenly to Hart as though he'd somehow wandered into the workings of one of Time's automatons, unable to see the true shape and purpose because of the sheer scale of the thing. He was a mouse inside a grandfather clock, an insect on a computer screen, trying to see things in terms he was used to, but unable to grasp the true concept and reality of where he was because his mind just wasn't complex enough.

A door slammed open on the far side of the room, and someone came striding through the maze of machinery with the ease of long familiarity. Hart pulled his drifting thoughts together and stood ready to meet Old Father Time. He thought he'd prepared himself for pretty much anything, but he was still taken aback by the slender young woman who finally stood glaring before him, her large tattooed fists resting angrily on her hips. Hart was hard pressed to think what sort of person would have looked suited to the room, but she definitely wasn't it. She looked to be barely out of her teens, dressed in battered black leather and chains, and going by her face she had a mad on for the whole world. She wore her hair in a spiky mohican, shaved high at the sides, and her face was half hidden behind a garish mask of black and white makeup. She had a safety pin piercing one ear, and a razor blade hanging from the other. Hart didn't know whether to smile and offer to shake hands, or back slowly away while reaching for a chair and a whip. In the end he smiled briefly, stepped back a pace and looked to Ash for help.

'This young lady is Madeleine Kresh,' said Ash easily. 'Call her Mad for short. Everyone does. She is Time's companion, assistant, social secretary, and anything else she can think of. She's not family, whatever else she is. She just turned up on his doorstep one morning, cold and shivering, he brought her in and gave her a bowl of milk, and she's been here ever since. She's a sort of combination bodyguard and watchdog, and everyone who wants to see Time has to get past her first. Isn't that right, Madeleine?'

'Don't call me that!' the young woman snapped in a deep harsh voice, her eyes digging holes in his face. 'And you can forget about seeing Time. He's busy. Now piss off.'

'Don't be like that, Madeleine,' said Ash calmly. 'You know your little heart goes pat pitter pat at the sight of me. I like the chains, by the way; they've come up nicely since you polished them. Now be a good girl and tell Time we're here. He's expecting us.'

'I said you can't see him! Don't come sniffing around me with your clever mouth, ghostie. I'm on to your game. You think the rules don't apply to you any more because you're dead, but that doesn't cut any ice with me. You're just another damned shade who didn't have the balls to go through the Forever Door. You're not seeing Time today. He's in the middle of an emergency. Now piss off or I'll set the dogs on you.'

'You don't have any dogs, Madeleine. You're allergic to them. And as for the emergency, Time is always in the middle of something important, that's his job. But he'll see us. Or rather he'll see James, here. He can't afford not to. Now then, my dear, your constant over-protectiveness stopped being sweet a long time ago, so stop wasting all our time and tell the old man we're here.'

Hart hadn't thought it was possible for Mad to get any angrier, but steam practically poured out of her ears as she advanced on Ash. A flick knife was suddenly in her hand, the blade snapping out with a short, flat sound that seemed unusually clear and distinct. Hart didn't like the look of her or her knife. They both looked extremely dangerous and equally inflexible. She stopped immediately before Ash and shoved her face into his.

'Bottom line, Ash, in words of one syllable or less. Get out of here or I'll cut you and your pretty boyfriend. I don't like you coming here, Ash. You've no business here, and you upset Time by getting him involved in things that are none of his business. I don't know why you're here and I don't care. You're banned from the Gallery. You're blacked, null and void, a waste of space. Now turn around and walk back the way you came or I'll see just how much damage I can do to that dead body of yours.'

Her voice was harsh and deadly and utterly sincere. Hart decided he believed every word she said, and looked urgently at Ash, who hadn't budged an inch. When he spoke, his voice was calm and even.

'You're getting above yourself, Madeleine. You've found yourself a nice little niche here, looking after Time, and that's good; someone has to do it, and most of us haven't the patience. But don't make the mistake of thinking you're in charge here, just because Time is starting to get a little vague as his death gets nearer. You may have the word HATE tattooed on both sets of knuckles, but that doesn't mean you're good enough to tangle with someone like me. Now be a good girl, and do as you're told, Madeleine.'

'Don't call me that!'

Mad brandished her knife in Ash's face, and then stopped and fell back a step. Nothing had happened but everything had changed. Without moving a muscle or saying another word, Ash was suddenly frightening, and very dangerous. Menace blew from him like a cold wind, chilling the heart and stealing its courage. Hart's flesh crawled, and it took all his self-control not to back away from Ash. He suddenly knew, deep down where it mattered, that Ash was exactly what he'd said he was; a dead man, walking. Death had entered the room, and would not be ignored. Ash reached out and took the knife from Mad's trembling hand. He smiled at her, and it was not a pleasant smile. Perhaps, Hart thought, it was not entirely sane, either.

'You speak very freely of death, Madeleine, but you don't know anything. Shall I show you what it really is, what it really means? Shall I teach you the secrets of the grave, and the comfort of the earth?'

Mad's face was drained of all colour, her makeup standing out starkly against her staring eyes. She was trembling violently, but even so she wouldn't retreat a step. Ash's smile widened, and there was no humour in it at all.

'All right, that's enough of that.'

The calm, dry voice broke the mood like a shock of cold water. Ash looked round to see who'd spoken, and Mad ran a shaking hand across her mouth, as though waking from a nightmare. Hart began to breathe more easily, and some of the ice went out of his veins. He looked briefly at

Ash with new eyes, and then looked to see who'd spoken. The newcomer walked unhurriedly out of the maze of machinery to join them; a gaunt man in his late fifties or early sixties, dressed to the height of mid-Victorian fashion. His long black coat was of a fine but severe cut, and apart from the gold watch-chain gleaming brightly across his waistcoat, the only flash of colour was the apricot-coloured cravat at his throat. He stood before them, smiling benignly, like a favourite uncle. An air of quiet authority hung about him like a cloak, only slightly undermined by a certain vagueness.

'You really must stop provoking poor Mad,' he said sternly to Ash. 'Just because you're dead, it doesn't mean you can forget your manners. Now give her back her knife.'

'Sorry,' said Ash, casually handing Mad her knife. 'It won't happen again.'

'No you're not, and undoubtedly it will, but let that pass for the nonce. It's good to see you here again, Leonard. Can I hope that you've finally decided to do the right thing, and pass through the Forever Door at last?'

'I can't go,' said Ash. 'Not yet. My parents still need me. It was their need that brought me back, and their refusal to let me go that still holds me.'

Time sniffed dismissively. 'You've told me that before, and I didn't believe it then. Still, it's your life, or rather your death, and I can't tell you what to do with it.' He turned to Hart, who straightened up and stood a little taller despite himself under the firm but kindly gaze. Time was handsome enough in an old-fashioned way, with a determined chin and a stern brow. He had a thinning mane of long white hair, brushed back from his high forehead and left to lie where it would, but it was his eyes that caught the attention. Time had very old eyes, old and more than a little tired. And very, very knowing. Hart felt six years old, and too impressed by the old man's sheer presence even to feel annoyed. Time smiled understandingly.

'So, you're Jonathon Hart's boy, are you? Yes, you've

your father's face. Never thought to see it here again, though I of all people should know better than to use the word never, hmm? Especially about anything to do with Shadows Fall.' He sniffed disparagingly and shook his head, and then a nearby dial caught his eye and he reached out to regulate the pressure with a few turns of a handy wheel. He glared at the dial, apparently displeased with what he saw, and rapped imperiously at the glass face with one knuckle. He waited a moment and then sniffed again, only just satisfied by the new reading. He turned back to Hart.

'Can't turn your back on anything round here; there's always something needs doing. Still, don't take anything you see here too literally, young man; not even me. We all tend to vary somewhat, according to the eye of the beholder. The human mind tends to adjust and tone down things it finds too complex or disturbing. Think of all this as a metaphor, if that makes you feel more comfortable. Now then, young man, we must talk. Things are happening, or will happen soon, and you're right in the middle of it.'

'Me?' said Hart. 'What did I do? I only just got here.'

'That was enough,' said Time. 'Your return has set in motion a chain of events that will affect us all; a wheel of destiny whose time has come round at last. And whether you like it or not, you are in it up to your lower lip and sinking fast. The prophecy will be fulfilled, no matter what you or I or anyone else can do.'

'I could leave Shadows Fall,' said Hart.

'No, you couldn't,' said Time, not unkindly. 'The town wouldn't let you.'

'But you're supposed to be in charge of everything here . . .'

'Hah! No, my boy, I'm more of an overseer, an umpire who sees that everyone sticks to the rules. I'm not even human, as you would understand the term. I am the physical incarnation of an abstract concept, both more and less than human. I exist because I'm necessary, but even I, more than anyone else, have to follow the rules. I'm not even immortal, strictly speaking. I live for exactly one year, age from babe to ancient, and then die and rise again from my ashes, which is a lot messier than it sounds. Each time I'm reborn I have access to all my previous memories, but am I the same person, or merely a new being with access to someone else's memories? It's an interesting distinction, and one I've been pondering for centuries without getting any closer to an answer. Still, that's Shadows Fall for you. I am the power that holds this town together, but it is the town that decides its future. All I get to do is nudge things in the right direction. Mostly I get the feeling I'm only along for the ride.'

'Nudge,' said Ash. 'Not quite the word I would have used. Speaking of the devil's henchman; where is Jack Fetch?'

'About my business,' said Time. His eyes were suddenly cold, but the smile he turned on Hart was reassuring. 'You don't want to believe everything you hear about Jack. He's my assistant; helps enforce the rules when necessary. Not the easiest of fellows to get along with, but I've always found him very loyal. He's not a bad sort, really, just rather direct in his methods.'

'Direct,' said Ash. 'That's another good word.'

'You're here on sufferance, Leonard,' said Time. 'Don't push your luck. Now then, my dear James, you're looking at me somewhat strangely. Is something wrong?'

'No, not really. I was just wondering, well . . . why *Victorian?*'

'Don't ask me,' said Time. 'It's your subconscious. I've no doubt Leonard sees me very differently, but then, being dead he's more able to bear the truth of my reality. I fear my true nature is a little too much for most people. Don't worry about it too much, my boy. However you see me, it's real enough. I'm just . . . translated by your mind into something more comfortable to deal with, hmm? You'll find a lot of things are like that in Shadows Fall.'

'So I can't see what you really look like, but Ash can?'

'The dead have few illusions,' said Time.

Ash shook his head firmly as Hart looked at him. 'Don't ask, James. Trust me on this. You don't want to know.'

'Let's get back to what you actually do,' said Hart, just a little doggedly. 'You decide how things should be, or the town does and you pass it on, and then Jack Fetch deals with anyone who disagrees. Right?'

'Pretty much,' said Mad, in the tone of someone who'd been left out of the conversation entirely too long, and wasn't at all pleased about it. 'Time makes the decisions that matter. He protects the town and the Door.'

'Protects?' said Hart. 'Protects from who?'

'Shadows Fall has its enemies,' said Mad flatly. 'And whoever controls the Forever Door controls the town. Time keeps us all safe. There's always some sneaky bastard ready to plunder the various times and realities, and to hell with the consequences. Thieves, conspirators and general ratbags. Time sniffs them out and sends Jack Fetch to fix their wagon. Jack kicks ass.' She smiled unpleasantly at Hart. 'You have to meet Jack before you go. He's dead interesting, is Jack.'

'That's enough, my dear,' said Time. 'Just because Jack isn't real, it doesn't mean that at heart he isn't a nice person. If he had a heart, that is. Jack has many fine and sterling qualities; it's just that in his line of work, he doesn't get to show them much. Now James . . . pay attention, young man! I'm not talking for the pleasure of hearing myself speak.'

'Sorry,' said Hart quickly, looking away from a clock face that had caught his eye. It was running backwards. 'I'm listening. Please continue.'

'Well,' said Time, a glint in his eye suggesting he was not entirely mollified, 'suffice to say I oversee and maintain the various times and realities that are attracted to Shadows Fall by its unique nature. People and places are constantly coming and going; it's that sort of place. I keep track of them all, through my portraits and other methods. I see all and know most, here, there and everywhere, and try not to trip over my own feet too often.' He broke off, and smiled at Mad. 'I seem to be getting a little dry. I'm not used to so much talking. Why don't you make us all a nice cup of tea?'

Mad nodded curtly, and glared at Ash and Hart. 'I'll be back in a minute.'

'I'm missing you already,' said Ash gallantly.

Mad gave him one of her best sniffs, turned on her heel and left. Her back radiated disdain.

Time started to say something admonishing to Ash, and then stopped and looked over Ash's shoulder. 'You wanted to see Jack Fetch, James, and it seems you're in luck. Here he comes now.'

Ash and Hart looked quickly back, and turned round sharply as they heard footsteps approaching outside the closed door. The footfalls were slow and steady and somehow . . . soft, as though whoever was approaching was wearing padded slippers. The thought disturbed Hart on some deep level, though he couldn't say why. The soft sounds were somehow too *diffuse*, not solid enough. They finally stopped outside the door, and in the long pause that followed, everyone seemed to be holding their breath. Hart could feel the hackles rising on the back of his neck, and was suddenly very sure he didn't want to see what was on the other side of the door.

And then the handle turned and the door opened, and Jack Fetch walked in on springy legs. He was a scarecrow, a thing of rags and sticks and straw. He should have looked quaint and old-fashioned, charming in a traditional rural way, but there was nothing reassuring or comforting about Jack Fetch. He was a human figure formed entirely of unliving, inanimate details, from his straw-stuffed shirt to his twiggy feet to the grotesquely carved turnip that was his head. He reminded Hart of a toy he'd once had, grown vague and frightening in his bedroom after the light had been turned off. Jack Fetch was made of things that did not live, and never should have lived, but moved now by the workings of some unnatural will. He wasn't a puppet or a tool, like Time's automatons; Jack was alive and aware and not in the least human. Hart could sense it, in his bones and in his water. The great turnip face turned slowly on its wooden neck, looking from Hart to Ash to Old Father Time, and of them all Time was the only one who met the dark, unblinking gaze. The scarecrow slowly advanced on them, the bound twigs of his feet making light scratchy sounds on the bare wooden floor, like rats scuffling across a barn's floor, and then he came to a halt before Time, bowed jerkily once, and was still. Hart looked at the unmoving creature and didn't know whether he wanted most to hit it or run away.

'Jack Fetch,' Ash said softly. 'In Shadows Fall mothers tell their children to be good, or Jack Fetch will come for them. And sometimes he does. How many have you killed today, Jack? There's blood on your hands.'

Hart looked automatically at the battered leather gloves that were the scarecrow's hands, and his heart jumped in his chest as he saw the dark stains that speckled the gloves. Time made a soft tutting noise.

'Jack, you know you're supposed to clean yourself up before you come to see me. What will our guests think, hmm? Even so, Leonard, I've told you before; you're not to be rude to him. His feelings are easily bruised, and you know how hard it is to get good help these days. Jack is my good right hand, and I rely on him to see that things are run as they should be run, for the town's sake. Even the most indulgent father must be stern on occasion.'

'Who did you send your dog after today?' said Ash flatly.

Time shrugged. 'The Lords of Order and the Dukes of Chaos have been arguing over fractals again and breaking up the furniture. This new science of Chaos Theory has caused more trouble on the aetheric planes than you'd think possible. I don't know why they can't just agree to disagree. Be that as it may, Jack quietened them down easily enough. He's a persuasive fellow, when he wants to be. Well done, Jack. Return to the Gallery of Frost, and I'll see you later.'

The scarecrow stood unmoving for a long moment, and then slowly turned his turnip head to stare at Hart. The carved smile and empty eyesockets held no warmth or sign of emotion, but there was a thoughtful deliberation to the stare that Hart found chilling. It was as though he was being studied and weighed and found wanting, in some silent Court from which there was no appeal. He fell back a step involuntarily, and the scarecrow moved after him. Time called sharply for Jack to stop, but the scarecrow went silently after Hart as he continued to back away. He made no sound, save for the scratching of his twiggy feet on the wooden floor, but still Hart could read purpose in his slow, unhurried advance.

Time came up behind him, calling the scarecrow's name with increasing anger, and finally took him by the arm. Jack Fetch shrugged him off without even looking round. There was an unnatural strength in the unliving body, and Hart knew on some deep primal level that if Fetch caught him, he could tear him apart as easily as a child might pull apart a stuffed toy. Hart's back slammed up against a wall, and there was nowhere left to go. His breathing was fast and shallow, like a bird in a cage being menaced by a cat, but still it never occurred to him to fight. He somehow knew there was no point, that Jack Fetch was not something that could be stopped by human strengths.

And then there was a cry and a scream and a black-clad figure threw itself furiously at the scarecrow, sending him staggering to one side. Madeleine Kresh rode the scarecrow's back like a jockey, her legs wrapped round his upper arms, her hands tearing at his turnip face. He quickly regained his balance, and reached up with his gloved hands. Mad spat at them, and cut at the nearest hand with her knife. Jack Fetch ignored her attacks, grasped her firmly by the arms and removed her easily from his person. He set her down, and pushed her firmly to one side. Mad stabbed him in his stuffed belly, her blade ramming home three times in swift succession, but no blood ran from the ragged cuts in his shirt. Mad stood there stupidly, and the scarecrow turned his attention back to Hart.

Ash stepped forward and stood between the two of them, his pale disquieting eyes fixed on the scarecrow's empty stare. And in that moment he drew his true nature about him again, and became terrifying. Mad felt its power and fell back despite herself. Even Hart could feel some of it, though it wasn't directed at him, and his blood chilled in his veins. Jack Fetch stood staring at the dead man, and then reached out with his gloved hands, took him by the arms and moved him gently but firmly to one side. Ash stumbled and almost fell, as though just the touch of the scarecrow's hands had drained the strength right out of him. Jack Fetch looked again at Hart, and stepped deliberately forward so that he was standing right in front of him. There was sawdust on his breath, stale and scratchy in Hart's throat as he breathed it in.

It's come for me, was all he could think. *It came for my parents, but they were already gone. So now at last it's come for me.*

The room had grown quiet, as Time and Mad and Ash watched helplessly to see what the scarecrow would do. Of them all, only Time had made no real move to stop him, presumably because he knew Fetch couldn't be stopped once he had been set in motion, that whatever was about to occur had the weight of destiny behind it. And as Hart watched with wide and staring eyes, Jack Fetch dropped jerkily to one knee and bowed his turnip head to him. And then he got to his feet, turned away and walked off, disappearing back through the door he had left ajar earlier. There was an almost explosive sigh of relief from those who'd been holding their breath, and Time looked strangely at Hart.

'In all the time I've known Jack, he's never done that to anyone. Not even me.'

'So what does it mean?' said Mad, reluctantly putting her knife away.

'I don't know,' said Time abruptly. 'But it is extremely interesting. I'm going to have to think about it.'

Hart had to swallow hard to clear his throat, but when he finally spoke his voice was cool and even. 'Did you send . . . that after my parents, when they decided to leave Shadows Fall? Is that why they never dared come back?'

Time pursed his lips thoughtfully before answering. 'The prophecy concerning you and your family was annoyingly vague, as most oracles are, but the sense seemed clear enough. The fate of the Forever Door, and that of the whole town, is linked in some way to you. You would not have been harmed, had you stayed. Only watched, and considered. We could have stopped you leaving, but we chose not to. For all our human and inhuman natures, Shadows Fall has always done its best to behave in a civilized manner.'

'Yeah,' said Ash. 'Jack Fetch is really civilized.'

'Well,' said Hart, meeting Time's gaze steadily, 'Now I'm back, what are you going to do?'

'Watch and observe,' said Time calmly. 'Please understand, James; Shadows Fall is important. The world needs a place like this, where the boundaries of the real can relax, and all lost souls can find their way home at last. The Forever Door is a pressure valve, where the world can let off steam safely, and let go those things that no longer fit. And you threaten all that, my boy, just by being here. If the Door were ever destroyed, or this town obliterated, the psychic shock would throw the whole world into madness and violence. Fires would be started that would burn for eternities, and the long night would never end. There are forces in the universe that will not be denied, James, both inside and outside Shadows Fall.'

'So what do you think I should do?' said Hart.

'I don't know,' said Old Father Time. 'But it seems to me that if there are answers to be found, they lie in your past, when the prophecy was made. Why don't you go and visit your old family home? Leonard can show you where it is.'

'Yes,' said Hart. 'I think I'd like that. Can we go now?'

'Of course, my boy, of course. Though do have a little something before you go, to warm the blood and keep the cold out.'

He gestured to Mad, who produced from somewhere a tray with four small porcelain cups on it. Time took one, sipped carefully, and smiled. Ash and Hart took a cup each, and Mad took the last. She was smiling suspiciously innocently, so Hart waited for her to sip hers first, which she did with great aplomb. Hart took a healthy gulp from his cup, and his eyes bulged as a small nuke went off in his throat. His tongue curled up and died and his eyes squeezed shut like they were never going to open again.

'What is this stuff?' he gasped, eventually.

'Saki,' said Mad, grinning. 'Powerful stuff, if you're not used to it.'

Ash looked wistfully at his cup, and smiled at Hart. 'Well, you can't say you weren't warned, James. Next time your future self tells you something, I really think you should pay attention . . .'

Hart glared at him through tear-filled eyes. 'You talk too much, Ash.'

4

Saying Goodbye

All Souls cemetery was a small affair, only a few hundred graves, tucked carefully away out of sight so as not to disturb anyone with its presence. Tall trees shielded it from passers-by, and there was only the one narrow gravelled path, wandering through the neat rows of headstones and out again. Shadows Fall was built around death, or at least passing through the Forever Door, but as in so many other places, no one really wanted to have to think about it until they were forced to by circumstances. All Souls was neat and tidy and efficiently laid out, with regular inoffensive rows of headstones, and no obtrusive crypts or statues or over-sized monuments. They weren't actually forbidden by any code or by-law, it was just understood that All Souls was not the place for such vulgar ostentation. Anyone who wanted such frills and fripperies was coolly encouraged to take their trade elsewhere. There were such places, even in Shadows Fall, but polite people didn't talk about them. All Souls cemetery was a place of peace and contemplation. Sheriff Erikson thought it was the most depressing place he'd ever been.

He stood resignedly beside Mayor Frazier and watched solemnly as Father Callahan ran smoothly through the reburial service for Lucas DeFrenz. The man who'd come back from the dead, claimed to be possessed by an angel, forgot what his mission was, and was murdered before he could remember. Now he lay at rest in a new coffin beside his old grave, waiting to be interred again, only this time, hopefully, for a somewhat longer stay. Erikson sneaked a look at his watch. The priest had been droning on for what seemed like ages, running through the special service for those whose rest had been disturbed, with more than usual care and emphasis, and even a certain sense of drama. Presumably because it wasn't a service he got to use all that often, and he was determined to make the most of it. Returning from the dead wasn't unknown in Shadows Fall, but it was still rare enough to be a novelty when it did occur.

Erikson sniffed, and shifted restlessly from foot to foot. He'd never liked funerals. Partly because they reminded him of his own mortality, but mostly because they bored the shit out of him. When you were gone, you were gone, and that should be the end of it. Erikson liked things neat and tidy, especially his own emotions. No doubt Father Callahan meant well, but the endless words of intended comfort had all started to run into each other, and Erikson just wished he'd get on with it. Erikson had never been one for standing around doing nothing; he needed to be active, to be occupied. It wasn't as if he'd known Lucas all that well. But his investigations into the man's second death had got absolutely nowhere, so all that was left was to attend Lucas's funeral, and hope something interesting happened.

He glanced unobtrusively at the Mayor beside him. Rhea Frazier was dressed elegantly but conservatively in black, with a little pillbox hat and a modest veil. She looked calm and composed, but then she always did. Rhea was a great one for being in control at all times. A mouse could run up her leg and her hat could catch fire, and still it wouldn't crack her composure. She hadn't got around yet to explaining what she was doing at Lucas's funeral, but Erikson was determined to get it out of her before she left. He glanced at her again, envying her cool composure in the face of mind-numbing boredom. Still, that was politicians for you; the polite smile and the hearty handshake, and a face that gave away nothing at all. He'd known Rhea for more years than he cared to remember, and he was still

96

no nearer understanding what made her tick. The thought disturbed him. Erikson believed in understanding people; in his job, knowing which way someone would jump could make all the difference. But Rhea stood there at his side, their arms almost touching, a friend since childhood, and she might as well have been on the moon.

Erikson sighed quietly and looked about him, not even bothering to hide it. None of DeFrenz's family had turned up for the ceremony. They'd been through the ordeal of his funeral once, and had no wish to put themselves through it again. He'd talked to them earlier, and they'd been polite but very firm. They'd said their goodbyes to the man they knew, and had no interest in the fate of the man who'd come back from the dead claiming to be someone else. One of them had sent a modest-sized wreath of flowers, but there was only the family name on it, and no note to identify the sender. It looked small and lost, standing alone by the headstone. There were no other flowers. Erikson wondered vaguely if he should have brought some. It had been a long time since he'd been obliged to attend a funeral, and he was a bit vague on the etiquette. And then it occurred to him that Rhea hadn't brought any flowers either, and the thought calmed him. Rhea always knew the right thing to do.

Apart from the two of them and the priest, the only other observers were two gravediggers, standing a respect- ful distance away and passing a single cigarette back and forth between them. They were talking quietly together, their words drowned out by the priest's loud and carrying enunciations. They were both tall and muscular, well but casually dressed, and didn't look much like gravediggers at all, as far as Erikson was concerned. Not that he had much idea of what a gravedigger should look like, apart from a vague feeling that they ought to be leaning on shovels. As it happened, there was no sign of a shovel anywhere. Presumably such things were kept carefully out of sight until the mourners had departed, so as not to upset them. Erikson smiled sourly. It wouldn't have bothered him if they'd turned up with a mechanical digger. He caught the priest looking at him narrowly, as though suspecting the Sheriff wasn't paying him proper attention. Erikson stood a little straighter, put on his best official functions face, and wondered wistfully how long it was till dinner.

Derek and Clive Manderville, the gravediggers and general handymen of All Souls cemetery, and half a dozen others as well, waited patiently for the service to be over so that they could get on with their job. It was a cold day, the grey and forbidding sky promising rain and sleet later in the morning, but they knew they'd work up a sweat fast enough once they got started. It was just as hard work filling in a grave as digging it, though not many people seemed to appreciate that. There was a lot about being a gravedigger that people didn't appreciate, as Derek often pointed out to his younger brother Clive. This was particularly true of towns like Shadows Fall (even though technically speaking there were no other towns like Shadows Fall), where you couldn't trust a person to stay where you planted them. You go to all the trouble of digging a decent-sized hole, lay them nicely to rest and cover them over respectfully, and the next thing you knew they'd dug their way out again, and there was mud and dirt everywhere. Derek thought there ought to be a law against it, to which Clive always replied that very probably there was, but you couldn't expect the newly-risen dead to give much of a damn about minor inconveniences like laws. Right, Derek would say, nodding his head firmly, as though he'd just made a particularly telling point. There were times, Clive thought as he passed over their one and only cigarette, that Derek got right up his nose.

'Maybe we should have dug this one a little deeper,' said Derek, accepting the cigarette as his due. 'Maybe putting another half a ton of dirt on top of him would help hold him down this time.'

'It couldn't hurt,' said Clive.

'I wouldn't mind, but he's not the first one to come back on me,' said Derek aggrievedly. 'That Leonard Ash was one of ours as well. You remember Ash; just over three years ago. Very nice mahogany coffin with gold scrollwork. Lovely job. Three years ago we dropped him in and covered him over, and just the other day I saw him walking around town, bold as brass. Some people just don't appreciate what you do for them.'

'You're not wrong,' said Clive, eyeing Rhea Frazier and wondering if she did. She looked as though she might.

Derek growled deep in his throat, and shook his head mournfully. 'The way they keep coming back these days, I don't know why they even bother nailing the lids down. They should just put in a revolving door and have done with it.'

'Are you going to hang on to that cigarette all day?'

'If you hadn't forgotten it was your turn to bring a new pack, we wouldn't be reduced to this. You wait your turn. At least we got this one back. What was his name again?'

'DeFrenz. Thought he was an angel.'

Derek sniffed dismissively. 'Talk about delusions of grandeur. Well, I'll tell you this, Clive, and I'll tell you it for free. If he sits up in his bloody coffin again, I'm going to brain him with my shovel. I'm not digging another hole for him.'

Clive nodded firmly as Derek finally handed him the last inch of the cigarette. They stood together in silence for a while, listening to Father Callahan winding down the service. Lovely speaker, Father Callahan. Such inspiring words. Well; Clive assumed they were inspiring. Half of them were in Latin. But they sounded inspiring, and that was what mattered.

'Course,' said Derek, 'to be fair, it's not always the stiffs that mess up this job. Remember that time we buried an empty coffin?'

Clive winced. 'Did they ever find out what happened to the body?'

'No; never did. Their own fault for having him exhumed. If they'd left well enough alone, they'd never have been any wiser, and we'd all have been a lot happier.

Then there was the time we planted that guy who turned out not to be a hundred per cent actually deceased.'

'He was by the time we dug him up again.'

'My very words at the time. Didn't go down well with the authorities. Not noted for their sense of humour, authorities.'

The service finally concluded, and Father Callahan made a series of ritual passes over the empty grave. He didn't normally approve of introducing white magic into Church ceremonies, but the service for reinterring the risen dead was quite specific, and he knew his duty. He had a responsibility, and through him the Church, to see that the DeFrenz family were not troubled again, and that Lucas DeFrenz could sleep soundly at last. Even if he had been a Godless blasphemer with delusions of grandeur. He gestured tartly at the coffin, and white fire crawled around it, sealing it shut for all time on both the material and spiritual planes. Another gesture, and the coffin rose into the air and then slowly lowered itself into the waiting grave. It quickly disappeared from sight, rubbing gently against the walls of the hole, and Father Callahan began a series of binding and protective spells that would hold until the final Day of Judgement, or he'd know the reason why.

Sheriff Erikson realized the service as such was over, and nodded to Rhea that they could move away from the grave. They moved off a respectful distance, both their faces calm and inscrutable, as much to reassure themselves as each other. Funerals are always hard on the living; especially when the deceased's murderer is still at large. Erikson stopped by an overgrown grave and glanced disinterestedly at the headstone. Time and the weather had worn away the stone until the inscription was barely legible.

NOT DEAD, ONLY SLEEPING.

He's not fooling anyone but himself, thought Erikson.

'Was there something about this grave that you wanted to show me?' said Rhea.

'No,' Erikson said quickly, 'But I did think we ought to have one last word about Lucas. There's still a lot we don't know, and I hate leaving cases unfinished. We were never even able to prove one way or the other whether he really was possessed, never mind what he was possessed by.'

Rhea nodded. 'We never found out what his mission was, either. All he could remember was that it was vitally important to everyone in Shadows Fall. And when he fixed you with those cold eyes of his, it was hard to disagree. He claimed his memory had been deliberately interfered with, by persons or forces unknown, but then, he would, wouldn't he? More and more it seems to me the man was just suffering from delusions. Coming back from the dead can't do your sanity a lot of good at the best of times. All right, I'll grant you he was pretty damn disturbing to be in the same room with, but that's hardly enough to prove him an angel, and a receptacle of God's will.'

'Maybe, if Michael really was an angel, he'll come back in another body,' suggested Erikson, and Rhea pulled a face.

'That would be all we needed. You know, the DeFrenz family wanted Lucas's body cremated, specifically so that it couldn't be repossessed, but Time said No. Very loudly and very emphatically. No reason given, of course. Heaven forfend that Old Father Time should start acting in a reasonable manner, and deign to let us lesser mortals in on what the hell is going on. Mind you, if he ever does I think we should all run for cover, because it probably means the end of the world is nigh.'

They both looked across at the clockwork automaton standing elegantly by a tree, some distance away. It had already been there when they had arrived for the service, but it had made no attempt to join the ceremony. It just stood there among the trees, half hidden in shadows, with no emotions on its painted face, seemingly as lifeless as the grave before it. But its eyes were Time's eyes, its ears Time's ears, and just the fact that it was there was significant. Old Father Time could have watched the funeral through one of the portraits in his Gallery of Bone, but instead he had sent one of his clockwork children, the

101

physical reminder of his presence and authority in Shadows Fall.

He knows something, thought Rhea. *He wouldn't allow Lucas's body to be cremated, and he wants us to remember that. Why?*

It could have been worse, thought Erikson. *He could have sent Jack Fetch.*

Rhea and the Sheriff studied the automaton for a while, but it made no move either to acknowledge or to ignore them, and eventually they turned back to watch Father Callahan perform his brisk magics over the open grave. So they never noticed the second watcher in the trees; a tall thin man dressed in black, hidden in the depths of the shadows. He watched Rhea, Erikson and Callahan through a pair of miniature binoculars, and now and again made a note on a pad. There was a handgun in a holster on his hip, and a rifle leaned against the tree beside him. There was something in his face that might have been anger or fear, or both. And also something very like disgust.

'It might be an idea to keep an eye on every death in Shadows Fall from now on,' said Rhea, with the easy assurance of one who knew she wouldn't have to do the job herself. 'Just in case Michael comes back through someone else.'

'I had already thought of that, actually,' said Erikson. 'Are you and the town Council ready to authorize the extra money it's going to take to pay for extra Deputies and round-the-clock surveillance?'

Rhea winced unhappily. 'I'll have to get back to you on that. The budget's a little tight this year.'

'The budget's a little tight every year,' said Erikson dryly. 'Especially when I want something.'

Rhea laughed softly, and Erikson had to smile. They'd fought more than their fair share of battles over money in the past, on one side or the other and sometimes both. For sheer complexity and vicious infighting, there's nothing quite like small town politics. Except possibly piranhas in a feeding frenzy. The Sheriff and the Mayor smiled uneasily

102

at each other, bound together by shared memories, neither of them sure if they wanted to pursue the sudden intimacy. The events of the past few weeks had brought them closer together, almost despite themselves. Erikson searched for something to say, and winced mentally as he realized the only subject he had wasn't one likely to make things any easier between them. But it had to be said. If only because it was his job, and it might just be important.

'Speaking of the newly-returned, I saw Leonard the other day. He looked good, all things considered. Did you know he's taken up with James Hart?'

'Yes,' said Rhea. 'I know. As if things weren't bad enough, James bloody Hart is back, and all anyone wants to talk about is the old prophecy. There must have been something else that could have happened that would have muddied the waters even more thoroughly, but I'm damned if I can think what. Sometimes I get the distinct feeling that everyone in town must have shot an albatross. These things come in threes, you know. First the murders, then James Hart's return. What next? The entire town being wiped out by a giant bloody meteor?'

'Hush,' said Erikson. 'Don't give Fate ideas.'

'I was thinking about Leonard anyway,' said Rhea. Her voice was cool and calm and perfectly steady. 'Today's funeral reminded me of his. There weren't any mourners there, either. Just you and me and his parents. It was wet and windy, and the florist had sent the wrong flowers. Not much of a way to say goodbye.'

'You should talk to him,' said Erikson.

'No. My Leonard's dead.' She gave him a flat, hostile look that told him she was going to change the subject. 'I understand you met James Hart. What's he like?'

'Surprisingly normal. Pleasant enough. A bit quiet, but encountering Shadows Fall for the first time will do that to you. He doesn't remember his childhood here at all. Leonard thinks he remembers him as a child, but I can't say I do. How about you?'

Rhea shook her head. 'No. I checked the old records, as

103

soon as I heard he was back. We were in the same class at the same school, all four of us, but neither you nor I nor anyone else I've contacted can remember him. That can't just be a coincidence. I think Time has been meddling with our memories again.'

'Leonard remembers him.'

'Leonard's dead. It's harder to hide things from the dead.'

'Maybe that's why Leonard took James Hart to see Old Father Time. Leonard always was one for getting to the heart of things.' Erikson smiled suddenly. 'I'd love to have had a bug on the wall during that conversation. But whatever happened there, they're all keeping pretty quiet about it. Hart's gone to look at his old family home. I hope he's prepared for a shock. No one's lived there since his parents did their disappearing act. I've got one of my Deputies keeping an eye on Hart, just in case. I don't know what's happened to Leonard, He hasn't been seen at any of his usual haunts. Still, I suppose Hart could have fallen in with worse company.'

'You don't really think they just happened to meet, do you?'

Erikson frowned. 'You think Time is interfering that directly?'

'Time, or the town.' Rhea shook her head and shrugged, and changed the subject again. Erikson let her do it. Even after all this time, Ash's name still had the power to hurt her. She looked out over the cemetery, and at the town beyond. 'Things are falling apart, Richard. The Hart prophecy has unnerved a lot of people. They're afraid for themselves, and for the town itself. No one trusts anyone any more. If it had been just the murders, or just Hart's return, I think we could have coped; but the two together are driving the town insane. And there's not a damn thing I can say to reassure them. We're no nearer finding the murderer now than when we found Lucas's body lying in its own blood on the floor of Suzanne's place. The town is looking for someone or something to blame, and if we don't provide a scapegoat soon, they'll find one for themselves. Everyone's waiting for the next murder, for the next shoe to drop. And when it happens, the people of this town will head for the brink like lemmings on amphetamines.'

'You always did have a gift for an interesting phrase,' said Erikson, just for the sake of saying something. He'd never seen Rhea look so down, so defeated. So vulnerable. 'We're doing everything we can,' he said lamely. 'My Deputies will protect Hart from attack, as long as he keeps a low profile. Apart from that, there's really not much else we can do. We've all kinds of forensic and magical evidence, and all of it together hasn't turned up one useful lead. We don't have a motive, a witness or a murder weapon. Or anything to tie the victims together. They could just be random targets, picked for reasons only a madman could understand.'

'That's right,' said Rhea. 'Go on. Cheer me up, why don't you?'

'If you're looking for optimism, you've come to the wrong man. The very fact that I'm here, hoping for a miracle, should tell you something.'

'Who knows?' said Rhea, shrugging tiredly. 'Maybe we'll get lucky. Cemeteries are special places everywhere, but especially so in Shadows Fall. Reality wears thin in the presence of so much death. And with all the recent comings and goings, maybe things have been disturbed enough to produce signs we can interpret. Did that really sound as desperate as I think it did? Don't answer that; I don't want to know.'

'Are you ready for the really bad news?' said Erikson, not looking at her. 'I wasn't going to say anything until I had some solid proof one way or the other, but what the hell. I have to talk to someone or I'll go crazy. We have two more missing persons. No warnings before they vanished, no reason for them to drop out of sight, and no trace of them anywhere now. It's too early to be sure, but would you like to bet whether they're going to turn up as victims eight and nine?'

'Two more?' Rhea closed her eyes tightly for a moment, as though she could somehow hide from the news. Erikson started to reach out a hand towards her, but the moment of weakness passed, and she opened her eyes and looked squarely at the Sheriff. 'What are the names? Anyone important?'

'Not really. An anthropomorphic, Johnny Squarefoot, and one of the Merlins, late European version. Both important to their friends and family, no doubt, but no great loss to the town. As with all the others, no obvious motive for their disappearance or murder. No problems, no enemies. Just two more poor sods plucked from our midst with no one noticing a thing.'

Rhea frowned, tapping a foot thoughtfully on the neatly trimmed grass. 'Are these new disappearances public knowledge yet?'

'Not yet. I'll keep it quiet for as long as possible, but there's a limit to how long I can sit on it. Someone always talks, eventually. Then it really will hit the fan. We were lucky to avoid a riot after the last murder was announced. I hate to think what two more will do to the town.'

'There must be something we can do!'

'I'm open to suggestions! I'm doing everything I can. If that isn't good enough for you, you can have my badge and my resignation on your desk within the hour.'

'Don't get touchy, Richard. I'm not mad at you. I just feel so . . . helpless.'

They stood together for a while in silence, not looking at each other. Father Callahan finished the last of his rites with a quick burst of Latin and a dramatic gesture, made the sign of the cross over his breast, nodded quickly to Rhea and Erikson and strode off without looking back. The two gravediggers looked hopefully at Rhea and Erikson, and then sighed resignedly as they realized neither the Mayor nor the Sheriff was showing any sign of being ready to leave.

'Since Michael claimed to be an angel,' Erikson said

106

slowly, 'Perhaps we ought to have a quiet word with Augustine.'

Rhea winced. Augustine was Shadows Fall's resident Saint. He was good and holy and forgiving, and got on everyone's nerves. There's something about never-ending pieties and good humour that drives ordinary people right up the wall. Augustine meant well, was always cheerful and smiling, and never had a bad word for anybody. Most people could only stand being in the same room with him for about half an hour before being seized with an over-whelming urge to swear, tell off-colour jokes about their relatives, piss on the potted plants and generally act up cranky. If he hadn't been so good at curing warts, rheu-matics and haemorrhoids, he'd have been run out of town long ago.

And besides, he could turn water into wine. By the gallon.

'I think we'll leave Augustine as a last resort,' said Rhea firmly. 'Things are confused enough as it is without getting him involved. Our accounting division still hasn't recovered from the time he insisted on exorcising the Internal Revenue computers, and wiped all their memory discs clean. All right, the computers stopped printing out blasphemies and stinking up the offices with sulphur, but it's the principle of the thing. You know, Richard, what with Saints and angels practically crawling out of the woodwork these days, do you suppose God is paying particular attention to us?'

'Now there's a spooky thought,' said Erikson. 'But when you get right down to it, it's just like Old Father Time. We know he's watching, but who knows what and why?'

'God moves in mysterious ways.'

'And has a very strange sense of humour.'

'Hush,' said Rhea, smiling in spite of herself. 'Show some respect. Or the odds are we'll all get struck by lightning.'

Bruin Bear and the Sea Goat watched the two humans talking earnestly together, and wondered if they should intrude. Bruin Bear was a four-foot-tall teddy bear with golden honey fur and dark knowing eyes. He wore a bright red tunic and trousers, and a bright blue scarf wrapped tightly round his neck. Most people found the colours a bit overwhelming after a while, but Bruin Bear wasn't people. Even if he did have one gold earring and a Rolex on his wrist. He'd been a very popular children's character back in the fifties and sixties, but he didn't move with the times, and was soon forgotten by all but a few collectors. Still, he tried to keep cheerful, and kept himself busy helping people in distress. That was what he'd always done in his many adventures in the Golden Lands, and he wasn't about to stop now just because he was real. He had many friends in Shadows Fall. People would do anything for him, because he'd do anything for them. He was that kind of Bear.

His companion of many years and even more adventures was the Sea Goat. People often loved Bruin Bear on sight, but few felt that way about the Goat. Wrapped in a long trenchcoat, he looked human enough from the shoulders down, as long as he kept his hands in his pockets, but he had a large blocky goat's head with long curling horns and a permanent nasty smile. His grey fur was soiled and matted where it showed, and his eyes were bloodshot. The coat was filthy, and half the buttons were missing. In one hand he carried a bottle of vodka that by some kind magic was never completely empty. He'd taken his fall from fame badly and didn't care who knew it, and only his long friendship with Bruin Bear kept him from the solace of the Forever Door. The Bear wouldn't go as long as he felt there was someone who needed his help and comfort, and the Goat wouldn't go on his own. At least partly because he knew how lonely the Bear would be without him.

'Maybe we should come back later,' said Bruin doubtfully. 'They look rather upset.'

'Of course they're bleeding upset. It's a bleeding funeral. What did you expect, paper hats and dancing?'

'I thought you'd agreed not to start drinking until after midday.'

'It's bound to be midday somewhere in Shadows Fall. Time,' said the Sea Goat grandly, 'Is relative. And I've never got on with my relatives. Smile, damn you, Bear. The jokes may not be much, but they're all I've got. Now are you going to brace these two realio trulios, or am I going to have to do it?'

'I'll do it,' said Bruin Bear. 'And please, let me do all the talking.'

'You're ashamed of me, aren't you?'

'No I'm not.'

'Yes you are. You're ashamed of me. I'm your best friend and you're ashamed of me. Course, you're quite right. I'm a mess. That's all. Just a bloody mess.'

The Sea Goat wept two huge tears that trickled slowly down his long muzzle. Bruin reached up and wiped them away with the end of his scarf.

'Stop that. You're my friend, and you always will be. So cut out the tears, or I'll piss in your vodka bottle when you're not looking.'

The Sea Goat snorted loudly and smiled, showing his great blocky teeth. 'Dear Bear, it could only improve the flavour. Now point me in the right direction, and I'll back you up while you tackle the dynamic bloody duo.'

Bruin Bear sighed quietly, pulled a smile from somewhere and walked towards the Mayor and the Sheriff with the Sea Goat stumbling along behind him. The humans looked quickly round as he hailed them cheerfully, and both of them had some kind of smile for him. He was that sort of Bear. They ignored the Sea Goat, but he was used to that.

'Hello, Bruin,' said Rhea. 'What are you doing here?'

'We heard that Johnny Squarefoot was missing. We're worried that something might have happened to him. Is there anything you can tell us?'

'We don't know anything definite yet,' said the Sheriff neutrally. 'As soon as we know anything for sure, my office will issue a statement. I'm sorry I haven't anything more for you, but it really is too soon to be seriously worried. You didn't come all the way out to All Souls just to ask me that, did you?'

The Sea Goat started singing softly in Gaelic. Everyone else ignored him and talked a little louder.

'No,' said Bruin. 'There was another funeral here, earlier this morning. Poogie the Friendly Critter died yesterday.'

'I'm sorry,' said Rhea. 'I didn't know.'

'We'd been expecting it for some time,' said the Bear. 'But that didn't make it any easier. He faded away so quickly, at the end.'

Rhea nodded. She'd seen it happen too many times before. Cartoon and fictional animals who ended up in Shadows Fall only remained stable as long as someone somewhere still believed in them. Once that last hold on reality was gone, they slowly reverted to their original template, becoming the actual animal they were modelled on. Bit by bit they lost their intelligence and their individuality, and lived short happy lives as beasts of the wild. Unless they found the courage to go through the Forever Door first.

Rhea had seen Poogie crying in the street a few weeks ago. He was never very definite to begin with; just another Saturday Morning cartoon who got cancelled after his first series. He was likeable enough, but too generic to last long on his own. Rhea found him sitting outside a shop, crying his eyes out because he couldn't add up the coins in his paw to tell whether he'd been given the right change. He understood numbers when he went in, but now they were a mystery to him. Not long after, he forgot how to talk. And now he was dead. Rhea wished she'd found him funnier.

There were all kinds of animals scattered throughout Shadows Fall, of varying reality and intelligence. They mostly kept themselves to themselves, living underground in the Underworld of the Subnatural. But now, with Johnny Squarefoot missing, presumed dead, it seemed the murders had touched even them, the most innocent and vulnerable of Shadows Fall's lost souls.

110

'There weren't many of us at Poogie's funeral,' said Bruin Bear. 'Most of us are afraid to go out, even in broad daylight. But we couldn't let his passing go unremarked. Father Callahan did a lovely service for him. Even managed a nice little eulogy at the end.'

'Yeah,' said the Sea Goat. 'Mind you, I'd have been more impressed if he'd got the name right.'

'Anyway,' said the Bear, 'He told us there was another funeral here, so the Goat and I waited, to pay our respects. Was Mr DeFrenz a friend of yours?'

'Not really,' said Rhea. 'But we thought someone ought to be here.'

'Damn right,' said the Sea Goat. 'Every man's death diminishes us. Only a Friendly Critter diminishes us rather less. How the hell can you forget a stupid name like Poogie?' He shook his head, and took a long swallow from his bottle. Rhea glared at him.

'How can you drink like that at this time of the day?'

'Practice, man, practice,' said the Sea Goat. He laughed hollowly, and belched. Bruin Bear gave him a hard look.

'You must excuse my friend,' said the Bear. 'He's a drunk and a slob, but he means well.'

'You'll be telling them I've a heart of bloody gold next.'

'We knew Lucas DeFrenz before he died,' said Bruin Bear, in the tone of someone determined to change the subject. 'Before he died the first time, I mean. He was a good man. Always ready to stop and talk. I think he liked the Sea Goat too. He was a man of great heart. After he came back from the dead we went to see him, but he didn't remember us. Michael didn't seem a very happy man, whoever he was. Do you really think he was an angel?'

Rhea was about to answer, when suddenly everything changed. The music came first. A choir of voices, massed beyond number, but still every note clear and distinct, like the plucking of a giant harp. The sound grew louder, impossibly loud, resonating in their bodies. They all put their hands to their ears, but the sound would not be muffled. It vibrated through their flesh and echoed in their bones. A light appeared in the sky, outshining the sun. It was too bright to be any specific shade or colour; a fiercely burning illumination like a star come down to earth, searing the eye even though they'd all squeezed their eyes shut. The light and the music filled the world. They had to open their eyes and look. And then the angels came down, and they were brighter and more beautiful than anything human or beast could bear to see for long.

They drifted down like blazing snowflakes, glorious and brilliant, every one unique and wonderful. Rhea wanted to look away, and couldn't. Tears streamed down her cheeks because they were so beautiful, too beautiful to be real. They were more than real, as though she and everything else were nothing but a rough, unfinished sketch. Erikson was watching and crying too, and Bruin Bear and the Sea Goat. They were in the presence of power and grace beyond the natural world, and they knew it.

The angels hovered above the open grave, and sang of love and loss and things left unfinished. They soared and glided on the air, never still, never settling, great wings beating slowly, and then they rose up suddenly and disappeared back into the sky. The blazing light and the thunderous sound snapped off, and the real world returned, though the echo of that glory still trembled within those who'd experienced it. Rhea fumbled a handkerchief from her sleeve and dabbed at her brimming eyes and wet cheeks. The world seemed a flatter and duller place without the angels, but still she couldn't find it in herself to be sorry they were gone. They were too beautiful, too perfect. They scared her. There was nothing in them of pity or forgiveness for human failings and weaknesses. No place for compassion, or mercy. They were angels, the Word of God given shape and form, and they did not belong in the human world. Rhea looked at the grave before her, and smiled slowly as she took in the clear colourless flame burning on top of Lucas's headstone. It burned unsupported, unmoved by the gusting wind, and Rhea knew without having to be told that it would burn that way for ever, in tribute to a man who for a time had carried an angel within him.

'Well,' said Erikson finally, his voice just a little shaky, 'I think that answers the question as to whether he really was possessed by an angel.'

'Yeah,' said the Sea Goat. 'Wow. Let's see them do that with their special effects.' He lifted the bottle to his mouth, and then lowered it again without drinking. For a time at least, he had no need for vodka. Something far more potent burned within him. He grinned at Bruin Bear, and then the bottle shattered in his hand.

The sound of the gunshot came a moment later. The Sea Goat stared stupidly at the broken neck of the bottle still in his hand. Erikson drew his gun and yelled for them all to get down. He dropped to one knee and glared wildly about him. Rhea hit the ground and lay flat, her hands digging into the grass as though she could pull it over her like a blanket. The Bear yanked at the Sea Goat's arm. There was the sound of another shot, and the Sea Goat lurched backwards a step. He looked down with wide, startled eyes at the widening bloodstain over his stomach. Bruin took a firm hold on the Goat's arm and pulled him down by brute strength.

Two more shots whipped past overhead, but the head-stones shielded them. Erikson finally made out the man standing in the trees, and fired two shots at him. The figure with the rifle didn't even flinch. Erikson swore briefly and took careful aim. It's a lot harder than most people think to hit someone with a handgun at any distance, even in Shadows Fall. Unfortunately the sniper had a rifle and what appeared to be telescopic sights. The moment the thought flashed through his mind, Erikson forgot all about aiming and dropped behind the headstone that was shelter-ing him. He'd only just got his head down when two bullets whined through the air where his head had been. Erikson quickly decided that the current situation called for common sense, rather than heroics. In particular, it called for keeping his head well down and not trying to fight it out with someone who had him completely outclassed in the weapons department.

He glared about him to make sure the others were safe. Rhea was lying flat on the ground a few feet away, shielded by the row of headstones. He could see her lips moving, but whether she was praying or cursing was unclear. Erikson thought he could guess, though. Bruin Bear was lying beside the groaning Sea Goat, trying to shield the seven-foot body with his own diminutive form. The two gravediggers had taken cover in the open grave. Any other time, Erikson might have found that funny, but right then he didn't have the time. He eased his gun round the edge of the headstone and fired two shots blindly, just to keep the sniper on his toes.

There was no return fire, and after a long moment Erikson peered very cautiously round the edge of the stone. The sniper had a hand radio, and was talking into it. Erikson smiled tightly. The sniper could talk to whomever he liked; there was no way he could get out of Shadows Fall, now he'd revealed himself. A sudden movement caught the Sheriff's eye, and he looked quickly round to see Time's automaton striding out of the trees towards the sniper. The man put his radio away, quickly brought up his rifle and fired. The bullet hit the automaton square in the chest. The metal figure shuddered under the impact, but kept on coming. The sniper fired again, and the automaton's head exploded. It stopped uncertainly where it was, and the sniper shot out its knees. The clockwork figure fell to the ground and lay there thrashing awkwardly. Erikson scowled. Time's automatons were pretty hard-wearing, but there was a limit to the kind of punishment they were expected to take. That was what Jack Fetch was for. He'd be here soon. Time wouldn't stand for this. Erikson shuddered at the thought, despite himself. The sniper might think he was in control of the situation, but the scarecrow would change all that. There was nowhere the sniper could run that Fetch couldn't find him. And

114

then Erikson heard the helicopter approaching, and knew immediately how the sniper was going to escape.

The sound quickly grew louder, and in a matter of seconds a black military-style helicopter with no markings was hovering over the graveyard. The trees bent reluctantly under the down-wash of the roaring blades, but the sniper held his ground. A door opened in the side of the helicopter, and a rope ladder fell down. The sniper shouldered his rifle and pulled himself up on to the ladder. Erikson raised his gun and took careful aim. *No you don't, my friend. Not that easily, you don't.* He fired once, but the ladder was swaying back and forth, and he missed. The helicopter turned to face him, and Erikson suddenly knew why.

Oh shit . . .

He crouched down behind the tombstone again, and the helicopter's machine guns opened up. Bullets flew around him, pounding against the stone and chipping away at its edges. Erikson curled into a ball, and tried to think himself smaller. *Who the hell are these people? Mercenaries? Who for?* He didn't have to see the sniper to know he was escaping up the rope ladder, but there was nothing he could do to stop him. He was pinned down, helpless in the face of superior firepower. There was nothing he could do. Nothing anyone could do.

But Bruin Bear wasn't just anyone.

He ran out from among the tombstones, his short legs moving him surprisingly quickly as he raced towards the helicopter. He had no weapon of any kind, but his small fuzzy face was completely determined, without a hint of doubt in it. Bullets hammered the ground to both sides of the Bear, but none of them hit him because . . . well, because he was Bruin Bear, and some of his old magic was still with him. He crossed the intervening ground incredibly quickly, and swarmed up the rope ladder after the sniper. His furry paw shot out and grabbed the sniper's ankle. The man kicked and shouted, but couldn't break the hold.

'Let go of me, demon! Hellspawn!' There was anger in the sniper's voice, but something that might have been fear and revulsion too. The Bear hung on grimly.

'You shot my friend,' he panted. 'You shot my friend!'

And then a man in military fatigues leaned out of the helicopter door and aimed a gun point blank at the Bear's head. There was a limit to Bruin's magic, and the Bear knew it. His paw closed harshly, crushing the sniper's ankle, and then he released his hold and fell back to the ground. He hit hard but was up on his feet in a second, watching helplessly as the helicopter flew away.

Back among the headstones Rhea and Erikson rose slowly to their feet and, for want of anything better to do, dusted themselves off thoroughly.

'Who the hell were they?' said Rhea, her voice not quite as steady as it might have been.

'I don't know,' said Erikson. 'But I'm going to find out.'

Bruin Bear came trotting back. 'Did you hear what he called me? He called me a demon! And hellspawn! I mean, do I even look like a demon? I'm a fucking teddy bear!'

He brushed past Rhea and Erikson without waiting for an answer, and knelt beside the Sea Goat, who had managed to sit up by bracing his back against a headstone. The front of his trenchcoat was soaked with blood. He was breathing in sudden little gasps, but his eyes were clear. Bruin Bear took the Goat's gnarled hand in his paw and held it firmly.

Rhea looked at the two gravediggers climbing out of the open grave. 'You two! Go get a doctor. Or a magic-user, if you can find one. Use my authority if you have to. Now move it!'

The gravediggers nodded and left at a run, as though their own lives depended on it. Rhea knelt down beside the Sea Goat, and started to undo his coat buttons.

'I wouldn't,' said Erikson quietly. 'It might be all that's holding him together. Leave it for someone who knows what they're doing.'

'Of course,' said Rhea. 'You're right. I just . . . wish there was something I could do.'

'Try a few prayers,' said the Goat hoarsely. 'Any deity. I'm not choosy.'

'How do you feel?' said Erikson.

'Bloody awful. Next stupid bloody question.'

'Save your strength,' said Bruin Bear.

'I saw your run,' said the Goat. 'Pretty good for a short arse. Scared the britches off that sniper.' He started to laugh, and then stopped painfully as blood started from his mouth. 'Damn,' he said thickly. 'That is not a good sign. Look, somebody do me a favour and drag me the hell out of here. I positively refuse to die in a cemetery. That's too sodding ironic, even for me.'

'We can't risk moving you,' said the Bear. 'Now shut up and lie still or I'll belt you one.'

'Not you, Bruin. Not your style, that. But thanks for the thought.'

Rhea got up and walked off a way, gesturing with her head for the Sheriff to join her. When they were comfortably out of earshot, Rhea looked Erikson straight in the eye. 'No more diplomacy, Richard. What are his chances?'

'Not good,' the Sheriff admitted. 'Gut shots are always bad. He's got an exit hole in his back you could stick your fist into, and from the way he's coughing blood, it's a pretty safe bet the bullet's at least nicked one of his lungs. If he was a man, he'd be in real trouble. Since he's . . . whatever he is, he's in with a chance.'

'Why shoot *him*?' said Rhea. 'If the sniper came all this way to kill someone, why not choose someone important, like you or me? A target that would be worth all this effort?'

'Good point,' said Erikson. 'I don't know.'

Rhea shook her head tiredly. 'What the hell is going on in Shadows Fall? First the murders, then James Hart, and now a sniper with military back-up. Has everyone gone crazy?'

'I don't know,' said the Sheriff. 'Maybe. But I think it's

more likely someone is following a definite game plan. That helicopter shouldn't have been able to get in here without setting off all kinds of alarms, natural and supernatural. Either our security is getting really sloppy, or . . .'

'Or there's a traitor in Shadows Fall,' said Rhea slowly. 'Someone has betrayed us to the outside world.'

5

Secret Places

Lester Gold's car took the corner at more than twice the speed limit, engine roaring, tyres screeching, and shot off down the empty road as though the Devil himself was in hot pursuit. Sean Morrison, bard, troubadour and late sixties rock-and-roller, hung on to his seatbelt with both hands, and watched with horrified eyes as his whole life flashed before them. An awful lot of it seemed to have been spent in bars, and Morrison fervently wished he was in one now, preferably with a large brandy in his hand. Brandy was good for shock. Lester Gold, Man of Action and Mystery Avenger, seemed blithely unaware that there was anything at all unusual about his driving, and continued to talk cheerfully about his past exploits as a costumed adventurer as he ran swiftly through the gears to squeeze every last ounce of speed out of the straining engine.

Morrison tried to remember whether his will was up to date, and listened incredulously as the old man at the wheel talked of his adventures in the thirties and forties as though they were yesterday. Under other, calmer, circumstances Morrison might have found them fascinating, but as it was he was more concerned whether the car would hold together much longer. If it had been a horse, it would have had wide, rolling eyes and froth at its mouth by now. The pressure of traffic increased as they headed out into the suburbs, and Gold reluctantly slowed to something nearer the speed limit. Morrison began to breathe more easily, and decided the next time the car stopped for a red light, he was going to hurl himself from the car and run like fun for the horizon. Except that the car didn't seem to be stopping for any red lights . . .

The suburbs flashed by in a blur of identical houses, with neatly trimmed lawns and cars in the drive. People stopped to wave at Gold's car, and he always waved cheerfully back. Morrison rather wished he wouldn't. He felt fractionally more secure when Gold had both hands on the steering wheel. Gold suddenly turned the car sharply to the right, not bothering with incidentals like mirror or indicator, and brought the car to a shuddering halt in the driveway beside a pleasant-looking house. Morrison decided he was going to sit very still for a while, until his legs felt strong enough to support him again. He took the opportunity to study Gold's house. It wasn't quite what he'd been expecting. It was an ordinary house in an ordinary street, situated right in the middle of Shadows Fall's quiet suburbs. Not too big and not too small, with a neatly laid out flower garden, and a stone bird bath full of murky-looking water. Down the end of the street someone was walking a dog, and half a dozen kids were kicking a ball about. Not exactly what he'd expected for the head-quarters of the Mystery Avenger.

Gold was already out of the car and round the other side, holding the car door open for Morrison to get out. He was still talking, something about the Blue Diamond murders and the Master of Pain. (Morrison could hear the capital letters quite distinctly.) He climbed out of the car just a little shakily, waited for a brief pause in Gold's story, and then nodded at the house.

'Is this it? The secret retreat of the Mystery Avenger?'

Gold grinned cheerfully. 'What did you expect? A Fortress of Solitude? I'm a retired florist on a pension. I'm rather proud of the garden, though. You should see it in the summer, Sean. It looks a treat in the summer. Now follow me, and keep clear of that flower bed. I've just put some bulbs in.'

Morrison followed Gold into the house, being very

careful where he put his feet, and found the house's interior exactly matched its exterior. A nice little commuter's house, with fitted carpets, comfortable furniture and paintings on the walls of those cute children with the big eyes. Morrison hadn't felt so nauseated since the time he'd mixed Polish vodka and Napoleonic brandy in the same glass to see what it would do to the taste. (Actually, it had tasted pretty good for the ten minutes or so he'd been able to hold it down.) He managed a polite smile, and Gold grinned back in a way that suggested he wasn't fooled in the least, but appreciated the thought.

'It's a small place, but my own. The Bank's paid off, and every inch of it is mine. It was supposed to be a retirement home for me and the wife, after we sold off the florist's. But Molly died only a year after we retired. I hadn't expected that. I always thought we'd have our autumn years together. But it wasn't to be. The old place seems rather empty without her. We'd planned so many things we were going to do; places to go, people to meet . . . but somehow they didn't seem nearly so attractive once I was on my own, so I never went. I stayed here, keeping the place clean and tidy and pottering about in the garden. I thought sometimes about selling the house and getting something smaller, but I never did. The rooms are full of Molly's things, and as long as they're still here I can pretend she's still about the place somewhere, in another room or just popped out for the moment. Silly, I know, but I do miss her. Now then, you're not here to listen to an old man's ramblings; you want to know about the Mystery Avenger. Come along.'

He started up the stairs to the next floor. Morrison pulled a face behind the old man's back, but followed obediently. *Probably going to show me his old costume, hanging up in a cupboard. Then I'll have to sit through all his old scrapbooks and photo albums. When am I going to learn to say no to people?* Gold stopped by the first door at the top of the stairs, pulled out a heavy brass key and unlocked the door. He pushed it open, and stepped back for

Morrison to enter first. He put on his best interested smile, nodded to Gold, and walked forward into another world.

It was an ordinary-sized room, but packed from wall to wall and from floor to ceiling with a lifetime's collection of souvenirs and paraphernalia celebrating one man's career as a costumed adventurer. There was a bookcase full of old pulp magazines and paperback reprints. A glass display case full of weird and unlikely objects, each carefully labelled as to which adventure they belonged to. There were photos of old friends and adversaries, and even a full-sized cinema poster from an old forties black and white movie serial starring the Mystery Avenger. And there was a costume, on a mannequin inside a polished glass case. It looked more like body armour, but it had a certain garish style. Morrison wandered slowly through the bookcases and display stands, and something of the small child awoke in him again, from a time when he still believed in heroes and villains. He looked back at Gold, grinning in the doorway.

'Welcome to my Batcave,' the old man said cheerfully. 'Most of it's junk, really. I should have a good clean out, make some room, but it all has sentimental value. Even if most of it never really happened.'

Morrison found himself standing before the cinema poster, with its huge photo of the Mystery Avenger in full costume, hanging on to the side of a speeding car, gun in hand. 'Is that . . . you?'

'No,' said Gold, 'That's Finlay Jacobs, the actor who played me on the screen. They never did get the costume right. Said it didn't look dramatic enough. Maybe, but at least I could go into a fight reasonably sure I wasn't going to trip over my own cloak. The serial made money, but not enough to make it worth shooting another. The studio already had the rights to the Shadow and the Spider, and they were both bigger than I ever was. Nobody else seemed interested. I can't say I'm sorry. They messed up all the stories, and got all the details wrong. Even had me swinging from building to building on a rope. Have you ever tried that? It gets very painful, very quickly. I used a car to get about, like everyone else. And before you ask, no, it wasn't a Batmobile. The whole point of a car was to get me quickly from place to place. The last thing I needed was some flashy motor that told everyone who I was. People would have mobbed it at traffic lights, demanding autographs.'

'I don't understand,' said Morrison slowly. 'The exploits in the magazines and books were really you, but the movie serial wasn't?'

Gold shrugged. 'I remember all of them, but none of them were real till I came here. I became real the moment I decided to stay in Shadows Fall, like any other legend. You have to be real, before you can die. But before that, there were so many versions of me that I lost count. So I decide what actually happened, and what didn't. Who else has a better right?'

Morrison nodded, and looked back at the display cases. One was full of toys and merchandising from the forties and fifties. He raised an eyebrow. That sort of thing was worth money these days, to collectors. Particularly if they came personally autographed . . . but that was in the outside world, and none of this would ever go there. He came to a leather-bound album, and opened it to flip through the heavy pages. The album was made up of a series of old newspaper cuttings, carefully mounted and dated, from the late sixties onwards. They all concerned the Mystery Avenger's involvement in strange and unusual crimes that had taken place in Shadows Fall. Sometimes he was just there as an adviser, sometimes assisting in the running of a case with other detectives, and occasionally there was a large photo of the man himself, in full costume, pictured at the scene of the arrest. There was something almost surreal in the way the costume remained the same, but the man inside grew steadily older. Morrison looked back at Gold.

'These clippings; they all really happened, here in Shadows Fall?'

'Oh yes. Officially I was retired, and I had the florist's shop to keep me busy, but every now and again the Sheriff of the day would run into something strange and baffling, and he'd quietly put the word out that he could use a little help. I always tried to do my best, and not disgrace my legend. I didn't wear my costume, except at photo calls. It's hard for an old man to look dignified in cloak and tights. I like to think I was helpful, but not a nuisance. They weren't what you'd call major cases, for the most part. That one you're looking at there was when I helped capture the Phantom Boggler, a semi-transparent gentleman in a long raincoat who went about flashing his insides at people. Rather unpleasant sort, as I recall. Not long after that, I rescued the Crampton child from a cave-in, and helped catch a woman who'd murdered her lover's wife, and then tried to pin the murder on him. Complicated case, that one.'

Morrison flipped through to the end of the album. The last cutting was dated three years ago. Half a column, no photograph. He closed the album respectfully, and looked back at Gold.

'This is an incredible room,' he said finally, trying to make it clear with his tone how genuinely impressed he was. 'I didn't know you'd been involved in so many . . . real cases.'

'They were all real, to me. I remember everything that was ever written about me, even the more outrageous ones at the end of my career, when they made a super-hero out of me. The events of those stories are as real to me as anything in that album. Even though they never really happened. I know it sounds complicated, but it isn't, to me. The world I live in now seems a little duller and greyer than it used to, but I suppose it seems that way to most people as they get older. The Mystery Avenger belongs in the past, in simpler times. I was just as happy running my florist's shop, with my Molly.'

Morrison nodded slowly. 'How many people have seen this room?'

'Not many. Only the most dedicated collectors remember me now, and no one else would be interested. Shadows Fall is full of fictional characters who became legends, and most of them are more famous than I ever was. I don't have any family of my own, and Molly's family were always rather embarrassed by my past. So I shut it all away in one room, and locked the door. I come in, once in a while, to dust and remember . . . But things have changed now. These new murders are getting out of hand. Sheriff Erikson's too young to remember me, but I haven't forgotten. I'm as sharp now as I ever was. It's time for me to come out of retirement. Shadows Fall needs the Mystery Avenger.'

If anyone else had said as much to Morrison, he would have looked away, embarrassed, or hooted with laughter, but something in Gold's voice and manner, a calm and sure dignity, made Morrison want to believe in him. For once in his life he was lost for words, and just nodded speechlessly. Gold smiled.

'Don't worry; I'm not going to wear the costume. Tights and cape are a young man's game. I'll just pick up a few things, and then we can be going.'

Morrison started to nod in agreement, and then lost it completely as Gold opened a display case and casually took out the biggest handgun Morrison had ever seen. Gold hefted it easily in one hand, checked to see that it was loaded, and then put it down to one side so that he could strap on a shoulder-holster. Morrison watched speechlessly as Gold slipped the gun into the holster and practised a few quick draws.

'Always choose a big gun, Sean,' Gold said casually. 'That way, if you run out of bullets you can always club the bastards to death.'

Morrison gave Gold a hard look, but he didn't seem to be joking. And then Gold reached back into the display case, and Morrison lost it again as Gold brought out what was very obviously a grenade.

'Lester; you have got to be joking!'

'A wise man always takes precautions,' Gold said calmly. He stopped and looked thoughtfully at Morrison. 'These . . . elves of yours; they're not going to be upset by a little firepower, are they?'

'No,' said Morrison. 'Trust me, Lester; they're going to love you.'

Gold looked at him narrowly, not entirely sure he liked the tone in Morrison's voice, and then he shrugged and pulled on his jacket, which had clearly been specially tailored to conceal the gun and shoulder-holster. He dropped the grenade casually into a jacket pocket, and politely pretended not to notice Morrison's wince. 'These elves of yours, Sean. Do we really have to go and see them? I mean, what use are a bunch of little people with wings and pointed ears going to be in tracking down a determined killer?'

'You've never met any of the Faerie, have you?'

'No. Never thought we'd have anything in common.'

'Well, first of all they're not *my* Faerie. They very definitely belong only to themselves, and would not take at all kindly to the idea that they might belong to a human. They don't exactly hold us in high regard. Except sometimes as pets. Secondly, they're not at all what you'd expect. They're an old people, savage and majestic. They are also proud, arrogant, and downright vicious. They delight in duels, vendettas and general slaughter, and most of the time no one within shouting distance of their senses should have anything to do with them. However, since I am also proud, arrogant and dangerous to know, we've always got on like a house on fire. People have mostly forgotten the old stories and legends that gave birth to the Faerie. Down the years people have censored and prettified and generally Disneyfied the hell out of them. Those versions are here too. In fact, there are areas where you can't move for the precious little fluttering things. They are not areas I care to frequent, especially when I'm sober. The Faerie are the real thing; old, brutal and desperately honourable. They keep to themselves, mostly, and every-body else is very happy to leave it that way.'

Gold looked at him dubiously. 'The more you tell me about them, the less sure I am this is a good idea. Maybe I should take along a rifle and a few incendiaries, just in case.'

Morrison smiled enigmatically. 'Couldn't hurt.'

Gold turned away, muttering, and filled his pockets with an assortment of presumably useful objects. Morrison looked at the covers of a handful of old super-hero comics, each individually bagged to protect the ageing paper. It was hard to relate Gold to the idealized, hugely muscular character on the covers. Gold was big enough, and in superb shape for a man of his age, but there was nothing superhuman about him. Still, he thought, you couldn't expect much realism from a medium where the women were habitually drawn with breasts bigger than their heads. He looked up and saw that Gold was ready, and looking at him expectantly.

'You know the way, Sean, so you'd better drive.'

Morrison smiled, and shook his head. 'That's not the way it works, Lester. The Faerie live in their own separate reality; the land beneath the hill. It's an old world, much older than ours, and entrances are few and far between. Once, long, long ago, it was otherwise, but the Faerie fought a bitter and savage war with something they still won't talk about. It's not clear whether they won or lost, but thousands of years ago they retreated beneath the hill and took most of the entrances with them. Which essen-tially means you can't get there from here. Unless you've got an invitation. Fortunately, I am on their guest list, because I am a bard, so all I have to do is snap my fingers and click my heels together, and we can be on our way.'

Gold looked at him thoughtfully. 'Sean; have you been smoking anything unusual recently?'

Morrison laughed. 'I know, it sounds crazy even for Shadows Fall, but the Faerie live by their own rules, and they don't think as we do. Trust me; I've done this before. Do you have a wardrobe?'

'Of course I've got a wardrobe. What kind of a question is that?'

'Can I see it, please?'

Gold gave him a hard look, strongly suspecting he was being silently laughed at, and led the way out of his den. He carefully locked the door behind them, and then showed Morrison into the next room down the passage. It was a bedroom, clean and tidy and almost completely devoid of personality. The fittings and furnishings looked like they'd been chosen by a committee, and a particularly unimaginative one, at that. Morrison allowed himself a brief internal wince, and then concentrated on the wardrobe. It stood solidly against the far wall, big and blocky and almost aggressively ordinary. Morrison nodded approvingly, walked over to it, and opened the door. Ranks of clothes stared back at him.

'And what are we supposed to do now?' said Gold. 'Shout hello, and wait for somebody to answer?'

'Not quite.' Morrison pushed a heavy coat aside and stepped into the wardrobe. 'Come along, Lester. There's plenty of room in here.'

Gold shook his head dubiously, and stepped in beside Morrison, hunching over to keep from banging his head. 'I don't believe I'm doing this. I'm just glad there's no one here to see me. They'd probably think we were indulging in some strange sexual practice.'

'I don't need to practise,' said Morrison briskly. 'I'm very good at it.'

Gold glared at him. Morrison laughed, reached out and pulled the door shut. For a long moment, nothing happened. It was dark, and extremely claustrophobic, but Gold found the familiar smell of his clothing reassuring. He could sense more than see Morrison beside him, but he slowly began to feel that there was a gap between them, gradually widening. There was a feeling of space all around him, as though the wardrobe was somehow growing, or he

128

was shrinking. He started to reach out to touch Morrison, but stopped himself. It would have been an admission of uncertainty, of weakness, and Gold didn't allow himself to be weak these days. Let the rot start, and there was no telling how far it might go. He might even start feeling old . . .

'Here we go,' said Morrison beside him, and Gold's stomach lurched as the floor beneath his feet suddenly descended like an elevator. The descent quickly picked up speed, but the darkness kept Gold from telling how fast they were moving. The coats had disappeared, left behind above, and Gold reached out cautiously to touch whatever was before him. There was nothing there, for as far as he could reach. He didn't step forward. He had a sudden alarming vision of himself and Morrison descending into the depths of the earth on a platform no wider than the floor of his wardrobe. He visualized an endless drop all around him, and cold beads of sweat appeared on his temples.

The speed of their descent slowed abruptly, the floor pressing up against Gold's feet, and then bright light burst through the darkness, and Gold cried out despite himself. He blinked rapidly, knuckled his watering eyes, and finally lowered his hands to look about him. He and Morrison were standing on a vast grassy plain, on a small wooden platform that seemed paradoxically to have risen *up* out of the grass. The plain stretched away into the distance for as far as he could see, and beyond. There were no buildings or other structures, the plain as smooth and level as a grassy sea. The midday sun was almost painfully bright, but the air was pleasantly cool. Morrison breathed deeply, and grinned almost giddily at Gold.

'It's good to be back, Lester. Welcome to the land beneath the hill.'

'I don't see any elves,' said Gold neutrally. 'In fact, I don't see much of anything except grass.'

'Patience, Lester. You can't hurry things here. The Faerie have a different sense of Time from ours. Which is probably why they're able to lead such an independent existence. Old Man Time has only the most elementary control over the Faerie. Eventually one or the other will push it just that little bit too far, and then there'll be the mother of a fight to discover which of them is really in charge here. But, since neither of them is actually all that sure about the outcome, they're mostly happy to go on as they are, with no one making any waves.'

'That's all very well,' said Gold, in a tone that rather suggested it wasn't, 'but where are they?'

'They're watching us. They know me, but they don't know you. Their war with whatever the hell it was has made them cautious, suspicious and not a little paranoid. As a rule, they don't care much for human visitors. Right now, they're deciding whether to let us in, or kill us both. Try to look charming and interesting, Lester.'

'Sorry. I was never written that way. I can do dangerous and menacing, if that's any good.'

'Don't put yourself out, Lester. And please, keep that hand away from your gun. Let's not give them ideas, eh?'

'I'm beginning to think this wasn't such a hot idea. I don't like this place, I don't like the way we got here, and I definitely don't think I want to meet the Faerie. How about we just turn around and go back again?'

'I'm afraid we can't do that, Lester. That's not the way things work here. We've stepped into their parlour, and we can't leave until they let us. Don't look at me like that; I know what I'm doing. I've been here dozens of times, and they've never turned me away. Of course, I never brought anyone with me before. Don't frown like that, Lester; you might get stuck that way. I am a bard, a singer of the old songs and teller of the old tales, and the Faerie have always had a soft spot for bards. They'll let us in, if only to ask who the hell you are, and why I brought you here.'

'That's a good question,' said Gold. 'What am I doing here?'

'You're a hero. The Faerie have a thing about heroes. They admire a bard, but they love a hero. If I can't persuade them with argument and reason, maybe you can charm them into it. We need them, Lester. If we can persuade the Unseeli Court to help us, they could find our mystery killer practically overnight. They have access to magics and sciences beyond the dreams of man. They also have their own unique viewpoint. No one sees the world as clearly as those who live outside it.'

'That's a lot of ifs and maybes.'

'Yeah, well, the Faerie are like that, mostly. Ah, there we are. The welcome mat.'

A great slab of turf had fallen away inwards, revealing a set of earth steps leading down into darkness. Gold moved warily over to stand before it. The earthen steps looked crude and ancient, as though cut from the earth in prehistoric times. They fell away for a dozen feet or so, and then were swallowed up by the darkness. Gold looked at Morrison.

'We're supposed to go down into that? There isn't even any light!'

'There will be. Trust me, Lester, I've done this before. Just suck it in and tough it out. The Faerie admire courage. And try to look impressed. I know as entrances go, this isn't up to much, but the Faerie are great ones for tradition. If something's worked in the past, they tend to hang on to it. I suppose that's what being immortal does for you.'

'Are they really immortal?'

'Actually, no, just very long-lived. But don't even suggest such a thing to their faces. They don't like to be contradicted.'

He strode forward and started down the stairs with every appearance of confidence. Gold shook his head and followed after him. They soon left the light behind, and darkness closed in around them. Gold stopped where he was. He could sense more steps falling away below him, but he didn't entirely trust his footing on the uneven steps without light to guide him. He scowled unhappily and peered into the gloom. He should have brought a flashlight. He'd

131

brought practically everything else he might need, but not a flashlight.

And then a bright spark of light flared up before him, bobbing on the air like a cork on water. More sparks appeared, a cloud of them, swooping and soaring all about him like molten butterflies. Their shimmering light filled the stairway bright as day, and Gold could see that the steps came to an end not far below, and gave out on to a tunnel. Gold reached out to try and touch one of the dancing lights, but they evaded his hands easily.

'Leave them be,' said Morrison from the foot of the steps. 'They're will-o'-the-wisps. Basically friendly, but they can develop a mischievous sense of humour if they're annoyed.'

'You mean they're alive?' said Gold, stepping down to join him. Morrison shrugged.

'Yes and no. I don't think anyone's really sure, including them.'

'Is there nothing definite in this place you've brought me to?'

'Of course not. This is the land beneath the hill. They do things differently here.'

He strode off down the tunnel, and Gold had to hurry to catch up with him. The will-o'-the-wisps moved along with them, bouncing brightly on the air, never still for a moment. Their light was surprisingly steady and uniform, but there was still something about it that disturbed Gold. He looked unobtrusively around him, and then realized with a sudden chill that neither he nor Morrison cast any shadow.

The way sloped gradually but steadily downward, for more than long enough to make Gold uneasy, and then levelled out into a broad tunnel deep beneath the grassy plain. The walls were bare earth, without buttresses or supports of any kind. Here and there worms the thickness of a man's thumb oozed and curled in the earth walls, and hung down from the ceiling. There was a good foot or more of clearance above Gold's head, but he hunched his shoulders anyway. He had a vague but definite fear of the worms falling into his hair. He tried to ignore the unsupported tunnel roof, but it kept pulling his eyes back to it. He thought about the sheer weight of earth pressing down above him, and then decided very firmly that he wasn't going to think about that any more. Morrison strode blithely along ahead of him, as happy and unconcerned as though he was walking down a suburban street. Gold glared at his unresponsive back, and stumbled after him.

They walked in silence for some time. Morrison wouldn't answer questions any more, and Gold didn't like how small his voice sounded in the tunnel. And if he listened very carefully, he thought sometimes he could hear the will-o'-the-wisps singing. They sang in high breathy voices, in a language he didn't recognize, but still the music sent tremors through his bones, as though he'd heard it before, in dreams.

Time passed. There were no landmarks by which distance could be judged, and Gold wasn't really all that surprised to find his watch had stopped working. The only measure left to him was the growing ache in his legs and hunched back. But eventually they came to a gate, and had to stop. It filled the tunnel from wall to wall and from floor to ceiling, huge and heavy, built from a pale, grey veined stone in the form of a giant head. It was some kind of animal, but there were elements of the snarling face that were disturbingly human. The muzzle stretched outwards into the tunnel, blocking the way forward with huge blocky teeth clamped together. The eyes were closed, but it looked as though it might be listening, and waiting. There was no way past the head, and Gold couldn't take his eyes off it. Every instinct he had was screaming at him to get the hell out of there. The sense of danger and menace was so thick he could all but feel it on the still air.

'They call it the Watcher,' said Morrison softly. 'Don't let the closed eyes fool you; it knows we're here. Don't ask me whether it's dead or alive. Legend has it the beast was alive when the Faerie set it here to guard their home,

133

and it sat here so long it petrified to stone. No one knows what its name or species might have been; whatever it was, it's extinct now. Even the Faerie don't remember.

'They say the Watcher can recognize truth and treachery in the soul, and know a true and honest man from a villain. It can see into the dark places of the heart, and see every little secret you ever had, even the ones you don't allow yourself to remember, except in dreams. Step right up and the jaws will open, and if you're brave and true you can walk on into the hidden home of the Faerie.'

'And if you're not?' said Gold, just a little more harshly than he'd meant.

'Then the Watcher will eat you up, soul and all. Pleasant little legend, isn't it? But that's the Faerie for you. Every story has a moral, every legend a sting in its tail. Well, Lester, what do you think? Do we turn back, or do we go on? It's up to you.'

Gold looked at the Watcher, and the closed stone eyes looked back at him. There were dark stains on the huge teeth that might have been old, long-dried blood. He looked at Morrison, who was regarding him narrowly, and smiled coldly. He was the Man of Action, the Mystery Avenger, and he'd faced worse than this in his time.

'We go on,' he said flatly. 'I faced the Gibbet of Doom and the Howling Skulls, the Phantom of the Bloody Tower and the Order of the Immaculate Razor. It'll take more than this to make me turn back or step aside.'

Morrison nodded approvingly, and Gold wished he was as certain as he sounded. Just staring at the Watcher made his hackles rise, and the gusting breeze passing in and out of the snarling jaws seemed more like breathing with every moment. He nodded politely to Morrison.

'After you.'

'Oh, no,' said Morrison. 'After you.'

'No, no, I insist.'

'Age before beauty.'

Gold gave Morrison a hard look. 'I thought you said you'd been this way before?'

'I have.'

'Then what are you being so cautious for?'

'I'm not! I'm just being polite.'

'Well, I'm feeling less polite by the minute, and I'm damned if I'm going in first. I don't like the look on this thing's face. It looks very much like the kind of creature that might have an extremely unpleasant sense of humour.'

Morrison raised an eyebrow. 'I thought you were supposed to be one of the great old superheroes?'

'I was. And I didn't get that way by taking dumb chances. Now, are you going to walk into that thing's mouth of your own free will, or am I going to have to pick you up and throw you in?'

'Well, if you're going to be like that about it,' said Morrison. He walked up to the huge grinning jaws, and the bobbing lights clustered thickly about him, as though fascinated to see what would happen. The jaws opened slowly, stone grinding on stone as they retracted into the floor and ceiling. A series of low creaking sounds filled the tunnel, as of ancient machinery stirring to life again, or the stretching of long unused muscles and tendons. Morrison stepped into the mouth of the beast, and looked back at Gold. 'You worry too much, Lester. It's a wonder to me you haven't got ulcers.'

'That's as maybe,' said Gold, watching carefully. 'My writers never intended me as cannon fodder.'

Morrison walked on and disappeared from sight, and the jaws slowly came together again to form their impenetrable barrier. Gold was almost sure the grin was now more pronounced. He glanced at the remaining will-o'-the-wisps hovering curiously around him, took a deep breath and squared his shoulders, and walked steadily forward. The jaws opened again, gaping wide before him. He never doubted for a moment that he was a good man and true, and therefore in no danger whatsoever, but still . . . there was no denying his life had taken many different turns since he became real. The real world was much more complicated, and he'd become . . . complicated too. He strode on into the maw of the beast, head held high, and his breathing slowly eased as he realized nothing was happening. He'd never doubted for a moment, but it was nice to know he was brave and true, after all. The tension went out of his back and shoulders, and he even managed a small if rather sour smile. For all he knew, Morrison had been pulling his leg. Still, it never hurt to be cautious. He looked back at the great teeth closing slowly behind him, and bowed briefly.

'Thank you, Watcher.'

You're welcome, said a dry rasping voice in his mind.

Gold glanced back, startled, and then looked suspiciously at Morrison, waiting patiently in the tunnel ahead. He wanted very much to ask Morrison if he'd heard the voice too, but he had a strong suspicion Morrison would just say *What voice?* and he didn't think he could handle that just at the moment. He shrugged mentally, and went on to join Morrison. You'd think living in Shadows Fall all these years would harden you to things like that, but his thirty years as a florist had cushioned him from most of the town's wilder aspects. Which was at least partly why he'd been content to stay a florist for so long. After eighty-seven adventures and forty-nine issues of his own comic, he felt he was owed a peaceful retirement.

He and Morrison walked on down the earth tunnel in their pool of shimmering light, the will-o'-the-wisps alternately darting ahead and falling behind but never quite losing touch with their charges. Nothing happened for a long time, and Gold actually started to get bored again. He studied the curved earth walls curiously. They were smooth, almost polished, with no signs of workmanship to suggest how the tunnel had been dug. Gold frowned slightly. There should have been something; tool marks, signs of bracing or transport . . . something.

Morrison stopped suddenly, and Gold stopped with him. The young bard cocked his head slightly to one side, as though listening to something faint or distant. Gold con-

136

centrated, but all he could hear was their own quiet breathing. They were far below the surface, a long way from the sounds of the natural world. And then, very faintly, he heard footsteps, slow and unhurried, approaching out of the gloom ahead. A few of the glowing lights started down the corridor to see who it was, and then apparently thought better of it, and hurried back to Gold and Morrison. The footsteps grew slowly louder, though still strangely muffled. Gold glared into the darkness ahead, and then stopped and looked back the way they'd come. The sound could have been coming from either direction. He glanced at Morrison, but he looked baffled too. And then a figure stepped out of the wall just ahead of them, like someone appearing out of a thick fog. Gold fell back a step instinctively, and Morrison's hand clamped down painfully tight on his arm to keep him from any further movement.

The figure hesitated before them, trembling slightly as though chilled by an unfelt breeze. It was basically human, but impossibly gaunt and desiccated, to the point where it seemed merely a collection of bones held together by skin and gristle. The face was barely distinct enough to hide the grinning skull beneath, and the staring eyes seemed very wide. The figure raised a bony hand in some kind of gesture, and then stepped forward and disappeared into the wall opposite, sinking into the solid earth like a ghost. Gold just had time to blink, and then more of the spindly figures trooped out of the right-hand wall, crossed before Gold and Morrison, and plunged into the opposite wall, all of them come and gone in a second, like a fleeting thought or impression. Morrison finally let go of Gold's arm, and he rubbed it pointedly to get the blood moving again.

'Sorry about that,' said Morrison, 'But I didn't want to risk you doing anything impulsive. Those things may look like they're knitted together out of pipe-cleaners, but they're actually pretty damned powerful in their own domain. They don't like strangers, they don't like being stared at, and most of all they don't like people. Not unless they're served with a nice white sauce and a few mushrooms to bring out the flavour.'

Gold frowned at the point where the figures had disappeared into the earth wall. It didn't look any less solid than any other part, and it certainly seemed firm enough when he prodded it with an inquisitive finger. He looked back at Morrison.

'Were those . . . elves?' he said finally.

'One kind. They're kobolds. Miners, basically, but they take care of any and all matters to do with the earth and what lies in it. And don't let the ghost act fool you; they can be incredibly strong, not to mention downright vicious, when they need to be. They're not very pretty, but then, in their job they don't get out much.'

'So they're the ones who dug this tunnel?' said Gold, with the air of someone trying to stick to the point despite numerous distractions.

'No. This wasn't dug. Wait a minute . . . oh, shit.' Morrison broke off, knelt down and placed one hand flat against the earth floor. 'Stand very still, Lester. You're about to get a look at what was responsible for this tunnel. If we're lucky, it won't get a look at us.'

He straightened up, his eyes fixed on the tunnel ahead. Gold looked quickly about him, but refrained from drawing his gun. Partly because he felt Morrison wouldn't approve, but mostly because he didn't have anything to aim it at. The tunnel floor vibrated beneath his feet, briefly at first and then in long surges, growing steadily stronger. Something was coming. Something very big and very heavy.

A dozen feet before them, the ground surged up and burst apart as something underneath it rose up out of the depths. The ground shook rhythmically, like a heartbeat in the earth, and something appeared in the widening crack. It was a sickly white, its surface glowing and glistening, ten feet across and more. It took Gold a long time to recognize what it was, because of the sheer size, but when a thick ridge appeared in the white flesh, followed some time later by another, he finally understood what he was looking at. It was a single segment of a giant worm, burrowing through the earth. Gold started to back away a step and then caught himself. His hackles rose and his stomach tightened, in simple instinctive fear. The white flesh glistened wetly as vast segments moved ponderously past the crack in the floor. Each segment had to be ten to twelve feet long, and there seemed no end to them as the worm ploughed on through the earth. Gold no longer needed to ask how the tunnel had been made.

'Cromm Cruach,' said Morrison softly. 'The Great Wurm.'

Finally the glistening segments sank back into the earth, and the crack closed over it. The rumbling below died away, and the tunnel floor was quiet again. Morrison breathed a little more easily, and smiled briefly at Gold.

'I hope you appreciated that. The Faerie must have laid it on specially to impress you. Cromm Cruach doesn't usually show himself to outsiders.'

'Why would they want to impress me?' said Gold. 'I doubt they've ever even heard of me. Besides, they don't know I'm coming.'

'Oh, they know,' said Morrison. 'You'd be surprised what they know. Let's get going. We're almost there.'

He set off down the tunnel, stepping carefully over the narrow crack in the floor, and Gold followed him. The air slowly grew warmer, and subtle scents replaced the acrid smell of wet earth. Dim, muffled sounds broke the tunnel's quiet, too distant to identify, but poignant with promises of meaning. The will-o'-the-wisps disappeared between one moment and the next, revealing a bright light somewhere up ahead. Gold was sorry to see the little spirits go. They'd seemed friendly enough, and he was beginning to think he could use a few friends in this strange new place Morrison had brought him to.

And then the tunnel turned suddenly to the left up ahead, and Morrison stopped. Gold stopped with him, and Morrison looked at him seriously.

'This is it, Lester. We've arrived. The land beneath the

hill, the last holding of the Faerie. From now on be careful, be courteous, and watch what you say. They have a largely spoken tradition of ceremony and law, so anything said can have binding properties. Don't accept anything to eat or drink from them, or accept any gift. But for God's sake be very polite about it. They're very keen here on duels, and they take their honour seriously. Remember, these people are aristocracy, the highest of the high. Don't show me up.'

'Relax,' said Gold. 'I know when to tip the butler, and which sleeve to blow my nose on.'

Morrison winced. 'This seems less and less like a good idea all the time. Let's go. I wish I felt lucky . . .'

He strode quickly forward and round the bend in the corridor, looking unhappy but determined, like a man late for a dentist's appointment. Gold followed quickly after him, and the two of them strode along side by side. The tunnel opened out into a vast cavern, hundreds of yards high, and so wide they couldn't see the far side. In that hollow was a courtyard big enough to hold a county fair and then some, with towering walls built from massive blocks of a blue-white stone. Sculptures of strange beasts and unfamiliar people stood scattered across the courtyard, along with a number of strange shapes without or beyond meaning. But none of that caught Gold's attention. To begin with, all he could see was that the courtyard had fallen to the jungle. Trees sprouted everywhere, thrusting up through the cracked and broken flagstones. Strange and fantastic plants and flowers rioted in thick profusion, and vines and creepers and a dozen sorts of ivy crawled over every available surface.

Small creatures ran and scuttled across the crowded floor, or threw themselves from branch to branch. Bright eyes watched from a hundred shadows, and unfamiliar cries and howls rang out on the air, along with harsh and raucous cries from brightly-coloured birds soaring high above the courtyard. Gold stood silently with Morrison before tall gates of rusting black iron, hanging drunkenly open from broken hinges. The air was uncomfortably warm and humid after the cool of the tunnel, and Gold could feel sweat breaking out on his exposed skin. The sheer variety of the jungle stunned his eyes, overwhelming him with detail. He didn't quite know what he'd expected of the land of the Faerie, of elves and goblins and forgotten dreams, but this sure as hell wasn't it.

Morrison gave him a few moments to get his breath back, and then plunged confidently forward into the jungle, following a path only he could see. Gold stumbled after him, eyes wide and his mouth all but hanging open. The air was rich with thick scents of life, of the greenery and all that thrived in it. Birds fluttered up as Gold and Morrison passed, sudden explosions of gaudy colours and beating wings, settling silently as they were left behind. Statues were everywhere, carved from some dark veined marble that was still smooth to the touch, despite their apparent age. Some of the faces were chipped and disfig-ured, and here and there a limb was missing, as though the smothering jungle had torn it away. Long strands of barbed creepers curled around bulging stone biceps and dreaming faces, hanging down in heavy, languorous coils. Something peered at Gold from out of the verdant gloom with bright shining eyes, only to turn and crash off through the trees as he and Morrison drew nearer. It was a man's size, but it didn't move at all like a man.

The jungle opened briefly to display two living figures, standing face to face, surrounded by coils of hissing roses. Gold didn't need Morrison to tell him that they were elves. They were tall, easily seven to eight feet in height, their bodies lean and wiry with no concealing fat to soften the muscles' outline. Their skin was inhumanly pale, and their faces were painfully gaunt. They had huge golden eyes and long pointed ears. They did not move as Gold and Morrison approached, but the roses coiled and twisted and hissed loud warnings not to draw too close. Only the slow rise and fall of the elves' chests showed that they were still alive. Their glowing eyes were fixed upon each other in endless fascination. The roses' thorns had pierced their flesh in a hundred places, but no blood flowed. Gold and Morrison passed them by and left them behind, and Gold wondered numbly how long they had been standing there, that the roses could have grown up around them in such numbers.

It took the best part of an hour to cross the vast courtyard, turning this way and that as the jungle dictated, but eventually they came to a tall, narrow gate in the far wall and passed through it, leaving the seething greenery behind. The gate opened on to a wide corridor, high-raftered and brightly lit from no apparent source, with towering walls and bare unpolished flagstones. Gold checked briefly, but as he'd expected there was still no sign anywhere of any shadow. Morrison strode confidently down the corridor, looking straight ahead, as though he'd been this way so often he felt no need to gawp like a tourist. Gold hurried to keep up with him, but every passing minute brought new wonders and marvels. Elves thrust out of the walls at intervals, as though they'd somehow grown from the stone or been immersed in it, sinking into the solid walls as into the warm embrace of a hip bath. The solid stone had closed around them, holding them fast for ever. They still lived, breathing slowly and shallowly, and sometimes their staring eyes would follow Gold and Morrison as they passed. Once an elf came striding down the corridor towards them, slow and stately in his height like a stilt-walker. Morrison bowed deeply, but the elf did not acknowledge his presence.

'What is this place?' Gold whispered finally, his voice low not through fear of being overheard, but rather through simple, overwhelming awe. The huge scale of the corridor made him feel like a child trespassing in the world of adults for the first time.

'This is Caer Dhu, the last castle of the Faerie, home to the Unseeli Court and all the elven kind who still exist. It's the land beneath the hill, the path that cannot be walked twice. The last holding of the shining ones. Don't ask me how old it is; I don't think even they know any more. It's older than Shadows Fall. Older than humanity itself. The Faerie are a dream that Nature had, but not for long. They were too splendid for the common world, and it passed them by.'

They walked on. Massive statues stood everywhere, of elves and men and astonishing creatures, some disturbing and disquieting in their lines and details, as though drawn from the kind of dream one chooses not to remember upon awakening. Wondrous machines stood abandoned in corners, huge and intricate beyond any hope of human understanding. Great suits of jointed armour moved slowly through simple movements, repeating them over and over without end.

Gold and Morrison turned a corner, and came upon a group of elves gathered around a great pit in the floor. They made no sound, staring down at what the pit held with unblinking eyes. Morrison stopped, and gestured for Gold to take a look. The elves paid him no notice as he cautiously eased his way through them, and stood at the edge of the pit, looking down. Two elves were fighting at the bottom of the pit, cutting and hacking at each other with a knife in each hand. Their bodies ballooned and shrank, leapt and distorted, to follow the fighters' needs. They made no attempt to defend themselves, accepting terrible injuries to inflict worse ones. Golden blood ran briefly from wounds that healed themselves in seconds.

The two elves fought in silence, the only sounds in the pit their explosive breathing and the continued dull impacts of steel cutting into flesh. The watching elves were silent too, but Gold could feel their tension as they followed each attack and counter-attack with rapt attention. They were all smiling, but there was nothing of humour in their faces. Gold started to back away from the edge of the pit, sickened by the almost palpable feeling of bloodlust all around him, thrumming on the air. The sheer intensity of the emotion was overwhelming, concentrated and held at an inhuman level. He eased his way out of the crowd, trembling slightly like someone who'd just witnessed a really bad street accident. One of the elves at the edge of the crowd turned to another and offered him his hand. The other elf produced a knife, took hold of the hand, and cut off one of the fingers. Gold stumbled backwards, his eyes fixed on the blood pouring from the mutilated hand. Morrison grabbed him by the arm and pulled him away.

'What the hell was that all about?' Gold said shakily as he followed Morrison along the corridor.

'That was a duel,' Morrison said easily. 'It's not actually as impressive as it looks. Elves can't die, except by extremely severe magics or destruction. Their wounds regenerate in seconds. The pain's real enough, but no elf ever gave a damn about that. Honour is everything. I've known fights like that to go on for hours, long after both fighters are exhausted.'

'And the bit with the hand?'

'He lost a bet. Elves love to gamble, but gold and silver have little meaning here. They wager pain or service or humiliation. The finger was a small thing. It'll grow back.'

'That's crazy. Sick.'

'No. Those are human judgements, and the elves aren't human. Not being able to die changes how you view things. Pain and injury are passing things. Loss of face and honour can last for centuries. That's why we can never really understand the Faerie. They take the long view. They think in terms of centuries, and the passing moment of the present doesn't have the importance for them that it does for us.'

Gold tried to visualize a life planned in terms of passing centuries, freed from the terror of death, and had to stop when it made him dizzy. 'How long do elves live, as a rule?' he said finally.

'As long as they choose. The only things that can kill them are certain powerful magics and sorcerous weapons, both of which are extremely rare.'

'Wait a minute. What about children? If they're immortal . . .'

'There are no children. New Faerie are born fully grown, created through sorcery to replace an elf who's died. And yes, I know that raises a whole bunch of new questions, but I don't have the answers. Some things the Faerie won't discuss at all, and that very definitely includes the origin of their species. I've got a feeling if we ever did find out, we wouldn't like it at all.'

They walked the rest of the way in silence, each occupied with his own thoughts, and finally they came to the Unseeli Court, the Gathering of Faerie. Two vast doors swung open unassisted as they approached, revealing a great chamber packed from wall to wall with the highest of the elven kind. Tall, lean and imposing, they dressed in complex robes of bright and furious colours, and every one of them wore a sword on their hip. Every face and form was perfect, without defect or blemish. They were beautiful, graceful, burning and intense. The sheer pressure of their presence was like facing a blast of heat from an open furnace. They stood perfectly still, inhumanly still, like an insect poised to attack, or a predator watching its prey to see which way it will run. Some wore masks of thinly beaten metal that covered half their face, while others wore the furs of beasts, with the heads still attached and resting casually on the wearer's shoulder. Strange perfumes scented the air, thick and heady and overpowering, as though someone had crushed a field of flowers and captured their essence in a jar. But most of all there was the silence, perfect and complete, unbroken by any murmur or whisper of movement. Gold and Morrison looked at the assembled elves, and the Faerie looked back, in a moment that seemed as though it would last for ever.

And then the elves at the centre fell back, opening up a path through the middle of the Court. Morrison stepped forward, calm and confident, and Gold went with him. The elves slowly turned their heads to watch the two humans walk among them, and Gold had to fight hard to repress a shudder. He could feel their gaze like a physical pressure, and there was nothing of friendship or welcome in it.

Morrison had made it clear early on that they had no guarantee of protection. Whatever the Faerie did, no one would or could call them to answer for it. Morrison might have been here before, as a bard and honoured guest, but that had been at their summons. This time he'd come unannounced and without invitation, and brought a stranger with him.

Anything could happen.

Gold and Morrison finally came to a halt before a wide raised dais, on which stood two great thrones, intricately carved out of bone. Shapes and sigils and glyphs of all kinds patterned the fashioned ivory, detail upon detail, complex beyond hope. And on those thrones, two elves. The man sat on the left, fully ten feet tall and bulging thickly with muscle, wrapped in blood-red robes that showed off his milk-white skin. His hair was a colourless blond, hanging loosely about a long angular face dominated by eyes of an arctic, piercing blue. He sat perfectly still, as though he had waited patiently there for an age, and would wait longer still, should it prove necessary. The woman sat on the right, dressed in black with silver tracings. She was a few inches taller than the man, lithely muscular, with skin so pale that blue veins showed at her temples. Her hair was black, cropped short and severe, and dark eyes watched thoughtfully from a heart-shaped face. She held a single red rose in her hand, ignoring the thorns that pricked her. Nobility hung about them both, like a cloak grown frayed through long familiarity. Gold didn't need to be told who they were, who they had to be. Their names were legend. Morrison bowed low to the King and Queen of Faerie, and Gold quickly did the same.

'My Lord and Lady, most noble Oberon and gracious Titania, I greet you in the name of Shadows Fall.' Morrison paused, as though expecting a response, but the silence dragged on. He smiled winningly, and continued, practically oozing charm and goodfellowship. 'I apologize for this intrusion, this uninvited appearance, but matters of great urgency have arisen which lead me to impose upon

146

your friendship and esteem. If you will permit, I would like to introduce my friend Lester Gold, a hero.'

Gold didn't need to be prompted to bow again, and did so as decorously as he could. It wasn't something he was used to, and he suspected it was one of those things you needed to practise a lot before you could bring it off really successfully. He straightened up to find neither the King nor the Queen had moved or acknowledged him in the slightest. Morrison stood at his side, smiling calmly, obviously waiting for a response. But the silence still dragged on, gathering a kind of weight and momentum that was both disturbing and dangerous. The endless stare of the packed Court seemed more and more threatening, and Gold had to fight to keep his hand from edging closer to the gun in his shoulder-holster. For the first time in his long career, he knew he was facing something that couldn't be stopped by naked courage and a well-placed bullet. Morrison smiled easily at Oberon and Titania, but Gold could sense the effort it took. The bard had been prepared for outright refusal, but the continuing silence that denied his very existence was getting to him.

'My Lord and Lady, have you nothing to say to me? I have been your bard in days past, sung your history and your praise before audiences both human and elven. In turn, you have honoured me with your friendship and your ear, and I need them both now more than ever. If I presume upon your patience, it is only because necessity drives me. Something has arisen that threatens humanity and Faerie alike, and I fear the town cannot hope to stop it alone. Your highnesses, will you not speak to me?'

A short, stocky figure appeared suddenly between the two thrones, grinning unpleasantly. Gold stared. It was the only elf he'd seen who wasn't perfect. The elf was easily as tall as the two humans, but the thrones and their occupants made him seem smaller. His body was smooth and supple as a dancer, but the hump on his back pulled one shoulder down and forward, and the hand on that arm was withered into a claw. His hair was grey, his skin the faint yellow of old bone, but his green eyes were alive with mischief and insolence. At his temples there were two raised nubs that might have been horns. He wore a pelt of some animal whose fur melded uncannily with his own hairy body, and his legs ended in cloven hooves. He laughed suddenly, and Morrison flinched at the naked contempt in the soft sound.

'Back again, little bard, little man, little human? Back to trouble us with your wit and worries, your passing consequence and transitory worth? And speaking of urgency, and matters arising, as though the frantic tick-tocking of your mortal span had any interest to us. You forget your place, little human. You come when you are summoned, at our pleasure and at our convenience. You do not intrude upon our Court and our business as and when the spirit moves you.'

'My Lord Puck,' said Morrison easily. 'A pleasure, as always. The harshness in your words pains me greatly. Am I not the bard of this Court, this Gathering? Have I not sung for you in this very hall, not six days past? You honoured me then with your praise, and gave me drink and bid me call you brother.'

'I never liked my brother,' said Puck, spinning casually on his hooves with surprising grace. 'Though I like humans well enough. They make such easy prey. They run with such touching desperation, and squeal so pleasingly when they are run to ground. The smallest things please them, and they'll fawn endlessly for a smile or a pretty word from their betters. They sniff at the rump like a randy dog, and kiss our perfect arse and think that makes us friends. You come at a bad time, human. Take what is left of our good will and leave now, while you still can.'

A brief movement went through the ranks of the Court, and Gold could all but feel the tension on the air. The weight of so many eyes, fixed and unblinking, was almost unbearable. Morrison didn't seem to be feeling any strain, but it was all Gold could do to stand his ground. Part of him wanted to turn and run, and keep running till he was

148

safely back in a world he understood. The thought steadied him somewhat. He wasn't going to run. He was a hero, and heroes didn't run. Though they did sometimes withdraw, for tactical reasons. He glanced casually behind him, checking how far it was to the doors, and how many elves were in his way. He thought again about the gun under his jacket, but kept his hand well away from it. There were hundreds of elves, and he had only a handful of ammunition. Besides, he had an uncomfortable feeling these majestic beings wouldn't be much bothered by anything as simple as a gun. He decided to concentrate on standing very still, and doing his best to look calm and unconcerned.

'Something has happened,' said Morrison flatly. 'Something has happened here, in this Court, in this land, since I was last here. But I have not changed. I am still your friend, your bard, your voice in the world of humans. I have not forgotten the gifts you gave me, or the nature and responsibilities of my position. It is a bard's duty to say what must be said, be he welcome or no. I have come from the town to speak with you, on a matter most vital, and I will be heard. The land beneath the hill is bound to Shadows Fall by oaths as old as Time itself. Am I now to understand that the word of the Faerie has become worthless, and all agreements null and void? Have the elves forsaken honour?'

Another brief movement went through the Court, and Gold could feel the subtle change from menace to anger. Morrison ignored them all, his unwavering gaze fixed on Puck. His voice had not risen once from its calm and reasonable tone, and his arms were folded casually across his chest. The imperfect elf leaned forward, his hooves clattering quietly on the polished floor. He glared at Morrison, all trace of smile and mischief gone, but the bard didn't flinch.

'Watch your words, little human,' said Puck. 'Words have power. They bind the speaker and the listener. If you would not hear words of power and portent, leave now. I will not make this offer again.'

'I came to speak,' said Morrison, 'And I will be heard. Do as you must, Lord Puck, but I'll not move another step. There are words that must be said, and matters that must be discussed, no matter what the consequence. The next step in the dance is yours, Lord Puck. I'll not be the first to break the faith between us.'

'So brave,' said Puck. 'So arrogant. So very, very human. Speak your piece, bard. It will make no difference. Your words have no meaning here. We do not hear them.'

'I have the right of audience,' said Morrison carefully. 'You made me your bard, for better or worse, and whatever falls between us that cannot be undone. I respectfully demand that two ranked members of this Court hear my words, and give judgement as to whether my words have meaning, and shall be heard.'

'Right? Demand?' Puck drew himself up to his full height, forcing his hump and shoulder back as far as they would go. 'Does a human dare to use such words, in our Court, in our land?'

'Yes. Their majesties Oberon and Titania gave me that right, in days gone past. Do you now deny their word?'

'Not I,' said Puck. 'Never I. Though there might come a time when you will wish I had.' He giggled suddenly, a strange and unsettling sound in the quiet of the Court. He spun on his hooves again, and dropped gracefully into a crouch. 'I like your gall, Sean. I always did. You remind me of someone I respect. Myself, probably. So, since you will not be told and you will not be warned, matters will proceed as they must. Lord Oisin, Lady Niamh; step forward.'

Two elves made their way through the Court, and came to stand facing Gold and Morrison, with their backs to Oberon and Titania. They bowed to Morrison, who bowed deeply in return. Gold bowed too, just to show he was keeping up with things.

Puck leant casually against Oberon's throne. 'The Lord Oisin Mac Finn. Once a human, now an elf, of long standing in this Court. The Lady Niamh of the Golden

150

Hair, daughter to Mannannon Mac Lir. They will hear your words. Do you accept them?'

Gold studied them both while Morrison took a long time to say yes. Oisin (once a *human*?) was six feet tall, which made him seem almost a dwarf when set against the rest of the Court. He had the same fierce eyes and pointed ears, the same lithe musculature and natural grace, but there was still something of the human in him. He was perfect, but not on the same scale. Niamh was a good eight feet tall, and looked even taller next to Oisin and the two humans. She had a sharp, handsome face and long golden hair that fell thickly to her waist, pulled back and kept out of her face with a simple headband. Gold found himself wondering, almost despite himself, how much time every day the poor girl had to spend washing and brushing and combing it.

He forced himself to concentrate on the matter in hand. Neither Oisin nor Niamh seemed particularly friendly or unfriendly. But there was something about the Court . . . the feeling he was getting from the packed hall had changed yet again. The anger and the menace were gone, replaced by something that had the flavour of resignation. As though by Morrison's insistence they had set out on a road none of them had really wanted to travel. Gold shook himself mentally. It was more than probable he was reading things into the Court's silence that weren't actually there. After all, they weren't human, and therefore weren't bound to think or feel as humans did . . . He glanced at Morrison, who had finally stopped speaking. The young bard seemed calm, almost relaxed. But then, he always did. Gold had always prided himself on being calm under fire and cool in a crisis, but that was thirty-odd years ago, and he hadn't met the Faerie then. Morrison bowed to Puck, crouching half-hidden behind Oisin and Niamh.

'I have my harp with me, to hand. You taught me how to get the best out of it, Lord Puck, and I will do your teaching justice. Hear my song.'

A guitar was suddenly in his hands. Gold blinked. He

would have sworn it wasn't there a minute ago. It would appear there was more to being a bard than owning a pleasant voice and knowing three chords. Morrison strummed the guitar casually, the soft gentle sound filling the quiet Court. Oberon and Titania sat forward a little in their thrones. Morrison began to sing in a strong tenor voice, and the Faerie listened.

It was a simple tune and a steady rhythm, that held the ear and then the mind, haunting and sublime. All who heard could no more have turned away than they could have stopped breathing. Morrison was a bard, and there was magic in his song and in his voice, the magic that comes from the heart and the soul, focused and given shape through the man and his song. He sang, and the world stood still.

He sang of Shadows Fall, and its unique nature. Of the lost and the fearful and the dying who came to the town when the world had no more use for them. He sang of the ancient and noble elves, and the long compact between Man and Faerie down all the many years. Of love and honour and duty, and how they held Man and Faerie together. And finally, he sang of the town's need in its hour of despair, of murder unfinished and unpunished. He broke off abruptly, and his music echoed on the still air for a long moment, as though it had unfinished business with those who had listened.

Tears stung Gold's eyes and there was an ache in his heart, and in that moment he could have denied Morrison nothing. He looked at the Faerie, at Oberon and Titania, Oisin and Niamh and Puck, and a cold breeze touched him. There were no tears in their fierce eyes, no sign in their faces that they had felt any of the exultation that had moved Gold so strongly. Instead, they looked tired and sad and resigned, as though the song had merely confirmed the need for something they would rather have avoided. Oberon and Titania leaned back in their thrones, and Niamh bowed to Morrison. He bowed back, the guitar disappearing from his hands.

'Your song moves us, as always, dear bard.' Niamh's gentle voice was music in itself, slow and steady and remorseless, like a tide sweeping up a beach. 'You have been our friend and our voice among the humans, and we would have spared you this if we could. But you have demanded the truth, as is your right, and we will give it to you, though it break your heart and ours. We know what is happening in Shadows Fall. The Wild Childe has come among you. He is the beast with every man's face, the killer who cannot be stopped or bargained with, because that is all he is. There is nothing you or we can do to stop him.

'Worse things still are coming. You are betrayed without and within. A vast army is gathering, to take the town by force. And we . . . are divided, friend Sean. For the first time in centuries, we cannot see our way. Our oracles speak of death and destruction and the ending of the Faerie. Some of us would form an army, calling up weapons and sciences long unused. Some would close the door between hill and town, and bar it shut for ever. And some would destroy the town and render it to ashes, in the hope we might then escape its fate.

'And so we talk and argue and debate and nothing is decided. We cannot find our way. The only thing we are sure of is that the darkness is closing in around us, and there seems no hope for man or elf. We have no help to offer you, friend Sean; only words of doom and warnings of disaster. Divided as we are, still we would have spared you that, if we could, rather than blight your hope or damn your spirit. We tried to turn you away, and give you harsh words in place of harsher truths, but you demanded to be heard, and we could not deny you.

'I think that in the end we might yet stand beside you, against whatever form our doom finally takes. Man and Faerie are bound by compacts older than Shadows Fall itself, and we would rather die than live without our honour. And we are fond of you, in our way. You are the children we never knew. I trust we will not desert you in your hour of need, no matter what the auguries say.'

'That is not yet decided,' said Oisin, his voice flat and heavy. 'Though many voices would rally us to humanity's need, there are as many and more who would have us stand clear of the town's fate, and turn our backs on the world of man for ever. We have a duty to survive. We have done all we can for you, and if the world must move on, then let it go. Like all children, humanity must learn to stand alone, for good or ill.'

'You must not go,' said Morrison, and there was no anger in his voice, only urgency. 'We need you. We need your glamour and your mysteries, your strangeness and majesty. The world would be a greyer place without your epic battles and intricate intrigues, your towering rages and immortal loves. You are humanity written large, and life roars within you. Don't go. We would be smaller without you to inspire us, and your going would leave a gap in us that we might never fill. You are the joy and glory of the world. You make us whole.'

Niamh smiled. 'Your words move us, as always, but I fear words have not the strength among us that once they had. Stay with us, Sean, and speak further. Perhaps together we can see our way clear again. You understand that I can promise nothing.'

'Nothing,' said Oisin, and it seemed that some of the Court whispered it with him.

Morrison bowed. 'I am at your service.'

'We have heard your words,' said King Oberon, in a voice that filled the Court. 'We shall consider them.'

'In the meantime, be our guests,' said Queen Titania. 'Ask for anything, and nothing shall be denied you.'

Niamh and Oisin turned to confer in lowered voices with the King and Queen, and the members of the Court talked quietly among themselves. Puck winked once at Morrison, spun sharply on his hooves and suddenly wasn't there any more. Morrison let out his breath in a long sigh, and all but slumped against Gold, his strength gone. He looked suddenly older and smaller, as though he'd poured something of himself into his entreaties. Gold supported him surreptitiously with an arm at his elbow. He had a strong feeling it would be a bad idea to show any kind of weakness at this time. He looked around him for inspiration, and his gaze fell upon a small table conveniently to hand, bearing a bottle of wine and two golden cups. He reached out for the wine, curious to see what the label said, and then stopped abruptly as Morrison's fingers sank painfully into his arm.

'Don't touch any of it!' said Morrison in a savage whisper. 'You can't eat or drink anything here; accepting it into your body ties you to the world that produced it. This is not our world, and the rules are different here. Time runs differently. As visitors, we can come and go unaffected. We'll return to Shadows Fall at the exact moment we left it, but to eat and drink here would make you subject to a different time. You could leave here after a few hours, and find that years had passed in the world you left. So please, Lester, remember what I tell you. This isn't the kind of place where you can afford to make mistakes.'

'Of course, Sean, I understand. Now will you please let go of my arm before my fingers drop off?'

Morrison let go of him, and Gold nodded stiffly. He'd never liked being lectured, but it was clear the bard knew the ground rules here, and he didn't, so he kept his peace. He nodded at the surrounding Court.

'What do you suppose they're talking about now?'

'Damned if I know. They don't think as we do. There was a time I might have managed an educated guess, but things here have changed so much . . . I knew something was up when Oberon and Titania wouldn't talk to me directly, but I had no idea things would get this out of hand.'

'Let me make sure I've got this right,' said Gold. 'Something really nasty is loose in Shadows Fall. Not only can the elves not help us, but some of them are actually

155

seriously considering wiping out the whole town, just in case it gets them too. Have I missed anything?'

'Not really. Once, I would have said this was impossible. The very idea of an elf breaking his oath would have been unthinkable. Which only goes to show how scared they are. I've never seen them like this before.'

'They said something about oracles. How accurate are these fortune-tellers?'

'Very. They tend to be a bit ambiguous, but they've got a hell of a track record. If the augurs say that the very existence of the Faerie is at risk, you can put money on it.'

'But what could possibly endanger a people who can't die?'

'The Wild Childe, presumably. Whatever that is.'

'That's another thing,' said Gold. 'I got the distinct impression they've known about this killer for some time. Why haven't they said anything before?'

'Because there was nothing they could do. They were ashamed. That's at least partly why they didn't want to talk to me at first. Partly because they were trying to hide the worst from me, but also because they didn't want to admit that they had failed in their oath to protect the town. They really believe we're all doomed. They didn't want me to know, for the same reason that you don't tell someone in hospital that they're going to die. Because it would be cruel to take away all hope.'

Gold looked at him steadily. 'Is it really that bad? We're all going to die, and there's nothing anyone can do?'

'I don't believe that. I won't believe it. They must have misinterpreted the oracle. Misunderstood it. I have to convince the Faerie not to give up without a fight. For their sake, as well as ours.'

'For their sake? Why?'

'Because if they believe they're going to die, they will. They'll just fade away. It's happened before, when an elf loses all hope. It's one of the few things that can kill them. We've got to convince them that there's still a chance, that you can't give up fighting just because the odds are against you.'

'What if it's not just odds? What if it's a certainty? James Hart has returned to Shadows Fall.'

'I can't think about that now,' said Morrison flatly. 'If I try to think about everything, I'll go mad. We have to concentrate on what we can do.'

'Pardon me for seeming dim, but what the hell can we do? What can a young bard and a hero well past his sell-by date do to save the Faerie and the town, that a race of immortal, unkillable elves can't do?'

'Beats me,' said Morrison, smiling suddenly. 'I guess we'll just have to improvise.'

Gold looked at him speechlessly for a moment, and then both of them realized the Court had grown silent again. They looked around the Unseeli Court, and found all eyes were on them. Gold stiffened. Something had changed again. He could feel it on the charged air; a strange mixture of menace and expectancy. Gold felt very like a rabbit staring into the lights of an approaching car. Something really unpleasant was headed his way, and he hadn't a clue which way to run. He looked to Morrison for guidance, but the bard looked just as thrown as he did. Niamh and Oisin bowed to them both, and after a moment Gold and Morrison bowed back.

Here it comes . . . thought Gold. *And whatever it is, I'm not going to like it one little bit.*

'This is a matter of great importance,' said Niamh. Her quiet voice seemed to fill the Court. 'It is not something to be decided in haste. We shall adjourn, and consider the matter at our leisure. In the meantime, their majesties Oberon and Titania will reside over the Games. You are welcome to join them, as honoured guests.'

'Oh shit,' said Morrison, very quietly.

Gold looked at him sharply. He thought for a moment the bard was going to faint. All the colour had dropped out of his face, and his mouth had gone a funny shape. 'Sean? Are you all right?'

'We'd be delighted to join their majesties,' said Morrison. 'Delighted. Wouldn't we, Lester?'

'Oh sure,' said Gold, picking up his cue. 'Always ready to watch some Games.'

Everyone took it in turns to bow to each other, and then the Faerie turned to talk among themselves again. Gold turned to Morrison.

'Oh *shit,*' said the bard, with great feeling.

'Sean; talk to me. What have we just agreed to, and why do I think from the look on your face that I should really be sprinting for the nearest exit?'

'Don't even think about it,' said Morrison sharply. 'Trying to leave now would be a deadly insult. You wouldn't live long enough to reach the door.'

'We're in trouble, aren't we?'

'You could put it that way. The Faerie have always been big on games. Challenges of strength and skill, wit and courage. You've already seen a duel, and their idea of betting, but they save the really heavy stuff for the Arena. They put on the kind of shows that would have shocked hardened Roman Circus-goers. They may not be able to die themselves, but they do like to watch other beings do it. Preferably in violent and inventive ways. We're talking combat to the death; man against elf, people versus all kinds of creatures, under all kinds of conditions. It's very rare for a human to be invited to attend the Games, except as cannon fodder.'

Gold frowned. 'Just how bad is this going to be?'

'Put it this way. If you have to puke, do it discreetly. They might take it as an insult. Whatever happens, you can't do or say *anything.* Or you could end up down in the Arena, on the wrong end of a Challenge.'

'I'm no weak sister,' said Gold. 'I've been around. I've seen a few things, in my time.'

'Not like this,' said Morrison. A little colour had returned to his cheeks, but he still looked as though he was recovering from a prolonged illness. 'And the joke is, we can't object. By their lights, they're doing us a great honour.'

'Some joke,' said Gold. 'Pardon me if I laugh later.'

Oberon and Titania rose unhurriedly to their feet, and the Unseeli Court fell silent. The two rulers turned to face each other, and in that moment something passed between them; something inhuman and utterly alien. Gold could feel the hackles rising on the back of his neck as the King and Queen of the Faerie gazed silently into each other's eyes. There was something in the air now, a rising pressure, as though something powerful and inevitable was about to happen, like the moment in a storm before the lightning strikes. The pressure rose unbearably, and then was gone in a moment as the world changed. The ground dropped away from under Gold's feet, and slammed back again even as he put out a hand to steady himself. The massed candlelight of the Unseeli Court was gone, replaced by a brighter, harsher light. Gold looked stupidly about him, the pressure of a gusting wind on his face. The Court was gone, and he and Morrison were standing in an ornately decorated private stadium, set high above the ranked seats, looking out over a vast Arena, spread out below an open sky.

The Arena was huge, a great oval of bare sand, without markings or limits, and the Faerie sat in ranks around it, thousands upon thousands of them. There was something simple and brutal about the open sands. This was not a place for sport, for the running of races or the competing of athletes. This was a place where you came to fight or die, and the roughly raked sands would soak up the blood of the victor or the loser with equal indifference. Gold pulled his gaze away from the Arena, and looked up. The sky was a boiling crimson, as though the air itself was on fire. There was no sun or moon or stars, only the bloody light of the sky. Gold felt suddenly dizzy, as though he was looking out over an endless drop, and might fall away up into the sky at any moment. He grabbed the raised side of the stadium with both hands, and the feeling slowly died away. He looked cautiously behind him, and found there were two chairs waiting, of simple but comfortable design. He stepped back and dropped on to the nearest chair, letting out his breath in a long slow sigh. He looked across at Morrison, who was still standing at the edge of the stadium, staring out over the Arena with a mixture of unease and anticipation.

'Sean; where the hell are we? How did we get here?'

'This is the Arena. And we're here because the King and Queen wanted us here. Their rule is absolute. Even time and space bend to the royal will.'

Gold decided he wasn't going to think about that for a while. He'd had enough shocks and upsets for one day and felt the need for a rest, physically and mentally. Morrison turned reluctantly away from the Arena, and sat down heavily on the other chair. A lot of the brashness and cockiness had been knocked out of him, and it showed. Whatever he'd expected from his audience with the Unseeli Court, this obviously wasn't it. He gripped his hands tightly together to stop them shaking, the knuckles showing white, but it took only a moment or two for his gaze to be dragged back to the open sands below.

He's been here before, thought Gold. *He knows what's coming. And he's scared.*

The sudden insight surprised him. He didn't feel scared. Apprehensive, yes, and curious, but he'd never scared easily, and he'd seen enough strangeness and cruelty in his days as a costumed adventurer for there not to be much left that could throw him. With all respect to the young bard, Gold didn't think the Faerie could come up with anything to match the outrageous exploits of his superhero days. Morrison sat back in his chair and tried hard to look calm and composed. Gold gave him a moment to get his second wind, and then leaned over to him.

'You've been to the Games before, haven't you?' he said quietly, and the bard nodded jerkily.

'Twice. It's supposed to be a great honour. Only they

160

know how humans react, so sometimes they use the Games to . . . test you. Sort out the lambs from the tigers.'

'What happens to the lambs?'

'They don't get invited back. To the Games or the Court. The Faerie have nothing but contempt for the weak. That's why they're so upset over the prophecies. They've never faced a threat to their very existence before. They're scared. A people to whom fear is the worst kind of weakness.'

Gold nodded slowly. A lot of things were starting to make sense now. 'Where exactly is this place?'

'God knows. The land beneath the hill is only loosely connected to the real world. Its borders are vague and its limits uncertain. It's only tentatively real, and the Faerie like it that way.'

'I don't know why I keep asking you questions. I never like the answers I get. Can we get back to Shadows Fall from here?'

'Not without the Faerie's help. Lester, whatever happens here, whatever you see; you can't make a fuss. The Faerie would take it as an insult, and they're very touchy about their honour. Remember; there are factions in the Court just itching for an excuse to attack the town.'

'I had worked that out for myself, actually,' said Gold. 'I've got eyes in my head. How long before the Games start?'

'Any moment now. We're just waiting for Oberon and Titania to signal their readiness. That's their private box, up there on the left.'

Gold looked across, and saw the two rulers sitting at their ease in a private stadium three times the size of the one he was sitting in. It had to be that large, to hold the two ivory thrones. Garlands of unfamiliar flowers decorated the stadium, with gold and silver scrollwork surrounding jewels of an impossible size and hue. Oberon raised his hand, and the murmur of sound from the packed ranks of Faerie was suddenly stilled. Oberon lowered his hand, and a tall elf appeared out of nowhere in the royal stadium. He

161

was naked, and blood dripped down his back from a recent whipping. He knelt before Titania, who handed him a silver chalice. He held it steady at his collarbone, and Titania produced a knife from her sleeve and cut his throat. Golden blood pulsed thickly from the wound, spilling down into the chalice. The elf's hands held it perfectly steady. Titania waited till the chalice was almost full, and then dipped a finger into the blood and smeared it in a line across her throat. Oberon leaned forward, and Titania traced a line across his throat too. The naked elf swayed slightly on his knees, but still held the chalice steady. Oberon gestured sharply, and the air swallowed up the kneeling elf. Gold turned to Morrison.

'All right. What the hell was that all about? Is the elf going to die?'

'Hardly; they've been using the same elf to open the Games for centuries. He's being punished, but I'm not sure if anyone remembers why. That's the Faerie for you; tradition is what matters.'

Oberon made a sweeping gesture with his hand. The air heaved and crackled, and the burning sky seemed to blaze more brightly. Oberon and Titania sat back in their thrones, and the Games began.

The sharks came first. Appearing between one moment and the next, a pack of sharks were suddenly swimming idly above the bare sands, whirling and gliding eerily in mid-air, as though buoyed up by some unseen ocean. They were huge beasts, some thirty feet long, their slack mouths studded with jagged teeth. They were a dull grey, with darker fins, curling around each other like drifting shadows. They swam back and forth in the middle of the Arena, as though testing the limits of a cage only they could see. Gold hoped the bars were strong. He'd encountered a few sharks in his time, but these were bigger and meaner-looking than anything he'd ever come up against. They should have seemed smaller at such a distance, but some magic inherent in the Arena made it seem as though they were only a few yards away. As though he could reach out a hand and touch them. Just the thought was enough to make Gold wince, and he kept his arms determinedly folded against his chest. One of the sharks rolled over slowly, so that it seemed to be staring at him with one black, emotionless eye. A chill ran through Gold that was at least partly instinct. There were no thoughts or feelings in the cold unblinking glare, only an endless, ravening hunger.

The crowd broke out into what seemed like spontaneous cheers, and Gold looked round in time to see the elves enter the Arena. There were seven of them, one for each shark. They were tall and spindly creatures, with a long elongated skull like a horse. They had no skin on any part of their body, so that the muscles and traceries of veins glistened wetly in the scarlet light. They marched out into the Arena as though to a silent band, and halted together some distance from the circling sharks. They bowed to the crowd, and then burst out into different shapes, stretching and swelling and contracting with insane speed and elasticity. They shrank to the size of children and ballooned up to twenty feet high, trading size and shape with dizzying ease. The crowd roared their approval. The sharks watched, unimpressed, and waited for their prey to come to them.

'What the hell are *they*?' said Gold.

'Spriggans,' said Morrison, unable to tear his gaze away. 'Guards, bully-boys, enforcers. They get all the dirty work, because they love it. Perfect match for the sharks. Now shut up and watch. And brace yourself. This is going to be bloody.'

The Spriggans started forward as one, as though in response to an unheard bell, and the crowd went quiet, eyes wide in anticipation. The sharks turned to face the elves, and the two sides fell upon each other. The sharks snapped viciously at trailing limbs, but somehow the arms and legs were always that little bit out of reach. The sharks whirled and pounced with breathtaking speed, but the Spriggans were never there, growing or shrinking at just the right moment. They danced among the sharks with

163

contemptuous ease, slashing at the blunt heads and pale bellies with their clawed hands. They had no weapons, but their claws dug deep, and blood spilled out on to the sand that waited for it. The sharks became frantic, maddened at the scent of blood and the elusiveness of the prey. Four sharks suddenly turned on the same Spriggan, boxing him in and then tearing at him with savage precision. More blood spilled out on to the sand, golden blood, and the injured elf grew and shrank in rapid spurts, as though trying to find some shape or size where the wounds wouldn't exist. The other Spriggans tore viciously at the sharks, forcing them away from the wounded elf. They backed off reluctantly, blinded by their own pain and blood. The elf's wounds were already closing, and within seconds he was back with the others, dancing round the sharks and taunting them.

The fight, or dance, couldn't have lasted more than ten minutes, but to Gold it seemed to go on for ever. It hadn't taken him long to realize the sharks stood no more chance than the bulls in a Spanish bullfight. The whole thing was a ritual, no doubt shaped by tradition, and the question was not if or when the sharks would die, but how. The elves killed them slowly, by the numbers, one after another, and though the crowd applauded the Spriggans' courage, Gold saw only the cruelty. Even sharks deserved better than this. He would have liked to look away, but he knew the Faerie would see that as weakness, or an insult, so he sat and watched and felt a slow anger build within him.

The last dying shark drifted to the sand, belly up, leaking blood from a dozen gut-deep wounds. The Spriggans tore at the bodies of the sharks, ripping off ragged chunks of flesh and eating them, and the watching crowd laughed and applauded. Morrison joined in politely, and after a moment Gold did too. The Spriggans and the sharks vanished, and the next Game began.

Seven Faerie in delicate golden armour took on three times as many walking corpses. It took Gold a while to realize this was a comedy turn. The liches were armed with swords and axes, and could take any amount of punishment, but you only had to behead them to stop them. Without a head, the bodies would wander aimlessly until their legs were sliced through, and then the bodies would just lie twitching on the sands, reaching out vaguely with their weapons. The skill lay in seeing how much an elf could cut away from a dead body without first beheading it, and without getting caught himself. The liches couldn't really hurt the undying Faerie, but to take a wound from a lich was clearly a disgrace. The battle, if you could call it that, seemed to drag on endlessly. Gold didn't appreciate the humour or the skill, but knew better than to look away. Eventually it was over, and the Faerie marched out of the Arena to riotous applause.

After that came skeletons bound together with copper wire, alive and screaming, and creatures of dancing flame. The Faerie dismantled the first, and pissed on the second. The werewolves did best. They were vulnerable only to silver, and fought with unmatchable ferocity, but in the end even they died. The Faerie ate their flesh too. Gold found the whole thing sickening, and yet still some deep primal part of him responded to the fighting and the blood, and he found himself wondering what it would be like to go head to head with a shark or a lich or a werewolf, just for the hell of it. He'd fought monsters in his time, but only through necessity, never for sport. And he'd killed only rarely, to save others; never for the joy of it. And anyway, he wasn't unkillable, like the Faerie. The Games might look impressive, but in the end none of the things the Faerie had faced had been a real threat. He said as much to Morrison, quietly, and the bard nodded briefly.

'This is just a warm up, Lester. The real challenges are yet to come. But you're right, it is rigged. The Faerie don't like to lose.'

A vast roar went up from the crowd, a howling baying from a thousand throats. Gold looked round sharply, and then stared open-mouthed at what had appeared in the middle of the Arena. He'd never seen such a thing before in the flesh, but he knew what it was. He'd seen its image all his life, in books and in films; the huge, towering figure with a wedge-shaped head that had stalked across an ancient landscape long before the birth of man, a merciless killer, unopposed and unstoppable. The two front limbs looked ludicrously small, set against the huge chest, but the strength of this beast lay in its terrible jaws, the great mouth filled with teeth. The massive legs stomped heavily on the bloody sands as the creature whirled and spun in the centre of the Arena, its long tail whipping back and forth behind it. It didn't seem possible that anything so huge could move so quickly. Gold stared at it in awe, sharp chills of instinctive, atavistic fear crawling in his gut. It was the devil out of ancient times. The great lizard, the tyrant king. Tyrannosaurus Rex.

It tilted back its great head and roared defiance at the baying crowd. Its teeth were like knives, the inside of its mouth bright pink, like cheap candy. Its gleaming scales were a swirling mixture of purples and greens, and dried blood caked its shrunken forelimbs. It stomped back and forth in the middle of the Arena, snapping its great jaws like a steel trap and screaming out its challenge, somehow held back from the crowds by unseen magics. It shook its wedge head angrily, tiny eyes glaring about for some weakness in the trap it had fallen into. And then it sensed something, and the great head turned slowly to stare at Oberon and Titania in their stadium. The beast stepped towards them, the huge mouth closed in a mirthless grin, and nothing happened to stop it. It picked up speed, and Oberon and Titania were on their feet in a moment as they realized the magic wards weren't protecting them any more. The elves in the seats below the royal stadium fought each other to get out of its way. Titania drew a sword. Oberon made a magical gesture, but nothing happened. He drew his sword, and the two rulers stood side by side and waited for the Tyrannosaurus to come to them. It halted before the royal stadium and turned its head this way and that, studying them first with one eye and then the other, as though deciding how best to devour them.

'How much danger are they actually in?' said Gold. 'I mean, they're unkillable, right?'

'Technically speaking, yes,' said Morrison. 'But being torn apart, eaten and digested by something that big might be too much to come back from, even for an elf.'

'Why don't they teleport it back where it came from?'

'I imagine they already tried that, and it didn't work. Something's happening here . . .'

'All right, why don't they teleport out?'

'They can't. It would be a sign of cowardice, a stain on their honour.'

'They'll be a stain on the floor of that stadium if they don't do something soon. Why isn't anyone helping them?'

'Because,' Morrison said patiently, 'The wards didn't just happen to fail. Someone sabotaged them. This is an assassination attempt. Some faction in the Unseeli Court has decided the present rulers are in the way. Either because they're too soft, or not hard enough. Oberon and Titania have to defeat the beast, to prove themselves worthy to rule. No one will help them, for fear of being associated with a losing side. And from the look of it, they're going to have to kill it without resource to magic. The assassins must be blocking Oberon's magic with their own, or he would have melted that thing down to a puddle by now. No, they're going to have to kill it the hard way, or die trying.'

'Can they kill it? Without magic?' said Gold, staring incredulously at the living mountain of muscle and scales.

'I don't know. I wouldn't put money on it. Normally the elves take on something like that in batches of a dozen or more, all armed to the teeth with magical weapons and devices. And even then someone always gets hurt. Oberon and Titania need a champion, but no one's that crazy. Lester; they're going to die. They're my friends, and there's not a damn thing I can do to save them.'

167

'Oh hell,' said Lester Gold, the Man of Action, the Mystery Avenger. 'Can't let that happen, can I?'

He climbed up on to the edge of the stadium, and Morrison looked at him blankly. 'You can't be serious. Get the hell down from there. This is a bloody Tyrannosaurus Rex we're talking about. Something our size is just a light snack as far as it's concerned. It's got a brain the size of your fist in a head the size of your car, and a heart protected by acres of muscle and hide. You could shoot it in the head with a Magnum 45, and it probably wouldn't even notice. Get down from there, Lester, please. I don't want to lose you as well.'

'Don't worry,' said Gold. 'It may be big, but I'm tricky.'

He jumped over the edge of the stadium, and ran quickly through the empty seats between him and the royal stadium. A man in his seventies, with grey hair and the body of a much younger man, a lot of heart, and the biggest handgun Morrison had ever seen. Going to do battle with certain death for two people he didn't even know, because it was the right thing to do. Because he was a hero.

'Who knows,' said Morrison quietly. 'He might just bring it off after all.'

Gold ran up through the ranks of seating, shouting at the top of his voice to try and draw the beast's attention. It ignored him, dipping its great head towards the royal stadium and its inhabitants. Oberon and Titania cut at its mouth with their swords, but though the blades bit deep enough to jar on solid bone the creature barely seemed to notice the pain. Its anger, and possibly something else, drove it on. Gold lurched to a halt beside the royal stadium, and had to rest for a moment to get his breath back. He wasn't as young as he once was. He straightened up, pushing back the passing weakness by force of will, and aimed his gun at the Tyrannosaurus's head. He was so close now he could hear the elves grunt with effort as they swung their swords, and the solid chunking of steel biting through scales into flesh. The beast stank too, of rotting meat and

168

other things. Gold pushed it all out of his mind, aimed carefully, and shot the Tyrannosaurus twice in the head.

The scaled flesh exploded as the high calibre bullets hit the thick skull and rebounded. The beast roared deafeningly, as much in rage as in pain, and swung its great head round to look at its new enemy. Its breath was foul beyond belief. Gold held his breath, leaned over the edge of the stadium, and shot the Tyrannosaurus carefully in the foot. One clawed toe was blasted clean away. Blood spurted out on to the sand. The creature paused a moment, as though unable to believe what had just happened, and then opened its mouth wide to scream its fury. Gold had already put away his gun, and had the grenade waiting in his hand. One of the things he'd put in his pocket before they left, just in case. He pulled the pin, tossed the grenade into the gaping mouth before him, and ducked down behind the royal stadium, yelling for Oberon and Titania to take cover. The huge mouth snapped shut on the grenade automatically, and the head reared back. Gold grabbed for his gun again, just in case. And then the beast's head exploded in a fountain of blood and bone and brains. It took the Tyrannosaurus a long moment to realize how badly it was hurt, and then the huge body lurched to one side, and fell heavily on the bloody sand. The legs still kicked, and the body still twitched, but it was already dead in every way that mattered. Gold straightened up slowly, and looked down at the body below. Eighty foot from head to tail. Had to be the biggest thing he'd ever bagged. Maybe he could have it stuffed and mounted . . . only, where would he display it? He heard movement beside him, and looked quickly round in time to see Oberon and Titania sheath their swords and incline their heads respectfully to him. On all sides of the Arena the crowds were going mad, shouting and cheering.

The Faerie do love a hero . . .

Gold smiled modestly. 'Glad to be of service, your majesties. I used to do this sort of thing all the time, when I was younger. Of course, I wasn't real then.'

169

6

Memories

On the outskirts of Shadows Fall stood two houses, a respectable distance apart. One empty, the other occupied, both haunted by remnants of a past that would not be forgotten or dismissed. The house on the right was a small and modest place, a little neglected and run down perhaps, but nothing that couldn't be put right with a little care and effort. It wasn't far out of town, but no one visited the house who didn't have to. Three women and a young girl took it in turns to stare out of windows on the first floor, but only one woman lived there. Her name was Polly Cousins, and something awful happened to her when she was a child. She couldn't remember what, but the house had not forgotten. Polly lived on the ground floor, but sometimes she would go up to the first floor and walk from room to room, looking out of the windows, sometimes pursuing a memory and sometimes trying to hide from one. In the room without a window, something breathed slowly and steadily.

Polly stood in the Spring room, looking out of the window at the first signs of leaves on a nearby oak tree. The air was bright and sharp and full of promise of the year to come. Polly, eight years old, had to stand on tiptoe to see out of the window. She was a pleasant enough child, with a blunt, handsome face and long blonde hair carefully brushed back and plaited into two long pigtails. She was wearing her best dress, which was also her favourite dress. She was eight years old, and something horrible had come into her life. She looked out of the window, but no one

171

came up the road from the town, no matter how long she watched and waited.

She was alone in the house. (Only that wasn't true, not really.) The view from the Spring room was the most promising, but it was also the most boring after a while, and eight-year-olds have a very low boredom threshold. Not for the first time, it occurred to her that she could open the window, and find her way out into the Spring scene before her. But she never did. There was something (in the house) that held her back. Polly Cousins, eight years old, sighed and kicked the wall briefly with a smart but sensible shoe, then turned her back on Spring and left the room.

As she walked out of the door she grew suddenly in size, shooting up to adult height with dizzying speed. She put out a hand to steady herself against the passage wall, finding a kind of comfort in its firm, unchanging nature. The change was quickly over, and she breathed deeply as the rush of new blood through new flesh briefly intoxicated her. She was eighteen years old again, back from relatives to live with her mother in her old house. There was something else in the house, but she didn't know what, then. She was tall, five foot ten and proud of it, with long blonde hair hanging limply round a square, pleasant face. She wasn't pretty and never would be, but she could have been good-looking if it wasn't for her eyes. They were a pale, washed-out blue, very cold and always wary. The eyes of someone who thought a lot but said little. She walked down the passage, opened the next door, and entered the Summer room.

Bright sunshine blazed from a sky so blue it was almost painful to look at. The sunlight splashed across the lawn below like liquid honey, and birds soared on the brilliant sky like drifting specks. Polly looked out into the world of Summer, and it was everything she ever dreamed of, but the house (or something in it) wouldn't let her go. She turned away from the window. She couldn't bear to look at the Summer for long. It brought back memories of the last time she'd known anything like happiness. When she'd come back to the house, not knowing what was waiting. She turned her back on Summer and walked out of the room.

Out in the passage, her shoulders slumped slightly as four years passed in an instant, and she was twenty-two again. Her eyes were lost and confused, and her hair had been cropped institutionally short. They did that at the hospital, the officially bright and cheerful place they took her to after she had her breakdown. She didn't care. She didn't care about anything then, except getting away from the house. She'd lived there alone after her mother died, and it was too much for her. After they told her she was cured, she went back to the house anyway, because there was nowhere else to go. She belonged there. She pulled back her shoulders, walked into the room opposite, and looked out of the window into Autumn.

Tatters of gold and bronze still clung to the oak tree, but most of the leaves were gone, and the branches stood revealed like bones. She liked the Autumn best. It was restful. It demanded less of her. This was the way it had looked when she'd needed the world not to bother her with its presence. At the same time, the passing nature of Autumn had given her confidence that the world could change, without her having to be strong. She stared out into the Autumn and then looked reluctantly away. She never stayed long, for fear it might grow stale and lose its comfort. She walked out of the room and into the passage, and thirteen years fell upon her, bringing her back to her real age, and there was only one window left.

She walked back up the passage and into the next room, empty as all the others were, and looked out of the window into Winter. It was cold and sharp, under a dark and threatening sky. Frost had patterned the lawn, and glistened on the sidewalk. She liked this scene the least, because this was now, the present, and the world went on without her, with no care for her needs. Winter became Spring became Summer became Autumn, on and on, world without end. She could walk downstairs and out of the house into Winter any time she chose. Except she couldn't. The house (and what was in it) wouldn't let her. She shopped by phone and paid by mail and never went outside.

Polly Cousins, thirty-five years old, looking ten years older. Painfully thin, almost gaunt, carrying a burden too heavy to put down. Not at all what the eight-year-old had expected to grow up to be.

Movement caught her eye, and she looked with mild surprise at a man walking up the street towards the house. She thought at first he must be lost. No one came this way unless they had to. There was nothing to see but the two houses, and anyone who knew about them knew better than to risk disturbing them. But the man kept coming, not hurrying, but showing no sign of fear or awe. He looked pleasant enough, even handsome in a dark and brooding way. He finally stopped outside the house opposite, and looked at it for a long time. The Hart house.

Polly felt a brief stab of regret that he hadn't come to see her after all, and then frowned as she realized the man's face was vaguely familiar. She scowled at his turned back, trying to grasp the elusive thought, but it evaded her, as so many of her thoughts did. She let it go. It would come back to her if it was important. The man suddenly strode forward, mounted the steps, and unlocked the front door. Polly blinked, taken aback. No one had been in the Hart house for twenty-five years, to her knowledge. Curiosity tugged at her like an unfamiliar friend, and she turned and left the Winter room. She strode down the passage towards the stairs, not letting herself hurry. It meant she had to pass the last room, the one with no window, but the door was securely shut and she passed it by with her head held high. She could hear something breathing, harsh and slow, but she didn't look into the room. There was nothing in there. Nothing at all. She listened to it breathing all the way down the stairs.

Downstairs, all the windows showed the same scene and the same Season. The ground floor showed the world as it was, and nothing more. Polly lived on the ground floor, and had made one of the rooms over into a bedroom. She spent as little time as possible upstairs. It held too many memories. But sometimes it called her, and then she had to go up, whether she wanted to or not.

She went to the front window and stared out at the Hart house opposite. As she did, the strange man looked out of the window opposite, and she saw his face again. She was sure she knew it from somewhere. Or somewhen. Her breathing quickened. Perhaps he was part of her past, from the years that were lost to her. From the time she'd chosen not to remember. The man turned away from the window and disappeared back into the house, but his face remained, dancing almost tauntingly before her mind's eye. She'd seen it before, when she was very young. It was the face of Jonathon Hart, who used to live with his family in the house opposite, when she was eight years old.

Do places dream of people till they return?

James Hart stood in the hall of the house he'd grown up in, and didn't recognize it at all. He felt disappointed and let down, even though he'd told himself not to expect too much too soon. As far as his memories were concerned he'd never been in this house before, but he hoped actually being here might stir up something. Unless what had happened here had been so awful that some part of him was determined not to remember. He still didn't know why his family had left in such a hurry. From what Old Father Time had said, the prophecy had been disturbing enough to throw a scare into anyone, but what had made his parents decide to just leave everything and run? Had someone threatened them; someone convinced that the Harts were a threat to the Forever Door and Shadows Fall itself? Or had his parents believed that, and left the town in order to protect it? He shrugged mentally, and moved over to try the first door on his left. It opened easily, without even a creak.

The room was bright and airy with pleasant, unremarkable furniture and rather bland-looking prints on the walls. A clock ticked slowly, steadily, on a cluttered mantelpiece. Hart frowned. He'd never liked slow-ticking clocks. He'd always thought that was because the dentist he'd been taken to had a slow-ticking clock in his waiting room, but perhaps that had just been the echo of an earlier fear . . . The room looked peaceful and undisturbed, as though the occupiers had stepped out just a little while before, and might be back at any moment. The thought disturbed him vaguely, and he looked over his shoulder, half expecting someone, some ghost, to be there watching him. There was no one there. He left the room and closed the door carefully behind him.

He made his way through the house, room by room, and none of it looked in the least familiar. Everywhere looked neat and tidy, as though a cleaning lady had just been through. And yet according to Old Father Time, no one had been in the Hart house since his family left it, though Time had been puzzlingly vague as to why that should be. There wasn't even any dust . . . nothing to suggest that anything had changed here in twenty-five years. He stood at the top of the stairs, and wondered what to do next. He'd looked in every room, picked things up and put them down, and still not a trace of memory had come back to him. It might have been a stranger's house for all it did for him. But he had spent the first ten years of his life here; he must have left some mark somewhere. He stood scowling for a long moment, tapping his fist angrily against his hip. There was nowhere else to look . . . and then a sudden inspiration hit him, and he looked up to see the attic trapdoor in the ceiling right above him.

It didn't take him long to figure out how to open it and pull down the folding ladder, and he scrambled quickly up into the attic. It was dark and cramped and smelled decidedly musty, but something in the place called to him. He could feel it. He reached out and turned on the single bare light bulb, and it was only after he'd done it that he realized he'd known where the light switch was without having to look for it. He took his time looking around him. The narrow space under the eaves was filled with old packing crates and dozens of paper parcels tied up with string. He bent over the nearest crate and pulled away the single layer of cloth that protected what lay beneath. It turned out to be more papers, bundled together and packed into paper bags with dates on. Hart pulled out a handful of papers and riffled quickly through them. Tax returns, financial records, hoarded receipts. Hart put them back. They meant nothing to him. He moved over to the next crate and jerked the cloth away. It was full to the brim with toys.

Hart stayed where he was, half crouching by the crate. All the toys you ever had and lost end up in Shadows Fall. The ones you broke and the ones your mother threw away, the stuffed toy that was loved till it fell apart, and the trike you outgrew. Nothing is ever really lost. It all ends up in Shadows Fall, sooner or later. It's that kind of place. Hart knelt down beside the crate, not taking his eyes off the toys for a moment, as though afraid they might vanish if he looked away. He reached into the crate and brought out the first thing his fingers found. It was a clockwork Batman figure, square and ugly and functional in garish heavy-duty plastic. He turned the over-sized key in its side, and the flat feet stomped up and down. Hart smiled slowly. He remembered it. He remembered sitting in front of the television, watching the old Batman show, with Adam West and Burt Ward. Same Bat time, same Bat channel. (Don't sit so close, Jimmy. It's bad for your eyes.) The memories were short and sharp, like stills taken from a film. He put the figure down on the attic floor and it stomped officiously off, whirring loudly and rocking from side to side. Hart wondered briefly if the Batman himself lived in Shadows Fall, but he thought not. The Batman was still popular. People still believed in him.

The next thing to come out of the crate was an old hardback Daleks annual. A spin-off from the Doctor Who series, back in the black and white days, when it was still scary. Hart leafed slowly through the book, and as he did memories surfaced in sudden little rushes; of sitting up in bed far too early on Christmas morning, reading his new annual when he should have been sleeping. The stories seemed instantly familiar as he discovered them, but the memories were complete in themselves. They didn't tell him anything of the boy who'd read them.

Thunderbirds vehicles. James Bond's Aston Martin, with the ejector seat. The Batmobile that fired rockets and had a chainsaw concealed in the bonnet. A box full of assorted model soldiers, all of them looking as though they'd led long and active lives. A gun shaped like a jet plane that fired sucker-tipped darts. Farm and zoo animals mixed carelessly together. Model trains, still in their boxes. Aurora monster kits.

Memories came and went, bringing back vague but strengthening images of a small boy, short for his age, shy and retiring, who played with his toys because there were few children his own age he could play with. And because, even then, there had been something odd about him . . . Hart sat beside the crate, letting Lego bricks trickle through his fingers like sands in an hourglass. Memories were surfacing slowly, brief and disjointed, giving him a vague feeling of the child he'd once been. It wasn't a comfortable image. The young James Hart had been cared for and loved, but spent much of his time on his own. He couldn't remember why, but he had a cold feeling he wouldn't like the answer when he found it. There had been something strange about his childhood. Something strange about him.

Something too strange, even for Shadows Fall.

A sudden shudder went through him, as though something had stirred briefly deep within him. He held his breath, waiting to see if it would return and take a more definite shape, but there was nothing more. He sifted indifferently through the layers of toys, but no other memories surfaced. He looked at the toys scattered around him on the attic floor, and all he could think was that there were collectors in the outside world who'd pay a small fortune for junk like this. Some of the Aurora monster kits weren't even assembled, still complete in their boxes. He studied the garish art on the box covers, the familiar images of Frankenstein and Dracula and the Wolfman, and smiled suddenly as it occurred to him that the original counterparts might well be at large somewhere in Shadows Fall, living in comfortable retirement. Maybe he could get them to autograph a few boxes . . .

He picked up the toys and put them carefully away again. He glanced at the other crates and packages, but felt no inclination to check them. Some inner voice told him they held nothing useful for him. The toys had brought him up to the attic, and he'd got all he was going to get from them. He clambered down the loft ladder, went back up again to switch off the light, descended again, and put the folding ladder back. He walked down the stairs, and then paused at the bottom. He had a strong feeling he wasn't finished here yet. There was still something waiting for him, something important. He looked around him and the hall looked back, open-faced and innocent. He moved slowly forward, drawn to a mirror hanging on the wall. His own face looked back at him, frowning and puzzled. And then, as he watched, the face changed in subtle ways, and his father was looking out of the mirror at him. His father, looking younger and more intense, and perhaps just a little scared.

'Hello, Jimmy,' said his father. 'I'm sorry I have to rush this, but time isn't on our side. You understand. I'm leaving this message for you just before we leave, pro-grammed to respond only to your presence. There are so many things I want to say to you. If you're back here, it means your mother and I are probably dead. I hope we had a good life together, wherever we end up. You're still a little boy to me, but I suppose you're a man now. Whatever happens, always remember that your mother and I loved you very much.

'We're leaving here because of the prophecy. I hope you'll never have to come back, and this message will

179

never be activated, but your grandfather, my father, is very insistent that you have the option to come back, if you choose. So, the prophecy; it's very vague. Basically, it just says that your fate is linked to that of the Forever Door, and that you are destined at some future time to bring Shadows Fall to an end. That will scare a lot of people, and people get violent while they're frightened. News of the prophecy hasn't had time to travel far yet, so we're leaving now, before someone decides to try and stop us. I don't know what kind of welcome you'll get if you do choose to return, but whatever happens, your grandfather will still be here to protect you.' Jonathon Hart stopped, glanced back over his shoulder, and then looked back at his son. 'Jimmy; we have to go now. Be happy.'

The face in the mirror was suddenly his own again. He looked pale and shocked. He'd never known his father as a young man; there were no photos or reminders from that period, and now Hart knew why. Tears stung his eyes as he turned away from the mirror. He never got a chance to say goodbye to his father and his mother. They drove off in the car like any other day, and the first he knew anything was wrong was when the police came to tell him they'd both been killed in a car crash. He wouldn't believe them at first; kept saying his father was too good a driver to have had an accident. He kept on saying that right up until he had to identify the bodies at the morgue. After that he didn't say much about anything for a long time.

'Goodbye, Dad. Goodbye.'

He sniffed hard, and blinked his eyes rapidly. He didn't have time for this. It wouldn't be long before the same people who ran his family out of Shadows Fall would learn of his return, and then all hell would break loose. He had to find out the truth about his family and the prophecy, and that meant looking for his grandfather. His father's father; the one who'd left him the map and instructions that had brought him back to Shadows Fall. The message in the mirror had seemed to imply that not only was his grandfather still living here, in the town, but he was actually powerful enough in his own right to be able to protect his grandson. Hart frowned. His parents had never talked much about family matters. He'd grown up without grandparents, uncles or aunts, brothers or sisters, and never thought it strange until his schoolfriends pointed it out. He'd asked questions then, but got no answers. His parents simply wouldn't talk about it. He had all kinds of fantasies after that. He dreamed he was adopted, or kidnapped, or that his father had been witness to a crime and put some big Mob boss behind bars, and had to stay hidden to keep safe. Finally he decided he'd been watching too much television, and let the matter drop. He always supposed that some day his parents would get around to telling him. And then they were gone.

A thought struck him. If his grandfather was still here, perhaps others of his family were too. Cousins, maybe, remote enough to have been overlooked by his enemies. That word stopped him short. Enemies. People who would hurt or even kill him, because of what he might some day do. He supposed he ought to feel threatened, even scared, but it was all too new, too strange. He couldn't take it seriously. Just as well, or he'd end up jumping at shadows.

Shadows. The word resonated within him like the tolling of a great iron bell, and glimpses of memories suddenly flickered through his mind, like the shuffling of a pack of cards. He tried to grasp them, but they slipped away, unformed and unfinished, until one memory hit him with the clarity of inspiration. He'd been lonely as a child, so he'd made up an imaginary friend. Called, with a child's logic and lack of sophistication, simply Friend. He talked to it and confided in it, and his shadow Friend protected him from all the monsters that frightened him at night. The memory surprised and charmed him. He'd never thought of himself as particularly imaginative. Pity his Friend wasn't around now; he could use some protection.

On an impulse, he raised his hands and made a shadow shape on the wall before him. He hadn't done that since he was a small child, but old skills quickly returned, as though that was only yesterday. A rabbit took shape, with twitching ears, and a bird with beating wings, a donkey and a duck. The shadows leapt and danced on the wall before him, rich with meaning. Hart smiled, and lowered his hands. And the shadows stayed where they were.

Hart fell back a step, his breath caught in his throat. His hands were at his sides but the shadows still clung to the wall, though there was nothing left to cast them. The shadows moved again, repeating the shapes with fluid ease, and then ran slowly down the wall to form another shape; his own shadow. He jerked his feet back rather than make contact with it, and it reared back, a human shape standing as tall as he did, but with folded arms.

Part of Hart wanted to turn and run, but after some of the things he'd seen in Shadows Fall, a shadow with a mind of its own wasn't really all that scary. And there was something almost . . . familiar about it. He'd seen this before, as a child. He remembered this. His Friend.

'And where the hell have you been?' said an acid voice. 'I turn my back for five minutes, and you disappear for twenty-five years! You might at least have left a note. Is this the thanks I get for looking after you all those years? When your father was at work and your mother was too busy? I was always there for you, and what was my reward? Twenty-five years in an empty house. No one to talk to, never any company; if I hadn't had the house to clean and tidy I'd have lost my mind. No one comes to call, the only neighbour is that crazy woman across the way, poor child, and the only television channel I can get shows nothing but soaps. Plus, not once but on three separate occasions, Father Callahan has tried to exorcise me. He should be so lucky. I'm a shadow, not a ghost, which by all accounts lead far more interesting lives. Well? Have you nothing to say to me?'

'I was waiting for a chance to get a word in edgeways,' said Hart.

'Well pardon me for breathing, which I don't, as it

happens. If you'd spent twenty-five years home alone you'd talk to yourself too.'

'Friend,' said Hart, 'I've missed you. Even when I couldn't remember you, there was still a part of me that missed you. How could I have forgotten you?'

'I wouldn't touch a straight line like that for all the tea in China. Well, don't just stand there. Where have you been, what have you been doing; tell me everything.'

'There was a prophecy. We had to leave in a hurry, or people would have hurt us. I would have taken you with me if I could, but even then I knew you couldn't survive outside Shadows Fall. I forgot everything when I left, but still, sometimes, I dreamed of you.'

'They took you away,' said Friend quietly. 'I knew you wouldn't have just gone off and left me. Oh Jimmy; I've missed you so!'

The shadow threw itself forward and wrapped itself around him like a living cloak of darkness. He could feel the weight of it in his arms, the heart beating rapidly against his own. It should have been scary, or at least disturbing, but it wasn't. It was rather like having an armful of warm puppy; all bright eyes and affection. Friend finally calmed down a bit, and drew back to drape itself down the wall again.

'It's good to have you back, Jimmy. Are you going to be staying here?'

'I suppose so. The house belongs to me now. My mother and my father are dead.'

'Oh Jimmy, I am sorry. Really. Look, obviously a lot's happened and I want to hear all about it, but there's no hurry, is there? You sit yourself down in the main room and take it easy, and I'll make you a nice cup of coffee.'

Hart raised an eyebrow. 'How are you going to do that when you don't have a body?'

'I'll improvise,' said Friend dryly. 'I've got as much body as I need to get things done. How do you think I kept the house clean and tidy all these years? Wishful thinking? Now do as you're told, and you can have some chocolate

183

chip cookies to go with your coffee. You always liked chocolate chip cookies.'

'Aren't they going to be rather dry after twenty-five years in the kitchen?'

'You're so sharp you'll cut yourself one of these days. The cookies are fine, like everything else in this house. Everything here is exactly as you left it. I knew you'd be back, some day.'

The shadow slipped away across the wall like rain sliding down a window, and disappeared in the direction of the kitchen. Hart blinked a few times, and then walked back down the hall and into the main room. Never a dull moment in Shadows Fall . . . He sank down into what had once been his chair, twenty-five years earlier. It seemed a lot smaller than he remembered, but then it would, wouldn't it? The room and its furniture seemed smart but dated, like the setting for a sixties sit-com. The television set in particular was large and blocky and looked like something from the Stone Age. He stared at it thoughtfully, hoping it would stir some memory of the programmes he used to watch as a child, and the child who watched them. The television stared blankly back, but slowly something stirred within him. TV shows came back to him that he hadn't thought about since he was ten years old, or younger.

Champion the Wonder Horse. Circus Boy. Wagon Train. Bonanza . . .

They flickered through his mind in swift succession, bright and cheerful and larger than life (*Lassie* and *The Lone Ranger*), but nothing came to him of what it had been like to watch those programmes, all those years ago. They were black and white snapshots, complete in themselves. Hart sighed, and leaned back in his chair. Perhaps the shadow Friend would be the key he needed to unlock his past. It seemed to know all kinds of things. It might even know who his grandfather was. The shadow . . . shadows had frightened him as a small child. He didn't like the sudden way they moved when you did, or sneaked around behind you. They watched him all the time, but he couldn't see their eyes. How could he have forgotten something that had so shaped his early life? There were shadows everywhere once the sun went down, watching silently. Waiting. Some nights he hadn't been able to sleep, even though his bedroom light was still on, because he was scared the shadows might jump him if he took his eyes off them. He could get rid of the shadows by turning off the light, but sometimes it seemed to him the dark was just one big shadow. So he made up a shadow Friend, to protect him from the other shadows. Only this being Shadows Fall, he ended up with a real imaginary Friend.

He looked up, startled, as he heard footsteps out in the hall. It couldn't be Friend; the shadow moved silently. Someone else was in the house with him. He got up and moved quietly over to the door, and then just stood there, his hand dropping away from the door handle. If Friend was real, perhaps the threatening shadows were too . . . A quick shudder went through him, but he pushed it firmly away. He wasn't a child any more. He had real enemies these days, and there was always a chance they'd kept a watch on the Hart house, just in case he was stupid enough to come here alone and unarmed . . . He pushed that thought aside too. It was just as likely his neighbour from across the road, come round to borrow a cup of sugar and scope out her new neighbour.

That crazy woman across the way. Poor child . . .

Hart shook his head. He'd better take a look in the hall while he still could. Any more of this and he'd scare himself into running for his life through the nearest window. He opened the door and stepped quickly out into the hall. There was no one there. He grinned shame-facedly, and didn't know whether to feel relieved or stupid. It was an old house, it was bound to make creaking, settling sounds from time to time. And then he looked down the hall, and saw that the front door was standing just a few inches ajar. He tried to remember whether he'd left it open, and couldn't make up his mind one way or the other.

185

He moved cautiously down the hall to the door, opened it and looked out. All quiet. No sign of anyone anywhere. He looked across at the other house, but there was no sign of his neighbour at any of the windows. Hart shrugged uneasily, closed the front door firmly and turned round just in time to see the knife heading for his throat.

He threw himself to one side with speed and reflexes he didn't know he had, and the knife just missed him. His attacker stumbled forward, caught off balance by the force of her own blow, and Hart drew back his fist. And then he hesitated as he realized his attacker was a thin, gaunt woman who looked almost as scared as he felt. Light gleamed off the knife blade as she prepared for another thrust, and the panicky determination in her face snapped Hart out of his paralysis. He had no doubt she meant to kill him, even though he'd never seen her before in his life.

The knife shot forward again. Hart dodged, and the blade buried itself in the wood of the door behind him. His attacker tugged at the knife, but it was stuck fast. Hart stepped quickly forward and seized her in a bear hug, pinning her arms to her sides. She struggled fiercely, but he was stronger than her, if only just. She subsided, and they panted in each other's faces for a moment. He saw the uprising knee in her eyes even as she planned it, and thrust her away from him. She lashed out at him with both fists, trying to force him away from the door so that she could get to the knife again. Hart warded off the blows easily enough, but even so they were strong enough to jolt his arms painfully. And then Friend came sweeping down the hall like a jet black tidal wave and dropped over the woman like an enveloping cloak. She struggled desperately to break free, but Friend was too strong for her, smothering her moves easily. She stopped struggling, and something came from inside the darkness that might have been sobs.

'Remember the crazy woman from across the road I told you about?' said Friend conversationally. 'Well, this is her. Polly Cousins. Spends a lot of time at the window, watching the world go by. Doesn't get out much, but you can probably tell that. A few guppies short of an aquarium, if you ask me. What do you want me to do with her?'

'For the moment, hang on to her like grim death,' said Hart, getting his breath back. 'Apart from that, I'm open to suggestions. Is the phone working? If it is, I suppose I should call the Sheriff.'

'No! Please don't do that.' Polly's voice was very small, like a child's. 'I'll be good, I promise.'

She looked so pathetic and helpless that Hart began to feel rather like a bully. A glance at the long knife still embedded in the front door was enough to dismiss that thought.

'Take her into the main room, Friend, but don't let go of her for a moment. There's a few questions I need answered before I decide what to do next.'

'It's your funeral,' said Friend cheerfully. 'My advice is to hand her over to the Sheriff, lock her up somewhere especially secure and then swallow the key, but what do I know? I'm just an imaginary friend.'

The shadow flounced back down the hall, dragging Polly with it. She didn't put up any resistance, but Hart followed them at a respectful distance, just in case. Back in the main room, Friend dropped Polly into a chair and settled across her lap like a throw rug, holding her firmly in place. Hart pulled up a chair and sat down opposite them.

'Talk to me, Polly Cousins,' he said evenly. 'Tell me why you tried to kill me, when to the best of my knowledge I've never set eyes on you before in my life. And while you're at it, give me one good reason why I shouldn't just hand you over to the authorities as a dangerous lunatic?'

'I'm sorry,' said Polly, her voice little more than a murmur. 'I panicked. I was looking out of my window, and I recognized you. You're very like your father, and I remember him well. When I realized who you were, who you had to be, all I could think of was the prophecy. The one that says you'll destroy the Forever Door and bring Shadows Fall to an end. I was scared. I need the Forever

Door, and the influence it has on the town; it's all that makes my life bearable. It's all that keeps me sane. I am sane; more or less.' She smiled briefly, sadly. 'Though I can understand you might find that hard to believe. You see, I'm . . . not always myself, and you caught me at a bad moment. I'm back in control.now. If you release me, I promise I'll behave.'

Hart sat back in his chair. She seemed sane enough, for the moment. Her knife was safely out of reach, and Friend was right there, ready to pounce on her again at a moment's notice . . .

'I have a strong feeling I'm going to regret this, but . . . all right, Friend; let her go. But stand ready, just in case.'

'Strikes me you're as crazy as she is, but you're in charge. Just don't blame me if she produces another knife from somewhere. She looks the type. But of course no one listens to me. I'm just a shadow, what do I know?'

'Friend; get on with it.'

It sniffed audibly (Hart couldn't help wondering what with), slipped away from Polly, and flowed up the wall behind her, adopting a human shape again. Polly stretched cautiously.

'Interesting friend you have there, Jimmy. I remember you telling me about it as a child, and I was never sure whether to believe you or not. You were always telling stories, then.'

'I prefer James, these days,' said Hart. 'You remember me as a child? What was I like? I can't remember anything from those days.'

'We went to school together, and we played together sometimes when our parents needed somewhere handy to dump us. Suzanne Dubois told me you were back in Shadows Fall. She saw it in her Cards. I knew you'd come back to the house, sooner or later, but it was still a shock, seeing you again. Rumours and stories have made you something of a bogeyman in your absence; a terrible sword hanging over all of us and everything we care for. I didn't realize how frightened of you part of me was, until I found

188

myself walking across the road to your front door with a kitchen knife in my hand. But I'm back in control now. There's . . . more than one of me, more than one person inside me. One of them is very young, and frightens easily.'

'You mean you're a multiple personality?' said Hart interestedly. 'I've heard of them.'

'It's not as simple as that,' said Polly hesitantly. 'It's the house, you see. My house; Four Seasons. Time has broken down there, and who I am and what age I am depends on where in the house I am.'

Hart looked across at Friend. 'Are you following any of this?'

'Oh sure, this is much more interesting than the soaps on television, and not nearly as complicated. I think we ought to go across the road and take a look at her house.'

'Can you leave here? I thought you were stuck in this place.'

'I was, till you came back, but now I can go anywhere you can. I'm your shadow. Do let's go, Jimmy, I mean James. I haven't been out of this house in twenty-five years, and Polly's place sounds absolutely fascinating.'

'Not five minutes ago, you were all for locking her up and forgetting where they put her. But you're right; it does sound fascinating. Lead the way, Polly. But if you even look like you're going for another knife, I'll have Friend drop on you like a ton of bricks. Is that clear?'

'Of course, James. I appreciate your need for caution. Please understand; this isn't easy for me. I haven't had a stranger in my house for more years than I care to remember. I'm going to have to talk about things I don't even discuss with myself. But I think it's time I talked to someone. And if you're as powerful as you're supposed to be, maybe you can find a way out of the hell I've made for myself.'

'I'm not powerful,' said Hart. 'I'm not anybody special. I'm just me.'

'I hope you're wrong,' said Polly. 'For both our sakes.'

189

She rose hesitantly to her feet, as though expecting him to change his mind at any moment, and led the way out into the hall. Hart stayed right behind her, ready to grab her or jump out of reach, as need be. She seemed sane enough now, but her knife had made a strong impression on him. People with knives were something he took very seriously. Polly stopped at his front door, glanced at the knife sticking out of the wood, and then pulled open the door and stepped out into the street. Hart went out after her, Friend bobbing along at his heels like any other shadow. He carefully locked the door behind him, and then the three of them crossed the road to Polly's house. It looked ordinary enough to Hart, but he'd been in Shadows Fall long enough to know that didn't mean a damn thing. *Time has broken down there . . .* Polly opened her front door and went inside. Hart and Friend followed her in, hanging back just a little.

There was something definitely wrong about the house called Four Seasons. Hart could feel it on the air; an unending tension, a sense of pressure, of purpose. Of someone or something waiting. He stepped into the hall-way, brightly lit by the afternoon sun, and had to fight an impulse to keep looking back over his shoulder. How could Polly live in a place like this? He'd only just arrived, and already he wanted to turn around and walk right out again. Polly looked back to say something, and he quickly made sure there was nothing in his face to betray his unease. For the first time he thought he understood the tension within her, that kept her always strained and agitated, like a guitar string pulled too taut too long. She blushed lightly as he stared at her, and put a hand to her dishevelled hair, as though realizing for the first time how she must look to him.

'I'm sorry; the place looks a mess, and so do I. If I'd known I was having company, I'd have made an effort. But only a few people ever come here, and mostly I like it that way. People think I'm crazy. Sometimes I think so too.' She looked around her, as though trying to decide where best to take him. 'You must understand, James; this place is dangerous. Time moves differently here. Something happened in this house, long ago, when I was just a little girl. Something awful. But I can't remember what. Suzanne told me you'd lost the memories of your childhood. I wasn't so lucky. I've still got mine. They haunt me, and this house. Upstairs, there are four different rooms, and in them I am four different people. Four different versions of myself. Down here, things are more stable. I'm allowed to be just me. Come on through to the kitchen. We'll be safe there, and it's far enough away from the rest of the house that it might not hear us talking.'

She led the way down the hall and into the kitchen, chattering nervously all the while. Hart couldn't follow half of what she was saying, but he listened carefully anyway, searching for clues as to what had happened long ago, to Polly and her house. The kitchen was a mess, but a comfortable mess; the kind of place where you know where things are without having to look. Every surface was buried under accumulated clutter, but there was no dirt or grime, and the floor was spotlessly clean. Polly cleared an old sweater off a chair, dropped it casually on the draining board, and gestured for Hart to sit down. He did so, checking unobtrusively that Friend was still with him, and watched Polly bustle round the kitchen as she made coffee for them. She kept up her chatter, perhaps because she was afraid of what might come to fill the silence if she didn't.

'Something bad happened to me when I was eight years old, and it's still happening, in a room upstairs. The room with no window. I haven't been in that room since it happened, but something's there, waiting for me.' Polly sounded strangely calm now, as though relieved at having someone she could talk to about it. 'I have tried to face it, in the past. I tried when I was eight, when I was twenty-two, and just recently, last year. I couldn't do it. I wasn't strong enough, and each time I failed, a room took a part of me and held it, like a fly trapped in amber. Now, when I go upstairs, the house makes me those people again. Not as a punishment. It took me a long time to understand that. The house is trying to cure me; to make me overcome what happened here by facing it. But I can't.'

She paused, and Hart chose his words very carefully. 'What actually happened to you, when you were eight years old? Can you remember any of it?'

'No. My mother was out, and I was alone in the house with my father. Something awful happened between us, something so bad I can't bear to remember it; something so terrible it still haunts this house and me.'

Oh my God, thought Hart. *She's talking about sexual abuse. Her father must have ... no wonder she doesn't want to remember.*

'Why don't you leave?' he said finally, when he could be sure of his voice. 'Just pack up and go, and leave it all behind you?'

'I can't. The house won't let me. As long as it has those parts of me upstairs, I'm not whole. Part of the house wants to cure me; part of it feeds off me. So I keep trying to face my fear, and every time I fail there's another fragment of me haunting the house. Soon you won't be able to move here for different versions of me, cluttering up the place.'

She tried to smile at her own joke, but it wasn't very successful. She bit her lip and turned away abruptly so that Hart wouldn't see the tears burning in her eyes. He sat there awkwardly, wanting to help, not knowing what to say or do for the best. Friend suddenly flowed up and over the kitchen table and wrapped itself around Polly's trembling shoulders like a shawl.

'Now, now, don't take on so, petal. It's all right, you're not alone any more. Your trouble is, you've been trying to face this thing alone for too long. Hasn't anyone ever tried to see this thing through with you before?'

'No. I never let anyone in here, not even Suzanne, who's my best friend. The only person who might have helped was my mother, but she wouldn't have understood. And she might have said it was all my fault. She died when

192

I was eighteen. Just before I tried to face the room the first time, and failed. And that part of me watched her funeral procession from its own window, after a child watched from another. Ever since then, there's only been me here, getting more and more alone as bits of me flake off and are held. No one comes here; they can feel the power building in Four Seasons. It's a jealous power, and it doesn't want anyone here who might try to break me free. I'm surprised you were able to come in. You must be very strong. Even when I was trying to kill you, part of me knew you were someone special.'

'I knew that, even when he was a child,' said Friend. 'Everything's going to be all right. James and I will see you through this. We'll start back with the earliest you, at eight, and work our way through the other yous until we finally get to what originally scared you. And then we'll kick its ass.'

'Excuse me just a moment,' said Hart, 'But do you think I could have a private word with you, Friend? Out in the hall?'

'Of course, James, but can't it wait?'

'No, I don't think it can.'

'Oh, very well then. Excuse us, dear, we won't be a minute. Will you be all right on your own?'

'Yes,' said Polly. 'I've had lots of practice being on my own.'

Hart got up and went out into the hallway, Friend sliding along the walls after him. Hart carefully closed the kitchen door behind him, moved a cautious distance down the hall, and then glared at his shadow.

'What the hell do you think you're doing? This woman needs competent psychiatric help! It's obvious she was sexually abused by her father as a child, and through fear and shame and guilt she's chosen to suppress the memory rather than face it. These other fragments could be nothing more than manifestations of a multiple personality. She needs professional help. There's no telling how much damage a couple of well-meaning amateurs could do!'

193

'If a shrink could have helped, she'd have found one by now,' said Friend calmly. 'She's been coping with this all her life, so you can be sure she's already tried all the obvious things. We can help her, Jimmy. We're special. You, because you've lost your childhood too, and me, because I'm not entirely real. Nothing can harm me, or frighten me, but I can protect Polly from pretty much anything. I learned how to do a whole lot of things while I was waiting for you to come back. And she's right, Jimmy. You do have power in you. I don't know what it is, but I can feel it, like the hum of underground machinery, just waiting for someone to throw the right switch. We have to do this, Jimmy. Polly needs us.'

Hart took a deep breath and let it out slowly. 'I've got a really bad feeling about this, Friend. There's something else in this house, apart from Polly. I can feel it, watching and waiting. And if there's any kind of power in me, it's news to me. But you're right; we can't just turn our back on Polly. If only because she might decide to stick a knife in it. If I'm going to have a neighbour, I'd rather it wasn't a looney tune with a knife.'

'You've grown very cynical, Jimmy. I'm not sure I approve.'

'The word is practical, and I thought we'd agreed on James, not Jimmy. Look, I said we'd help, didn't I? I just think we'll all be a lot safer going into this with our eyes open. All right; let's get this show on the road, before I suffer an attack of good sense.'

He smiled and Friend shook its head, and they went back into the kitchen. Polly was standing with her back to them, looking out of the window. She was hugging herself tightly, as though suddenly cold, or perhaps just to stop herself shaking. She didn't look round as they came in.

'I was always afraid, before you came,' she said slowly. 'Afraid of what might have happened in the past, afraid of whatever's in the room with no window, and afraid that at any moment it would call to me again and I'd have to go to it. But I didn't know what fear really was, until you came and offered me hope. I want so much to be free of all my pasts, but the thought of trying and failing scares me so much I can hardly breathe.'

'Don't worry,' said Hart. 'Whatever happens, I won't leave you here alone. If I can't find a way out of this for you, you're welcome to come and stay in my house, across the road. You'll be safe there.'

'You don't understand,' said Polly. She turned round to face him at last, and there was no hope in her cold gaze. 'I *can't* leave. The house won't let me. Whatever it is that's in this house with me, I helped to make it; I gave it power over me. And I know, beyond any doubt, that it would rather kill me and you than let me go.'

Hart wanted to step forward and hold her in his arms, and comfort her, but the pain in her face was a barrier he couldn't cross. 'All right,' he said briskly. 'This is what we're going to do. We're going upstairs and into the room where you're eight years old, and then we'll go from room to room, collecting all your other selves and reintegrating them into one you again. We'll make you whole again, and then we'll see what's in the last room, and deal with it.' He smiled briefly. 'I'm trying hard to sound confident, like I know what I'm doing, but really it's up to you. Trust me, Polly. I can't think of a single good reason why you should, but try. We were friends once, even if I can't remember it, and I swear I'll do everything I can to help. Friend will too. You failed before because you were on your own, but we're here now. We won't let you down. We won't let you fail. Are you ready?'

'No,' said Polly. 'But let's do it anyway.' She unfolded her arms and came to stand before him. 'You were a scruffy little kid. Your clothes were always dirty and your hair was a mess. And I was always so clean, so spick and span. But there was no one I'd rather have been with, and I told you things I wouldn't have dreamed of telling anyone else. When you left, I thought it was the end of the world, and I hated you for going and leaving me behind. Leaving me with the awful thing that had happened. I think that's partly why I tried to kill you earlier, if we're being really honest with each other. But now you're back, and I've started to hope again. The house feels different since you came into it. Maybe you were meant to come back here, to help me. Shadows Fall is like that, sometimes. But James . . . there might be a power in you, but there's definitely a power here, built by years of guilt and suffering. It's real, as real as I am, and it doesn't want me to come together again. I don't know what it'll do once it decides you're an enemy. You don't have to do this, James.'

'Yes I do,' said Hart. 'We're friends. Even if I don't remember it. Lead the way, Polly.'

She smiled, put a finger to her lips and then pressed it to his. She walked out into the hall, not looking back, and Hart and Friend followed close behind. Polly's back was very straight and she held her head high, and only the tension in her shoulders showed the forces and emotions warring within her. The hall seemed somehow darker, more claustrophobic, and Hart felt a rising need to reach out a hand to the walls to assure himself they weren't closing in. He didn't do it, though. He didn't want to do anything that might distract Polly now that she'd screwed up her courage to the sticking point. He only had a vague idea of how much courage Polly had, to face a fear she'd been living with most of her life, but it was more than enough to impress the hell out of him. He wasn't sure why, especially after the episode with the knife, but he liked Polly, and he was determined to do whatever it took to free her from her past. Whatever it took. Polly stopped suddenly before a closed door, and Hart almost bumped into her.

'This is where it all began,' she said softly. 'I was eight years old. Playing on my own while my mother was out. Daddy was upstairs. He called to me, and I went upstairs. And then it happened, whatever happened, and my life was never the same again.'

She took a deep breath, opened the door and stepped unflinchingly into the room beyond. She stepped to one side just inside the door, so that Hart could join her. He did so, his hands clenched into fists, though he couldn't have said why. The room was almost offensively ordinary, with nice comfortable furniture in a tasteful setting. The afternoon sun shone brightly through the window, and pooled on the carpet like golden wine. Polly stepped forward and sank to one knee before the empty fireplace.

'Here I was, a podgy little thing with immaculate pigtails, working on a jigsaw puzzle, not particularly successfully. It was too old for me really, but I wouldn't admit it. I took challenges personally, then. Part of me's still here, picking up the pieces and putting them down, waiting for my Daddy to call.'

'*Polly! Come up here. I need you.*'

The voice was hoarse and strained. A man's voice. It seemed to echo on and on in the room, an echo from the past still resonating in the present. Polly got to her feet and walked out of the door. Hart hurried after her. Polly walked unhurriedly down the hall and stopped at the bottom of the stairs. Without looking round, she held out a hand to Hart. He took it, and together they walked up the stairs, and into the past. It seemed darker, as though the sun had gone in. There were shadows everywhere, and Friend clung to their heels like a guard dog. Hart could feel the tension growing in Polly like a bowstring pulled to its fullest extent, but there was control there too, and if it was the control of desperation rather than courage, it still did what was necessary. Hart gripped her hand tightly, trying to pass some of his own steadiness on to her.

If you're there, Polly's father, I'm coming for you. If you're still alive in some way I'll kill you, and if you're dead I'll dig you up so I can spit on you. I don't remember you at all, but I hate you for what you've done to Polly. I'll do whatever it takes to break her free of you. Whatever it takes.

They reached the top of the stairs, and Polly squeezed Hart's hand painfully tight. She strode forward without waiting for any response, and pushed open the door before

197

her. She hesitated in the doorway as the door swung open, and Hart tensed, expecting something to happen, but nothing did.

'I was eight years old, all alone, and I heard my Daddy call me. I came in here first, because I was trying to put off going in to him. I can't remember why, only how scared I was. I'm scared now.'

'You're not alone this time,' said Hart. 'Friend and I are right here with you.'

'I'm still scared. It just isn't enough to stop me, this time.'

She walked into the room, and bent over sharply, as though caught by a sudden stomach cramp. She shrivelled and shrank, falling in upon herself like a fold-up toy. Her dwindling hand slipped out of his, and she stood there before him, a child again, in a child's bright and cheerful dress. She looked up at him briefly with an adult's eyes, and then turned away to look out of the window. Hart moved in beside her, and looked out at the Spring.

'I've been here so many times,' said the little girl. 'The voice would call and I'd come, because if I didn't, it'd just keep calling me until I did. It's a strange feeling, knowing that whatever happens, I'll never have to come here as a child again. I've never known what it's like to put away your childhood for ever, never to experience it again. Part of me will miss it, but it'll be worth it, to be free at last.'

She put up her tiny hand for him to hold again, and he took it carefully in his own. It looked very small and very fragile, and anger flared up in him again, pushing out the fear and uncertainty. She turned and left the Spring room, and walked out into the passage. She looked briefly at the room opposite, and then looked away and went on down the passage, to the next door. Hart looked back at the closed door of the room with no window. He could hear something breathing heavily behind the door. It didn't sound entirely human. Hart could feel the mixture of fear and attraction that door had for Polly, even though she wouldn't look at it.

Polly led him to the next room, pushed open the door and walked straight in. Her height shot up, her hand crawling in his as it grew, and in a moment she was a teenager again. He could see in her the beginnings of the woman she'd be, with her steady gaze and determined chin. Outside the window it was Summer, and the room was flooded with light. Tension trembled on the air like the crash of a slammed door. Polly looked out of the window at a long ago Summer with a face older than her years, and when she spoke her voice was quiet but perfectly steady.

'This was the first time I tried to answer the call, to face my fear and conquer it. I'd heard him call on and off down the years, but I never got past that first room. I was always too scared. I felt so ashamed, even though it wasn't any ordinary fear. It was more like a silent scream that went on and on and on. But my mother was dead and I was eighteen, a woman, and I thought I should be beyond childhood fears. So I walked up the stairs and into the first room and out again, quickly so I couldn't change my mind, and then I stood staring at the closed door opposite. Something moved inside, waiting. And finally I turned away, and came in here instead. I think it was then I realized I was never going to be free of the fear. I stood and looked out of the window at the Summer, and finally, I turned and went back down the stairs again.'

She turned and left the Summer room and walked out into the passage again. Her hand was trembling now, and her shoulders were slumped as though carrying a weight too heavy to put down, but her back was still straight and the determination in her face was so cold and fierce it was almost inhuman. She pushed open the door to the Autumn room and stepped inside, and years piled on her again. She looked suddenly very tired and her hair was brutally short.

'I had a nervous breakdown when I was twenty-two. I started to remember, you see, and I wasn't strong enough to deal with it. So I fell apart at the seams, quite suddenly one afternoon. Nothing too dramatic. I just started crying

199

and couldn't stop. So they put me away somewhere nice and restful, until I was able to forget again. I came home after a while, and the voice called to me, and I was so numb I thought I could face it. I was wrong, and a part of me is always in this room now, lost and confused and just a little weaker than before.'

She turned and left without looking out of the window, and Hart had to hurry to keep up with her. She strode determinedly down the passage, pushed open the next door and walked into the Winter room. Thirteen years passed in a moment, and her hair grew out again in a sudden rush, spilling down to her shoulders. The tension in the room was almost unbearable, the pressure so strong Hart could feel it throughout his body. It was like facing into a howling wind, or struggling against the rising tide that bears you remorselessly back out to sea no matter how hard you swim.

'I almost made it, this last time. I didn't care any more. I thought nothing could be worse than living like this. I was wrong, again. I stood in this room all through the morning and late into the afternoon, and couldn't bring myself to do the one thing that might have freed me. Such a simple thing, just to go into the next room . . . I hated myself because I was so weak, so scared, but hate wasn't enough. In the end I went back downstairs again, leaving another part of me behind. This is as far as I ever got. I can't do any more, not on my own. Help me, Jimmy. Please.'

Her hand was limp in his, as though all the strength had gone out of her. Her shoulders were slumped and her head was bowed, like the horse at the end of a race it's just lost.

'Polly! Come here. I need you.'

The voice was louder now, right there in the next room. Hart tried to read some kind of meaning or context in the voice, if not the words, but it remained stubbornly ambiguous. Polly stood before him, calm and relaxed and completely still, come finally to a state where anger couldn't move her and fear couldn't touch her. Whatever happened next, it was up to him.

I don't want this kind of responsibility! I don't know what to do!

'She's gone as far as she can,' said Friend quietly, pooled around his feet. 'You have to decide, James. Do we go on, or do we go back?'

'I don't know! I thought I did, but . . . look at her. If just the thought of the next room can do this to her, what effect will the room itself have? She's already had one breakdown; I don't want to be responsible for another.'

'She came this far because she believed you when you said you'd stand by her. Are you going to let her down now?'

Hart shook his head, almost angrily. 'What the hell is in that next room, that it can do this to her? What did her father do to her?'

'I wondered that,' said Polly, in a slow, sleepy voice. 'I spent years wondering what there could be in that room that could be so frightening. For a long time I wondered if it might have been some kind of sexual abuse. You hear a lot about that, these days. But I can't believe that of my father. I loved him and he loved me. So why does just the thought of seeing him again scare me so much I can scarcely breathe?'

'Only one way to find out,' said Hart. 'Let's do it.'

He took a firm hold on her hand and headed for the door, Polly going with him like a small child. Out in the passage, night had fallen. The only light shone from under the door to the fifth room. The steady breathing sounded louder, harsher, as though roused by anticipation. Hart walked slowly forward, Polly at his side. The passage stretched away before them, impossibly long. Hart didn't know what to think any more. He'd been so sure sexual abuse had been at the root of everything, but Polly had already thought of that and dismissed it. So what was in that room, breathing so loudly? They walked on through the darkness, and the door drew nearer very slowly, as

201

though something was drawing the moment out to savour it. But finally they stood before the door, and Hart hesitated, unsure what to do for the best. Polly reached out a steady hand, turned the handle and pushed the door open, and she and Hart went into the room together to face what was there. The door slammed shut behind them.

The room was brightly lit, and smelt of sickness and medicines. A man lay in the bed, gaunt and withered from the strain of long suffering. His eyes were closed, his breathing laboured, as though every inhalation was an effort. Polly looked at him silently. Hart looked around him, baffled. There was nothing else in the room, just one extremely sick man who didn't even know they were there.

'I remember,' said Polly. 'My father had cancer. There was nothing the doctors could do, back then, so they sent him home to die. He took a long time dying. I was scared of him. Scared of losing him, of him going away for ever. Death is hard enough to understand when you're only eight years old, but when it's your father . . . For a long time I couldn't believe it would actually happen, and then I wouldn't believe it. But finally he took to his bed and stayed there, and I realized he wasn't ever going to leave it again. Then I believed.

'I prayed for a miracle. Prayer after prayer, promising God I'd do anything, anything he wanted. I even said I'd be a nun if he would just save my Daddy. And all the time the cancer ate away at my father, leaving less and less of him in the bed. I couldn't look at his hands on the covers without seeing the bones, couldn't see his face without seeing the skull. It was as though he was becoming death. And I stopped going in to see him, because it scared me so much. Even when he asked for me, I wouldn't go.

'And then one day my mother had to go out, and I was left alone in the house. Alone with my father. I lost myself in my jigsaw. That at least was a puzzle I could solve, if I just tried hard enough. It was just after midday when he called out to me. I wouldn't go. I was scared. He called again and again and finally I got up and went out into the hall. I stood at the bottom of the stairs for a long time, and then I went up, very slowly, step by step. I hid in the room opposite, and he called to me again. I stood outside his door, listening to him fight for every breath. And then the breathing stopped.

'I went in, and he was dead. He didn't look like my father at all, not the way I remembered him. It was as though this dead cancer thing had come and taken my father's place. And all I could think was, if I'd gone to him when he called, he might still be alive. Maybe I could have done something, said something, and he wouldn't have died. But I hadn't . . .

'So I ran out of the room and told myself I'd never been in there. Kept saying it over and over, till I believed it. But the guilt wouldn't let me forget, not completely. Not all that long afterwards, I started hearing him call me again. My guilt and fear had built something in this room and given it power over me. To punish me as I should be punished. That isn't my father there. It's something else, something awful. I think once it might have been a part of me, but that isn't true any more. It belongs to itself now. And it hates me.'

Hart looked at the dying man on the bed, and then back at Polly. The expression on her face worried him. Her words had the sound and power of an incantation, as though she was calling up something. And then the man in the bed sat up. Polly fell back a step, and grabbed at Hart's arm. The man on the bed smiled at them both, and there was something horribly hungry in his gaze. Cancers suddenly bulged out of his skin like bunches of black grapes, boiling up out of his flesh as though driven by some internal pressure that couldn't be denied. His face grew swollen and misshapen as blood-engorged tissues turned his features into a demon's mask. He was still smiling.

'Hello, Polly,' he whispered. 'You finally came to see me. Come and kiss your Daddy, and I'll share what I've got with you. You know you deserve it. And then you and

I can stay here together in the dark, growing strange and different, and we'll never die. Never die . . .'

Polly looked at him silently, tears spilling down her cheeks. The cancer figure giggled.

'Come to me, Polly. You look so good I could just eat you up.'

'That's enough of that,' said Friend, and threw itself at the cancer figure. He fell back, startled, and Friend billowed out into a vast black shape, with massive fangs and claws. It dropped on its victim, and the cancer figure disappeared in the darkness. For a moment there was silence, and then Friend screamed. It burst apart, shrieking horribly at the cancer man as he effortlessly tore the shadowstuff apart. Friend spilled down the sides of the bed like dirty water, and fled across the floor to gather at Hart's feet again, whimpering like a hurt child.

'Sweet,' said the cancer figure, 'but a little light and frothy for my taste. Polly's the one I want. I've waited for this for so long, my dear. The house tried to protect you, by giving you chances to escape, but you never took them, so you're mine now, body and soul. Especially body. I'll enjoy your flesh in so many ways, and when I'm done with you, you won't know yourself.'

'Go to hell,' said Hart, and stepped forward to put himself between Polly and the cancer man. He looked at Hart thoughtfully, light glistening wetly on his bulging skin. The air was thick with the stench of rotting meat.

'You have no place here,' said the cancer man. 'You don't belong here. She made me and she belongs to me. This is what she wants, even if she won't admit it. Leave now, or I'll kill you. And you don't want to know what I'll do to your poor defenceless body afterwards.'

'She was only a child,' said Hart. 'She didn't understand. She was afraid.'

'It's too late now for pleas and excuses. I'm going to take this woman and stir my sticky fingers in her flesh, and there's nothing you can do to stop me.'

The figure swept aside the bedclothes with a swollen

hand and swung his elephantine legs over the side of the bed. He swayed to his feet, the cancers bulging in his flesh like diseased fruit. He started forward, a malignant nightmare given shape and form, and Hart raised a hand to stop him. Something stirred within him then that he had no name for. It was a power, or a potential, like nothing else he'd ever known, and it answered him when he called on it. Not for his own sake, but for Polly, who'd been hurt too much already. He beckoned brusquely to the cancer figure, and his voice was short and sharp.

'You. Come out. Come out of him now.'

Black streams of living cancers burst out of Polly's father, to fall in coils around his feet. Dark shapes split the skin and running foulness seeped out of every pore as his body convulsed, helpless in the grip of a greater power. And finally Polly's father stood before them, pale and trembling but unmarked, and on the floor around him the cancer lay steaming and twitching, like something newborn in the darkest part of the night. As Hart and Polly watched, the cancer slowly grew still and lifeless, and the last of the life Polly had given it went out of it for ever. She turned and looked at her father, started to move forward, and then stopped herself.

'Daddy?'

'Hello, Princess. Look at my lovely little girl, grown up so fine and tall. It's been a long time, honey, but I'm back now. I'm back.'

Polly threw herself into his arms, and they hugged each other tightly like they'd never let go. There were tears on both their faces, and neither of them gave a damn. Hart turned away to give them some privacy, and looked at the shapeless darkness around his feet.

'Are you all right, Friend?'

'I've felt better. Ask me again when I've had a chance to recover, in a year or two. How the hell did you do that? I didn't know you could do that.'

'Neither did I,' said Hart.

He looked at Polly and her father. They'd finally released

their hold on each other, but they were still standing as close as it was possible for two people to get. Polly sniffed away the last of her tears.

'Daddy; this is Jimmy Hart. He saved you. He brought me here and believed in me, even when I wasn't sure myself.'

'Jimmy Hart?' The man looked at him strangely. 'You look at lot like your father, Jimmy. Thank you, for what you did for my daughter.'

'Oh Daddy, I'm so sorry. I know I should have come to you long before this, but I was so scared . . .'

'Hush, Princess, I know. I understand. You were just a kid.'

'And you don't blame me for . . .'

'I don't blame you for anything.' He looked at Hart again. 'Eventually, I hope someone is going to explain exactly what happened, but for the moment I'm just glad to be here and happy to be alive. Part of me's been here for years, held by that . . . thing, but I don't remember much of it. It was more like a fever dream, a nightmare I couldn't wake up from.'

'It's all over now,' said Polly. 'You're alive, and everything's going to be fine.' Her face fell suddenly. 'Oh Daddy, you don't know. Mother's dead.'

'I know. I felt her go, a long time back, but there was nothing I could do, then. It's all right, Polly. If she were here, I'm sure she'd be just as proud of you as I am.'

'But I treated her so badly . . .'

'She understands,' said her father. 'Wherever she is, I'm sure she understands.'

Polly smiled at Hart. 'Thank you, James. Thank you for . . . everything. I never dreamed . . . I had no idea you had such power.'

'Neither did I,' said Hart. 'It seems there are a lot of things about myself I don't know. I'm going to have to do something about that.'

7

Something Bad Is Coming

Suzanne Dubois woke slowly to the sound of music, and lay in bed for some time without opening her eyes. The clock radio turned itself on automatically every morning at nine o'clock, set carefully just out of reach so that she'd have to get up to turn it off. She lay still with her eyes closed, letting the quiet music wash over her without actually listening to it. Waking up was always a slow process for her, and it wasn't as if she had to rush to get anywhere.

Her bed was pushed right up against the wall, so that she could reach out a hand and feel its strength and presence without having to get up. The wall was a comfort to her, solid and real and unchanging. Ever since she'd come home to find Lucas's dead body lying on her floor, she'd felt the need for constant little reassurances that her home was still strong and intact. The unexpected presence of death still haunted her, and her little shack was no longer the safe haven it had been. It took her a long time before she could sleep at nights without having to leave the light on. During the day she could distract herself with people and routine, but the night found her as weak and vulnerable as a small child. She lay in her bed stiff as a board, ears straining for the slightest sound until her eyes adjusted to the gloom, and then she watched the dark shadows around her till finally she fell asleep through sheer exhaustion. The door was locked and bolted, the only window secured, but it was still going to be a long time before she felt really safe again.

Suzanne lay bonelessly in her bed, listening to the morning, putting together a picture of her world through the sounds around her. The radio murmured quietly to itself, and above that she could hear the soft creaking sounds her bed made as she stretched lazily. She'd had the bed more than twenty years now, and they'd adjusted to each other in all the ways that mattered. The mattress supported where it should, and gave where necessary. The years had formed a long hollow down the middle that she fell into naturally, fitting her perfectly from head to heel. The wooden shack made brief, sharp noises around her as it settled its weight, the wood swelling appreciatively under the morning's warmth after the cold of the night. Outside, she could hear a barge chugging slowly down the river Tawn, the brisk cheerful sound full of places to go and things to do. Suzanne sighed, sat up in bed, and opened her eyes.

She hugged her knees to her, rested her chin on them and looked around her. Her one-room shack was a mess, but then, it always was. She liked it that way. Clothes lay scattered casually here and there, and all three chairs were buried under piles of old magazines and newspapers. Fast-food cartons from yesterday's dinner and late supper still lay where she'd dropped them. That last thought moved her mind vaguely in the direction of breakfast, but she wasn't awake enough for that yet. Preparing breakfast was too complicated a task to be considered until her body had woken up enough to listen to her mind. Or was it the other way round? Suzanne shrugged. She was used to not making much sense in the mornings. It was that kind of blithe casualness that had infuriated her last lover, a tall bony guitarist from some heavy metal band she'd never heard of. He'd been pleasant enough company, and almost as good at the horizontal bop as he'd thought he was, but he used to positively leap out of bed in the mornings, ready to attack the day and grab great handfuls of whatever it had to offer. Of course, he was fifteen years younger than her thirty-five, and in the mornings she felt every one of those extra years. Which was at least partly why she hadn't been too devastated when he left her.

She pushed back the sheets, swung her legs over the side of the bed, and sat there quietly, ruminating. She had a strong feeling she should be up and about today, but she couldn't quite place why. No doubt it would come to her, eventually. She scratched at her ribs, more for the pleasure of it than anything else. Suzanne slept in the nude, except in the coldest of winters, when she reluctantly swathed herself in thick pyjamas. She'd never taken to nightclothes; they always seemed to wrap themselves around her in the night, till she woke up wrapped in what felt uncomfortably like a straitjacket.

She got up, looked vaguely about her, and got through the business of getting dressed without having to wake up any further. A leisurely visit to the outside toilet took care of that. She returned, still yawning, and stood in the middle of the room. It seemed to her that something important was due to happen today, but she was damned if she could think what. It didn't bother her. She often felt that way. She moved unhurriedly over to study the broad mirror balanced precariously on her dresser. Curling photographs of old beaux stared back at her, and a single lipsticked message from herself.

Company's coming.

Suzanne stared blankly at the mirror, and her reflection looked doubtfully back. A tall, leggy blonde who dressed in odd assortments of this and that because she could never bring herself to throw anything out. Suzanne felt about fashion the way she felt about religion; all right for those who believed in it, but too much of a bother for her. The only thing she believed in was getting enough sleep. She often formed sentimental attachments to odd bits of clothing, and clung on to them long after they'd outlived their purpose. This blouse was lucky, that scarf was the one she'd worn when Grant first asked her out, those shoes were just too pretty to throw away . . . And so on and so on.

In the mirror, her face was all wide eyes and prominent cheekbones. Without her makeup on, she looked like her mother. Suzanne made a face at the mirror, and made herself up with quick, practised strokes. Far too early in the day for such blasphemy. She looked critically at her long braids. They hadn't looked that tidy to begin with, and sleeping in them had not improved their appearance. She didn't really have the touch or the patience for braids, but she kept trying. She looked good in braids, and they were practical, too. She liked to feel she was practical about something.

The radio had started playing elevator music, something slow and smooth with too many strings, so she turned the dial till she found something loud with a good beat. Good old-fashioned, no-frills rock-and-roll. The music got into her blood and brought her fully awake at last. She stomped happily about the room, bopping to the beat, picking things up and dropping them in one great pile in the corner. *Company's coming.* She remembered about that now. The Cards had been very specific last night, or at least as specific as Tarot Cards ever were, that she'd be having an important visitor early this morning. Someone she'd known for a long time, but hadn't seen in ages. She pondered happily as to who it might be. The description covered a lot of ground, not to mention ex-boyfriends. There was always someone coming or going, and sometimes both. She never bothered to keep track of them, but she liked to think it was part of her charm that she was always glad to see them whenever they reappeared in her life. As long as they didn't get possessive. Suzanne might be possessive about things, but never people. It caused too many complications, and Suzanne was a simple girl at heart.

There was a knock at the door, firm but somehow hesitant, as though the caller was unsure of their welcome. Suzanne looked quickly about the room. She hadn't so much cleared things up as redistributed them, but it would have to do. She checked her appearance in the mirror, went to the door and opened it, and then the smile froze on her face as she saw who it was.

'Hello, Suzanne,' said Polly Cousins. 'It's been a long time, hasn't it?'

'Polly . . . Is that *you*, Polly? You haven't been here in . . . I don't know how many years!'

'I know. But I finally got myselves together, so . . . Can I come in?'

For the first time Suzanne realized that Polly was white-faced and trembling, more from strain than the morning chill.

'Of course! Come on in!' Suzanne grabbed Polly by the arm, pulled her in, kicked the door shut behind her, and then enveloped Polly in a fierce bear hug. They clung to each other with almost frantic strength, as though each afraid the other might disappear if they didn't hold on to them hard enough. Tears ran happily down their cheeks as they both tried to say how glad they were to see each other. The words made no sense, but they didn't have to. Eventually they let go, and held each other at arm's length to get a better look. Suzanne gestured speechlessly at the two chairs by the table, and they sat down facing each other. Polly looked around the cluttered room, and smiled for the first time.

'I thought I remembered what a tip this place was, but you have to see it to really appreciate it. For my birthday, let me clean up in here. You've probably got two or three old boyfriends buried somewhere under all this junk.'

'You leave my place be,' said Suzanne. 'It suits me just fine the way it is. It's comfortable. Polly; I'm so glad to see you, after so long. What is it now; ten years? I never thought to see you outside that damned house again. What happened? Something must have happened! Tell me all about it, fill in all the juicy, sordid details. I want to hear *everything*.'

'Slow down,' said Polly, smiling so hard it hurt. 'Give me a chance to get my breath back. This is the first time I've left my house and travelled any distance since I started to fall apart, and I'm still a bit shaky. I got a taxi to bring me here, but for most of the time I couldn't even bear to look out of the taxi's windows. The world's just so big, and I'm not used to that. Even the short walk down the riverbank to get to your shack was enough to set my heart racing. It's going to take me a while to get used to being free again.

'Do you remember, when we were younger, how we used to go everywhere together? Parties, dances, concerts and protest marches, there we were; two bad girls on the razzle. Bimbos from Hell. Teenage tormenters; no man was safe. We put streaks in our hair over your mother's kitchen sink, because we thought it made us look more slutty. Being a slut was *in*, then. Remember going to discos and checking our makeup was just right in the powder room, arguing over which boys we were going to let pick us up that night? It all seems like another world to me now. I can barely believe that person was me. I seem to have gone from teenage queen to old maid without touching the ground in between.'

'Stop that,' said Suzanne firmly. 'None of it was your fault. You had your problem, or rather it had you, and you coped with it as best you could. Anyone else would have broken under the weight of it years ago. I always knew you'd break free eventually. Oh God, it's good to see you again, Polly! Talking on the phone for hours kept us together, but it's not the same. Now will you please tell me what the hell's happened, before I go into meltdown mode!'

'Someone came to see me,' said Polly. 'Someone I'd known before, when we were both children. He broke me free of my past. His name's James Hart.'

'You're kidding! You've met James Hart? I saw his return in the Cards about a week ago, and I'd heard he was here, but I haven't met anyone who's actually talked to him. What's he like? Is he handsome? Is he spooky? Is he *available?'*

Polly laughed for the first time. 'Yes, no, and you'll

212

have to ask him yourself. He's an amazing man. Doesn't say much, but there's a power in him you wouldn't believe. He has the potential to become someone quite extraordinary, even if he doesn't realize it yet.'

'Of course he has,' said Suzanne calmly. 'The Cards have been telling me that something really powerful was headed this way for months. Though I have to admit, I wasn't expecting it to be James Hart. I don't think anyone expected him, except possibly Old Father Time. And you found him first . . . Has he really put you back together again? All of you?'

'Every last one of me. I'm whole again. But he didn't just stop at that . . .'

'You mean there's more? What else did he do; build you a new house?'

'He brought my father back. My father is alive again, thanks to James Hart.'

'Wow . . . Polly; you and I are in dire need of a stiff drink. Possibly several stiff drinks.' Suzanne got up, still shaking her head, went over to a cupboard and brought out a bottle of brandy and two glasses. She put the glasses on the table, mouthed the word *Wow* again, and poured out two generous measures of the brandy. 'Polly; where exactly is he now?'

'Gone to see my mother's grave. Or did you mean James? I'm not entirely sure where he is now. He said something about looking up the rest of his family, but we're going to meet up again later this evening. We're meeting in a bar he knows. A bar! Do you realize how long it's been since anyone bought me a drink in a bar? I don't know if I can do it. I mean; going out is hard enough, without having to face a whole bunch of strangers as well. Maybe I should tell him I can't go. Put it off until I'm feeling stronger.'

'Oh no you don't,' said Suzanne immediately. 'You're out of your shell now; you can't go back. Don't worry; you'll be fine. I'll come along too, staying discreetly in the background, of course. I'd better find someone to escort me, so I don't stand out.'

'Who is it this week?' said Polly, grinning. 'I never can keep up with your tangled love life. You're the only person I know whose life really is like a soap opera. The last one I remember is Grant. Is he still current?'

'More or less. Nice guy. Guitarist with a group you've never heard of. Heavily into brooding in corners and looking enigmatic. A bit young for me, but I like a challenge.'

'You always did,' said Polly dryly. 'Is he a good guitarist?'

'How would I know, dear? You don't bring a guitar to bed. Officially, we're separated, because I didn't recognize his genius. Which essentially meant not being able to keep a straight face when he talked about it. I'll give him a ring later on today, see if he's still sulking.'

Polly looked at her thoughtfully. 'Do you hear much from Ambrose these days? You don't talk about him as much as you used to.'

'He pays the rent on this place, and drops me a cheque now and then when he thinks of it, but mostly he's civilized enough to keep his distance. We should never have married. You warned me about him. Hell, everyone and their brother warned me about Ambrose, but I wouldn't listen. Living with him was like being married to a quick-change artist. I never knew which aspect of his personality I was going to wake up beside. It was fun at first, like being married to several men all at once, but it got old very quickly. Even I like a little stability in my life. In particular, I prefer my men not to change personality in mid-conversation. We're much happier, now we hardly ever see each other.

'I really ought to get around to divorcing him, but things are convenient the way they are, and it would be so much bother and effort. Why rock the boat? He keeps me financially stable, and I don't turn up to embarrass him in front of his upwardly-mobile friends. I'm happy with my painting, and my sittings with the Cards. And frankly, my dear, the thought of having to go out and earn my living fills me with horror. I mean, can you see me rushing to work every morning, like a good little commuter, saying yes sir and no sir to the boss, and clocking in and out? I'd rather die. I am not a practical person, and have no desire to learn how to be. I am a happy little parasite, warm and secure in my snug little nest, and I see no reason to change anything.'

'Money . . .' said Polly. 'That's something I haven't had to think about for a long time. It's not like I have any expensive habits. I inherited the house from Daddy, and a fair amount of money. Only most of that's gone, now. It trickled away, down the years. I haven't got around to telling Daddy about that yet. I keep waiting for the right moment to bring it up, but there never seems to be one. Besides, he's got enough problems already, trying to adjust to all the things that have changed while he was . . . away. It's not the life he remembers.'

'Drink up,' said Suzanne. 'The world's too cold and dark a place to face sober.'

'Suzanne; it's only half past nine in the morning! And there's enough brandy in this glass to have me paralytic by half past ten.'

'Best thing for you,' said Suzanne briskly. 'If more people got smashed of a morning, the world would be a kinder place. They wouldn't get much done, but then, they wouldn't be in any shape to care, would they?'

Polly smiled, and shook her head. She'd phoned Suzanne every day for years, talking endlessly about nothing and everything, but she'd forgotten how exhilarating conversation with her could be, in the flesh. You had to work to keep up with Suzanne when she was on a roll. Which was half the fun. Polly sipped her brandy carefully, relaxing almost despite herself as its warmth glowed in her stomach. Suzanne was drinking and talking practically simultaneously, a skill she'd spent years acquiring through diligent practice.

'Are you still having problems with Father Callahan?' Polly said finally, just to get a word in.

'Of course. He doesn't approve of my Cards, but then he doesn't approve of anything fun or interesting. I think he's secretly a Puritan at heart, and believes people like me should be banned on general principles. Never had a drink or a woman in his life, that one. Keeps calling me a Bad Example in his sermons, which is fair enough, and prophesies all kinds of doom for anyone who dares consult me. But since I have a much better record in the prophecy department than he does, the customers still keep coming, bless their timid little hearts. I don't know what a man like Callahan is doing in Shadows Fall anyway.'

'How about your parents?' said Polly, cutting in quickly before Suzanne could launch into her favourite tirade.

'Relations are still strained, and likely to stay that way for some time. As long as we don't actually see each other, we get on quite well. Drink up, you're falling behind.'

Polly took another sip obediently. She wasn't used to booze. She'd never kept any in the house. It would have been too easy to drink or drug herself into a stupor, and that would have been dangerous. She'd needed all her self-control to keep what was left of her together. But she didn't have to worry about that any more. The thought sank slowly through her, tinged with exhilaration. There were a lot of things she didn't have to worry about any more, and that thought was more intoxicating than the brandy could ever be. She took a large swallow, breathed deeply for a moment, and then looked thoughtfully at Suzanne.

'Did you really see James Hart's return in your Cards?'

'Damn right. The Cards have been full of him for weeks. Maybe now he's finally got here, they'll calm down again.'

'Read mine,' said Polly impulsively. 'Tell me my future, now I'm free.'

'Sure; why not?' Suzanne drained her glass, got up and went to fetch the Cards. She kept them in the drawer of her dresser, held casually together by a rubber band. They didn't look like much when she shuffled them and laid them out on the table. They were old and battered, and just a little greasy from constant handling. The designs were creased and faded. Suzanne laid out the Cards one at a time, muttering to herself as she produced the necessary patterns. She laid down the last Card, sat back, and looked at what she'd done. She said nothing for a long time, and then looked at Polly oddly. Her eyes were cold, and her mouth had lost its shape.

'What is it?' said Polly anxiously. 'What do you see? Is something bad going to happen to me?'

'I was wrong,' said Suzanne, in a voice like someone else's. 'It wasn't Hart I saw in the Cards. Something bad is coming. Something bad is coming for the whole town.'

In the Great Cavern, far below the town of Shadows Fall, deep in the dark earth where only moles and the things they feed on feel very comfortable, the Underworld of the Subnatural had come together in a Gathering. Every fictional and mythical creature that ever lived in the imagination of the world is a member of the Subnatural. Dragons and unicorns, sasquatches and wendigos, wyverns and cockatrices, all the beasts of the wild that never were but should have been. Super-intelligent dogs from fifties TV series, Saturday Morning cartoons that never made it past the first season, politically aware animals from daily comic strips that the times have left behind; all are welcome in the Underworld, the wide network of caves and dens and warm earth tunnels that lie beneath the town where dreams come to die. The Great Cavern is the place of debate and judgement, where the animals Gather once in a blue moon, to decide what must be done and why.

Actually, it's much sillier than that.

The Great Cavern was brightly lit by a thousand candles, but the place was covered in dust and cobwebs and wax droppings that no one ever got around to clearing away. The setting was based on what the animals thought a place of judgement should look like, but as animals never were

217

very strong in the imagination department, they'd ended up cribbing a lot of it from illustrations they'd seen in books. The end result was like something out of a Victorian children's book. One of those dutiful, moral-laden tales featuring dastardly villains with twirling moustaches, and heroes so brave and true and pure they'd make an owl puke.

The Judge sat at the front, peering down at the Court from a wooden desk so tall that some animals got nose-bleeds just from looking at it. To his left sat the Jury, on extremely uncomfortable wooden benches, so they wouldn't nod off if the case got boring. The Jury consisted of a dozen animals whose hearts were brave and true, chosen mainly by the simple expedient of grabbing anyone who couldn't run away fast enough. To the Judge's right stood the dock, a grim wooden box with spikes on, just so that the accused would be under no misapprehension as to why they were there. It stood alone on a raised platform, so that the onlookers could throw things at it, if they felt so inclined. And mostly they did. Facing all of this were rows of pews for the onlookers, witnesses, those who had business with the Court, or were just feeling nosey and in need of a good laugh. All animals, whether fictional, mythical, or highly unlikely, share a common sense of curiosity, and a gleeful urge to kick someone while they're down.

This particular Gathering had been called to decide what to do about the shooting of the Sea Goat by an unknown assailant. The Usher, a large hyena standing on two legs and wearing a scholar's mortar board and gown, announced this in ringing tones, and there then followed a brief burst of conversation as half of the spectators explained what 'assailant' meant to the other half. There had already been a great deal of general discussion about what to do. On hearing that the Sea Goat had been shot, but would survive, a sizeable majority of animals had suggested shooting him again, and getting it right this time, dammit. They were voted down on a point of order, and because

Bruin Bear was standing beside the Sea Goat's wheelchair, carrying the biggest bloody gun the animals had ever seen. A voice at the back pointed out that it was against the rules to bring weapons to a Gathering. Bruin Bear pointed out that heckling was also against the rules, and that he felt quite capable of enforcing that rule with as much ammunition as necessary. He glared at the spectators, swivelling the gun casually back and forth, and everyone immediately replied that they took his point, and quite agreed. The Bear turned his back on them and sat down beside the Sea Goat, and heads slowly began to appear above the pews again. The Judge looked down on all this, and sighed heavily.

The Mock Gryphon was acting as Judge. It should have been the Mock Turtle, but he was feeling a bit depressed, and had gone off somewhere quiet to have a nice lie down. The Mock Gryphon had been voted in as replacement Judge, over his loud objections, because his voice had been the loudest in declaring a need for a new Judge. He was therefore not in the best of tempers, and was quietly determined to find as many people guilty as possible. Someone was going to suffer for this indignity, and it sure as hell wasn't going to be him. He slammed his gavel down hard, and the general chatter died away as the spectators looked interestedly to see what was happening. The Mock Gryphon wondered what to do next. Banging his gavel had pretty much used up his knowledge of legal matters. Gryphons, on the whole, didn't have a lot to do with the law. They tended more to biting smaller animals' heads off, and then being politely regretful to their meal's next of kin.

'If I might have your honour's attention,' said a loud and carrying voice, and the Judge looked hopefully down at his official Prosecutor. The current holder of this office was an Ostrich wearing pince-nez and a somewhat supercilious expression. He had been the subject of a large number of political cartoons in his day, and had been insufferably condescending ever since. He spoke loudly and confidently at all times, on all kinds of issues, whether he knew anything about them or not, but was continually undermined by the bucket of sand he carried around with him, just in case he felt the need to bury his head in a hurry. He glared around at the packed Court, and sniffed loudly in a way that suggested he had better things to do with his time than stand around waiting for Certain Individuals to be quiet. The spectators, who knew a good sniff when they heard one, settled down happily and passed pieces of spoiled fruit among themselves, ready for the first witness they didn't like. The Ostrich struck a dignified pose, and cleared his throat. Given the length of his neck, the process was a long and intimidating one, and the Ostrich made the most of it, glaring disdainfully at the spectators all the while. They loved it. This was what a Court was all about.

'My Lord and honoured members of the Jury, we are Gathered here today on a most solemn matter. One of us has been shot and injured by an outsider. We must determine why, and how, and where.'

'In the stomach!' said the Sea Goat loudly. 'Then out my bleeding back, and after that I lost track of it.'

'Silence in the Court!' said the Mock Gryphon, gavelling for all he was worth. 'Order! Order!'

'Chaos!' shouted a punk llama at the back, just to be contrary. 'Anarchy! Riot! Don't vote, it only encourages them!'

It then spat defiantly in all directions, until the Court Usher suppressed him with a solid blow to the side of the head with a large croquet mallet. A trio of young ducks in sailor suits took advantage of the llama's dazed condition to rifle its pockets for anything interesting or smokeable.

'My Lord,' said the Ostrich, 'I must insist on silence. This is a most important matter, and must be discussed in depth.'

'Bollocks,' said a nervous-looking unicorn. 'All that matters is we're under attack. The hunting fraternity have finally found us. I say we should all disappear into the deepest holes we can find, pull them in after us, and stay put until someone comes down to tell us it's all over. Head for the depths and batten down the hatches, lads. I'll lead the way.'

'You'll stay where you are,' snapped the Mock Gryphon, gavelling like fury. 'No one's going anywhere till we've talked this through, and the Jury have made a decision.'

'What, that rabble?' said the Sea Goat, glaring incredulously at the dozen assorted creatures on the Jury benches. 'I wouldn't trust that lot to guess my weight. I've seen more intelligent-looking life forms lying on their backs in butchers' windows. The only reason they're staying put is because their ankles are chained to the benches. Be honest, did we really choose these geeks, or did we just draw straws and they lost?'

'It was all done quite properly, in accordance with tradition,' said the Ostrich, curling its beak in disdain. It rather liked the effect, and did it again, even though beaks as a rule don't normally curl all that well. 'All members of the Jury meet the necessary requirements.'

'Yeah,' said the Sea Goat. 'They're warm and breathing.'

'Hold your peace!' snapped the Ostrich.

'What, in public?' said the Sea Goat. 'I'm not in the mood. And even if I was, I wouldn't want to be looking at you while I was holding it. You are definitely not my type.'

'You will be called to give your evidence in good time,' said the Ostrich. 'Kindly remember where you are.'

'Kindly get on with it,' said the Sea Goat. 'Or I'll tie a knot in your neck.'

The Ostrich decided that it hadn't heard that, and turned to face the Jury, most of whom had already lost interest in the proceedings, and were trying to bribe some of the spectators to take their place. One was trying to raise interest in a friendly game of chance. Another claimed to have a deck of pornographic playing cards, but as all the pictures were of ducks, it was hard to be sure. The Usher confiscated the cards and ate them, just to be on the safe side. The Ostrich cleared his throat again, and the Jurors glared at him mutinously.

'My noble ducks, voles, squirrels . . . and small furry mammal with a Disgusting Habit, I must regretfully insist you give your full attention to the evidence as it is presented to you,' said the Ostrich firmly. 'Otherwise we'll be here all bloody day, and some of us have got homes to go to.'

The Jury nodded approvingly. This was the kind of language they could understand. They put on their best paying-attention faces, and looked expectantly at the Ostrich, who swelled visibly under their gaze. He did so love to be the centre of things. He hadn't had an audience this large in years, and had every intention of making the most of it.

'I call my first witness,' he said grandly. 'Call the Glorious Radioactive Terrapins.'

Several people took it in turn to call the Terrapins, including a handful of spectators, who were just trying to be helpful. There was an embarrassingly long pause, and finally the Usher went to see what was happening. He returned almost immediately, shaking his head.

'You're going to have to do without the Terrapins,' he said flatly. 'Apparently they got into an argument over who got top billing on their late lamented TV show, and they are currently duelling each other to the death, or until they get bored. Either way, there are steel weapons flying in all directions, and I'm not getting one inch closer to them than I absolutely have to. Call someone else instead.'

'Very well,' said the Prosecuting Ostrich, wishing he had some teeth, so he could grind them. 'Call the gopher of gloom, Robbie Rabbit.'

A great many creatures called for Robbie Rabbit, having acquired a taste for it, and the Usher had to move among them with his croquet mallet to restore order. The Mock Gryphon gavelled like there was no tomorrow, but no one took any notice, apart from a handful of disreputable-looking weasels, who were busily taking bets on which direction the gavel head would fly when it finally worked loose. The Hyena laid about him with his mallet with verve and vim, until he finally achieved an uneasy silence, with vague undertones of mass rebellion. The Hyena grinned toothily, and looked hopefully around for someone else to intimidate. He'd rather taken to being an Usher. It opened up whole new vistas of legally approved mayhem.

Someone cleared their throat, and raised a hesitant hand. There was a sharp intake of breath from everyone in the vicinity, followed by a mass moving away at speed in all directions, to get out of the line of fire. The Hyena's grin widened, and several of the more timid onlookers fainted dead away. Mostly on the grounds that if they were going to end up unconscious anyway, they preferred to do it in a way that didn't involve extensive bruising. The Usher made his way through the crowd, creatures parting before him like waves, and fixed his best intimidating stare on the animal with its hand in the air.

'Yes?' said the Hyena, hefting his mallet meaningfully.

'I don't mean to be a nuisance, and I could be wrong, but I think I might be the one you're looking for. I think there's a possibility I might be Robbie Rabbit.'

The Hyena lowered his mallet, and blinked at the Rabbit. 'Either you are, or you aren't. Aren't you?'

The Rabbit sighed wistfully. 'If only it were that simple . . .'

The Usher grabbed the Rabbit round the throat with one bulky paw, and removed him from the crowd in much the same way as one plucks a weed from among flowers. He made his way back to the front of the Court, the Rabbit hanging limp and uncomplaining from his fist, and dropped him into the dock, which was also serving as the witness stand. Mostly because no one had got around to building a witness stand yet. The Ostrich provided a chair for the Rabbit to stand on, and the Rabbit peered dolefully over the edge of the dock. He wasn't much to look at, being basically short, thin and very grey. Even the bits of him that weren't grey somehow gave the impression of being

223

so drab and lifeless that you couldn't help feeling they ought to be grey too. His whiskers drooped, and his long ears bent in the middle. His face seemed to consist almost entirely of a pair of exceedingly doleful eyes above a twitching nose, and he looked very much as if he'd have to cheer up considerably just to feel depressed.

'Your honour,' said the Ostrich, 'Allow me to present my first witness.'

'Guilty,' said the Mock Gryphon immediately.

'But your honour, he's just a witness!'

'Are you sure? He looks guilty.'

'Quite sure, my Lord. If I might continue . . .'

'Don't you know?'

The Ostrich decided to rise above that, and turned the full force of his personality on the Rabbit, whose ears drooped a little further in response.

'You are Robbie Rabbit, the loopy lupine, the hare with a hang-up?'

'Well, that's a difficult question to answer,' said the Rabbit sadly. 'I could say I was, but how could I be sure? Just because I look like him in the mirror, that's no reason to go jumping to conclusions. I remember having been him, but those memories could have been artificially induced. Or hallucinations. So could you. All of you. For all I know, this whole Court could be nothing more than a particularly depressing delusion I'm having. In which case I'm talking to myself, and I do wish I wouldn't. I think I'd like to go home now, please. I'm not feeling very real.'

'I could prove you're real,' said the Hyena. 'If I smack you round the ear with the business end of this mallet and you feel it, which you will, that'll prove you're real.'

'Not necessarily,' said the Rabbit. 'I could just be imagining you hit me.'

'Oh no; not the way I'd hit you. You'd have no doubt at all that you'd been hit.'

'But how does that help prove that I'm Robbie Rabbit?'

'Because I'd tell you you were, just before I hit you!'

'But how would you know you weren't just imagining

it? You could be suffering from the delusion that you're hitting people with a croquet mallet, when in reality you could be doing something else entirely, like reading a book or picking flowers. I mean, how do you even know you're really a Hyena? I see one when I look at you, but how can you trust my fallible judgement on something so important as your identity?'

The Usher opened and shut his mouth a few times, and then sat down on the steps beside the dock to have a bit of a think. The Ostrich, being made of sterner stuff, tried again.

'I say you're Robbie Rabbit, and since I'm the Prosecutor in this case, what I say goes. Now, will you please tell the Court what you observed of the attack on the Sea Goat.'

'I don't know what I saw,' said the Rabbit sadly. 'If I saw anything at all, and wasn't really somewhere else at the time. I'm not even sure I'm here. And if I am, I wish I wasn't. I think I'd like to go now, if I haven't already gone.'

The Judge leaned over the top of his desk and gave the Prosecuting Ostrich a hard look. 'Get this Rabbit out of my Court, before he convinces us we're not here either, and we all disappear up our own . . .'

'Quite, quite,' said the Ostrich quickly. 'That will be all, Robbie Rabbit. You may step down.'

He gestured for the Rabbit to leave the dock, but by this time the Rabbit had decided he really didn't exist, or the Court didn't, or both, and either way there was no point in responding to an order he probably hadn't heard anyway. The Ostrich gestured wearily for the Usher to remove the Rabbit, which he did with some gusto, having decided that he personally must exist, because he was having such a good time. Particularly when it included using his mallet. He dragged the uncomplaining Rabbit from the dock and dropped him at the front of the spectators' benches, where he was promptly put to use as a foot rest.

'I think that I think, therefore I think that I am. I think

. . .' murmured the Rabbit sadly, but no one paid any attention, not even him.

'Call the next witness,' said the Ostrich, just a touch desperately. 'Call the Sea Goat.'

'I'm already here,' snapped the Goat. 'And no, I can't get out of this wheelchair, so there is no point in trying to get me into the dock. Just wheel me over to it and I'll lean against the bloody thing.'

Between them, Bruin Bear and the Goat wrestled the wheelchair into position. The Ostrich looked meaningfully at the gun the Bear was carrying.

'Self defence,' said the Bear, casually allowing the muzzle to drift in the Ostrich's direction. The Ostrich decided he wouldn't press the point. He gave his full attention to the Sea Goat, who was sucking noisily at his vodka bottle. The Goat was not looking his best, but then, he never did. The bloodstained bandages round his middle seemed out of place in the animals' world.

'You are the Sea Goat?' said the Prosecuting Ostrich.

'If I'm not, the wife's in for one hell of a surprise when I go home tonight. Of course I'm the bloody Sea Goat; what do you think I am, a bleeding platypus? God, those things are ugly. Living proof that the Creator has a sense of humour, and it's a bloody nasty one at that.'

'You have to confirm it for the Court,' said the Ostrich doggedly. 'State your name, and tell the Court exactly what happened at the cemetery.'

'I'm the Sea Goat, and some bastard shot me. Right, that's it, Bear; wheel me out of here.'

It took a little time, and not a little patience on everyone's part, but the Court finally got a detailed picture of what had happened out of the Sea Goat. The spectators muttered uneasily among themselves. Most had never had a real enemy in their lives, never mind someone who shot from hiding and then got away in a military-issue helicopter. The Goat took comfort from his bottle and fixed the Ostrich with a bloodshot glare.

'When are we going to get down to what really matters; namely, working out what the hell to do about this?'

'That is what this Gathering is here to decide,' said the Mock Gryphon, and then rather wished he hadn't, when the Goat fixed him with his glare. Being shot had done absolutely nothing to improve the Goat's disposition, and he didn't care who knew it. He looked at the assembled spectators, and then at the Jury.

'You have got to be joking. This lot couldn't decide to take a piss if their boots were on fire.'

The Judge banged his gavel. 'That's enough of that! Any more and I'll find you in contempt of Court.'

'No you won't,' said Bruin Bear.

'I have to agree with the Bear,' said the Prosecuting Ostrich. 'Mainly because he's pointing a gun at me.'

The Mock Gryphon looked down at the Bear and his gun, and decided the Ostrich had a point. 'The witness is excused, and may leave the witness stand. He may also go to hell, if it isn't too much trouble.'

The Bear wheeled the darkly muttering Sea Goat away, and the Mock Gryphon looked very hard at the Ostrich.

'One more witness like that, and we might as well all pack up and go home.'

'Early days yet, my Lord,' said the Ostrich breezily. 'I call my next witness; Scottie, the Wee Terror.'

Before anyone else could take up the Call, the Court was suddenly disrupted by a series of startled screams, as something small but very violent made its way through the packed rows of spectators. Animals of all shapes and temperaments hurried to get out of its way. Those at the front scattered as a small but extremely determined looking dog emerged from the press of bodies.

It was a Scottish terrier, wearing a cut-down leather jacket with steel studs and chains. Its collar had spikes on, there was a safety-pin through its nose, and for such a small dog it seemed to have an extremely large mouth, positively crammed with teeth. There was an air of menace and mayhem about the dog, and the cock of its head suggested it was the kind of creature that didn't suffer fools gladly. If at all. It padded forward, sniffed disdainfully at the Ostrich, raised a leg and pissed against the dock. The smell was appalling, and steam rose on the air. The dog glared about to see if anyone dared object, and then jumped up on to the chair in the dock and fixed the Ostrich with an arrogant glare.

'I trust there'll be none of this Are you Scottie nonsense? Everyone knows who I am, and if they don't, then to hell with them.'

The Ostrich nodded quickly, and turned to face the Jury. It seemed safer to look at them. 'My noble ducks, voles, squirrels . . . and small furry mammal that's Still Doing It, allow me to present to you Scottie, the Wee Terror, a beast of great distinction and high standing in our community.'

'Damn right,' said the small dog. 'Give me any trouble and I'll rip your head off. Now get on with it, you oversized pigeon. I'm not here for my health, you know.'

'Scottie has travelled far and wide in the town, searching for news of our enemy, and through persistence and determination has put together a disturbing picture of the problem we face. I should like at this time to call for a vote of thanks for his devotion to duty.'

'Are you trying to take the piss?' said the dog sternly.

'Well, really,' said the Ostrich, flustered.

'Ah, shut up and get on with it, or I'll set fire to your trousers.'

'I'm not wearing any trousers.'

'That's your problem, pal. Now shut your face and give your beak a rest, it's my turn to talk.' The dog looked out over the packed Court. 'We are in dead trouble. No one in town knows exactly how the enemy got in here, but it's bloody obvious they couldn't have done it without inside help. Which means there are traitors among us. It's also clear the enemy's no damn amateur. He's well armed and well equipped, and you can bet he'll be back, in force. If you're expecting the humans to protect you, you can think again. They don't know any more than we do. Right now, they're running around in ever-decreasing circles and disappearing up their own backsides. I've seen cats stoned out of their tiny minds on catnip that looked more organized than the humans do right now. Which means, for those of you who've been paying attention, that we're on our own. It's up to us to defend ourselves. We are in deep shit, and it's going to get a lot worse before it gets better.'

For a long time, no one said anything.

'So, in your opinion,' said the Ostrich, 'things are looking rather glum?'

'Are you trying to be funny, pal? Did you not hear a word I've been saying?'

'Of course, my dear chap, but we mustn't let ourselves get down-hearted. I'm sure we can rely on the proper authorities to do what's right on our behalf.'

'What proper authorities? The Sheriff can't even find a bloody murderer, let alone stop an invasion force, and Old Father Time has holed up in his Gallery, and won't talk to anyone. The only person I've seen with the right idea is that bloody Bear with his gun.'

'You're not having it,' said Bruin Bear icily. 'Find your own gun.'

'You're not listening, damn you! The enemy's coming, and he's coming in force. What are we going to do?'

The Ostrich buried his head in his bucket of sand.

Scottie sighed tiredly. 'We're on our own. No one's going to help. We can't afford to be funny any more.'

Rhea Frazier brought her car to a halt outside Leonard Ash's house, and tried to convince herself she was doing the right thing. She was here on business, as Mayor of Shadows Fall, because she needed to know what Ash could tell her about James Hart. She was concerned about what Hart's return meant for the town, particularly since Old Father Time had granted him an audience so readily. Time wasn't usually that accommodating. She was here on business, nothing more. Rhea sighed, and looked at herself in the rear-view mirror. Maybe if she said it often enough, she'd be able to believe it. Maybe.

She looked at the Ash house from the safety of her car. It was a pleasant-looking detached house, modern and cheerful, set comfortably back from the road. A wide gravel path led through the sculptured grounds to the front door. Hearing the gravel crunch under her tyres on her way up the drive had brought back all sorts of memories. She'd come here often when Ash was still alive, sometimes with Richard Erikson, sometimes not. Mostly not, towards the end. She'd come sweeping up the drive, feeling her pulse race just a little as she looked for her first glimpse of Leonard. He was always there, opening the front door as her car ground to a halt, waiting for her with a smile and a kiss and an arm round her waist. They'd been so happy, so much in love . . . but that was three years ago, before he died, and many things had changed since then.

There was no sign of him now, and Rhea shook her head as she realized she'd been unconsciously waiting for him to make his usual appearance. Either he wasn't in, or her arrival didn't matter to him any more. Leonard lost interest in a lot of things, after he died. She shrugged quickly, turned off the car's engine, and listened to the silence. The Ash house stood on the outskirts of town, away from the hurly-burly of its many realities. There wasn't even a bird singing. Probably had ordinances against that sort of thing in this neighbourhood. She opened the door and stepped out of the car, doing it quickly so she wouldn't have the chance to think about what she was doing, and change her mind. She'd already changed it half a dozen times on the way here. She locked her car door, absently enjoying the quiet thump of all the locks closing. She liked it when machinery worked the way it was supposed to. It made her feel secure. There'd been little enough of that in her life, these past three years.

She walked up to the front door, trying hard to look calm and confident, just in case . . . anyone . . . was watching. She was still wearing her smart black outfit from the funeral earlier, though she'd left the pillbox hat with its veil back in the car. Leonard didn't like hats. He never wore them himself, and tended to make desperately humorous remarks about those who did. She didn't think she could stand his sense of humour, not on top of everything else. She stopped before the front door, took a deep breath, and pushed the doorbell. She could hear it ringing faintly inside the house. There was no other response. Somewhere, a bird was singing. It sounded lonely.

A dark shadow appeared beyond the opaque glass of the door, drawing unhurriedly nearer, and Rhea felt a sudden surge of relief as she realized it wasn't tall enough to be Leonard. The door swung open, and Leonard's mother smiled with genuine warmth on seeing Rhea. Martha Ash was a short woman, barely five feet tall, with a frizz of dark curly hair and calm grey eyes. She wore smart, sensible clothes, understated jewellery, and gold-rimmed spectacles that she was always misplacing. Rhea had always got on well with her, and she realized with something like shock that although she'd once thought of Martha as a friend, she hadn't been to see her once since Leonard came back from the dead.

'Rhea, my dear; it's so good to see you again. Do come in. We'll have some tea; I've got a kettle boiling.'

'Thank you,' said Rhea automatically. 'Tea would be nice. Is Leonard home? I need to talk to him about something.'

Rhea wanted to wince at the awkward words even as they left her mouth, but if Martha was aware of her unease, she gave no sign of it. She stepped back to let Rhea enter, and her voice was calm and unconcerned.

'Leonard's out at the moment, but he won't be long. Go on through into the lounge, and I'll be with you in a moment. You do remember the way?'

'Yes, thank you. I remember.'

Rhea moved past Martha into the spacious hall, and the

familiar scents of the Ash house hit her as though she'd never been away. There had been a time, not all that long ago, when this house had been as familiar to her as her own home. She recognized the framed prints on the walls, and the feel of the thick pile carpet under her feet. The hall was open and airy, and her shoes made no sound on the carpet. A sudden sense of peace washed over her, and it seemed to Rhea that she was walking through her memories, that she was back in the past, when the world still made sense. Any minute now Leonard would come running down the stairs to greet her . . . Rhea forced herself out of that train of thought. That was then, this was now. Things were different now.

The lounge was open and airy and very comfortable. Rhea put her purse down on the handy table by the door, and walked slowly forward into the huge room. Ash's parents were supposed to be quite rich, though they always preferred to refer to themselves as comfortably well off. A polite euphemism that appeared to mean loaded, but not ostentatious. Out beyond the open french windows lay a vast expanse of garden, lovingly tended and bullied into line by Thomas Ash, Leonard's father. Thomas spent a lot of time in the garden. On days when the weather wouldn't permit it, he tended to pull up a chair before the french windows and sit watching the garden, as if to make sure it wouldn't misbehave in his absence. He'd never had much to do with Rhea, though he was always polite, in a mumbling, absent-minded way. At first Rhea had thought it was because she was black, but it didn't take her long to discover that Thomas was like that with everyone, including Martha and Leonard. It wasn't that he disliked people. He just didn't have much to say to them. Unless you were interested in gardening, and then you couldn't shut him up. The weather was clear and fine at present, so presumably he was out there now, staring thoughtfully at some inoffensive bush with a pair of secateurs in one hand, and his pipe clenched firmly in one side of his mouth.

Rhea turned away from the windows as she heard

movement behind her, but it was only Martha, carrying a silver tray loaded down with all the necessities for making tea. There was even an assortment of chocolate biscuits on a plate. Rhea smiled. She'd always had a soft spot for chocolate biscuits, and Martha never failed to provide a few, just to tempt her. The two women pulled up chairs on opposite sides of a low table, and busied themselves with the tea things. Finally they both had a cup just the way they liked it, and sat back in their chairs. Martha looked at Rhea appraisingly.

'You've lost some weight since I last saw you, dear. Are you eating properly?'

'Yes, Martha. Though with the pressure of work just recently, it's not unusual for me to have to eat on the run.'

'You should always make time for a proper meal. Dashing back and forth does nothing at all for the digestion.'

And then they sat for a while in silence. Martha was waiting for Rhea to make the first move, and they both knew it. She felt uncomfortable under Martha's calm gaze; there was a time she could have said anything to Martha, anything at all, but not now. She ran through a dozen possible openings in her mind, but they all sounded false, or trite. Martha would see through anything, except the truth.

'I need to talk to Leonard. It's town business.'

'I thought it probably must be, to bring you out here again. Leonard's out walking. He does a lot of that, these days. He doesn't sleep any more, you see, and that makes him terribly restless. But he'll be back soon. He had a feeling you'd be along some time today.'

Rhea raised an eyebrow. 'Does he often have . . . feelings like that?'

'Oh yes. And they're usually quite accurate. He says he sees things much more clearly since he died.'

That last word hung on the air between them, refusing to be ignored or overlooked. Rhea opened her mouth to say something and then shut it and tried again.

'How do you cope with him being dead?'

Martha sighed, and looked away. Her gaze lingered on the garden, as though looking for her husband for support, but after a moment she turned back and met Rhea's gaze with her own.

'It's not been easy. The first Thomas and I knew of his return was the night after the funeral. We'd gone to bed early. The house had seemed so empty without him. We were still suffering from the shock of his death. He died so suddenly. I always worried about him riding that motorcycle, but I never really thought . . . but then, I don't suppose anyone does, really. Motorcycle crashes are things that happen to other people.

'We were in bed, the lights out, both of us wanting to hide from the day in sleep, but neither of us able to. And then the doorbell rang. I sat up and turned on the light, and looked at the bedside clock. It was barely half past twelve. Thomas got up and put on his dressing-gown, muttering all the time about being disturbed at such an hour. I got up too, and went down the stairs with him. I don't know why. Or perhaps I did, on some deep, basic level. We stopped at the front door, and Thomas asked loudly who it was. And on the other side of the door a voice said *It's me, Dad. I've come home.*

'We looked at each other, but we didn't say anything for a long time. And then Thomas unlocked the door, and opened it. Leonard was standing there, smiling slightly, looking neat and presentable, just as he'd looked in his coffin before the funeral. He looked from Thomas to me and back again, as though unsure of his reception. I took him in my arms and held him as tight as I could. I had some crazy idea that if I didn't hold on to him hard enough, make it clear how welcome he was, he'd disappear and we'd never see him again. I was crying so hard I couldn't talk, and Thomas kept patting first me on the shoulder and then Leonard, as though he wasn't sure who needed him most.

'I finally let go of Leonard and took his hands in mine. They felt cold. Not unnaturally so, but as though he'd been standing out in the night too long. I brought him back in and made him sit by the fire, and his father sat with him while I went and made some tea. Thomas was still patting Leonard on the shoulder over and over, saying how good it was to see him. We'd heard about such things happening before, this is Shadows Fall after all, but we had no reason to believe . . . that sort of thing only happened to other people. Like motorcycle crashes. But he was back, and that was all that mattered. We didn't ask any questions.

'It was a few days before we noticed the changes. It was definitely Leonard, no question of that, but . . . not all of him. As though when he came back, he left part of himself behind. He didn't eat or drink any more, or sleep. He used to sit up all night reading, or watching television with the sound turned down so as not to disturb us. He lost interest in all the things that used to fill his time. Things . . . and people. A lot of his friends came round, the moment they heard. Richard Erikson was here within the hour. But none of them stayed long. Leonard was always scrupulously polite to them, but they all felt uncomfortable in his presence, after a while. He wasn't the Leonard they remembered. He'd been somewhere they could never understand, and he carried its dust on his shoes. So they all left, one after the other, and they never came back. Leonard made no effort to hang on to them. The spark wasn't in him any more.

'I hoped it was just a temporary thing, that he hadn't "woken up" all the way. I kept waiting and hoping, watching him for some sign of what was missing, but it never came. He was my son, I never doubted that, but . . . not all of him. Only part of him came back. Is that why you stayed away, Rhea?'

'No. I don't even have that excuse. When I first heard, I couldn't believe it, and then I wouldn't. I didn't want to. The man I loved was dead and buried. The last thing I wanted to see was some double with his face and voice. I kept telling myself it wasn't really him, and eventually I managed to convince myself, on every level but the one that mattered. You see, I was Mayor. I knew better. I knew people come back, sometimes. It is him, isn't it? It's really him.'

'Yes,' said Martha. 'It's him.'

They sat for a while in silence, looking at everything but each other, and then Martha leaned forward and put her hand on Rhea's. 'You've always known it was him, dear. Why did you never come? Do you know why?'

'Yes,' said Rhea quietly. 'Because I knew that even if he had come back, it wasn't to stay. It never is. Sooner or later, the reason for his coming back will fade, until it isn't strong enough to hold him any more, and then he'll go away again. He'll die and he'll stay dead. I couldn't face losing him a second time.'

For a moment Rhea thought she might cry, but she didn't. It was an old hurt, and it didn't have the power over her that it once had. And anyway, she was a politician, and used to being in control of her emotions. These days, she only cried when it was expedient, and only then if the cameras were around. She sniffed once, and then smiled briefly at Martha to show everything was all right. They both heard the front door open, and Rhea was quickly on her feet, as though part of her wanted to run and hide from what was coming. She made herself stand still, trembling slightly, and in the end it was Martha who got up and went out into the hall. There was a brief murmur of voices, and then Martha's voice rose clearly on the quiet.

'Leonard, dear, come through into the lounge. You have a visitor.'

Rhea braced herself, but it was still something of a shock when Ash appeared out of the hall to smile at her the way he always used to. Her heart was racing slightly, not exactly from pleasure. He looked much as he always did; his clothes were casual and sloppy, and his hair needed a good combing. He stepped forward to greet her, and for one horrible moment Rhea thought he was going to put out a hand for her to shake. She couldn't have touched him, not for anything. In the end, he just smiled and nodded to her amiably, and perhaps a little absent-mindedly, as though part of his attention was somewhere else, fixed on some other, more important matter.

'Hello, Rhea,' he said calmly. 'It's good to see you here. I take it mother's been looking after you all right . . . ah yes, the chocolate biscuits are out. You should feel honoured, Rhea; mother doesn't get the chocolate biscuits out for just anyone.'

'I need to talk to you,' said Rhea brusquely. 'It's important.'

'I thought it must be, to have brought you out here after so long. Let's go upstairs. We can talk in my room. It'll be more private there.'

'You're welcome to the lounge,' said Martha. 'I can disappear, if I'm in the way.'

'That won't be necessary,' said Ash. 'I prefer to talk in my room. I feel more concentrated there.'

He turned and left the lounge without waiting to see if Rhea was following him. She gave Martha a quick smile of thanks, and hurried after him. She remembered the way to his room, even though it had been some time since she'd last seen it. Not since he'd died, and she'd gone to his room on a kind of pilgrimage, to say goodbye to his things. Now old memories came crowding around her, jostling for her attention, but she held them firmly at arm's length. She was here on business. Nothing more. Ash was waiting for her at the top of the stairs, holding open the door to his room. She walked past him, and then stopped just inside the room. It was exactly as she remembered. Nothing had changed. Nothing at all.

'I spend a lot of time in here,' said Ash quietly. 'It's full of memories for me to hang on to. I don't sleep any more, but I spend hours lying on the bed. Thinking, remembering, trying to keep a grip on all the things that make me *me*. It helps to have my things around me; my books and my records, the brush and comb and deodorant on my dresser. All the little things that the living use every day and never think twice about. I don't use them any more, but I like to look at them. They help me . . . pretend.'

'I'm here on business,' said Rhea, a little more forcefully than she'd meant. 'I need to talk to you about James Hart.'

'Yes. I thought that might be it. Take a seat, please.'

There was only one chair, and Rhea sat on it, crossing her legs primly. Ash sat on the edge of the bed facing her. Rhea pulled back her feet just a little, so they wouldn't touch Ash's. He looked at her encouragingly, and she had to look away for a moment. He was trying so hard to be helpful, and somehow that only made it more difficult. She looked around the room to avoid looking at him, and everything she saw brought back memories of the times they'd spent together in this room, in the past, when he was still alive. The poster on the wall of the concert they'd been to, the book on the dresser she'd got him that he always meant to get around to reading, but never had. Or perhaps he had, now he had more time.

'You look good in black,' said Ash. 'Very smart. If I'd known you were going to look that good, I'd have died earlier.'

'It's not for you. I was at a funeral earlier today. Lucas DeFrenz.'

'Yes; I heard about that. I was worried you might have been hurt in the shooting. But I should have known you'd be all right. You always were lucky.'

'Why are you wearing black?' said Rhea, more to put off what was to come than because she cared.

Ash grinned suddenly. 'I'm in mourning for my sex life.'

Rhea groaned, and smiled in spite of herself. 'Being dead hasn't done a thing to improve your sense of humour. Leonard; let's make this as easy as we can for both of us. I'm not here to see you, I'm here to pump you for whatever information you might have about James Hart. Strange things have been happening, strange even for Shadows

238

Fall, and all of them started the day James Hart came home. Tell me about him. What's he like?'

Ash pursed his lips. 'Just an ordinary guy, nothing special. If he is responsible for whatever's going on in town, I'm pretty sure he doesn't know about it. He doesn't remember the town at all. Apparently I was at school with him, but I don't remember anything definite. Of course, my memory isn't what it was.' Ash stopped and frowned suddenly. 'There was one thing . . . I took Hart to see Old Father Time, and Jack Fetch was there. Large as life and twice as nasty. Rhea; *the scarecrow knelt and bowed to Hart.* I've never seen Jack Fetch do that to anyone, not even Time himself. I could be wrong, but I think Old Father Time was taken aback too. And that's not something you see every day.'

'I'll be damned,' said Rhea, frowning. 'I didn't think Jack Fetch acknowledged any authority but Time. He certainly never bowed to me, the few times our paths crossed. Not that I'd have known what to do if he had. Unnatural thing. I'd banish him if he wasn't so necessary. And if I thought he'd take any notice of me. What else can you tell me about James Hart?'

'That's it, really. He seemed a friendly enough sort, wasn't too thrown by Shadows Fall, which would suggest either great strength of character or an extremely limited imagination. He was good company, but pretty reserved. Didn't talk about himself much at all, now I come to think of it. I don't know what else to say.'

'I was hoping for more than that, Leonard.'

'Sorry. That's all I've got.'

'Then it's time I was going.' Rhea stood up, and Ash was quickly on his feet again. She smoothed the creases out of her dress, carefully not looking at him. 'Nice visiting you, Leonard. We must do this again some time. Now I must dash. A hundred things to do.'

'Don't go, Rhea. Please.'

'We don't have anything more to talk about.' Rhea

forced herself to meet his gaze. 'I was here on business, Leonard. Nothing more.'

'There's so much I want to say to you.'

'I don't want to hear it.'

'I don't believe that. You finally came to see me, after all this time. That has to mean something. I've missed you so much. There isn't an hour in the day that I don't think of you, and the time we shared. Sometimes I think it's only those memories that still hold me together.'

'Stop it! That was somebody else. The man I loved is dead and buried and gone! He's not a part of my life any more.'

'I'm still me, Rhea. I'm dead, but I'm still me. I'm the same man who held your hand when we were out walking, who sat around waiting downstairs while you agonized over which outfit to wear. The same man who told you he loved you more than life itself. Your face just changed, Rhea. It's that cold, empty face you always put on when you don't want to hear something. The shutters come down in your eyes, and your face says there's no one home. Don't hide from me, Rhea. Not from me. I'm so alone.'

'Don't do this to me, Leonard.' Rhea met his gaze unflinchingly, but she could feel her legs trembling. Tension, or strain. Nothing else. 'There's nothing between us any more. Love is for the living, for people with a future.'

'You think I don't know that? You have no idea what it's like for me now. I know I'm not really Ash. I'm a memory of who I used to be, given shape and form. And that isn't enough. A man of hidden shallows; that's what you used to call me. Only now it's true. I'm starting to forget things, Rhea. I'm losing all the things that make up me. Every day I remember a little less. The words of a favourite tune, the colour of a friend's car; gone, and nothing left to fill their space. Only little things, for the moment, but they add up. Or rather they subtract, from me. I'm fading away. Every day there's that much less of me left. Eventually everything will be gone, and I'll really

240

be dead. Just a ghost, an image of someone who doesn't exist any more. Help me, Rhea. I'm scared. I'm so scared.'

The anguish in his voice tore at her, and pain rose up inside her, the old bitter pain that she'd never shared with anyone. She looked at Ash angrily, refusing to give in to the tears that burned in her eyes. 'You didn't come back because you loved me. You came back because your mother needed you!'

'No. That's not how it happened.'

'Then why did you come back? Why did you have to come back, and ruin all our lives?'

'*I don't know!* I'm here for a purpose, but I don't know what or why. I said my parents needed me because I had to say something. I didn't mean to hurt you. I never meant to hurt you. You're everything that ever mattered to me, Rhea. I would have died for you. I would have stayed dead for you, if I could. That's why I stayed away from you all this time, because I wanted you to be free, to get over me. But something brought me back, and holds me here. And day by day there's less of me. I can't live, but something won't let me die. I need you, Rhea. If you ever loved me, love me now.'

Rhea reached out and took his cold hands in hers. 'If I ever loved you? Leonard, my dear . . . I never stopped loving you.'

Ash reached out to hold her, then hesitated, and Rhea had to pull him into her arms before he could really bring himself to believe it. Rhea buried her face in his neck and let out her breath in a long, shuddering sigh.

'I don't know what to do, Leonard. Nothing in my life makes sense any more. Shadows Fall is coming apart at the seams, despite everything I do to hold it together. It's all happening so *fast*. I can barely keep up with the reports. I suppose that's really why I'm here. I came to you for help, even if I didn't want to admit it. I felt such a failure. After you were gone, all I had left was my job. I worked hard at it. And since all I had was the job, it took over my life.I came here to use you, Leonard; to get information from you I could use to control Hart. To put me back on top of things again.'

'I don't mind,' said Ash. 'Use me all you want.'

They both managed some kind of laugh, and stood back from each other so they could stare into each other's eyes. Ash held on to Rhea's hands, and she squeezed them gently in return. They were still cold.

'Whatever happens, Leonard; I'm not going to lose you again. We're back together, for better or worse. Death didn't part us after all.'

'I'm glad,' said Ash. 'Whatever's left of me is yours. For as long as it lasts. I wish I had more to offer you.'

'We'll find a way to be together always,' said Rhea. 'There's got to be a way. This is Shadows Fall, after all.'

'For as long as it lasts. I've been getting some very strange feelings just lately. Premonitions. Bad ones. I think something really bad is coming our way. Something powerful enough to threaten the whole town.'

'Not you as well, Leonard. Everyone's gone paranoid these past few weeks. Could you at least be a little more specific?'

'Sorry. Being dead, I get to see things more clearly, but it's more feelings than anything else. There's something out there, outside the town, watching and waiting for just the right moment, but I've no idea what. It's alive, if that's any help.'

'Not a lot.'

'I didn't think so.'

'You must have thought about this, Leonard. What do you think it is?'

'I don't know,' said Ash. 'But I did wonder if maybe this was the reason I was sent back. There has to be a reason.'

'I'm sure there is,' said Rhea. 'Maybe I brought you back, because I needed you so much.'

'Maybe. Stranger things have happened, even in Shadows Fall. That's a very pretty dress you're wearing. Can I help you with the zip?'

*

242

Far below Caer Dhu, Court and Castle of the Faerie, deep in the heart of the land beneath the hill, three figures walked unhurriedly in a wide earth tunnel. Two were tall and fair and one was not, but they all carried nobility with them, like a scarred and scoured shield that had taken punishment from more than one battle too many. It was dark in the tunnel, but will-o'-the-wisps in their hundreds danced on the air around the three figures. Their blue-white light was sharp and piercing, glistening on the smooth earth walls, but still none of the three cast any shadow.

Oberon and Titania and the withered elf called Puck finally came to a halt before a great trapdoor, set flush into the earth floor. It was fully twenty feet square, stretching from wall to wall, thick boards of centuries-old oak held together with steel bands and silver rivets. Words and phrases from a language much older than man's had been carved into the wood of the trapdoor, and etched with acid into the steel bands. There was no ring or other mechanism by which it might have been lifted, had anyone the strength to stir its massive weight. Oberon, King of the elven kind, stared silently at the trapdoor. No visible thought or emotion moved in his icy blue eyes, or stirred his colourless features. He was ten feet tall, built almost entirely of muscle, and wrapped in robes the colour of blood, but still he stood before the trapdoor like a suppliant unsure of his welcome.

Titania, his wife, Queen of the Faerie, stood at his side. She was a few inches taller than he, dressed in blackest night with silver trimmings, but beneath the short black hair the pallor of her face was that of a ghost. They had been through much together, he and she, and if they had been human they might have wondered if it was love or memories that still held them in union. But they were Faerie, with larger and brighter emotions than any human could ever know or stand, and their love was eternal.

Puck, malformed and broken, the only imperfect elf, squatted on his hairy haunches by the trapdoor, one arm hanging lower than the other by virtue of his humped back. The hand on that arm had withered into a claw, and he scratched his sharp nails idly across the ancient wood. Static sparked about his fingers as thin parings of wood curled up from the trapdoor. Beneath the nubs of horns protruding on his brow, his green eyes burned with mischief, though his face was properly solemn. He scratched absently at the furred hides he wore, in marked contrast to the graceful robes of his companions. Puck cared little for grace or dignity, since his twisted form denied him both.

'It is not too late,' said Oberon softly. 'We could yet turn away from this. The destiny of Shadows Fall has been made known to us. It cannot endure. The Wild Childe is loose among them, unkillable and unstoppable, and they are betrayed by those they trusted. We need not share that fate. Much as it would pain me, I would see the town destroyed and everything in it dead and gone before I would risk the future of our people.'

'We all heard the oracle,' said Titania, her voice calm and steady. 'Shadows Fall cannot be saved or protected, but we need not fall with them. We could still turn away from this, withdraw into Caer Dhu, and wait out the passing of the town. The Faerie would survive.'

'To what purpose?' said Puck, not looking up from the trapdoor. 'We could save our precious lives, but only by giving up what we value most. We are sworn to protect the town, at any and all cost. Just as the hero, Lester Gold, protected you from the dread beast. Shall we allow them to outdo us? What are the Faerie, if they know not honour? Would we break our sacred oaths, undo our trust, discard what we have always treasured most in ourselves, just to survive? I think not. The humans might be capable of such duplicity, but we are not. It would destroy us. No; the Faerie must fight. A simple choice, in a complicated world.'

Oberon stirred unhappily. 'Time has turned his back on us. For the first time in uncounted centuries we cannot see the future. We have always known this time would come, when even our oracles would be struck blind and deaf, but we chose not to think of it. Now, we no longer have that comfort. We look for the future and see only darkness. Some greater power clouds our sight. But what power is there, greater than us? There was only ever one, and they are gone.'

'The Fallen,' said Puck, and the word seemed to echo on and on in the quiet of the tunnel.

'Speak not their name so loud,' said Titania. 'They might waken.'

'Not easily,' said Puck. He chuckled unpleasantly. 'Shadows Fall will be destroyed and Caer Dhu thrown down in rubble before the Fallen ever waken again. Come, my noble King and Queen, the time for talk is past. The Court has debated this up and down and back and forth. There is only one answer. We cannot turn our backs on honour, either by destroying or ignoring the town, so all that is left to us is to open the ancient Armoury, draw forth our ancient weapons, and wake our sleeping blood to wrath. The Faerie must go to war once more, with or without the comfort of prophecy. It matters not who our enemy may be. In all our wars, in all our history, the Faerie have never been defeated.'

'Yes,' said Oberon. 'Our glory and our curse. You have the right of it, Puck, Weaponmaster. It is time. Open the door and let us in.'

'Prepare yourselves,' said Puck, and for the first time there was no humour in his eyes. 'I will awaken the Sleeper.'

He lifted a hooved foot and slammed it down on the trapdoor twice. The sound was disturbingly loud on the quiet, echoing on long after it should have died away, as though it had an immeasurably long distance to travel. And far away, beyond the limits of sight or hearing, something from outside the waking world stirred in its long slumber and awoke. It turned its awful gaze on the three Faerie, and they looked away, unable to face it. But wherever they looked the Sleeper was there, staring back at them, and they shuddered in anguish and loathing as change was thrust upon them.

It was the pride and glory of the Faerie that they were not bound to one shape or nature. Not for them the human logic of yes or no, either/or; they lived by wider parameters. To the elven kind, shape and form were as fleeting as thought or imagination, and past, present and future were equally accessible. They shared one basic form by common consent, partly for aesthetic reasons but mainly through the force of tradition and custom. There was a reason for that custom, that centuries-old tradition, but few chose to remember it. The Sleeper knew. It wasn't capable of forgetting. And then, there was always honour. The Faerie needed honour; it was the only thing that could bind their thoughts and aspirations, and keep the elves from destroying each other on a moment's whim. But now all these things were gone, swept away by the Sleeper's gaze. The three Faerie were stripped of their spontaneity, locked in their shapes and anchored in the present; condemned to the mundanity of unchanging reality. Titania and Oberon clung together, trembling violently, and even Puck lost much of his dark merriment. He lifted his horned head and stamped his hoof on the trapdoor again.

'Open the door, Sleeper. Our enemies are upon us, and the sword must be drawn from its sheath!'

The massive trapdoor stirred in response to his voice and the ancient code words. Dust sprang away from its outline, and the trapdoor rose slowly upwards, pivoting gracefully on silent hinges, revealing a great black mouth. The will-o'-the-wisps fell back, seething agitatedly, and would not go near it. The elves held themselves stiffly, clinging to dignity though all else had been taken from them. They had committed themselves willingly to a single form in order to gain access to their long-abandoned Armoury, and the mighty weapons it contained, but it had been so long . . . they had forgotten the horror of unrelenting order. Only the Faerie could withstand the Sleeper's gaze, and embrace the shape and structure of ultimate reality.

Humanity would have shrivelled under that gaze like a burning leaf under the magnified glare of the sun. Even the Faerie were much diminished, which was why the Armoury had gone so long unvisited. It was a price the Faerie had not paid for centuries beyond counting, not since they emptied the Armoury and went forth to face the Fallen, so very long ago.

The trapdoor stood open, its uppermost edge scraping against the earth roof of the tunnel. Before it lay the huge black opening, a gaping mouth of unrelenting darkness that turned aside the massed light of the will-o'-the-wisps with contemptuous ease. Looking down at that blackness was like staring up into an endless night sky that had never known a moon. Vertigo tugged at the elves, but their pride held them still at the edge of the opening. The darkness seemed to fall away for ever, or at least further than any material thing should. The Armoury was too powerful and too tempting to be left where just anyone might stumble upon it, so the Faerie had taken it out of the world and hidden it where only they could find it. Puck looked at Oberon and Titania and bowed mockingly.

'After you, my noble King and Queen.'

'No, loyal Puck,' said Oberon. 'We would not take the honour from you. You are Weaponmaster, and shall go first.'

The withered elf laughed softly, and stepped forward into the darkness. A wide step of shining steel appeared out of nowhere to meet and support his hoof, and another step appeared below it. Puck strode unflinchingly down the gleaming steps as they appeared before him, and Oberon and Titania followed close behind. The bobbing will-o'-the-wisps circled uncertainly round the opening, but would not follow any further. The trapdoor swung forward and settled smoothly into place, cutting off the land beneath the hill from the other place, the place the Faerie had made to hold and protect the Armoury. A light glowed in the darkness far below, a steady crimson glare like an unblinking watching eye. The Faerie descended carefully towards it, though afterwards they could never agree for how long. There was only the steel steps and the dark, and a growing sense of distance. But finally Puck stepped down from a steel step on to bare concrete, and the Armoury appeared about him as though it had always been there.

It was vast beyond reckoning, an endless vault that stretched away into infinity in all directions. Crimson lights set at regular intervals glared down from a ceiling some fifty feet above. And all around, in that hellish light, stood row upon row of gleaming steel shelves, stacked in endless profusion with weapons and machinery of all kinds. All the many forms of destruction the Faerie had created, in the days when they depended on science rather than magic. There were projectile weapons and energy guns, plasma generators and high energy lasers. Bombs beyond counting, guns beyond number. Vast mechanisms that could tear apart an army or a world with equal ease. Huge viewscreens stood waiting to reveal an enemy's plans and positions, and computer banks stood ready to undo them.

The three elves stared slowly about them. It had been a long time, and they had forgotten much, by their own choice. They had enjoyed the Armoury's power too much. In the aftermath of the war against the Fallen, it had not taken them long to realize that the next inevitable step would be for one faction of the Faerie to employ these weapons against another, to the destruction of both. And so they turned their backs on the Armoury and all that it held, and buried it deep in their minds, so that it would only surface again in the direst emergency, when the land beneath the hill itself might be endangered. Now they were back, and memories returned like water unleashed from a dam. Memories of slaughter and destruction, and the wild thrilling of the blood. Puck smiled and stretched slowly, like a cat in the summer sun. It was good to be back.

'Puck, Weaponmaster,' he said crisply. 'Acknowledge.'

A shimmering purple light stabbed down from above, holding him in place like a butterfly skewered on a pin. He could not move, or blink, or even breathe, but Puck knew better than to try and fight it. Until the Sleeper acknowledged his identity and rank, it was still in command, and it would kill him without hesitation if it considered him a threat. That was, after all, how he'd programmed it, all those centuries ago. The light sank into him like a slow chill, mapping his physical structure and genetic makeup and comparing it with those in its records.

'Acknowledged,' said a calm, inhuman voice in his head. 'Welcome back, Weaponmaster.'

'Activate all systems,' said Puck. 'I want all weapons back on line and ready for inspection.'

'Of course, Weaponmaster. My sensors detect two other life forms in your immediate vicinity. They must be scanned and cleared before inspection can take place.'

Puck nodded to Oberon and Titania, and they announced their names and suffered the examination of the shimmering light. Puck watched, not bothering to hide his amusement. It had been a very long time indeed since the King and Queen of Faerie had had to bow to any will save their own. They took it surprisingly well. Probably because they were starting to remember all the mighty weapons the Armoury held, and were as impatient as he to get their hands on those wonderful toys again. The Sleeper acknowledged Oberon and Titania and made obeisance to them. Viewscreens blazed with light on all sides, displaying endless information on which weapons were ready for immediate use, and which would require time to be made ready. Puck grinned until his cheeks hurt. How could he ever have wanted to forget all this? There was enough firepower here to level Shadows Fall in a matter of hours. Enough engines of destruction to pound the world into rubble. Many he had used himself in the war against the Fallen, and something warm and darkly pleasant stirred within him as he remembered wielding this weapon or that, and how he had wrought death and devastation at his will.

There was the Spear of Light, which could not be stopped

or evaded once thrown, and could seek out one enemy among thousands. There was the Cauldron of Night, wherein the dead could be raised and sent out to kill again in the name of the Faerie, no matter what side they might originally have fought on. There was the Bone Ripper, the Howling Tide, the Shatterer of Dreams and the Spirit Thief. Nightmares of destruction given shape and form, as potent and as deadly now as when the Faerie first created them, millennia ago.

Oberon and Titania walked unhurriedly in the Hall of Weapons, pausing occasionally before this viewscreen or that, savouring some particular memory of suffering or slaughter. Glorious mechanisms of destruction revealed themselves to their masters, who considered the prospect of a world in flames, and found it pleasing. The time had come again when the Faerie would test their courage and skill and honour on the only grounds that really mattered: the field of battle. The elves knew that they were not what they had once been. Immortality has many drawbacks, the chief of which is boredom. They had grown soft through lack of challenge and dreamed away their long lives, but that would end now. They would heat their blood in the kiln of battle, and rediscover their greatness in the blood of their enemies.

Puck stood alone before a giant viewscreen, his thoughts elsewhere. His time as Weaponmaster had made him what he was now; the only imperfect elf. He had exposed himself to forces and energies that had yielded immeasurable power, and had paid the price. He had twisted and shrivelled in the heat of strange tides, his flesh running as wax runs down a candle to escape the flame. He had been Weaponmaster of the Faerie, and he was only now beginning to remember what that had entailed. War had been his life, his cause, his reason for existence. He gloried in death and destruction, and the trampling of worlds. He plucked a weapon from a shelf, primed and aimed it without hesitating, and blasted a wide hole in the shelving. The roar of the explosion echoed loudly in the Hall of

Weapons, and jagged pieces of metal shrapnel fell out of the air like hail. Puck breathed deeply, still grinning. It was good to be back.

He turned his thoughts inward, and reached out beyond the material world. His inner gaze fell upon a path of roaring power, channelled energies burning with unquenchable vigour. More paths blazed around him, crackling and howling in the hollow places between the worlds, ready to be tapped and exploited by those with the power and audacity. It was the work of a moment to reach out and tap into the nearest path, and power beyond mortal control or hope of reckoning beat within him. And it was only then that Puck remembered the source of those paths of energy, and his laughter rang loud and savage in the Hall of Weapons.

It was the Fallen, in all their millions; dead but not destroyed, vanquished but not released, suffering endlessly as their destruction was stretched across the warp and weft of time. The Fallen were dying, and always would be.

'Tremble, all the worlds that be,' whispered Puck. 'The elves go to war once more.'

Sheriff Richard Erikson pushed open the tall wrought-iron gate and stepped through into a nightmare of overgrown greenery. Trees and bushes crowded together at the edges of the single paved path, and thick creepers hung down from lowering branches. A breath of movement stirred the surrounding trees, rustling through the thickly-knit branches, but no wind blew and the air in the garden was deathly still. It was early in the evening, but already dark, and deep impenetrable shadows filled what gaps there were in the greenery. The quiet seemed to grow more brittle the further into the garden he walked, and every sudden rustle or whisper of movement sounded clearly in the hush. The air was full of perfume, thick and sickly sweet, like flowers left too long in a hothouse, and gone to rot.

Erikson stopped, and looked casually about him, taking his time. Nothing definite met his gaze, but he had a strong feeling this would be a bad time to show any sign of weakness. He could feel the weight of his gun and his baton on his hips, but he kept his hands away from both. He didn't want to start anything. There was a vague sense of settling, of relaxing, and all around him the garden and the darkness grew still and quiet. Some of the tension went out of Erikson too, and he began to breathe more easily. He strode unhurriedly along the narrow path, heading for the great hulking house before him. It was a squat, ugly place with ivy crawling everywhere. There was a light at one window on the ground floor; the others were dark and empty, staring back like watching eyes. Erikson sniffed, unimpressed. He'd seen uglier places, in his time. Shadows Fall was not a town for the faint-hearted, especially if you were the law. He scowled at the gloomy, glowering house and sighed quietly. Whatever the good Doctor Mirren wanted to see him about, it had better be important.

The call had come through on his car radio half an hour ago. Doctor Nathaniel Mirren needed to speak urgently with Sheriff Erikson. He wouldn't say what about, only that it was vitally important that the Sheriff contact him immediately. He'd stressed the word vital. The dispatcher tried to put him through to one of the Deputies, but Mirren was having none of that. It had to be Erikson. Anyone else, Erikson would have sent a polite, reassuring reply, and got around to it when he had the time, but Mirren was different. The good Doctor was an important member of the community, well-connected, and, it must be admitted, often able to see things in the present and in the future that other people missed. Just what the town needed; another politician with ambition who dabbled in sorcery.

Necromancy, to be exact; trafficking with the dead. Though of course no one ever said that out loud. It wasn't actually illegal, but it wasn't exactly popular either. In the Sheriff's experience, people tended to get rather squeamish at the thought of their dearly departed having their final rest disturbed, just so that Doctor Mirren could pursue the answers to questions he shouldn't have been asking in the first place. Still, Mirren was connected to all the right people, in social as well as political circles, and he was the best doctor in Shadows Fall; a positive genius at diagnosis. So everyone made allowances. Lots of them.

Erikson finally reached the front door, and looked for a bell to ring. There wasn't one, but there was a large black iron knocker on the door, cast in the shape of a snarling lion's head. It was a large knocker, easily twice the size of Erikson's fist, and he felt strangely reluctant to use it, as though afraid it might suddenly come to life and snap at his fingers. He pushed the thought firmly to one side, took a good hold on the knocker and banged it twice. Even through the door, he could hear the sound echoing through the house. Everything else was quiet, save for the occasional stirring or rustling in the garden behind him. He didn't look back. He didn't think he wanted to know. A thought struck him, and he rummaged in his jacket pockets. He came up with a packet of mints, popped one into his mouth, and sucked it noisily. It wouldn't do for Doctor Mirren to be able to smell alcohol on his breath.

Erikson didn't think of himself as a heavy drinker, but he liked a glass of something, now and again. These days, now and again were a lot closer together than they used to be. His search for the murderer was getting nowhere fast, and more and more pressure was coming down on him from all sides. He was doing everything he could, driving himself and his seven Deputies unmercifully, but so far he had little enough to show for it. Just ten dead victims, and no trace of their killer anywhere. No clues, no suspects; they hadn't even been able to positively identify the murder weapon yet. A blunt instrument was the best they could do, wielded with almost inhuman force. But no fingerprints or footprints. No witnesses, no traces of the murderer's passing, nothing to show the bastard had ever been there, apart from his victim. No leads, no theories, nothing. So Erikson took a little drink, now and again. He had to. He needed something to keep him going.

He glared at the wide, towering door before him. All that rush to get him here, and now Mirren couldn't even be bothered to open his damned door. It was a pretty impressive door, though. Eight feet tall if it was an inch. The kind of door expressly designed to keep people out. Almost, one might say, the door of someone under siege. The door of someone with enemies. A gleam of light at the top of the door caught his eye, and he looked more carefully. His eyes had grown used to the gloom, but even so he only just made out the outlines of the security camera set just above the door. No wonder Mirren was taking so long. He was having a good look at his visitor first.

What have you been up to, Doctor? What's got you so scared?

The door swung open, and Doctor Mirren looked out at the Sheriff. His face was pale and strained, and he had a shotgun in his hands. Erikson stood very still. Mirren looked at him closely. The Doctor's mouth was trembling but his hands were steady, and the gun never wavered. Mirren's clothes were a mess, and going by the dark circles under his eyes, he hadn't been getting much sleep lately. He looked past the Sheriff and out into the darkness, his eyes darting back and forth as though trying to catch something by surprise. Erikson cleared his throat cautiously.

'You asked to see me, Doctor, so here I am. You did say it was important.'

'It is. Very.' Mirren lowered the shotgun, but didn't take his finger away from the trigger. 'Sorry; I don't trust the camera any more. There are lots of things that don't show up on the monitor.'

Erikson chose his words carefully. 'What kind of . . . things are you expecting, Doctor?'

Mirren looked at him coldly. 'Talk to me, Sheriff. Tell me something only you and I could know. I need to be sure you're really who you seem to be.'

'Doctor; we've known each other the best part of ten

years now. We've sat on opposite sides of the table at town Council meetings more often than I can count. Now you told my dispatcher you needed to see me about something vital. Right now I'm in the middle of a murder inquiry, in case you've forgotten, and my definition of vital is getting pretty damn thin. So either invite me in and tell me what the hell this is all about, or I'm leaving. I have work to do.'

Mirren smiled slightly, though it didn't reach his eyes. 'Yes; you're Erikson. I'm sorry, but I have my reasons. Come in, and I'll explain.' He stepped back, and gestured for the Sheriff to enter. He seemed a little calmer, but even so Erikson kept a watchful eye on the shotgun as he walked past the Doctor and into his hall. Mirren shrugged apologetically, and lowered the gun so that it was pointing at the floor. He glared suspiciously out at his garden one last time, then slammed the door shut, and locked and bolted it. The sight of the closed door seemed to steady him, and he nodded for Erikson to follow him with some of his old arrogance. 'This way, Sheriff. We can talk in my study.'

He set off down the hall at a fair pace, and Erikson had to hurry to keep up. He felt a little more secure now that the shotgun wasn't pointing in his direction, and took the opportunity to take a good look about him. He'd never been in Mirren's place before, though he'd heard rumours. The hall was certainly impressive. It was vast, that was the only word for it, and only dimly lit, with shadows on every side. Wood-panelled walls gleamed dully behind heavy antique furniture, and a scattering of paintings. Erikson didn't recognize any of them, but they had the dull, dark look of age and value. There was even a suit of armour in an alcove, looking like it could do with a good polish. If the rest of the house was on the same scale as the hall, Mirren must rattle around in it like a single pea in a pod. A place this size needed a large family and a flock of servants to fill it. But Mirren lived alone, and always had.

Erikson scowled briefly. He wouldn't have liked to spend a single hour here on his own, day or night. The place was spooky, even for Shadows Fall. There was a strong atmosphere of foreboding, of imminence, of something about to happen. The Sheriff kept wanting to stop and look back over his shoulder. He was beginning to think he should have taken the hint out in the garden, and got the hell out while he still could. The thought disturbed him, and he sniffed angrily. He was the Sheriff of Shadows Fall, and it would take a lot more than a spooky old house to put him off his duty. A hell of a lot more.

The study turned out to be surprisingly cosy. It was a large room, but not imposing, and well-lit. Tightly-packed bookshelves covered three walls, and two overstuffed and very comfortable chairs lay on either side of a crackling open fire. Mirren sank into the nearest chair and gestured for Erikson to take the other. He laid the shotgun across his knees, holding on to it so tightly that his knuckles showed white. He watched impatiently as the Sheriff settled himself. He seemed to want to say something, but wasn't sure where to start, or even if he should.

'Doctor; you asked me to come here,' said Erikson finally. 'Now what is so important I had to leave an ongoing murder investigation just to talk to you? Under normal circumstances, being a member of the town Council gives you certain privileges, but circumstances these days are far from normal. Now, why am I here? Is it connected to the murder inquiry?'

'I'm not sure,' said Mirren, almost apologetically. 'Perhaps.'

'Perhaps isn't good enough.'

'Please, Sheriff, be patient with me. My situation is . . . complicated. Tell me about the murder investigation. How is it going?'

'It isn't. My men and I are running ourselves into the ground trying to find something, anything, that might open up the case, but we've got damn all to show for our efforts. No clues, no motives, no suspects. Just bodies. And as if that wasn't bad enough, Old Father Time has locked himself away in the Gallery of Bone, and won't see anyone. Not a word of explanation, never mind an apology. Just a short written warning, left with that punk girl who lives with him.'

'A warning?' Mirren sat forward in his chair, something like life coming back into his strained features. 'What did it say?'

'*Beware the Wild Childe.* That's all. Does it mean anything to you?'

'No,' said Mirren, sitting back in his chair again. 'I can't say it does.'

He looked older suddenly, as well as exhausted, and Erikson felt a fleeting sympathy for the man. Whatever Mirren's problem was, it had clearly taken a lot out of him. Erikson began to wonder if this might not be a wasted journey after all. Something had happened here, something bad enough to scare ten years off a man who dealt with the dead every day for fun. What could scare a man like that? Erikson decided to keep talking, and see where it led him.

'I've got my people working in the Libraries, and talking to various Powers in the town, trying to track down what this Wild Childe might be, but so far we've turned up nothing. I can't even get two answers the same as to why Old Father Time might have decided to isolate himself from the town. As far as we can tell, it's never happened before.'

Mirren nodded slowly. 'How long has Time been incommunicado?'

'Nearly twelve hours. His automatons are still out and about, though; I'm getting reports of them turning up all over the place. Even had one out at the site of the latest murder, while the body was still warm. You won't have heard about this one yet. Keith January. Psychic Investigator from a series of stories in the late sixties. Never really caught on, and hasn't been reprinted since. He was found dead in his own front room. Put up a pretty good fight from the look of it. The room was a mess. My people are going over it with a fine tooth comb. We'll find something this time. A thread from a piece of clothing, mud from the killer's shoe. Something.'

'Did you know him, Sheriff?'

'Yes. I knew him. Worked with him on a few cases. Pleasant sort. Got a few results I might not have, without his help. I'd have a drink with him, now and then. I was round at his place just a few nights ago, sharing a drink. Talking about this and that. Now he's dead, and I don't seem to be able to do a damn thing about it. All my years of training, all my experience, and I can't even find my friend's murderer.'

'Was there anything . . . unusual, about this murder?'

'Yeah. No sign of a forced entry, which suggests the victim knew his murderer. Also, Jack Fetch was there. Turned up not long after the automaton. Didn't do anything. Just stood there, watching, and scaring the shit out of my people. That was unusual. The scarecrow usually only turns up when there's unpleasantness to be done. The more I think about that, the less I like it. Time's hiding, and Fetch is on the loose. It must mean something . . .'

They sat looking at each other for a while, across the crackling fire. Erikson felt a little embarrassed at having opened up so much in front of Mirren. It wasn't as though they were friends. Just acquaintances. He didn't think Mirren had any friends. He wasn't what you'd call outgoing. But Erikson needed to talk to someone. It was either that, or explode.

'Can I offer you a drink, Sheriff?' said Mirren abruptly. 'I could do with one, and I don't like to drink alone. Bad habit for a doctor to get into.'

'I wouldn't say no to a small glass of something, if you're offering,' said Erikson, careful to keep his voice casual and easy.

Mirren put aside his shotgun, got up and quickly produced two brandy glasses and a decanter from an ornate wooden cabinet. He poured out two generous measures with steady, controlled hands, and brought them back to the fireplace. A log cracked in the fire, and Mirren jumped, just a little. He handed one glass to Erikson, sat down carefully again, and put the shotgun back across his knees, almost absently. He gently swirled the brandy around in the glass to release the bouquet, and then sipped approvingly. Erikson tried his. He didn't know much about brandy, but he knew an expensive one when he tasted it. He had to stop himself from emptying the glass in quick swallows. He didn't want to look unappreciative.

'Tell me about the town,' said Mirren. 'I know; you're waiting for me to get to the point, and wondering if I'm just putting off the moment when I'll have to tell you why you're here. Well, perhaps I am, partly, but please believe me, I have a reason for asking these questions. What is the town's mood, this evening?'

'Scared,' said Erikson flatly. 'Rattled. People are starting to panic. There's never been anything like this in Shadows Fall before. Murders just don't happen here. There are supposed to be forces working in the town to keep us safe from things like that; if we can't depend on them any more, what else might we be vulnerable to? Wait till people find out that Time's locked himself away. It'll really hit the fan, then.

'Some people have already tried to leave the town. They didn't get far. When Time dropped out of sight, barriers came up all around the town. For the moment, no one can get in or out. The Mayor is putting the pressure on me, because the town Council is putting the pressure on her, but then, you'd know all about that, wouldn't you, Doctor? The only useful idea the Council's come up with is to arrest James Hart, presumably on general principles. It's not a bad idea. Unfortunately, Hart has disappeared. Dug himself a hole, climbed down into it, and pulled it in after him. You know what I've been reduced to, Doctor? As soon as I leave here, I'm going down to Suzanne's place, by the river, and have her read the Cards for me. Maybe she can at least point me in the right direction.

'Look, Doctor; I've been very patient, but this is as far as I go. Either you get to the meat of the matter and tell me what the hell I'm doing here, or I'm leaving. And I won't be back.'

Mirren sighed, and took a long drink from his glass. 'Something bad is coming, Sheriff. Something very powerful and quite deadly. Strong enough to raze this town to rubble. I'm not going to tell you how I know; you wouldn't approve. Draw your own conclusions. Just believe me when I say the whole town is under threat. You're going to have to start making decisions about how best to defend the town. Some parts may have to be abandoned, to protect others. And Sheriff; you don't have much time. The clock is running.'

Erikson frowned, but kept his voice scrupulously polite. 'Can you be more specific about the nature of this threat?'

'No, I can't. But the threat is real. You must believe me.'

'And that's what you brought me here to tell me? Something bad is coming? Doctor; I hope to get more than that from Suzanne's bloody Cards!'

'That's not all I brought you here for, Sheriff. I suppose the bottom line is . . . I'm scared. You see, I can't afford to die. Not yet. If I die, the dead are waiting for me. I've done . . . questionable things, in the pursuit of knowledge, and the dead will make me pay. Already things are starting to go wrong. You've read my report on what happened when I tried to raise Oliver Lando's spirit for Mayor Frazier, so that we could ask it questions about who killed it. Something else came in its place. Something old and awful and very powerful. I haven't been able to perform a successful ritual since, but . . . things have started appearing anyway, without my summoning them.

'They haven't been able to break through my protections yet; I've spent a good many years making this home and its grounds secure. I'm not a fool. I knew the dangers. But I'm starting to see things. I look in the mirror and something else looks back at me. Things come and go at the edges of my vision, laughing and whispering. I hear voices at night, and footsteps outside my bedroom door.

They're coming for me, Sheriff. The dead are coming to take me back with them.'

Erikson got to his feet, and Mirren rose uncertainly to his. Erikson looked at him expressionlessly. 'I don't see what I can do to help, Doctor. The dead are out of my jurisdiction.'

'You can take me into protective custody! I want full police protection. There are half a dozen major sorcerers working for or with the Police Department; they could set up a ring of major league defences that would keep anything out. At the very least that should buy me some time to figure out what to do next. There are things I can tell you, Sheriff. I told you about the coming threat; surely you owe me something for that!'

'For a vague feeling that some force you can't name or describe is heading our way? Doctor; my sorcerers and Deputies are all working sixteen-hour days and more on the murder investigation, and I need every one of them. And they need me. I've spent too long here as it is. I can put you in touch with some private protection agencies, but I'll warn you, there's a big demand on their services just at the moment. Now I really must be going.'

He realized he was still holding his glass in his hand, and drained the last of the brandy. It left a trail of warmth behind it as it went down, but it did nothing to touch the bone-deep cold and weariness that was always with him now. In the past, he'd always had the booze to lean on when things got rough, but these days he didn't even have that. He didn't know whether that was a good thing or not. He put the empty glass down on the arm of his chair and looked coldly at Mirren.

'You made your own bed, Doctor, now it's up to you to lie in it. I told you often enough your nasty little hobby would turn around and bite you one of these days. It occurs to me your best bet would be to find yourself an understanding church and ask for Sanctuary. Those kind of people tend to be more forgiving than me. Maybe they can protect you, if you're serious about regretting what

261

you've done. If you're not, then you're on your own, Doctor. Don't bother to show me out. I can find my own way.'

He strode out of the study and down the great hall without once looking back. He'd never liked Mirren, and felt obscurely guilty about not feeling sorry for the man. But if half the rumours he'd heard about Mirren were true, then he deserved every damned thing that was coming his way. He let himself out, and pulled the heavy door shut behind him. The gardens seemed full of restless movement, with shaking branches and loud rustlings. He wasn't sure, but he thought he saw quick, furtive shadows stirring at the edges of the path. Erikson smiled coldly, rested his hand on his belt near his gun, and walked slowly but steadily down the path and out of the front gate.

Something bad is coming . . . I've got news for you, Doc. I think it's already here.

Back in his study, Mirren sat alone before the fire, his shotgun forgotten in his hands. The outsiders would reach the town soon, bringing death and destruction with them, and then that fool of a Sheriff would get what was coming to him. Him, and a lot of other people who thought they were in charge here. The Warriors had promised him that, in return for his work on their behalf. But they'd better get here soon, or their promises of protection wouldn't mean a thing. The Sheriff deserved everything that was going to happen to him, and his precious town. He'd had his chance. If Erikson had agreed to protect him, he would have told him all about his dealings with the outsiders. There might still have been enough time left to set up some kind of defence. But now the town and the Sheriff had abandoned him, and he was all alone, as usual. Had he really done anything that was so bad? All he'd ever wanted was the truth . . . and perhaps a little company. That was why he'd made his deal with the Warriors. They'd offered him access to centuries of accumulated mystic knowledge. How could he have turned that down? Mirren shivered, despite the warmth of the fire. He'd risked so much,

262

including his soul, but if the Warriors of the Cross didn't get here soon, it would all have been for nothing. The dead were coming for him, and they wouldn't take no for an answer.

As a rule, Derek and Clive Manderville didn't tend towards doing much in a hurry. As gravediggers and general handymen, or Cemetery Technicians, as their mother preferred to put it, their work tended to be sporadic and leisurely. When you weren't waiting for a funeral service to finish, or a storm to blow over, there was still plenty of time for the odd philosophical discussion or a crafty drag on a hand-rolled. Neverthless, the brothers Manderville could still act quickly when the need arose, and at present the speed with which they were packing two suitcases would have startled even an observer from the *Guinness Book of Records*. Clothes, toiletries and other essentials were being thrown in the direction of the suitcases with quite astonishing speed and accuracy. In short, Derek and Clive could have packed for the Olympics.

This was not their preferred mode of existence, in or out of work, but the brothers Manderville were more than capable of recognizing a threat to their continued livelihood, especially when it knocked them to the ground, planted a metaphorical knee on their chest and started growling right in their faces. They also had no difficulty in deciding how to meet such a crisis. They were panicking.

Derek and Clive lived with their mother in a pleasant little house overlooking All Souls cemetery. The view wasn't up to much, but at least it meant they didn't have far to go to work in the morning. They had good jobs, excellent health, and a secure if limited future. They were both young, in their early and mid-twenties respectively, and were tall, muscular and handsome in a way that had fluttered several female hearts, and lifted a few skirts into the bargain. Money wasn't exactly flowing in their direction, but they weren't short of the price of a pint either. So basically, all things considered, they should have been happy with their lot. On top of the world, so to speak. Instead, they had left work early, run all the way home, and were presently up in their bedroom packing two suitcases at speed, prior to making a moonlight flit.

Of course, since it was barely mid-afternoon, the moonlight part would have to go by the board. Flight was the important part, and they were all for it, as soon as humanly possible. Unfortunately, the packing wasn't going particularly well. They were supposed to be taking only the barest essentials, but Derek and Clive were having great difficulties agreeing on what they couldn't live without. They'd been packing for almost half an hour now, and still didn't have a lot to show for it. Tempers were growing strained. They'd both started snatching things out of each other's suitcase, and taken to breathing hard through flared nostrils. Clive was wearing his Deep Fix Live Tour T-shirt, and a pair of jeans so filthy they could have walked to the laundry room on their own. Derek, on the other hand, had taken the time to change into his best suit, complete with shirt and tie. He couldn't do up all the buttons on the former, and the latter was half strangling him, but at least he'd made the effort.

'At least I'm not going to make my getaway looking like a tailor's dummy,' said Clive, cuttingly. 'We've buried people who looked more at ease in a suit than you do.'

'If we don't get a move on,' said Derek scathingly, 'Someone will be burying us, with or without a suit, and irregardless of whether we happen to be still breathing at the time.' He paused for a moment, rather pleased with the irregardless. It wasn't a word you got to use often. 'The suit is a disguise, right? Who's going to expect to see me in a suit?'

He put on a pair of dark glasses, to add to the effect. Clive sniffed, unimpressed. 'Great. Now you look like a spy. The whole point of this exercise is to get out of town without being spotted, remember? You go out looking like that, and everyone we know will be coming up to us and asking who's died in the family.'

'If you were dressed up too, they wouldn't be able to recognize us,' said Derek patiently. 'What I thought was, you could dress up in some of Mum's old clothes, and we could pretend to be man and wife.'

Clive looked at him dangerously. 'You're not turning *funny*, are you?'

'All right, all right! It was just an idea!'

They both broke off as their mother came in. Mrs Manderville was wearing a nun's habit and wimple, as usual, and being both rather short and somewhat dumpy, resembled nothing so much as a motherly penguin. She wasn't what you'd call religious, but she'd been dressing as a nun ever since her husband died three years previously. She was carrying a tray with two tall glasses of lemonade on it. The brothers looked at the lemonade, and winced.

'Here you are, dears,' said Mrs Manderville cheerfully. 'I've brought you both a nice cool glass of lemonade.'

'Thanks, Mum,' said Derek and Clive together. They took a glass each and stood there holding them awkwardly.

Mrs Manderville beamed at them both, blinked at the open suitcases on the bed, and then turned and left, happily humming an old Country and Western song. Mrs Manderville liked Country and Western. She was never happier than when singing along with someone else's tale of heartbreak and suffering. Basically, Mrs Manderville lived in a world all her own, where she didn't have to remember her husband was dead, and just visited the real world on occasion to make sure her boys were all right. They'd told her they were leaving several times, but it hadn't taken. She tended not to hear things she didn't want to. A lot of people are like that, but Mrs Manderville had raised it to an art form. Derek and Clive waited until the door had closed behind her, and then put the glasses of lemonade down on the dresser next to the six other glasses she'd already brought them. Once Mrs Manderville got an idea in her head, there was no shifting it. Derek glared at Clive, who glared right back at him. Derek sighed heavily.

'Look; we don't have time to argue. The Warriors are

coming, and our continued good health depends on us being a comfortably far distance away from Shadows Fall when they get here.'

'Are you sure they're coming?'

'Does the Pope crap in the woods? They'll be banging on our door sometime in the next twenty-four hours, and when it happens I for one intend to be out. They think we've been working on their behalf all these months, preparing the way for their invasion of the town. They are in fact presently labouring under the misapprehension that we have been diligently sabotaging the town's defences all this time, in return for the not inconsiderable amounts of money they paid us. In advance, the fools. They are not going to be at all pleased when they get here and find we have in fact done naff all to earn it. They think we are politically committed ideological terrorists. They are not going to be at all impressed by two Cemetery Technicians who still live with their mother. I don't know about you, but I am heading for the nearest horizon.'

'Have you finished?' said Clive, cuttingly. 'Surprisingly enough, I had managed to work most of that out for myself. May I remind you of whose fault it is that the Warriors believe we are such hot stuff? Who told them we had personal contact with Old Father Time, had blackmail material on every member of the town Council, and helped design the town's defences?'

'All right, so I got a bit carried away . . . the point is, we will both be carried away in matching body bags if we don't stop messing about and get the hell out of here. Which means, to get back to the point, we don't have the time to be arguing over non-essential items like these!'

He made a grab at a stack of tape cassettes, but Clive snatched them up first. 'I can't leave these! These are my Benny and the Jets bootleg tapes!'

'Clive, our time and suitcase space is severely limited, not unlike your brain. We have to stick to essentials.'

'You're taking your teddy bear.'

'He's a mascot.'

266

'Pathetic! If you can have your bear, I'm having my tapes.'

'All right! Anything for a quiet and hopefully prolonged life. But no more luxuries!'

They continued their packing in silence, watching each other like hawks. Clive glanced at the glasses of lemonade on the dresser.

'I still say we ought to take Mum with us.'

'She wouldn't go without Dad, and we haven't the time to dig him up. She'll be safe enough. The Warriors aren't going to harm a nun, are they? No; they're going to have much more important things on their mind. Like what to do when Shadows Fall gets its act together and starts kicking the Warriors' ass all over the countryside. I mean; it's not as if they had any chance of winning, is it, the poor bastards?'

'Well, yes,' said Clive. 'There is that.'

They both chuckled unpleasantly, and snapped their suitcases shut.

'Right,' said Derek, trying to sound organized, 'All we have to do now is phone our various employers and explain we won't be in tomorrow. We have in fact come down with something sudden and drastic and highly contagious.'

'With spots,' said Clive. 'Spots are always good for upsetting people.'

'Right. All over?'

'Mostly around the unmentionables. That'll do it.'

Derek felt briefly itchy all over, but rose above it. 'While I'm doing that, you take the cases downstairs and load them into the car. As soon as I'm finished, we'll head straight for the park, and hide out there till it gets dark.'

'Wait just a minute,' said Clive. 'What's this wait in the park till it gets dark bit? You never mentioned that before. I wouldn't spend a night in the park if I was armed with two bazookas and a flame-thrower! In case you've forgotten, the park has this nasty tendency to fill up with dinosaurs the minute it gets dark.'

'Exactly! That's the whole point! No one will think to

look for us there. I mean; would you do it if you didn't have to?'

'I do have to, and I'm still not doing it.'

Derek sighed heavily. 'I think in a previous incarnation your brain must have been used as a doorstop. The thing to remember is that the Warriors are coming, in force, and will be here very soon. Anything that will give us a scrap of advantage has to be a good thing. And it's not really all that dangerous. I mean, given the size of the park, and the size of us, what are the chances of a brontosaurus just happening to stumble over us?'

'Pretty damn good, the way our luck's been going lately.'

They broke off again as Mrs Manderville came in with a tray and two glasses of lemonade. They all nodded and smiled at each other, the boys took their lemonade, and Mrs Manderville left, happily humming something about a train wreck. Clive looked at the glass in his hand.

'It's not as if either of us particularly liked lemonade . . .'

'That doesn't matter,' said Derek firmly.'We're still going to have to empty all these glasses before we go, or Mum'll be upset.'

Clive looked at the dresser. 'If I have to drink five glasses of lemonade, I'm going to be upset. My mouth'll shrivel up permanently.'

'We're not going to drink them, you pratt. We'll pour them down the toilet.'

'Oh, we can't do that,' said Clive. 'You can't just throw away good lemonade. I mean; there are millions starving in China.'

'So what do you want me to do? Pack the lemonade up and send it Air Mail? Go downstairs with those cases and get the car started.'

'All right. Give me the keys, then.'

Derek looked at him. 'I thought you had the keys.'

'No; I haven't got the keys.'

'If you've packed them in that bloody suitcase, I'm going to tie your legs in a square knot. Turn out your pockets.'

Clive scowled unhappily, and emptied out his pockets on to the bed. It took some time. Derek stared at the growing mound of not particularly sanitary objects with the kind of fascination usually reserved for especially unpleasant car accidents. He also decided that if he had to sneeze at any time in the future, he definitely wasn't going to ask if he could borrow Clive's handkerchief. The keys were the last item out, of course. It had been that kind of a day. Clive put it all back into his pockets, apart from a lump of chewing gum he removed from his handkerchief and stuck behind his ear for later.

'Who gets to drive?' he said suddenly.

'I do,' said Derek. 'I'm the eldest.'

'I've got more experience.'

'Yeah, at reversing into things.'

'That was an accident! My foot slipped.'

'Yeah, well, that's why I'm driving. Mine doesn't.'

'You know,' said Clive thoughtfully, 'we still haven't really decided where we're going when we leave here. I still like New York. Or Hollywood. Somewhere glamorous and romantic.'

'You want glamour and romance, you can forget about New York. That's not a city, it's evolution in action. I'd feel safer with the dinosaurs. No; I think we'd better stop by Switzerland first. That's where the Warriors said the bank with our money was.'

'Oh yeah; get the money first. Then Hollywood, and as many groupies as I can get my tongue around.' Clive scowled suddenly. 'You know, I'm starting to feel just a bit guilty about disappearing like this. I mean; there are graves waiting to be dug. We've never let people down before.'

'We've never been faced with imminent bloody death before, either. If Father Callahan's worried about a few graves, he can roll up his sleeves and dig them himself. Bit of hard exercise wouldn't do him any harm. They say he's a secret eater, you know. Munches biscuits while he takes Confession.'

'Oh, I don't like to think of the Father digging graves,' said Clive, just a little shocked. 'That wouldn't be proper . . .'

'I wouldn't worry about it,' said Derek. 'He'll find some other poor mugs to do the digging. Probably hand it out as a penance. Three Hail Marys, and I want six foot of dirt shifted before you go home.'

'Don't let our Mum hear you talking like that, or she'll wash your mouth out with soap again.'

'Take the suitcases down to the car,' said Derek firmly. 'I'll start phoning round.'

'Are you going to ring Sadie, and tell her goodbye?'

'Don't see why I should. She's your girlfriend.'

'No, she isn't,' said Clive. 'I thought she was your girlfriend.'

They looked at each other. 'No,' said Derek. 'She's not my girlfriend.'

'Well, that's all right then. We don't have to ring her. I never did know what you saw in her . . .'

Father Ignatius Callahan stared glumly at the empty candy jar. There should have been enough chocolate and vanilla fudge in that jar to last till the end of the week, and here it was empty and only Thursday. He used to have more will power than this. He sighed wistfully, and turned the jar upside down to empty out the few remaining crumbs on to his palm. Chocolate flared briefly on his tongue and then was gone, like the fading memory of a kiss. He arched an eyebrow as the simile crossed his mind, and then he looked down at his prominent stomach and sighed again. Apart from his stomach he was in pretty good shape. In fact, for a man only a few months short of forty, he was in damn good shape. He exercised every day, jogging in the mornings and walks in the evenings, but still his taste for candy betrayed him. There was a time he could eat practically anything and burn off the calories through sheer nervous energy, but a man slows down as the years accumulate, and these days he only had to sniff at a cookie for his waistline to expand another inch. He'd cut down a lot, since his waistline hit forty before he did, but he still allowed himself a little chocolate and vanilla fudge now and again. As a special treat. A quarter pound of each, per week. No more. But here it was Thursday afternoon, and already the jar was empty.

And Lent was coming up soon.

He scowled determinedly. He could beat this. He'd done it before; he could do it again. Less food, more exercise, and a damned sight more will power. He wasn't going to sit around stuffing his face and slumping into fat, like his father had. Callahan felt a familiar urge to look around and see if his father was watching him, and aware of his disrespectful thoughts. He fought down the impulse sternly. His father had been dead of a heart attack almost twenty years now. He didn't have to fear the man's spite and vindictiveness, his sudden angers and flying fists. He was free. He was safe. He didn't have to be scared any more.

Callahan's scowl deepened as the old hatred burned in him again, the helpless rage of the defenceless child against a vast and overpowering parent. Vile man, evil man. Callahan smiled shakily at how easily just the thought of his father could still disturb him, even after all these years. He concentrated, and deliberately put aside the anger, denying it power over him. He was a man of God now, a man of peace, and there should be no room left in him for hate. That was from another time, another life, and if he couldn't find it in himself to forget or forgive, he could still pray for the strength to live his own life, free from his father's ghost. He smiled sadly at the familiar thought, and shook his head. How far we come from what we were, and how far we always are from what we would be. There was a sermon in that, somewhere. He looked about him for pen and paper, and then the front door bell rang, and he lost track of the thought. It didn't matter. It would come again, if it was worth anything. He got to his feet, carefully put the lid back on the candy jar, and went to see who had come looking for him. He wasn't expecting anyone.

He opened his front door and found himself face to face with a man wearing gleaming black body armour, set off with brave flashes of red and blue, and topped with a long dark cape. The man was tall and blockily muscular, with the body of a young and active man, but his hair was grey shot with silver, and his face was heavily lined. Lester Gold, the Man of Action, the Mystery Avenger, grinned at the surprise on Callahan's face.

'Hello, Nate. Sorry to drop by unannounced, but something's come up. I need to talk to you.'

'Of course,' Callahan said quickly. 'You're always welcome here, you know that. Come on in. You're looking . . . good.'

Gold seemed even larger and more imposing as he stepped into the cramped hallway. Callahan shut the door, and then belatedly shook the hand Gold put out to him. It was a large hand, flecked with liver spots. An old man's hand, but the grip was firm and strong. Callahan frowned slightly as he led the way down the hall and back to his study. Gold was looking good. There was a bounce in his step and a gleam in his eyes that Callahan hadn't seen in a long time. But then, he hadn't seen Gold in costume for nearly three years now. It had been his understanding that the Mystery Avenger had retired. Something must have happened. Something really important, to have changed Gold's mind. Callahan felt the first faint stirrings of unease, but he clamped down on them hard as he waved Gold through into his study. For a moment they busied themselves settling comfortably into the two chairs by the fire, and then Gold leaned forward and fixed Callahan with a steady, disquieting gaze.

'Strange things have been happening in the town,' he said flatly. 'Strange even for Shadows Fall. Disturbing things.'

And then he broke off, as though uncertain where to start, or how much it was safe to reveal. Callahan waited patiently. The Mystery Avenger's costume was even more impressive at close quarters, almost overpowering, but the face was that of a man with doubts, troubled by dilemmas of the soul. Finally Gold sighed and leaned back, his powerful hands resting uneasily on the arms of the chair, as if they felt there was some important business they ought really to be about.

'How long have we known each other, Nate?'

Callahan smiled. 'Must be almost twelve years now. Most of it seemed to make some sort of sense at the time. Yes; almost twelve years since I came knocking nervously at your door with a copy of your very first magazine in my hand, for you to autograph. You were very gracious, and when you showed me your private collection of memorabilia, I thought I'd died early and gone to heaven.'

Gold laughed. 'You don't know how thrown I was. I'd never had a priest as a fan before. How's your collection going these days?'

'Pretty good. There's still a few items I haven't been able to get my hands on, but I'm keeping my eyes open. It's the price that puts me off, these days. You wouldn't believe what some of the rarer comics are going for. But you didn't come here to talk about that. What's the problem, Lester? How can I help you?'

Gold leaned forward in his chair again, as though bracing himself, and his eyes were suddenly very cold.

'Nate; what can you tell me about the Warriors of the Cross?'

Callahan raised an eyebrow. 'Now there's a name I didn't expect. What do you want to know about them?'

'Everything. Who they are, or were. Their purpose, their reason for existence. The name has been cropping up in prophecies and warnings just recently, all across the town, but no one seems to know anything about them. I was headed for the Library, but I'm hoping you can save me a journey.'

'Do you see them as a threat to Shadows Fall?'

'I don't know. Maybe.'

'I really don't see how. They're a fringe group of extreme fanatics who believe in the imposition of their particular brand of Christianity through brute force. Militant hard-liners to some, Christian terrorists to others. They preach revolution and hellfire, and fund all kinds of right-wing governments across the world. Heavily into faith healing and fund raising. They've even got their own satellite broadcasting system. They've been investigated several times on charges of brainwashing and programming their converts, but nothing's ever been proved. They've been hailed by some as Christianity's last chance for survival in an increasingly secular world. But why their name should suddenly be appearing in prophecies concerning Shadows Fall is beyond me.'

'The prophecies see the Warriors as some kind of threat. One seer even used the word *invasion*.'

'No,' said Callahan firmly. 'I can't believe it. If anything like that was in the wind, I would have heard something by now. I promise you, Lester, we're in no danger. It's much more likely we're all feeling the strain of the recent murders. Helpless, frightened people will grab at any gossip or rumour if it seems to promise an answer. We mustn't allow ourselves to be caught up in the hysteria; it's important that people like us keep our heads. People look up to us. But you already knew that. You didn't come here for a briefing on the Warriors of the Cross. Something's worrying you, isn't it? Something . . . spiritual.'

'Yes,' said Gold, in a voice so quiet Callahan could barely hear it. The big man's hands had closed into fists, and he looked at the floor rather than meet the priest's eyes. 'I've been to the land beneath the hill, and spoken with the Faerie. I've seen . . . strange things. Disturbing things.'

Callahan nodded slowly. 'You shouldn't have gone there, Lester. It's no place for a Christian. The land beneath the hill is an evil place, steeped in sin and wickedness. No good can come of it, or the creatures that live there.'

'They're supposed to be immortal. They were very beautiful, but so cruel . . . civilized, but still savage.'

'They're full of contradictions.' Callahan struggled to keep his voice calm and even. Gold had come to him for comfort, not a stern lecture. 'Lying is a part of their nature. They know nothing of faith or certainty. They are immortal because they have no souls, so when they die they are denied Heaven or Hell. They have rejected God and cursed his teachings. They're demons, Lester; everything you saw or thought you saw was nothing more than glamour; sorcerous illusions designed to hide their true hideousness. In reality they are vile and awful creatures, ugly beyond belief, living in a squalid hell of their own making. Their gold is false, their food is poison, their word is worthless. They exist only to tempt Man away from his faith and his duty.'

'You really don't like them, do you?' said Gold, and Callahan had to smile.

'Sorry; I was getting a bit worked up, wasn't I? Trust me, Lester; the Faerie are evil, and nothing good can come of them. How did you come to meet them?'

'Sean Morrison . . .'

'Sean? Say no more; if ever a soul was born to trouble, he was. He has a fine singing voice, and entirely too much charm, but there's no room in him anywhere for the holy word. He's a Pagan, damned by his own arrogance and folly. You've fallen in with bad company, Lester. These are troubled times; we must cling to what we know to be true.'

'I'm not sure what I believe in any more,' said Gold. 'It's hard to have faith in Heaven and Hell when you live in a town where the dead come back to life as often as not.'

'Well, not quite that often,' said Callahan. 'But I do know what you mean. I reburied Lucas DeFrenz earlier today.'

'Was he really an angel, do you think?'

'No; just a poor deluded soul, driven mad by his passing. He's at peace now, in the arms of the Lord.'

They sat in silence for a while. Gold still looked worried, disturbed on some deep, fundamental level. Callahan wished there was something else he could say to ease his friend's anxiety. Obviously there was something else on Gold's mind. The old hero looked up suddenly, as though he'd just made a decision. He met the priest's eyes squarely.

'Let me throw another name at you, Nate; see if you recognize it.'

'By all means.'

'Wild Childe.'

Callahan waited a moment to see if there was anything more, and then leant back in his chair and pursed his lips thoughtfully. 'I can't say it rings any bells. In what context did you hear the name?'

'From the Faerie. Sean asked them who was responsible for the murders in Shadows Fall, and they said the Wild Childe.'

'You can't trust the elves, Lester. The delight in deceit and trickery. Anything you get from them cannot be trusted.'

Gold nodded slowly, but he didn't look convinced one way or the other. Callahan decided it was time to change the subject.

'Let me try a name on you now, Lester. What can you tell me about James Hart?'

'I thought we might get around to him. It seems like his name is on everybody's lips just now. I was talking with the town Council earlier; they're going crazy over Hart. Apparently he's disappeared. Dropped out of sight a few hours ago; so completely that neither the Sheriff's people nor the Council's pet sorcerers can find any trace of him. Lots of people claim to have met him, talked with him, but it's hard to find two accounts that agree. Have you met him?'

'No. He worries me. I can't believe it's just coincidence that so many bad things started happening at exactly the same time he returned. I've heard some of the stories they tell about him. They say he cured a sick woman of her illness, and Jack Fetch knelt to him. One of the St Laurence mystics said he was an avatar of change, an agent of possibilities. I went to the Library and looked up the original prophecy. It's surprisingly straightforward and unambiguous. James Hart will bring about the end of Shadows Fall. No ifs or buts or maybes.

'I'm sorry, Lester. You came here for help and comfort, and I can't even offer a little hope. Just remember what I said. The Faerie cannot be trusted, and you can forget about an invasion by Christian terrorists. Stick with what matters; the murders. Great things are happening all around us, Lester. All we can do is cling to the things we understand. And just maybe things aren't as bad as they seem. Who knows; maybe Shadows Fall has to be destroyed, so that something greater can take its place.'

'Thanks a lot, Nate. Very reassuring.'

They both chuckled quietly, and then Gold got to his feet, and Callahan got up and escorted him out of the study and back down the hall to the front door. Gold paused there a moment, as though searching for some last thing to say, something brave and meaningful, but in the end he just smiled and shook Callahan's hand, and left. The priest watched him walk slowly back to his car, and pursed his lips thoughtfully as he closed the door. Things were coming to a head sooner than he'd expected. He walked back down the hall and into his study, and sat down at his writing desk. This was where he sat and marshalled his thoughts when he wrote his sermons, and he always preferred to sit there when he had anything important to decide.

He pulled open the bottom drawer of the desk and pulled out a pure white telephone. It looked perfectly ordinary, but it wasn't connected to the town system in any way, and he'd been assured by those with reason to know what they were talking about that there was no way it could be listened in on by any outside agency, magical or technological. Callahan still hesitated to use it. This was Shadows

Fall, after all. He sighed quietly, and picked up the receiver. There was no dialling tone, just a quiet hum, and then a voice said his name.

'Yes, it's me,' said Callahan, and immediately felt foolish. Of course it was him; no one else could hear anything on this phone but him. That was the way it had been designed. 'You must warn your superiors; things are getting out of hand here. If you don't begin the invasion soon, you'll lose all advantage of surprise. Your name is turning up on oracles' lips all over Shadows Fall. They don't know what it means yet, but it won't take them long to find out. On top of that, there are too many unknown factors confusing the issue. First the murders, then James Hart's return. Now he's disappeared, and the Faerie are threatening to involve themselves in the town's business.'

'Is there any chance of your role being discovered?' said the voice at the other end. It didn't sound particularly concerned.

'I don't know. I took a lot of risks smuggling your man in, and even more arranging the holes in the town's defences, so you could send in that helicopter to pick him up. You should have told me he was an assassin!'

'You didn't need to know. Keep your head down and you should be safe enough. Say again about the Faerie. Are they involved in the town's defences?'

'I don't know. They might be, in the future.'

'That must be discouraged. Such demons are powerful and unpredictable. We will eradicate them in good time, but the timing is unfortunate.'

'They are creatures of the night,' said Callahan dismissively. 'They cannot stand against the Warriors of the Lord.'

'Of course not. But they could do great damage to our forces during the invasion. We haven't come this far to risk losing the object of our assault. Do what you can to prevent the town turning to the Faerie for help. It won't be long now. We will be coming soon, and then every demon and hellspawn will fall before us. We are the

Warriors of the Cross; God's chosen warriors, and none can stand against us.'

Sean Morrison dived head first into the plastic snowscene, and the shock of the sudden bitter cold knocked the breath right out of him. Snow and ice whirled around him as he tumbled through the air. Light from somewhere in the night showed him the snow-covered ground far below. He managed a short, shuddering breath and the cold stabbed through him again as freezing air filled his lungs. Morrison gritted his teeth and concentrated on turning his fall into a controlled dive. The ground still looked a long way away, but he'd done this before so he could do it again. From what he remembered of the last time he'd done it, the landing was going to be hard and painful, but in the end still the kind you could walk away from. Which was all that mattered.

Old Father Time really didn't care for uninvited visitors. He had even less subtle ways of discouraging people who weren't warned off by the long drop, but Morrison wasn't worried. Well, not much. He frowned suddenly as he realized the air was growing thicker and more buoyant around him, slowing his fall. At first he thought that Time had relented, and decided to make things easier for him, but it only took him a few moments to realize that not only had he stopped falling, he was practically hovering in mid-air, buffeted on all sides by the storm. He glared into the swirling snow and pulled himself down through the storm, swimming through the freezing air with more purpose than grace. The ground began to rise again with increasing speed. Morrison had learned a few things from the Faerie over the years, mostly to do with will power and determination. And just a little magic. The blizzard parted suddenly before him, and the ground rushed up to hit him in the face.

The thickness of the packed snow cushioned his landing, but even so it was a good minute or two before he felt strong enough to climb out of the hole he'd made. He hugged himself tightly, trying to hold in some warmth in the face of the storm, and looked about him. Not all that far away, All Hallows Hall called to him like a beacon. It couldn't hide from him, no matter what Time did. In the Gallery of Frost, the Forever Door called to him as it called to all those who should have passed through it, but hadn't. He headed for the Hall like a horse returning to its stable, and part of him wondered at how strongly he responded to the call, as though part of him, deep down, wanted to go through the Door and find peace. He smiled mirthlessly. There'd be time for peace later. Right now, he had things to do.

The storm's fury increased, but it couldn't stop him. He'd come a long way to talk to Old Father Time, and he had a few pointed and rather urgent questions to put to him. Like, for example, why someone with Time's power and resources still hadn't been able to locate or identify the murderer who'd been terrorizing Shadows Fall. And why he hadn't warned the town about the coming of the Wild Childe. Whatever that was. And most of all, when was Time going to get off his ancient arse and do something? Morrison wanted to make it very plain that he and others in the town weren't going to just sit back and wait patiently for Time to get his finger out. They had a few plans of their own to protect the town. Like unleashing the Faerie. Morrison grinned. That ought to light a fire under Time. Whatever happened, he was going to get some answers. Morrison was a firm believer in the virtues of personal confrontation. It was a lot harder for people to ignore you when you had your face pushed right into theirs.

All Hallows Hall loomed up out of the snow before him, huge and dark and not at all welcoming. The intensity of the storm increased again, as though making one last attempt to keep him away, but he just hunched his head down and trudged on through the snow, step by step. The wind howled, hitting him first from one side and then the other, and the bitter cold sank remorselessly into his bones, leeching his strength. But still the inner voice spoke within him, calling him on, and it didn't take him long to find the single unmarked door. He kicked it open, and a bright golden light spilled out into the storm.

He stumbled inside, put his shoulder to the door and slammed it shut against the pressure of the wind. The roar of the storm fell away to a murmur, and warmth seeped slowly into his body. He stood with his back pressed against the door, staring at nothing as his laboured breathing slowly returned to normal. He grimaced as returning circulation drove pins and needles into his fingers, and then set about beating the accumulated snow from his clothes. There seemed to be rather a lot of it. Time really didn't want visitors. He decided that if he ever had to do this again, next time he'd remember to choose a heavier coat first. He sniffed, and looked about him. The huge medieval Hall stretched away into the distance, shadows clustering about the sparsely-placed gas lamps. High above him, something stirred briefly in the rafters, and then was still again. The Hall hadn't impressed Morrison the last time he'd been here, and it didn't this time either. Mostly it looked like it could use some modern lighting and a good clean.

'Put the kettle on, Time! You've got a visitor!'

Morrison waited as his voice echoed loudly on the quiet, but there was no response. He'd have been surprised if there was. Time had already made it clear through the snowstorm that he wasn't at all welcome. He set off down the Hall, stamping hard to loosen the last of the snow from his shoes, and to beat some feeling back into his frozen feet. The call of the Forever Door was louder and clearer now, but he tried not to listen to it any more than he had to. He hadn't come here for that. He had too many things to do. There'd be time for the Door later. Much later.

He had to keep thinking that. It was the only way to stay sane.

By the time he reached the Gallery of Bone, his hands and his feet felt as though they belonged to him again. He strode past the portraits on the walls without even glancing at them, ignoring the moving images and the sudden bursts of sound. He didn't have time to be distracted. Which was why the arm that shot out of the portrait on his left caught him so completely by surprise. He lurched to a halt as the clawed hand closed on his collar and then shook him effortlessly like a dog shakes a rat. Morrison tried to grab at the hand, but couldn't reach that far behind him. The hand spun him round, and Morrison found himself staring into the portrait of a huge hulking beast with wide staring eyes and a crimson maw studded with jagged teeth. Great muscles bulged in the arm as the beast dragged Morrison kicking and struggling towards it, and saliva spilled smoking from its mouth. Morrison stopped struggling and stepped forward, to gain himself a little slack, and then kicked the beast squarely between the thighs. If he'd been kicking a football, it would have travelled the full length of the field. As it was, the beast's eyes bulged and then squeezed shut, and the hand let go of his collar. He stumbled backwards away from the portrait, and tensed, waiting for the beast to come after him again, but nothing emerged, and after a moment he relaxed a little and set off down the corridor again.

Morrison scowled as he pulled his coat back into a more comfortable position. Things like that weren't supposed to happen.

In fact, it was supposed to be impossible for anyone or anything to travel through the portraits except Time's automatons. If Time was losing control of the Gallery, things were even more worrying than he'd thought. In many ways, Old Father Time was the glue that held Shadows Fall together, that made its many overlapping realities possible. What the hell was happening, that Time himself could be affected? Morrison increased his pace a little, carefully keeping to the middle of the corridor, just in case some other portrait's occupant was feeling frisky. He tried not to look at them as he passed, but almost in spite of himself he kept catching glimpses of scenes full of sound and fury, with wild faces and sometimes the flicker

282

of flames. Time's attention was elsewhere, and the town knew it. Morrison was so preoccupied with the portraits that he didn't hear the steady footprints coming up behind him until they were almost upon him.

Some instinct warned him at the last moment, and he stopped and spun round to find himself almost face to face with a towering metal automaton. It loomed up before him like a clockwork giant, its gleaming brass and silver parts tick-tocking quietly as wheels revolved and armatures swung. Metal arms shot out to grab Morrison, but he evaded them easily. He danced around the metal figure, blushing with anger at how close he had come to being caught again. Time wasn't going to stop him that easily.

He darted in and out, slapping and pushing the automaton while staying always out of reach, just to prove it couldn't touch him. The thing was fast enough and strong enough to catch any normal man, but Morrison had lived in the land beneath the hill. Finally he ran out of patience, tripped the automaton and sent it crashing to the floor. He left it thrashing on its back like an overturned turtle and hurried on down the corridor. He'd have to be on his toes from now on. He had no friends in the Gallery of Bone.

He jogged along the corridor, conserving his strength, dodging into nooks and crannies and the occasional cul-de-sac to avoid more automatons as they appeared silently out of portraits on the walls. Presumably Time was too busy with whatever was filling his time these days to turn his full attention on who was running loose in his Gallery, but there was no telling how long that would last. He ran on, evading automatons where he could and dancing his way past those he couldn't. Screams and howls echoed from the portraits, and chilling sounds of violence and rage. But finally he came to Time's private sanctum, and stopped outside the door for a moment to get his breath back. He didn't want Time to think he was in any way rattled. Morrison took a deep breath, kicked the door open and strode in like he owned the place. First impressions are always important.

Unfortunately, he'd wasted that impression on an empty room. He scowled, and glared about him. The place looked much the same as the last time he'd seen it; a riot of psychedelic lights and colours, like a Rorschach blot of the sixties. Patterns of light seethed and bubbled on the walls, and the air was thick with incense. Throw cushions lay scattered across the floor, and a huge Indian hookah stood nonchalantly in a corner. There were flowers and peace signs everywhere, and the gentle strumming of guitars murmured from hidden speakers. It felt rather like he was having a flashback. In a way, it was almost like coming home again . . . but Morrison stepped on that thought hard. He couldn't afford to give Time any openings. Besides; such thoughts were dangerous. They led to the Forever Door.

'What the hell are you doing here?'

Morrison smiled genuinely as the harsh voice erupted behind him. He turned unhurriedly and nodded amiably to the young punkette in the black leather and chains standing in an opposite door that hadn't been there a moment ago.

'Dear Mad; don't ever change. It's part of your charm.'

'Cut the crap, Morrison,' said Madeleine Kresh as she advanced on him, scowling. 'You're not supposed to be here. No one's supposed to be here. Time isn't seeing anyone.'

'He'll see me,' said Morrison easily. 'I have something important to discuss with him.'

'Look, dickless, Time has shut himself away and locked the door. He won't even see me. So you can turn around and strut right out of here. Whatever Time's up to, he doesn't mean to be disturbed.'

'Did I mention you're looking particularly revolting today?'

'Flattery will get you nowhere.'

'Come on, Mad; something's wrong and you know it. Time's never locked himself away before when there were genuine emergencies to be dealt with. You're closer to him than anyone. Have you noticed anything . . . unusual about his behaviour just recently?'

Mad scowled unhappily, her black and white patterned face seeming briefly young and vulnerable. 'Hard to tell with Time, but . . . yeah. Spends all day walking up and down the Gallery, staring at the portraits. Since he can see them all perfectly well from here anyway, it beats the hell out of me what he thinks he's doing. Or what he's looking for. He's called in all his automatons; I don't think there's one left anywhere in the town. And he's stopped talking to me. Usually he's always going on and on about his work and what valuable lessons there are to be learned from observing him, and it's all I can do to get him to shut up. But he's changed. Ever since James Hart came to see him, he's been . . . distracted.'

'You've met James Hart?' Morrison looked at her with new interest. 'What's he like?'

'Surprisingly average. The way Time talked about him, I thought he'd have two heads and be carrying a personal thermonuclear device under his arm. As it was, I thought he was a bit of wimp. Until Jack Fetch knelt and bowed to him.'

'You actually saw that? I couldn't believe it when I heard.'

'I was there, and I have trouble believing it. Scared the shit out of me at the time. I mean, if you can't rely on Jack Fetch to be consistent, who can you trust? I suppose I should have known that if Fetch had gone crazy, Old Father Time couldn't be far behind. I can't get you in to see him, Sean. He won't even talk to me. After everything I've done for him . . . the ungrateful bastard. He could trust me. He could trust me with anything. Something's wrong. Something apart from all the crazy things that have been happening in the town just recently. I could be wrong, but . . . I think Time's scared.'

'Scared? He's immortal, unkillable, all-knowing and supposedly all-powerful. What the hell could there be that could scare him?'

'I don't know. Don't think I want to know. I just wish this was all over, and we could get back to what passes for normality around here. In the meantime, you can bog off and stop bothering me or I'll carve my initials in your forehead.'

'How can you say that, Mad, after everything we've meant to each other?'

'We have never meant anything to each other. I have about as much feeling for you as I have for what I scrape off my boots in the morning. Now, you are not going to see Time, so you might as well leave, while your body is still reasonably intact and functioning.'

Morrison had a strong feeling that charm was largely wasted on Mad, but he persevered anyway. It wasn't as if he had anything else to do. He smiled winningly at her, and then both of them looked round sharply as they heard footsteps approaching from out in the corridor. A dozen of Time's automatons filed into the inner sanctum, one after the other, in perfect step. They fanned out to block off the door, and Morrison backed slowly away from them, glancing warily from one clockwork figure to another. Their blank painted faces showed no trace of emotion, but there was a cold, casual menace in their deliberate, unhurried movements that chilled Morrison's blood.

'It's all right,' said Mad. 'He's just leaving. Back off, and he'll go. Right, Morrison?'

'I'm definitely considering it.'

'You're not helping, Morrison.' She looked warily from one automaton to another, but none of them seemed to be paying her any attention. 'I said, I'm handling this. Now bog off back to wherever you came from, and let me get on with it. Right?'

'I don't think they're listening to you,' said Morrison. 'I think they're here to make sure I leave. Unfortunately for them, I'm not ready to go yet.'

His guitar was suddenly in his hands, as though it had always been there. He strummed a few chords, grinned unpleasantly at the automatons, and launched into one of his old songs. One of the songs he used to sing in the sixties, before he came to Shadows Fall, when his voice and music had been known across the world. He hadn't sung it for years. It reminded him too much of when he'd been real. But he sang it now, and his voice filled the chamber.

All the old power was there, roaring in his song and in his voice, a force and energy that would not be denied. It was a kind of magic; the all-encompassing, overwhelming rush that can fill a concert hall and bring the audience surging to its feet, when the band is in the groove and you can feel the beat of the music pulsing in your veins. The song washed over the automatons and drove them back, their unliving forms unable to comprehend or deal with the wild emotions that were howling around them.

They fell back, one by one, step by step, until their backs were pressed against the walls and there was nowhere left to go. Except back through the door. They filed out, backwards, their painted faces unable to reflect the power that was driving them from the sanctum, the power in that music, and in that voice. And then the last of them was gone, and the door shut behind them, and the song broke off, its unfinished chorus still ringing on the air. Mad looked at Morrison with something very like respect.

'Not bad,' she said finally, trying desperately to sound nonchalant. 'Bit before my time, but not too shabby. Know any Stranglers?'

'Don't blaspheme,' said Morrison. He looked down at his guitar and grinned cheerfully. 'Good to know I can still light a fire when I have to.'

And then he broke off and looked back at the door, and Mad looked too. There was the sound of rustling cloth and the brushing of twigs on the floor, and Jack Fetch strode into the sanctum, a fixed smile carved on his turnip face, and only holes where his eyes should have been. The scarecrow Jack Fetch, come to do what the automatons could not. He stopped just inside the doorway, his empty gaze fixed on Morrison.

'Oh shit,' said Mad. Her flick knife was quickly in her

hand, the long blade snapping out with brisk efficiency. She glared at the scarecrow, remembering the last time she'd tried to use the knife on him, and looked uncertainly at Morrison. 'Sean; maybe you could come back some other day.'

'No,' said Morrison. 'No, I don't think so.'

'Sean, don't fuck about. Jack Fetch is a mile and a half of bad news. You haven't seen what he can do. He's dangerous, he's vicious, and Time isn't here to restrain him.'

'Maybe he's come to bow to me.'

'I wouldn't put money on it. Sean; get the hell out of here. Please.'

The scarecrow was suddenly moving again, heading for Morrison with new purpose. Morrison strummed his guitar and raised his voice again. Emotion filled the room; warm and fine, like a hot drink on a cold day. Mad swayed unconsciously, caught up in the flow. Life and love and all it meant cascaded over Jack Fetch, but it didn't stop him. The music crashed against the walls, and Morrison's voice rose and fell like the ocean at high tide, powerful and unstoppable, and still the scarecrow advanced on him. A gloved hand shot out and plucked the guitar from Morrison's hands. Jack Fetch looked at it for a moment, as though unsure what it was, and then he ripped the guitar apart as though it was made of paper. The unfinished song still echoed on the air as the broken pieces fell to the floor, and Morrison licked his dry lips. He fixed the scarecrow with a glare that held all his old arrogance, and sang again, unaccompanied. His voice filled the room like an unstoppable presence, resonant with all the old power that had stunned his audiences and left them gasping. And then Jack Fetch was upon him, cold and implacable. A gloved hand shot out and grasped Morrison's shirt front, pulling him close. Morrison stopped singing, and in one last defiant gesture, grabbed the turnip head with both hands and kissed it square on the carved lips.

'All right; that's enough of that.'

Jack Fetch released Morrison immediately, in response

to the tired, flat voice, then stepped back and stood still, his arms at his sides, waiting for new orders. Morrison took a long shuddering breath as relief flooded through him, and then turned to look at the figure who had appeared in the opposite doorway. Old Father Time looked back at him with a mixture of affection and exasperation. He was dressed in a long flowing kaftan, complete with sandals, beads and a headband. His grey hair fell to his shoulders, and his long beard had been neatly braided. He looked like an archetypal sixties guru, a sort of low market Gandalf. Which was how Morrison always saw him. Except this time he looked older, frailer, as though his years were catching up with him. Morrison was shocked at the extent of the change, and a quick glance at Mad revealed she was too.

'Most people can take a hint,' Time said sternly. 'I can't stop to talk to you, Sean. Something bad is coming, and I must prepare to meet it. I know about the murders, and the Wild Childe. They'll have to wait. I'm not sure I could do anything about them anyway. There are forces in the universe that will not be denied. I'm sorry, Sean. Go home. There's nothing you can do here, and I'm doing everything I can. And yes, I know about the Faerie too. I don't think you really understand what you've let loose there. But you will. Goodbye, Sean. If we both survive what's coming, we can talk then.'

And then he was gone, disappearing with the abrupt finality of a burst soap bubble. Jack Fetch turned silently and left the sanctum. Morrison and Mad looked at each other.

'I think he means it,' said Mad.

'I think you might be right.' Morrison knelt down and gathered up the remains of his guitar. It was clearly shattered beyond mending, and he nursed it for a moment like a dead child. He finally shook his head, and the guitar vanished. He rose to his feet, looked at Mad, and shrugged. 'It seems my journey was a waste of time. He already knew everything I was coming to tell him. His answers weren't exactly comforting, but then that's Time for you. I suppose I could hang around and clutter up his sanctum, just to annoy him, but I don't really see the point. He's obviously said all he's going to, and I can't just hang around doing nothing. Unless you'd like me to stay and keep you company, Mad.'

She smiled sweetly. 'That'll be the day.'

Morrison laughed briefly, blew her a kiss, and started towards the door. Mad watched until he was almost gone, and then cleared her throat. He stopped and looked back. Mad looked at him thoughtfully.

'Your name wasn't always Sean, was it?'

'No,' said Morrison, 'It wasn't.' He grinned at her, turned, and left the sanctum. A little of his voice lingered on the air behind him, like the echo of a softly-whispered name.

One moment James Hart was walking down the street, with his shadow Friend darting back and forth around his feet like an over-eager puppy, and the next he was at the beach. He stopped and blinked a few times, to give the world a chance to go back to what it should be, but the scene remained obstinately the same. He was standing on a pebbled beach that stretched away to the left and to the right for as far as he could see. Before him, the ocean lay spread out beneath the midday sun like a smooth grey blanket. There were no waves, no wind to disturb the surface of the sea, only the gentle swelling of the tide, sweeping in and out with slow, languorous tranquillity. The air was sharp, and just a little on the cool side, suggesting the end of Summer. High above, a gull hung on the sky like a drifting shadow, calling out its plaintive cry. Hart thought it was the saddest sound he'd ever heard. He frowned slightly. There was something almost familiar about that thought, as though it was something he'd thought before.

His frown deepened. He didn't recognize the beach at all, but he had a strong feeling he knew it from somewhere.

That he'd been here before in the time that was lost to him; the first ten years of his childhood. Maybe his parents had brought him here, on some Summer vacation. The beach seemed more familiar the more he looked at it. He walked slowly along the beach, pebbles sliding and crunching under his feet. It occurred to him that he was taking it all surprisingly calmly, but that was Shadows Fall for you. After a while, it was hard to be startled by anything. He came across a rock pool, lying just out of reach of the advancing tide, and he knelt down beside it, nudged again by *déjà vu*. A bright orange starfish was lying at the bottom of the pool, pretending to be dead. A crab that had to be all of an inch in width waved its claws threateningly, poised to run at any sudden movement.

'I've been here before,' Hart said quietly.

'Of course you have,' said Friend briskly, running up Hart's back to peer over his shoulder at the pool. 'Your parents used to bring us here every Summer. You used to sit there at the edge of the water and throw pebbles out into the sea. I never could see the point in that. I mean, it's not as if the ocean was difficult to hit . . .'

'What's this place called?' said Hart, picking up a pebble and hefting it thoughtfully.

'Now there you've got me. I never was very good at names, and it was a long time ago.'

'All right, try this one on for size. What the hell are we doing here?'

'I summoned you,' said a slow, familiar voice. 'There are things that must be said. Things that must be discussed. And, though I hate to say it, we're running out of time.'

Hart looked sharply back the way he'd come, and reclining in a deckchair that hadn't been there a few moments before was Old Father Time. He was dressed in the same Victorian outfit as previously, but his socks and shoes were lying neatly piled to one side, and his trousers were pulled up to the knee, as though he intended to go paddling at some point. He looked older and very tired, but he still had a smile for Hart.

'I see you've found your Friend. I was hoping you would. You were inseparable as children.' He looked unhurriedly about him, taking in the scene with quiet pride, as though he'd personally arranged it. 'I always liked this beach. I would have liked to come here with you and your parents, but it wasn't possible. Sometimes I'd come here on my own, after you and your family had left, so I could feel near you. Take off your shoes, James. Pebbled beaches are best enjoyed in bare feet.' He stirred the pebbles with his toes, and smiled again.

'Hold on a minute,' said Hart. 'Run that by me again. You know about Friend?'

'Of course. I know about everything. It's my job.'

'Then perhaps you'd be so kind as to tell me why I've been brought here.'

Time raised an eyebrow. 'Do I detect a note of anger in your voice, James? If this is a bad time, I do apologize, but we must talk. Events are coming to a head despite all my best efforts, and you must be prepared to meet them. There are things I need to tell you; important things that I couldn't mention the last time we met.'

'Why not?'

'Too many ears.' Time gestured, and a second deckchair appeared beside him. 'Take a seat. You're going to need to be sitting down for some of the things I have to tell you.'

Hart studied the deckchair dubiously, and then sank cautiously down into it. Contrary to his expectations, it didn't immediately collapse under him. In fact, it was surprisingly comfortable. *Only in Shadows Fall*, he thought wryly. He looked across at Old Father Time, who was staring out to sea.

'All right,' Hart said impatiently. 'I'm here, I'm ready, I'm prepared. Talk to me.'

'Your father was Jonathon Hart,' said Time. 'But you never knew your grandfather.'

'No. I never knew any of my grandparents. My parents would never talk about them. There weren't even any photos. There weren't any aunts or uncles, either; just us.

When I was a kid, I used to wonder if perhaps we were the black sheep of the family, thrown out of the clan for something too dreadful even to discuss. When I found my grandfather's map and letter among my father's papers after the funeral, I didn't know what to think. I suppose that's one of the reasons why I finally decided to come here. I was looking for answers. Instead, all I ended up with were more questions, about things I never even dreamed of before.' He broke off suddenly as a thought occurred to him. 'Did you know my grandparents? Is that what this is all about?'

'Yes. Your parents didn't want you to know about Shadows Fall. They were worried you might want to come back here, searching for the rest of your family. And the prophecy made that far too dangerous. They wanted you to lead a normal life. But there were some things they never told you, about the prophecy and your family, that you need to know, so it falls to me to tell you now. It all begins with the prophecy, long before you were born.'

'Wait a minute,' said Hart, sitting up sharply in the deckchair. 'The prophecy was made when I was ten years old. That's why we had to leave Shadows Fall in such a hurry.'

'No,' said Time. 'Your grandmother made the prophecy, not long after giving birth to your father, Jonathon Hart. And shortly after that, she died. The prophecy was kept secret. Even then, it was clear what a bombshell it would be. They wanted time to study the prophecy, and make sure of what it really meant. So, the only ones to know were your grandfather, and later your father, after you were born. He didn't believe it. He didn't want to believe it. But it's hard to keep secrets in a town like this, and eventually it got out. When you were ten.'

Hart lay back in his deckchair, frowning fiercely as he tried to fit all the new information together. Friend pooled across his lap like a throw rug, trying to provide comfort by his presence. Hart sighed, looking out over the still

293

expanse of the sea. What he'd heard explained a lot, but it raised as many questions as it answered.

'So, he said finally. 'Who was my grandfather; Jonathon's father?'

'I am,' said Old Father Time.

The words seemed to hang on the air as Hart looked incredulously at Time. 'But . . . that's not possible! I thought you couldn't have children!'

'I thought so too. And for centuries upon centuries, I was right. But then I met your grandmother, and for the first time in my long lives, I fell in love. She was no one particularly special or important, except to me. She was a warrior woman from some old television future that no one remembers any more. No one was more surprised than us when she became pregnant. I almost left her, convinced the baby had to be someone else's, but it didn't take long for me to discover that vast latent potential of the foetus, or recognize the power the child might be able to wield. It was my power; Time's power. We kept the knowledge to ourselves at first. We had no idea what it meant. The pregnancy turned out to be long and hard, and in the end it killed her. And I was left with nothing but a dead love, a baby who showed no signs of any power, and a prophecy that made no sense.

'I didn't want any of them. I went a little crazy for a while. Though given the nature of my job, it was a while before anyone noticed. I've seen deaths beyond number in Shadows Fall, but none of them ever hurt me the way hers did. I didn't want the baby. I had no experience or interest in raising a child, even if I could have come up with some story to explain him. So I gave him to the Harts. They'd just lost a baby and were glad to take him. And I put it all behind me, and set about my job again.

'After a few deaths and rebirths I was able to look at things a little more clearly. There's nothing like growing old and dying a few times to calm you down. I kept an eye on Jonathon. He grew up to be a perfectly normal child, with never a trace of the power I'd sensed in him. Time passed, and I allowed myself to lose track of him. But then suddenly he was a man, and married, and his wife was pregnant. You were such a tiny thing as a baby. For a long time they worried about you, and wondered if you'd live. But I never doubted it. I could see the power within you, latent but potent, blazing like the sun. I kept a close watch on you. I hadn't been able to be a father to Jonathon, but I tried to be a grandfather to you, if only from a distance.

'And then, just after you turned ten, somehow the prophecy got out. I went to your parents, and told them everything. There wasn't time for recriminations or reconciliations; you had to be got to safety. They packed the barest essentials, and I got them out of town without being seen. It seemed the best thing to do, to buy us all some breathing time. And for a while, everything was quiet.

'Then your parents were murdered.'

Hart felt as though he should have jumped in his chair, or said something, but really all he felt was numb. He'd felt too many things already. He realized Time was looking at him, waiting for a response. He licked his dry lips and cleared his throat.

'Who . . . who killed them?'

'The Warriors of the Cross. They're a long-established extremist organization, an army of Christian terrorists dedicated to preserving their version of Christianity by wiping out anything that might threaten it. They mostly work behind the scenes, using political lobbying and economic pressure, but they're not averse to getting their hands bloody on occasion. They've been trying to locate and attack Shadows Fall for centuries. Partly because they see us as a town full of demons and unnatural creatures, but mostly because they want to get their hands on the Forever Door. They believe it will give them direct access to God.'

'Why would they want that?' said Hart, just to be saying something.

Time shrugged. 'Who knows? Perhaps they have some pointed questions to ask him about the nature of the world. And perhaps they don't really know themselves. Like all extremist organizations, they get a bit flaky around the edges.'

'Could the Door really give them access to God?'

'Maybe. But only on a one-way basis, like everyone else.'

Hart shook his head slowly, trying to put it all together and make it make sense. Friend flowed up around his shoulders like a shawl and hugged him comfortingly.

'Take it easy, Jimmy,' it murmured in his ear. 'Don't let him throw you. Just take things one step at a time. And remember, you're not alone. I'm here with you.'

Hart nodded briefly, and looked at Time. There was really only one question that mattered. 'Why did the Warriors kill my parents?'

'So that you would return to Shadows fall, and activate the prophecy.'

Hart jerked in his chair as though Time had hit him. 'Are you saying it's all my fault? They died because of me?'

'No, it's not your fault. Don't ever think that. The Warriors must take full responsibility for their actions, and what those actions will bring. They see you and your prophecy as a lever they can use to pry open the town. I doubt if they give you or your parents a second thought. Shadows Fall is protected by all kinds of guards and shields, but it's become increasingly clear of late that there are traitors among us. I have therefore taken an unprecedented step. The only power left to me. I have closed the Forever Door and shut the town off completely from the outside world. A desperate step, I know.

'I don't dare keep the Door closed for long; the pressure of passing souls is growing all the time, and eventually it would literally blow the town apart. People don't realize how precarious the nature of this town is. If the balance were ever seriously upset, you'd have to move Heaven and earth to put it right again. Possibly literally.

'But for the moment, I'm largely helpless. I should be able to tell who the traitors are, but I can't. The Warriors are shielding them from me, even though only a few months ago I would have said that was impossible. I can't see their actions either. I've always been able to see everything that occurs in Shadows Fall, in all its dimensions, past and present, but not now. Things are hidden from me. It's very uncomfortable; not unlike having gaps in my mind. Let me show you.'

Hart jerked in his deckchair as the world suddenly changed. He was flying over the town, so high he could see everything, and yet at the same time he was in the middle of everything, like a spider in its web. Nothing happened that he didn't know about, nothing moved that he didn't see, down to the minutest detail. He saw a thousand scenes simultaneously, and heard the roar of a thousand voices gabbling all at once. It was all so huge, and he was so small. He had to fight to hang on to his own sense of identity, drowning in a sea of information. But even as he floundered he saw the beginnings of patterns, and felt the skeins of the town run through his fingers. Given time, he felt he could make sense of it all, and feel the world turn about him. And yet here and there were blank spots, places he could not go, people he could not see, like an itch he couldn't scratch. And then suddenly the beach was back, single and solitary, and Hart let out a long breath as he slowly relaxed back in his chair.

'You get used to it after a while,' said Time. 'You have the power in you, James. My power. Coming back to Shadows Fall has awakened it in you. It's still largely dormant; presumably because the world couldn't cope with two Father Times at once.'

'Am I supposed to be your . . . successor?' said Hart.

'I don't know. Perhaps. I'm supposed to be immortal and unkillable, but you never know . . . You saw the blank spots. They're supposed to be impossible too, but a lot of impossible things have been happening in Shadows Fall, just recently. You never met the archangel Michael, did you? He came down to earth specifically to warn us about the coming changes and what they meant, but someone or something interfered with his memory, so that he couldn't complete his mission. He was murdered, or rather the body he was possessing was murdered, before he could remember. I'm pretty sure it was the Warriors messing with his mind, but I don't think they killed him. That was the Wild Childe. I'll tell you about him later, after we've survived the Warrior invasion. If we survive . . .'

'An invasion?' Hart sat up again in his deckchair, so suddenly he almost turned it over. 'What do you mean, an invasion? Do these Warriors have an army, or something? When are they coming?'

'The Warriors are an army, and they'll be here soon. They have agents everywhere, and their own military training camps.'

'If they're that big, why haven't I heard of them before?'

'You probably have. They exist in many forms, with many names, but they're all Warriors at heart. They have great, if indirect, power, and are extremely dangerous. Unfortunately for them, Shadows Fall can be pretty dangerous too, and we have powerful friends. I have a strong feeling we're going to need them.

'I gave orders that DeFrenz's body should not be cremated, just in case the angel Michael might come back, but so far he hasn't. Apart from that, I'm pretty much out of ideas. Which is why I brought you here. You have all my power, buried somewhere deep within you. I always feared the prophecy meant you were destined to use it to destroy Shadows Fall, but now I wonder if perhaps you were meant to use it to protect the town from the Warriors. It is possible.

'I can't really appeal to you as your grandfather. You don't have much to thank me for, and I don't have much experience with children. Mad comes close, but it's not the same. I don't even have much practice being human. The job takes up most of my life, and for centuries I was happy to leave it that way. Things were different after I met your grandmother. My Sarah. She taught me the joys and limitations of being human. I'm still not sure whether that's made my job easier or harder. I have to keep a certain distance, or I couldn't do what this job sometimes entails. But I try to do what must be done with compassion as well as efficiency.

'If you won't do it for me, James, do it for the town. It's a special place, and the Warriors would destroy it trying to make it what it isn't, what they think it ought to be.'

'But . . . what is it?' said Hart slowly. 'What is Shadows Fall, really?'

'You've heard a dozen explanations, I'm sure, but at heart it's really quite simple. The world can only believe in so much at a time. Old dreams must make way for new. This is where old dreams come to die and be forgotten, and those for whom reality has proved too much can find final comfort.

'Shadows Fall is necessary; it eases the pain of the world.'

They sat together in silence for a while, looking out at the placid sea. The wind was pleasantly cool, and two gulls glided high above, calling to each other plaintively.

'How long before they get here?' said Hart finally.

'Out in the real world, not long. But time moves differently here. You can take as long as you need to make your decision.'

Hart nodded, reached down, and picked up a pebble from the beach. It was smooth and cold and faintly damp. He hefted it in his hand, and looked at Time. 'Did you ever throw pebbles into the sea?'

'No, I can't say I ever did. Is it a human thing to do?'

'Yes. It's a family thing, too.'

And James Hart and Old Father Time took it in turns to throw pebbles out to sea, sometimes for distance, sometimes to watch them bounce, all through the long, unending afternoon.

Sapphire Lake had started out as a kids' holiday camp, but that didn't last long. It changed hands rapidly over the years as one outfit after another tried to make it profitable, and failed. There were the health nuts, the orienteering nuts, and experts in survivalist training. Who were a whole different kind of nut. Outfits came and went, the camp getting just a little shabbier each time, and no one who lived anywhere near by was at all surprised. Sapphire Lake camp lay in the midst of some beautiful countryside, but it was just too far from anywhere. The surroundings were pretty enough, but nothing you couldn't find elsewhere in cheaper and more accessible locations. So the huts and dormitories lay empty and abandoned, and the world forgot all about Sapphire Lake. Which suited the Warriors of the Cross just fine.

William Royce, Imperial Leader of the Warriors, strode briskly through the packed camp, nodding approvingly at the controlled chaos all around him. Men in military uniforms were marching and drilling in their hundreds, the barked orders from their non-coms sounding loud and fierce in the quiet evening. The sun was going down, and generators were starting up all around the camp. Jeeps roared back and forth on urgent missions, and over in the next clearing helicopter gunships were warming up, ready for weapons tests. Everywhere Royce looked, his army was preparing itself for war with pride and efficiency. His heart swelled, and he allowed himself a brief smile. In less than twelve hours he would finally be ready to lead his army of light against the devil's spawn currently infesting Shadows Fall. Blood would flow, and the ungodly would perish in their thousands, and he would walk in triumph through the streets he'd dreamed of for so long.

Royce was a short, stocky man in his mid-forties. He had strong, angular features, dominated by a hatchet nose and a disturbingly direct gaze. He knew his gaze upset people, and he used it like a weapon to separate the men from the boys. He'd lost most of his hair, and didn't give a damn. He'd had a good career in his country's army, rising slowly but steadily, until the Lord called him to leave and form his own army, an army of light. He'd found the Warriors of the Cross almost by accident, though later he realized the Lord had meant him to find them all along. They'd fallen apart in recent times, split into feuding factions, but he'd come to them with his vision and his military experience, and within a year he'd transformed them into an army worthy of the Lord. All they'd really needed had been a goal to unite them, and he'd found that in Shadows Fall.

He'd dreamed of the town ever since he was a child, but he knew it was not for him. Not yet. Not as long as demons and unnatural creatures walked the streets with impunity, and witches practised their foul magics openly. Shadows Fall was a human place, meant for humans only. He'd seen all this in dreams, and more, and vowed that one day he would come to purge and cleanse those streets. And now, after years of planning and training and waiting, he was finally ready. He'd turned the Warriors into a professional fighting force, leasing them out as mercenaries in a hundred undeclared wars across the globe, so that they would be tempered by pain and experience. They'd done him proud, time and again; and if some had died nameless and alone in foreign fields, they had not died in vain. The Warriors remembered them, and fought all the more fiercely in their memory. No one ever complained or objected. They knew they did the Lord's work, and were content.

Aides came running up to him with plans and papers and last-minute problems, and he dealt with them all calmly and efficiently. He took the time to be courteous with them all, never too rushed or unsettled by the news they brought. A leader must always inspire confidence in his men. Even when he was so tightly wound inside he felt as though he might explode at any moment.

He stopped outside the long customized trailer that was his mobile Headquarters, and looked out over his people. They were good men and women, Christians all, uncorrupted by the pleasures and weaknesses of the modern world. They would stop at nothing, hesitate at no extreme, to carry out his orders. Either you were a Warrior, and beloved of the Lord, or you were a sinner and worthy only of destruction. They were his children, and he would lead them to victory. It was ordained.

He pulled open the door and stepped into his Headquarters. The trailer had started out fitted with all manner of comforts and conveniences, but he'd had most of them torn out. In their place he'd had fitted banks of computers and monitor screens, and all the necessary technologies of the modern soldier. In his Headquarters he was never more than a phone call away from any of his people, anywhere in the world. Trained men and women sat always before the monitors, missing nothing. They even had their own satellite to ensure constant communications. Half a million soldiers of the Lord, scattered across the world, ready to kill or die for the cause at a moment's notice, waiting only for the word from him. It made him feel humble, sometimes.

He nodded to his secretary at her desk, and she smiled radiantly at him as he passed. As his secretary she protected him from unnecessary visitors and paperwork, and as his bodyguard she protected him from the enemies of the Lord. She was very good at her job. He moved on into his separate office, and closed the door firmly behind him. He felt the need for a little quiet and meditation, while he had the chance. But first, the paperwork.

He sat down behind his desk and leafed quickly through the day's accumulation, signing where his secretary had initialled, and ticking the necessary boxes to show he'd read the relevant passages. Everything seemed to be in order, but he couldn't escape a growing conviction that somewhere along the line he'd forgotten something. Something important. He went slowly through his mental checklist one more time. The last of the helicopter gunships and troop transporters had arrived, and the engineers were checking them now. The last consignment of guns and ammunition had arrived, from various army bases that probably hadn't even noticed they were missing yet. And every man and woman of the Warriors had answered their Call Up and checked in.

From all walks of life they came, from all social standings and economic backgrounds, united by their faith in the Lord and their hatred for anyone and anything that didn't fit the Warriors' definition of a Christian. All the filth-mongers and atheists and bleeding-heart politicians had a lot to answer for, and the Warriors would see that they did, once Shadows Fall had fallen to the army of light. Every station had been contacted and placed in readiness, waiting only his word to launch the invasion. He'd done everything to prepare himself and his people. All that was left was prayer. And that was what he'd forgotten. He closed his eyes and put his hands together, and sent his words up to God. His God.

Dear Lord, hear me. Grant us the power and strength to wipe out the vermin infesting your glorious city of light, Shadows Fall. Guide our weapons, and damn all who dare to stand against us. Every death shall be a gift to you, another soul sent for judgement. We shall prevail, no matter what the odds, for you are with us in this glorious Crusade. Just as our ancestors fought to free the holy lands from the heathen, so shall we purge Shadows Fall, and then the world. The Warriors shall rule supreme, in your holy name.

The guilty will be punished.

He opened his eyes, and looked at the television set standing in the corner of his office. He'd had to do many things over the years to build his army, to revitalize the Warriors and hold them together. Some he regretted more than most. One in particular still troubled his dreams, if not his conscience.

He pushed his chair back from his desk, and stood up. He pulled open the top drawer, took out the television remote control and aimed it at the set like a gun. His mouth was dry, and his hand was shaking just a little. He licked his lips, and slowly lowered the remote. This was not a time for fear, or weakness.

I fear nothing, for the Lord is with me.
Oh yeah; which Lord?

It was in his head, but it didn't sound like his voice. He squeezed his eyes shut, and then opened them again and stared at the television set. It stood alone, compact and ordinary, inside a chalked pentacle. It wasn't plugged in, and it had no aerial. Royce took a deep calming breath and triggered the remote. The television turned itself on, and grey static sparked and spat on the screen. Then it cleared, and a game show host in a sparkling suit stood in a sea of fire, the flames licking up around him. He smiled, and his teeth had points. There were nubs on his forehead that might have been the beginnings of horns.

'Well, well, and who have we in our audience today? Hey folks, its William (I'm in charge) Royce, Imperial Leader of the famous (or should that be infamous) Warriors of the Cross; paragon of virtue and all around good guy. Defender of the meek, as long as they worship the right God in the right way, and punisher of the unworthy, and to Hell with what the Law says. Well, what do you say, folks? Give the man a big hand, and one hell of a welcome! William Royce; come on down!'

Agonized screams erupted from behind the figure, the sound of countless people in unbelievable, indescribable pain. The flames leapt up for a moment, filling the screen, and then fell back to reveal the game show host transformed into a heavy metal rock-and-roller, complete with long hair, leather and chains. His face was puffy and swollen from too many excesses and gratifications of the flesh. The horns curled up blatantly from his forehead. He smiled, and a forked tongue flickered briefly between his pouting lips.

'Don't look so surprised, William. Isn't this what you always suspected? I have many forms and many faces, and my name is Legion. I know, it's an old gag, but we're great ones for tradition down here. I'm every rock-and-roller who ever played too loudly for your precious ears. When you play a record backwards, it's my voice you hear, if you listen hard enough. But only as long as you want to hear it. You're not smiling, William. Doesn't this form please you? You know I'll do anything for you, as long as you're out there and I'm down here. Perhaps this is more to your liking.'

He was a choirboy in a pristine white surplice, nailed to a wooden cross. Blood ran thickly from his wrists and ankles, and his eyes were very cold. He opened his rosebud mouth and sang. 'Jesus wants me for a sunbeam . . .'

'Enough!' A bead of sweat ran down Royce's face, but his voice was firm and commanding. 'Cut the crap, demon. I summon you in the name of the Lord, and command you to assume a more pleasing countenance.'

'Spoilsport,' said the choirboy. The flames leapt up again, and when they fell back, a teenage girl in jeans and sweater was sitting in a wicker chair, legs casually crossed to show off their magnificent length. 'Remember me, Billy? I was the first girl who ever smiled at you, back in high school. You had all kinds of dreams about me, but you never did work up the courage to actually talk to me. You could have me now. You could do anything you want with me. All you have to do is break the pentacle and let me out, and I can be everything you ever dreamed of.'

'The hell you say,' said Royce. 'Don't you ever get tired of these pathetic routines? I know who you are and what you are, and I do not feel your temptations. I am sworn to the Lord, and his strength is mine.'

'Wouldn't doubt it for a moment, Billy boy. Only, if you're so pure and holy, and your cause is so damn righteous, how is it you ended up coming to me for the power you needed? And you do need me, Billy. Prayer and fasting's all very well, but it won't take a town for you. All the armies and traitors in the world won't get you past Shadows Fall's defences. You need me and my kind for that. And when the day is over and the battle's done, I'll be standing right there at the front of the line, demanding payment. And all the prayers in the world won't save you then, Billy boy.'

'Liar and Prince of Liars,' said Royce calmly. 'You obey me because the Lord is with me, and you cannot disobey his word.'

The demon shrugged prettily. 'There's none so deaf as those who will not hear. What do you want from me this time?'

'Tell me of Shadows Fall. Do any of them suspect our invasion is imminent?'

'A few are beginning to have their suspicions, but they know nothing of what is to come. We have hidden the future from them, and clouded their minds. Relax, Billy. Your agents and mine are in place. Nothing will go wrong.'

'And the traitor angel Michael?'

'My brothers and I still combine to keep him from returning to a human host. Such fun. Don't you find it amusing, Billy dear, that a man who claims to soldier in God's name should traffic with one of the fallen against one of God's host?'

'Your words do not sway me. I do what is necessary.' Royce was careful not to let his voice waver. 'I will use whatever weapons I can find, to fight the good fight. I will use evil to fight evil, if I must. The archangel Michael is a traitor to the Lord and the Lord's work. He would defend the unnatural creatures that plague Shadows Fall. If I must soil my hands to work with such as you to stop him, I shall not hesitate. God is with me.'

The demon giggled charmingly. 'That's what they all say . . .'

'Enough! Don't think to tempt or confuse me, demon. You are corrupt and evil, and I know you too well. Now begone.'

'Not just yet,' said the demon casually. 'We're having such an interesting chat. And your wards have grown very weak.'

Royce looked automatically at the chalked lines of the pentacle around the television set. They were still intact. And yet suddenly it seemed uncomfortably warm in his office. A blisteringly hot breeze wafted out of the screen towards him, thick with the stench of sulphur. Screams of pain and horror rose again in the background, but nearer now, and mixed with awful laughter. The demon rose from her chair and strode forward, filling the screen. The flames jumped and danced. She put out a hand, and it thrust out of the screen and into his office. Her fingernails were long and sharp, the colour of blood. Royce fell back a step in spite of himself, and the demon laughed mockingly. Horns thrust up out of her brow, curling and twisting like a goat's.

'Did you never hear the saying, sweet Billy, that when you sup with the Devil, you should use a long spoon? Well, your spoon wasn't long enough. The game's over now. You lose. Time to play another game, more to my liking. Time for me to come out, and all my friends. We're going to have one hell of a time.'

The television screen stretched and widened, looking less like a window and more like a door with every moment. Royce tore his gaze away from the laughing demon, and took a deep breath. The remote control was still in his hand, and the familiar weight of it calmed him. He met the demon's gaze again. It had started to pull itself out of the screen, and it didn't look much like a girl any more.

'I'm not afraid of you,' said Royce. 'I summoned you and I can dismiss you. You entered into a compact with me, and are bound by its terms. I know your true name, and so I have power over you. Back to the flames, hellspawn, till I have need of you again.'

He hit the off button on the remote control, and the television began to shrink. The demon was sucked inexorably back in, despite all its struggles. It snarled and spat and clutched desperately at the edges of the screen, but in a moment it was back inside, and the television was its normal size again. Royce hit the off button a second time, and the scene disappeared from the screen, as though it had never been. The set turned itself off, and all that remained was the uncomfortable warmth, and the smell of sulphur. Royce sat down behind his desk, put away the remote control, and turned up the air conditioning.

The intercom buzzed, and he nearly jumped out of his skin. He waited a few moments to let his heart settle before answering. It wouldn't do to sound upset or flustered. His people needed to believe in him. And it definitely wouldn't do for them to suspect the forces he was dealing with, on their behalf. They wouldn't understand. He leaned over the intercom.

'Yes?'

'Frank Morse is here to see you, Leader.'

'It's all right, I'm expecting him. Send him through.'

Royce settled himself behind his desk, and put on his most stern and unreadable face. This wasn't going to be at all pleasant, but it had to be done. The door opened, and Morse came in. He marched up to the desk, crashed to attention and stood there silently, staring fixedly at a space just above Royce's head. Morse was young, barely into his twenties, but his heart burned with the holy fire of the zealot, and he would have died for Royce, or the Lord. Sometimes he seemed to have them confused. He'd been the obvious man to send into Shadows Fall, to perform one simple task, but somehow it had all gone wrong. Royce was pretty sure he knew why, but he wanted to hear it from Morse's lips. He nodded to Morse to relax, and he crashed into parade rest, still not meeting Royce's eyes.

'I've read your report on your trip to Shadows Fall, Frank. It doesn't make very good reading. I'm really very disappointed in you, Frank. You were sent in with strict instructions. Kill the Sheriff and the Mayor, and leave immediately without being spotted. This would have been a test run for other missions.

'Instead, you allowed yourself to be distracted by one of the town's lesser creatures, and I had to send a helicopter in to get you out. Have you any idea how many agents I had to jeopardize to get you and that helicopter safely out of Shadows Fall? Answer me, Frank. I'm not talking for the pleasure of hearing my own voice.'

'You're entirely right, Leader. I allowed myself to be distracted. I saw . . . visions. Things that pretended to be angels, in all their glory, to test my faith. And then, when I saw the demon standing there, in a Christian cemetery, blatantly revealing its goat's head and horns, I let my anger get the better of me. I failed in my mission. I accept any punishment you deem necessary.'

'Oh you do, do you? I wasn't aware I needed your permission. I'm not interested in punishment, Frank; only atonement. You have sinned against me and against the Lord, and you must make amends. You will be at the front of our forces when we attack the town. You will go naked and without weapons, armoured only in your faith. If that is strong enough, and if it is God's will, you will survive and be reinstated. That's all, Frank. Dismissed.'

'Yes, Leader. Thank you, Leader.'

Morse crashed to attention again, spun round, and marched out of Royce's office. He didn't seem too upset by his penance. If anything, the cocky young prig looked quite pleased at a chance to show off his faith. The intercom buzzed again, and Royce looked at it as though it was a hissing snake.

'Yes?'

'Martyn Casey is here to see you, Leader.'

'Yes, of course he is. Send him in.'

Royce grimaced disapprovingly. He must be getting tired. He'd forgotten all about this meeting with his Second in Command. And he still had to find some time to get a little rest before the off. Tired people make mistakes. The door swung open, and Casey came in, smiling pleasantly. Royce smiled and nodded in return as though he didn't have a care in the world.

'Ah, Martyn, good to see you. Take a seat. Now then, I understand you have a problem.'

Casey sat down, looking immediately relaxed and at ease. He was just a little shorter than average, with a bland open face and pale, guileless eyes. He was in his early fifties, and looked at least ten years younger. His self-control was legendary, and no one had ever known him raise his voice in anger, let alone lose his temper. His speciality lay in taking general aims and translating them into specific plans and missions. He was the perfect Second in Command, and Royce kept a careful eye on him at all times. Such men were ambitious, and therefore dangerous.

'Everything is going as scheduled, Leader. The troops are prepared, our agents in Shadows Fall have all been contacted, and everyone is ready to move out at a moment's notice. The town is being quietly but systematically stripped of its defences, and soon will lie helpless before us. In every way that matters, the war is already over. They just don't know it yet. However, we do have one small problem . . .'

He paused for effect, and Royce glowered at him. 'Get on with it, Martyn.'

'Yes, Leader. There is still the enigma of the Wild Childe. Intelligence has been able to turn up remarkably little on this individual, other than that he is thought by the town to be responsible for a series of recent murders. Not particularly important in itself, this man is still an unknown factor, and therefore not one we have prepared for.'

Royce smiled tightly. 'I don't see one sneak-in-the-dark murderer giving our soldiers much of a problem. I see no reason to change any of our plans. The invasion will go ahead as scheduled. There can be no place for doubt in us now, only faith. That's all, Martyn. You may go.'

Casey bowed briefly, got up and left, closing the door quietly behind him. Royce sighed. He was so close to success now he could almost taste it. All the years of planning, to get to this place, this moment. Everything he'd done, so that he might enter the Gallery of Frost, and stand before the Forever Door. He knew exactly what he'd say. He'd waited a lifetime to say it.

8

First Strike

Sitting alone in his office, Sheriff Richard Erikson looked at the bottle of whisky on his desk, and the bottle looked back. It had been full when he'd taken it out of the bottom drawer of his desk, but somehow he'd got through almost a third of it in under an hour. Just shows you what a man can achieve, if he puts his mind to it. It was good to know he was still good for something. He couldn't catch murderers, or protect the townspeople, but he could still get himself stinking drunk. He smiled harshly. It was almost a cliché: the hard-nosed cop who dives into a bottle when things get too tough. Play it one way and it's tragedy, play it another and it's comedy. Except he didn't feel like playing. He was just a man who needed a drink.

He'd always thought of himself as a strong man. A strong, competent man. Someone reliable you could lean on when the going got hard. But then the murders began, one after another, and he found out he wasn't the cop he'd thought he was. On quiet days, he used to dream of what it would be like to solve a murder. Do a Sherlock Holmes, and astound everyone with his detective skills. Only now his dream had come true after all, and it turned out to be a nightmare.

Twelve bodies. Eight men and four women, all killed in the same way. No murder weapon and no witnesses. No suspects, no clues, nothing to link the victims to each other or their murderer. Erikson and his Deputies had been working sixteen-hour shifts and more, trying to find something that would open up the case, and all they had to show for it was shortening tempers and dark circles under their eyes. The one time the town depended on its Sheriff, and he'd let them down. He was no nearer catching the killer now than the night he'd knelt by the body of the first victim at Suzanne's place down by the river.

Murders weren't supposed to happen in Shadows Fall. Such a thing was impossible. At least, that was what he'd always been led to believe. The town policed and regimented itself, with a little covert help from Old Father Time. And occasionally Jack Fetch. Erikson scowled. In theory, he had authority over the scarecrow, but he'd always known Jack Fetch took his orders only from Time. He'd kept his mouth shut and looked the other way on occasion, because Time had always seemed to know what he was doing. The scarecrow did what was necessary to protect the town, nothing more. Only now Time had abused the trust Erikson placed in him, by turning out not to be infallible after all. The murders were tearing Shadows Fall apart, and Time and Jack Fetch were nowhere to be found. Great. Just great.

Erikson poured himself another large drink. There was something rather disturbing about drinking whisky out of his favourite coffee mug. Almost . . . sacrilegious. The thought amused him, but he didn't have it in him to smile. It wasn't as if he liked whisky all that much. Tasted like weasel piss. He looked at his mug broodingly. It had a picture of Judge Dredd on the side, and a speech balloon saying I'm in Charge! Yeah. Right. Judge Dredd looked accusingly back at him, and Erikson turned the mug round so he wouldn't have to look at him. He looked at his watch. It was getting late. Another hour or so and it would stop being late and start being early. He ought to go home and get some rest, but he was too tired to move. Too tired, and too drunk.

Too drunk to drive, probably. Have to give himself a ticket. He giggled at that, and the high, sudden sound surprised him. He wasn't the giggling sort, as a rule. He

312

could call a taxi. He could, but he wasn't going to. Word would soon get around about his . . . condition. He had to keep up appearances. The town had to be able to believe in its Sheriff, even if he didn't, any more. Besides, it wasn't as if there was anybody at home waiting for him. Never had been. He'd always been alone. He allowed his lower lip to pout self-pityingly. Once, there had been Leonard and Rhea, but now Leonard was dead and Rhea was Mayor. The job had been his life, and now even that was being taken from him. He'd given up all hope of love and marriage in order to concentrate on the job, and then it went and did this to him. Destroyed his dream by proving he wasn't worthy of it. He wasn't Sherlock Holmes. He wasn't even Doctor Watson.

He drank his whisky and glared about him at his empty office. No one home, and no one here, either. All his Deputies were out, somewhere, working on the murders. Maybe he'd go down and sleep in one of the cells. Leave a note he wasn't to be disturbed. They'd understand. They all felt the pressure. Some of them were even looking to him for comfort and support, which only went to show they weren't as bright as they thought they were. He sighed, poured more whisky into his mug, and looked at it tiredly. He ought really to be out there with them, scouring the town for clues, searching for the one break that would blow the case wide open, and make everything make sense. That was what any television detective worth his ratings would be doing. Instead, he was wasting time getting drunk and allowing himself to be distracted by the likes of Doctor Nathaniel Mirren.

Now there was a man with problems. Erikson scowled unhappily. Much as he hated to admit it, even a son-of-a-bitch like Mirren was entitled to protection, but he was damned if he could see what he could do to help. The dead were out of his jurisdiction. He smiled briefly. Good line, that. He'd have to remember it. He sighed, and sat back in his chair. Maybe he could ring around a few Churches, see what they suggest. Not now, of course. Wrong time entirely to be ringing Churches. Even if he did find somebody up, they might ask awkward questions about the state of his voice. Priests could smell whisky, even down a phone.

He looked at the row of half a dozen telephones before him, and shook his head slowly. He'd ring in the morning. He looked about him for his jotter pad, to make a note, and his gaze stumbled over the stack of papers he'd pushed to one side some time ago. They didn't matter. Just a bunch of reports, and since they weren't concerned with the murders, they didn't matter at all. He picked up the top report so he could officially sneer at it. Apparently Lester Gold had been seen in town wearing his old Mystery Avenger outfit. Stapled to the page was another report that other superheroes and costumed adventurers were turning up all over the town, some new and some out of retirement, as though in response to some unspoken need in the community. Great. Just what he needed. A bunch of well-meaning amateurs and old men in tights and cloaks with no colour sense, getting in the way and messing things up. He picked up the whole stack of papers and slammed them down on the letter spike.

One of the phones rang, and he looked at it stupidly. Whoever it was, they shouldn't be ringing him. He wasn't supposed to be here at this hour, and anyway, he didn't feel like talking to anyone. The dispatcher should have known better than to put the call through. The phone persisted, the ringing shrill and piercing, and in the end Erikson picked up the receiver just to make it shut up.

'Sheriff Erikson, and this had better be important.'

'Deputy Briers, Chief. We've got problems. We've been getting reports on disturbances from all over town. I'm heading out to Darkacre, and Collins and Lewis are over at Mansion Heights. We're getting reports on fires, fighting, even explosions. It all sounds pretty ugly. What's that? Wait a minute, Chief, someone's trying to . . . what?'

The voice broke off abruptly, but Erikson could hear another voice gabbling excitedly in the background. He squeezed his eyes shut, and tried to concentrate on what the Deputy had been saying. Disturbances? What did he mean, disturbances? Briers's voice came back again suddenly, hurried and perhaps just a little panicked.

'Sorry, Chief, I'm going to have to go. Things are getting out of hand here. I can see flames on the horizon. Word's coming through of open fighting in the streets, even people killed. Fire-fighters and ambulances have been contacted, but there've been so many emergency calls we might have to just sit tight and take a number. You'd better get out here, Chief. Things are going to hell in a hurry.'

The Deputy broke the connection without waiting for an answer. Erikson had only just started to replace the receiver when the phone next to it rang. This time it was Deputy Hendry, out in the Haymeadow suburbs. More disturbances, damage to buildings, people hurt. Another phone rang, and another. Disturbances, more disturbances. People with guns, shooting in the streets, tanks and troop carriers heading in from the outskirts. Erikson tried desperately to make sense of it all, the alcohol still clouding his mind. He tried to get details of what was happening, but the Deputies, like the town, had been taken by surprise. He was trying to calm one man down and get him to talk coherently when there was the sudden sound of an explosion in the background, followed by screams. Another explosion, louder, and the phone went dead.

Erikson looked at the receiver in his hand, and shook it, as though trying to persuade it to work again, but the lines stayed dead. He put the receiver down slowly, staring at the suddenly silent phones. His town was under attack. The whole damn town. He tried to think what to do, and the whisky swirled through his thoughts, thick and heavy and confused.

Polly Cousins carefully made her way down the narrow, dimly-lit steps that were the only entry to the Cavern. The cellar club didn't believe in fripperies like easy access and exterior lighting. The door finally loomed up before her, and swung open as she approached it. Harsh light spilled out into the gloom, blocked off almost immediately by the huge form of a bouncer apparently descended directly from King Kong. And not descended all that far, either. He was easily seven feet tall, and seemed almost as broad across the shoulders. He looked Polly over carefully, just to be sure she wasn't carrying any visible weapons, and then stepped reluctantly back to let her in. Polly strode past him with her nose in the air, and her hands clenched into fists at her sides to keep them from shaking.

It had been a long time since she'd last been at the Cavern; a long time since she'd been able to leave the house at all. But now all her personalities had merged again, she was going to celebrate if it killed her. She'd spent most of the day travelling round the town, getting to know places again, and trying to get some kind of control over her nerves. No; nerves was the wrong word. She'd been scared. Sick to the stomach, trembling-in-every-limb scared. It had taken several hours, but she finally had her nerves under control. She felt only a mild terror now at the thought of her first date in years. It helped that she'd arranged to meet James Hart in the Cavern. She'd spent some happy times here, when she was younger and her life was still her own.,

She stopped abruptly in front of a wall mirror just before the main door. She looked good. She was dressed in long flowing black, with heavy eye-makeup and black finger-nails, and looked the quintessential Goth. The Gothic look had been very in the last time she'd been here, which only went to show how long it had been. She was still fashion-ably thin, and dressed in her best she looked several years younger than the troubled stranger she was used to seeing looking back out of mirrors. At least, she hoped she did. She wanted to look her best for James. She lifted her chin again, pushed open the main door and strode determinedly into the club.

Loud and vibrant music washed over her, along with the

roar of massed voices, stopping her in her tracks. The air was thick with mingled smoke, incense and company, and she looked desperately about her for something familiar. Luckily the bar was close at hand. She made her way through the crush, ordered a large drink, and then steeled herself to look about her. The Cavern looked very sixties tonight, but then it always had. In two golden cages hanging from the ceiling, two go-go dancers in feather bikinis were frugging energetically to the music of the live band. Down below, the happy crowd were bopping enthusiastically to the beat, dressed in a clashing collection of fashions. Waitresses moved unhurriedly between the tables at the far left, wearing low-cut blouses, leather mini-skirts and knee-high boots. A tall and slender man strode out of the crowd with a girl on each arm, smiling at everyone. He was wearing the bright red military coat of the Chelsea Pensioners, and a pair of ridiculously narrow sunglasses. Polly had to smile. Very Penny Lane. Very Sergeant Pepper. It occurred to her that most of the young people currently dancing their hearts out before her probably wouldn't even recognize the references, but she refused to allow the thought to depress her. Her drink finally arrived, though when she heard the price she nearly sent it back. She'd forgotten how pricey club drinks were. She smiled thinly. It seemed some things hadn't changed while she'd been gone. She sipped at her drink resignedly, and looked about her for James Hart.

She was on time, but she hadn't spotted him yet in the crush of bodies. She hoped he wasn't the sort who deliberately arrived late, so that his date would, theoretically, be all the more eager to see him. She wasn't sure her courage would hold together much longer, drink or no drink. Her heart was all but kicking its way out of her chest. Suzanne Dubois was supposed to be here somewhere, to give her moral support, but there was no sign of her anywhere either. Polly looked about her, keeping a firm rein on her emotions. Her gaze stumbled across a group of Beats sitting around a table, all wearing heavy duffel coats and

317

dark glasses, despite the gloom. They huddled together as if for comfort, trying to look cool and waving books of privately printed poetry at each other. No one was paying them any attention, which was probably what they were looking so annoyed about. Sitting at the next table were a bunch of slightly faded-looking hippies; all wide eyes and dreamy smiles, long hair and flower power. The Cavern was heavily into the sixties tonight, though there was a fair sprinkling of other times and fashions to be seen.

And then James Hart was suddenly there before her, appearing out of the crowd in an instant. He smiled at her easily, and she smiled back, suddenly so nervous again she was practically hyperventilating. They shook hands rather formally, and Polly realized he was just as nervous as she was, which made her feel a whole lot better.

'Nice place you suggested,' said Hart, leaning forward and raising his voice to be heard over the hubbub. 'You've nearly finished that drink. Would you like another?'

'Peach brandy and lemonade,' said Polly automatically. She drained her glass and handed it to him, and he weaved through the crush at the bar with practised ease. He caught the barman's eye and ordered her drink and one for himself. Polly was quietly impressed. She'd never been able to catch a barman's eye that easily, unless the bar was deserted and she was all but clinging to the man's shirt-front. She hadn't really wanted a second drink so soon, but she hadn't wanted to turn James down and appear stuffy. She shook her head angrily. She'd been living alone too long; her social skills had atrophied through lack of use. The evening was going to be a disaster; she could feel it. Panic ran through her like a lightning bolt, and it was all she could do to stand her ground and not run screaming from the club. She clamped down hard. James wouldn't let the evening go wrong. She didn't know why, but she trusted him.

Hart paid for the drinks with only the slightest wince, and glanced back at Polly. She was staring out at the dance floor, apparently lost in thought. She'd been a bit nervous when they met, he could tell, but she seemed to have calmed down now. She was bound to be finding this difficult, after so long in enforced isolation. He'd just have to be extra understanding, and make things as easy for her as he could. After all, she couldn't be as nervous as he was. He'd never been very good on first dates. He'd actually got here half an hour early, so he could check the place out. He never felt comfortable in a new place until he'd had a good prowl round. He needed to know what the bar was like, and where the toilets were. Things like that.

He was glad to see Polly again. She looked great. The outfit was a bit extreme, but he'd seen worse. She certainly seemed younger and more at ease now that she was out of the house and away from its influence. Hart was only too aware that he was wearing the same clothes he'd been travelling in all week. He'd set out on his search for Shadows Fall pretty much on impulse. He hadn't bothered to pack a suitcase, just dumped a few things in an overnight bag. The more he thought about it, the less like an impulse his departure seemed, and more like a response to some hidden instruction, as though Shadows Fall had been taking over his life even then. It hadn't bothered him before, but now he wished he'd taken the time to pack some decent clothes. He wanted to look his best for Polly. She deserved the best he had to offer. He realized he'd been standing there with the drinks in his hands for some time now, and hurried over to give Polly her peach brandy and lemonade. He winced mentally. How she could drink the stuff was beyond him. They stood together, smiling at each other over their drinks, neither of them sure what to do or say next.

There were a lot of things Hart would have liked to discuss with Polly. His talk with Old Father Time was still ricocheting around inside him, unable to settle. He had to talk it out with someone soon, or he'd explode. And yet part of him wanted to forget it all, bury it so deep he'd never have to look at it again, so he could concentrate on having a good time with Polly. He desperately wanted to feel normal and ordinary, even though his relationship to Time suggested he wasn't, and never had been. To distract himself he looked around for a free table, and then double-taked as he took in the live band for the first time. He turned to Polly, who followed his gaze and then shrugged smiling.

'Oh, they often turn up here,' she said off-handly. 'The place wouldn't be the same without them.'

'But I thought . . . I mean; they're all dead, aren't they? They all died in that plane crash . . .'

'Being dead's no handicap in Shadows Fall. We're not prejudiced. People believed in them once, and that's all that matters.'

Sitting at a table hidden in the shadows of a far corner, Suzanne Dubois kept a sharp if unobtrusive eye on Polly and Hart, just to be sure everything was going all right. She wasn't sure what she was going to do if she decided they weren't, but she'd promised Polly she'd be there for her, and a promise was a promise. Suzanne didn't normally keep promises, on principle, on the grounds that they made her predictable, but that just made this one all the more important. She took her eyes off Polly and Hart just long enough for a quick look round, and shuddered fastidiously. She didn't think much of the Cavern, and never had. Nostalgia was all very well, but it wasn't what it was. Suzanne believed very firmly in living in the present, and occasionally the future, through her Cards. Never look back, she was wont to say, especially after a few drinks. All you see are the mistakes you made; and catching up on you, as like as not. She was wearing her usual mixture of fashion and tat, thrown together with more haste than style. She didn't believe in dressing up, or down, for the occasion. Take me as I am. What you see is what you get. Suzanne was full of little sayings like that, mostly to hide the fact that she had long ago given up trying to make a good first impression. It just wasn't in her.

She looked fondly at the man sitting beside her. One good thing about going out with Sean Morrison was that whatever you were wearing, it was bound to look good compared to him. He was wearing his usual T-shirt, jeans and leather jacket, all of which looked as though someone else had slept in them, and had an extremely restless night as well. Sean had never been known to give a damn. He always maintained he had more important things to consider than the vagueries of fashion. Suzanne was pretty sure this was just a mask for a total lack of taste, but she kept a diplomatic silence. At the moment he was watching her watching Polly and Hart. She could feel his eyes on the back of her neck. She turned back to face him, and he smiled at her, his expression half amused and half exasperated.

'You know,' he said calmly, 'when you called me up and said you needed my company this evening, this wasn't quite what I had in mind.'

'Sorry,' said Suzanne, 'but I want everything to go right tonight. Polly's had a lot of bad luck in her life, and she's entitled to a little happiness. She's going to have a good time tonight, or someone's going to suffer.'

'And you think she's going to find happiness with the mysterious and enigmatic James Hart? I don't want to worry you, Suze, but from what I've heard he's not exactly Prince Charming. Word is, the guy is downright spooky. Though truth be told, he doesn't actually look like much. I was expecting someone taller.'

'You're in a bad mood tonight, Sean. What's got under your skin?'

'Nothing much. I just talked the Faerie into leaving their land beneath the hill, to come here and help hunt down our murderer. Only it's been ages, and I haven't seen sight nor sound of any of them yet. They're up to something, and I have a strong feeling that when I find out what it is, I'm not going to like it at all. When the Faerie start plotting, the only sensible thing to do is keep your head down and run for cover. I have a strong feeling bordering on certainty that I have unleashed a hurricane. And everyone is going to blame me for the storm damage.' He broke off as Suzanne sneaked another look at Polly and Hart. 'Look, what exactly are you planning to do, Suze? Wait for him to say something that upsets Polly, and then rush over and pound on him? Leave them be. They're both well over twenty-one, and quite capable of looking after themselves.'

'You're quite right,' said Suzanne. 'Talk to me, Sean. Distract me.'

'All right. What happened to your current beau; the teenage guitar wonder? Isn't he allowed out this late, or did he have some homework to do?'

'You are going to suffer for that,' said Suzanne sweetly. 'Suffer long and horribly. He's currently off sulking with his friends because I didn't recognize his tortured genius. Or at least I got tired of hearing him talk about it. Punks can be a lot of fun, but they do tend to be terribly single-minded. If it was sex I wouldn't mind, but he will keep going on about his music . . . If that was what I was interested in, I'd buy a musical dildo. I'm not worried. He'll be back. They always come back. Even you, Sean.'

'Are you implying that I'm easy?' said Morrison, raising an eyebrow haughtily.

'Perish the thought.'

'I saw Ambrose the other day,' said Morrison, casually. 'He was doing his eye of newt and tongue of dog bit for some visiting Japanese businessmen. He's done very well since he moved into Exchange and Securities.'

'Oh, I've still got a soft spot for Ambrose; it's a deep marsh just outside town. One of these days Ambrose and I are going to pay it a visit, along with something heavy to weight him down. Never forget, Sean; I left him, not the other way round. We should never have got married in the first place, but you do these things when you're young and stupid, and don't understand the difference between love and sex.'

Hart and Polly sat companionably together at a table comfortably far away from the band and the dancers, nursing their drinks and trying not to think about the things that really concerned them.

'So,' said Polly brightly. 'What have you found out about your background?'

'More than I bargained for. It's . . . complicated. What's your father doing, now he's back in the land of the living?'

'Trying to catch up on everything that's happened since he . . . left. Shadows Fall has changed a lot in the past few years. Where's your Friend?'

'I left him back at the house, stuck in front of his beloved soaps. I didn't feel the need for a chaperone tonight.'

They fell silent again. It was hard to think of things to say when they both had so much they didn't want to talk about. Hart felt his brows lowering into a frown, and tried not to. He didn't want Polly to think he was bored or angry with her. But it was hard to make small talk when most of the things they had in common were too disturbing to discuss. He wasn't even sure how he felt about Polly. What they'd been through together had forged some kind of link, but that was more to do with circumstance than personality. *Great basis for a relationship; I resurrected her father and helped her get her heads together.*

Not that he was much better. How could she feel anything that mattered about him, when even he wasn't sure who he really was? Hart decided he was thinking too much and talking too little. Polly would be thinking he'd taken a vow of silence. The best thing would be to stop worrying about trying to impress her, and just relax, let things happen as they would. He was safe here; just another face in the crowd, with nothing expected or feared of him. He smiled at Polly, and she smiled back, sensing the change in his mood and responding gratefully.

The lights went out, and there was a sudden drop in the noise as the amplifiers cut out. The band stumbled raggedly to a halt, and a sudden silence filled the club as people's conversations broke off. The first questions had just begun when the building suddenly trembled. There were shouts and a few screams in the pitch darkness as the floor shook under foot and then was still. A loud and confident voice presumably the Manager, started saying calm and reasonable things, but no one was listening. Hart reached out in the gloom and held Polly's hand. It was trembling violently, and he squeezed it in what he hoped was a reassuring manner. The club shook again, more violently this time. People cried out as they were thrown to the floor, and everywhere there was the sound of glass breaking. Screams rose up on all sides as people began to panic. Some were already shouting and cursing as they fought their way through the darkness to where they thought the exits were.

And then there was a roar so loud it hurt the ears, and one side of the Cavern club exploded inwards. Brick and stone and splintered wood flew on the air like shrapnel, cutting through the panic-stricken crowd with grisly efficiency. Blood flew and people fell and men and women screamed in fear and agony. Hart was thrown over the top of his table by the force of the blast, and slammed into someone before hitting the floor. He hoped it wasn't Polly. Something struck his elbow hard, and his arm went numb. He could feel blood trickling down his face, but didn't know whether it was his or not. He called out to Polly, but his voice got nowhere in the bedlam. He got one foot under him and lurched to his feet. He reached out in the darkness for Polly, and there was another explosion, louder than the first, and the ceiling came down. Screams were cut off suddenly, drowned in the roar of collapsing rubble, and then and for a long time after there was only silence in the Cavern club.

Ash and Rhea lay cuddled in each other's arms in Ash's bed. It wasn't really big enough for two people, but neither of them felt like complaining. Rhea stretched languorously, enjoying the way her skin brushed smoothly against Ash's, and buried her face in his neck. It was pleasantly cool in the bedroom, and the two of them lay naked under a single sheet. Ash reached out across her and shook a single

324

cigarette out of the pack on his bedside table. He stuck it in his mouth, and touched the tip of his index finger to the tip of the cigarette. It glowed brightly under his touch and was instantly alight.

'Those things'll be the death of you,' said Rhea sleepily.

'Oh, most amusing.' Ash lay on his back, staring up at the ceiling, smoke drifting up out of his slack mouth. 'So, how was it; making love with a ghost?'

Rhea raised her head and considered the matter for a moment, running her fingers lazily through his chest hair. 'I thought you gave a very spirited performance.'

Ash groaned. 'I'd forgotten how sex affects you. Everyone else gets hungry, or fancies a cigarette; you come up with bad jokes.'

'They have to be bad to be good. Anyway, it's your own fault for asking. Why do men always have to ask how it was? What do you want; points for technique and endurance?'

Ash shrugged, and enjoyed the way it moved her body against his. 'I just wondered if it seemed at all . . . different, now that I'm dead. There are bound to be differences. I'm not the person you used to know. I'm the memory of a man, made flesh and blood through an act of will, but my memory isn't perfect. For example, you've been lying on my left arm with all your weight for some time now, but it hasn't gone to sleep. I'm trying to be everything I can for you, Rhea, but I can't be everything I was. I'm sorry.'

'No, don't. It's all right. I understand.' Rhea buried her face in his neck again, her lips moving against his skin as she spoke. 'I know there are differences. From the way we were thrashing about it's a wonder the bed held together, but you never raised a sweat and you never got out of breath. You feel just a little cold to the touch, and you never warm up no matter how tight I hug you.'

'Does it matter? I loved you with all my heart while I was alive, and I love you just as much now. That hasn't changed. It never will.'

A sudden high-pitched bleeping filled the room, and Rhea groaned angrily. 'That's another thing that never bloody changes. My office has noticed that I've been out of touch for more than five minutes, and my entire staff are having a collective panic attack. If I had any sense, I'd throw the damn bleeper away and swear blind I lost it. Can I use your phone? There's always the chance it might be something important.'

'Sure. Go ahead.'

Rhea sat up in bed, knuckling at her eyes, and Ash sat up with her. He leaned back against the headboard, and watched happily as Rhea dialled a number from memory on his bedside phone. He liked having Rhea in his bedroom, using his things. It was just like old times. Rhea reached out and took the cigarette from his hand as she listened to the phone ringing at the other end, and managed two quick jerky puffs before someone answered her.

'This is Mayor Frazier. And if this call turns out to be not one hundred and one per cent necessary, your ass is grass. Talk to me.'

And then she stopped and listened. The bleeper cut off. Ash tried to read her face as the silence lengthened, but she seemed perfectly calm and composed. It was her professional, political face. He took his cigarette back from her, and she didn't notice at all. She grunted and mumbled a few times, her eyes far away, and finally asked in a perfectly calm voice how bad it was. She listened and then nodded slowly, as though that was the answer she'd been expecting.

'All right, I'll come straight in. Call in the rest of the Council, and keep them together till I can get there. Keep trying to contact Sheriff Erikson, and send someone into the Gallery of Bone to hammer on Time's door. He can't just abandon us like this.' She put down the receiver with barely contained violence and looked at Ash. 'The shit has just hit the fan. Shadows Fall is under attack by an unknown but extremely powerful force. The whole town. Whoever our enemy is, they have what appears to be an entire army at their disposal, and a bloody well-trained one, at that. They've already taken control of several key positions, and are trying to disrupt our communications network. They're shelling some parts of the town. Tanks, trucks and helicopters are entering the town from all directions, without opposition. Our defences have collapsed. No one knows why.

'My people are panicking. Time won't talk to them. He's closed the Forever Door and isolated the town. No one can get out, though the invaders are having no trouble coming in. Our good Sheriff is not in his office, and none of his Deputies know where he is. Probably off drinking somewhere. I've got to get back, Leonard. The invaders are just sweeping our people aside. There must be something I can do to get our forces organized . . .'

'I'm coming with you,' said Ash. 'I haven't found you after all this time just to lose you again. Besides, you might need someone to watch your back.'

Rhea nodded quickly, and swung her legs out of bed. She and Ash got dressed with desperate speed, hauling clothes into place by brute force. Rhea finished first, and hurried out of the door and down the stairs. Martha Ash was waiting at the bottom. Rhea stopped before her, suddenly aware of her dishevelled appearance, and what Leonard's mother must be feeling, but Martha just smiled warmly.

'I'm glad you're back together, dear. He needs you.'

'Yes. I think so too. But we have to be going. Something important's come up, back in town.' She hesitated, and then continued. 'Martha, I think it would be best if you and Thomas were to stay indoors for a while. Don't answer the door to anyone, and stay away from the windows. It's just a precaution.' She broke off as Ash came clattering down the stairs, still doing up his shirt buttons. 'Move it, Leonard, or I'll leave you behind. I'll see you again, Martha. 'Bye.'

She pecked Martha on the cheek, and then hurried down the hall and out of the front door with Ash right behind her. They piled into her car, Rhea behind the wheel, and the motor caught right away, just for a change. She slammed home the gears and had the car down the drive and out on the road before Ash even had time to do up his seatbelt.

'I know it's not really necessary in my case,' he said calmly, tugging at the belt to make sure it was secure, 'But I like to pretend. It helps me feel more real. Nice car, by the way. A lot better than the old junker you used to drive around in. The Council finally got around to agreeing the money for an official car, did they?'

'No,' said Rhea, taking a corner tightly and scowling at the road ahead. 'I just got tired of waiting, bought a car anyway, and sent them the bill. They're still arguing about it in committee.'

Ash smiled, but it didn't last long. 'Who do you think they are? The invaders?'

'Damned if I know. There's supposed to be a whole army of them, but that could just be imagination and exaggeration. Most of the reports describing them sounded pretty hysterical. But it doesn't matter how many of them there are, the town's shields and defences should still have kept them out. Someone fell asleep at the switch, and once I find out who I'll have his balls, when this is all over.'

Ash frowned suddenly, his gaze turning inwards. 'Slow down, Rhea. There's something up ahead, just around the next corner . . .'

Rhea hit the brakes automatically, and they rounded the corner with plenty of time to slow down before reaching the road block manned by six soldiers in generic military uniforms. The road block consisted of concrete posts strung together with rolls of barbed wire; quick but efficient. Rhea brought the car smoothly to a halt, but didn't turn off the engine. The soldiers approached the car, and Rhea realized only then that they were all armed with machine pistols. The soldiers looked young, tough and very professional. Rhea glared at them anyway.

'Who the hell are you, and what do you think you're doing, blocking the road? I could have had an accident.'

'Turn off the engine and get out of the car,' said one of the soldiers. From the way he said it, and from the way the other soldiers reacted to him, he was obviously in charge of the group. 'I'm Sergeant Crawford, of the Holy Order of the Warriors of the Cross, the Army of God. This town is now under our protection, and martial law has been declared.'

'Under protection?' said Rhea, making no move to leave the car. 'Who the hell are you protecting us from?'

'The Warriors who?' said Ash.

'Get out of the car,' said Crawford flatly. 'If you won't do it voluntarily, I'll have my men drag you out. Guess which we'd prefer.'

He opened the door on Rhea's side. He didn't look at all like he was kidding. Rhea sniffed, turned off the engine, and got out of the car as though it had been her intention all the time. Ash got out the other side. His feet had barely touched the ground when he was grabbed by two of the soldiers, swung round, and bent over the bonnet of the car with unnecessary force. One Warrior held him down while the other frisked him with professional thoroughness. Rhea glared at Crawford.

'Are you planning to search me too?'

'I don't think that will be necessary. But I will need to inspect your handbag.'

Rhea sniffed, and thrust it at him. He opened it and turned it upside down over the bonnet. He stirred through the junk with a finger, and then picked out her driving licence. He studied it as she swept her things back into her handbag, and then raised an eyebrow as he checked the name.

'We've struck lucky, boys. This is Mayor Rhea Frazier. She helps run this cesspit of a town. Your name is on my Red list, Mayor Frazier. You know what that means? Well, firstly it means you are to be detained for questioning by my superiors. It also means we can do anything we want

329

to you, as long as we don't damage you so much you can't answer questions. They won't even slap our hands. My superiors really don't like you at all. Now, I'm sure there are all sorts of unpleasant surprises awaiting an invading army in this town. You're going to tell us all about them so I can warn my people.'

'Or?' said Rhea.

'Or you get to watch us use your friend here as a punchbag. So unless you want to listen to your friend screaming, you'd better be very cooperative, Mayor Frazier.'

'We've got plenty of time,' said one of the other soldiers. 'We're well ahead of schedule. Plenty of time for fun and games. I think we ought to soften her up a bit first, you know? She looks like she could be very cooperative, with a little persuasion.'

'Don't touch her,' said Ash.

The soldier turned with startling speed and slammed a fist into Ash's gut. The force of the blow bent Ash forward, and his face came down to meet the soldier's rising knee. Rhea cried out and Crawford grabbed her from behind, pinning her arms to her side. Ash leant back against the bonnet of the car, shaking his head. The soldier grabbed him by the shirtfront with both hands, and slammed him back against the side of the car, again and again. The car rocked under the impact, and Rhea listened sickly to the sound of Ash's body hitting the car. He never once cried out. The soldier stopped to get his breath, grinning cheerfully.

'Subtle as ever, Kamen,' said Crawford dryly.

'He's alive, isn't he?' said Kamen. 'For the moment, anyway. Why don't you take madam there and find somewhere comfortable to lie down, and we'll have a little fun with our new friend here. Oh, and Sergeant; be a gentleman. We don't want damaged property when it's our turn.'

'Trust me,' said Crawford. 'See if you can persuade your new friend to make a little noise. Might help persuade our good lady Mayor to be a little more cooperative. More . . . responsive.'

Rhea stamped down hard on his foot, and his grip loosened, as much in surprise as pain. She jerked free from Crawford, and started towards Ash, but two of the other soldiers grabbed her before she'd managed more than a few steps. Crawford moved over to stand before her. They were both breathing more heavily, but he was grinning. He grabbed a handful of her blouse and ripped it open.

'Don't touch her,' said Ash.

The soldiers turned and looked at him. There was something new in his voice, something . . . disturbing. Kamen fell back a step, and Crawford's hand fell away from Rhea's blouse. Despite the punishment Ash had taken there was no sign of any blood or bruising on his face. In that moment, without doing or saying anything more, Ash was suddenly frightening. He wrapped himself in what he was, a dead man walking, and showed the soldiers what it meant. Their blood ran cold and they all stumbled back away from him, terror clutching at their hearts. They didn't bother to raise their guns. They knew it wouldn't make any difference. They saw death in Ash's face and heard it in his voice, and none of them could face it.

Kamen broke first, running into the woods at the side of the road, without once looking back to see if his friends were following. They quickly bolted after him, their minds empty of everything but fear and panic. Crawford was crying as he ran, and didn't know why. Rhea watched them go. The fear had barely touched her, but she'd felt enough of it to know why the soldiers ran. She also knew she'd never feel quite the same about Ash again. But he looked perfectly normal now, the fear just a memory, and she hurried forward to be sure he was unhurt. He waved for her to get in the car.

'Drive, Rhea. Get us out of here.'

She nodded, and got behind the wheel. Ash got in beside her, and she had the car round the barricade and down the road while he was still shutting the door. She drove quickly but carefully, mindful of other road blocks, and her knuckles were white where they gripped the wheel.

'I thought you handled that rather well,' she said finally, trying for her usual professional calm, and not quite making it.

'It's easy to be brave when you know nothing can harm you any more,' said Ash. 'I was just worried for you.'

'I'm worried about the town,' said Rhea. 'If those bastards are typical of the invaders . . . We've got to get somewhere safe, regroup, make decisions. If there is anywhere safe any more . . .'

'Drive,' said Ash. 'Just drive.'

The Warriors of the Cross came howling into Shadows Fall like a pack of wolves maddened by the scent of blood. People ran screaming before them, and the Warriors shot them down as they fled. The soldiers' orders were to terrorize the town's inhabitants and render them incapable of resistance, and for a long time they swept on unopposed. Tanks rumbled inexorably through the emptying streets, taking every opportunity to shell buildings with any connection to authority, blowing them to rubble. Flames leapt up behind the invading army, and there was no one left to put them out. Smoke billowed up into the sky, blotting out the sun. The Warriors brought death and destruction to Shadows Fall, and they laughed and joked and sang the praises of the Lord as they headed remorselessly for the centre of the town, and their final objective; the Sarcophagus of Time.

Three members of the town Council had gathered in their meeting chamber before the Warriors found them. The officer in charge checked their names against a list, and ordered one of the Councillors to step forward. He did so, blinking uncertainly, and the officer calmly ordered his soldiers to shoot the man. The other two Councillors were still gaping disbelievingly as the Warriors' bullets lifted the man off his feet and slammed him back against the wall behind him. He slid slowly to the floor, leaving a long bloody smear on the wall. The Warriors hustled the two remaining Councillors out of the chamber, and they went unresistingly, their eyes wide with shock. The officer gave instructions for the building to be torched, and his men laughed as they set the fires. They were doing the Lord's work, and it felt fine, so fine.

But even as the invaders swept through the outskirts and on into the more complex inner circles of the town, the advance began to slow. Maps were useless. One road might become another as they were driving down it, or even reverse itself without them noticing. Time changed suddenly, without warning, from day to night and back again. The invaders had a list of strategic buildings and locations to occupy, but none of them were where they were supposed to be, as though the town itself was working to confuse them. They stopped people at random or dragged them out of houses, demanding directions, but even though the townspeople were too frightened to lie, it did the invaders little good. There were worlds within worlds inside the boundaries of Shadows Fall, and even the laws of nature were not constant. Boiling summer became freezing winter, and there were places where the engines of the tanks and transporters would no longer function, though there was nothing wrong with them. One group thought it saw another armed force coming to confront them, and opened fire, only to discover they were shelling their own rear. Other groups found themselves lost in jungles or open plains, or maddened by alien landscapes without sense or reason.

One platoon became separated from the main thrust of the advance and was soon hopelessly lost. They gathered round a signpost, hoping for useful clues, only to find the words on the signpost changed when they weren't looking, or even when they were, giving useless or conflicting information. The Warriors cursed it, and it cursed them back. They riddled it with bullets, and it crashed to the ground. The sign read *Oh I am dying*. The soldiers converged on it, stamping and kicking and shouting. They

333

sprayed the surrounding buildings with gunfire in their frustration, and laughed at the screams.

Any living thing that wasn't clearly human was shot on sight. The Warrior officers had declared them demons, devils, unnatural beings whose very existence was a mockery of the Lord. The soldiers shot down unicorns and griffins, cartoon animals and childhood friends. Some tried to surrender, but the Warriors had no mercy for anything inhuman. The Underworld of the Subnatural fled, disappearing into secret hiding places and burrows, scattering as they ran so that the invaders couldn't hope to find them all. But some couldn't run fast enough, and others were tracked down and dragged kicking from their boltholes, to die from a bullet in the head or the battering of rifle butts. Pathetic little corpses lay in bloody heaps among the burning buildings, innocent eyes empty and unseeing.

The Warriors did finally manage to find the main train and bus station, and occupied it, to prevent further townspeople from escaping and to keep out any help that might be coming in. There was clear evidence that some people had already fled, but the soldiers looked uneasily at the strange names and destinations on the departures board, and would not go after them. The local television and radio station was the next to fall, and the Warriors began broadcasting instructions. Everyone was to remain calm and stay in their homes. Attempts to flee would be taken as a sign of guilt. All non-human life forms were to be handed over to the occupying forces for execution. The penalty for harbouring such creatures was death. The penalty for resistance was death. Television screens showed gutted buildings with shattered windows, burning freely. Bodies lay everywhere, the dead and the dying alike ignored by the Warriors as they pressed steadily, mercilessly inwards.

There was resistance, here and there, but it was scattered and isolated. The speed and surprise of the invasion had caught the town unprepared, for all its forebodings. The Warriors pressed remorselessly on, despite everything the town could do to slow or stop them, heading for the one crucial objective of the invasion; control of the Sarcophagus, and through it access to the Galleries of Frost and Bone. To Old Father Time, and the Forever Door. It took hours, and some said days, but eventually the leading force streamed into the park, and found itself faced with real resistance for the first time. From everywhere they came; a great swarming army of metal automatons, running gleaming from every direction to fall on the Warriors with silent fury. Blood sprayed from metal fists, but the expressions on the painted faces never wavered as they tore into the invaders, killing and maiming and crushing with cold, calculating efficiency.

The Warriors retreated, to give themselves a free field of fire, and then opened up with automatic weapons. The bullets ricocheted more often than they penetrated, but even so some automatons fell as gunfire smashed vulnerable joints or openings. The clockwork figures ignored their losses, pressing always forward, and step by step, foot by foot, the Warriors were driven back from their objective, until finally they were outside the park again. They regrouped as best they could, their military professionalism shattered for the moment by their losses and the inhuman unstoppability of their enemy, and as they hesitated a thick mist rose up, filling the park. The automatons fell back, one by one, disappearing silently into the fog. A strained quiet fell across the scene, and the Warriors slowly lowered their weapons. In a while they would fortify their position, and radio for reinforcements and more powerful weapons, but for the moment they just stood there, staring into the fog, feeling the first intimations of defeat shuddering through them.

Some parts of Shadows Fall are older than others. In one of the oldest, an ancient circle of standing stones greeted the dawn as it had for uncounted centuries, still and silent, waiting only to be woken and put to use. In that circle, a hundred men and women put aside their differences and came together to form a new circle within the old. Druids stood with Jews, Christians with Muslims, interspersed with followers of Wicca and the Golden Dawn. There was a time they would have argued hotly with each other, struck blows with fists or knives, but they had found a new union in the town's need. The same inner voice had called them to the standing stones, to defend Shadows Fall against the Warriors. For after all; the enemy of my enemy is my friend. Or at least my ally.

They joined together, hand in hand, as the first light of dawn spilled across the stones, and an ancient music stirred within them, bursting forth in song. The magi sang, and power burned within them; the old, wild magic from the dawn of Time, before man discovered reason and science, and chose to stand aside from the natural order. It was a vast, capricious, whimsical magic, fierce and raging, but the magi drew on the long-established power of the stones and bent it to their will. They drew power from all the old sources, from the moon and the tides, the ley lines and the bustle of the hedgerow, from the light that burns in all the living world. The wild magic built within the circle of the magi, racing round and round in search of an outlet. The pressure built and built, screaming for release, but still the magi held it back. They tapped the barest fraction of it and sent their minds soaring out above the beleaguered town, to see how far the Warriors had advanced. They watched and they learned, and their hearts grew cold as stone.

The Warriors of the Cross streamed into Shadows Fall from all sides; long columns of tanks and trucks and marching men. Helicopters hovered overhead like angry insects, spying out the way ahead. The Warriors came in their thousands, howling through openings in the town's defences that could only have been made from within. The soldiers of a jealous God fought their way inexorably inwards, heading for the heart of the town, burning and killing as they passed. The townspeople fled screaming before them, and devastation lay in their wake, and the cries of the dying.

The magi witnessed the butchery of the Subnatural and the destruction of the town, and could hold their rage back no longer. The wild magic leapt out, given shape and form by the cold fury of the magi, and fell upon the advancing Warriors. From that moment, the soldiers of the Lord were hexed. Machines broke down, motors stopped running, accidents happened. Men fell, and broke their legs. Petrol became water. Guns could not fire, or exploded in soldiers' hands. And helicopters fell out of the sky like dying bees. The Warriors' advance stumbled to a halt, all across the town.

But then the Warriors of the Cross revealed their hidden hand: a cache of sorcerer priests dedicated to their vision of the Lord, and fanatically devoted to the way of the Warriors. Their magic came from the dark places of the world and the darker places in their hearts, though they would never admit it. The end justified the means, they said, when they would speak of it at all; anything is justified if it is done in the name of the Lord. They raised their bitter magics and lashed out at the magi. Only the ancient power in the standing stones protected them, and their hex was broken in an instant. Motors roared and guns fired, and the advance began again. The magi steeled themselves, raised their voices in song, and sent out the wild magic again.

This time it roared through the natural world, and the weather turned against the Warriors. Storms blew up out of nowhere, and blinding rains fell from the skies. Snow and hail and ice froze the soldiers, and blazing suns boiled the blood in their veins. Thunder roared, shaking the world, and lightning stabbed down to shatter tanks and throw helicopters out of the sky like burning birds. But once again the sorcerer priests struck back, breaking the hold of the magi on the natural world, and the weather settled and grew still once more. The priests were strong in their fanaticism, and had the faith of their whole army to draw on. The magi had only themselves and the power of the stones, and they knew that wasn't going to be enough. Especially now the sorcerer priests had located them.

A platoon of soldiers split away from the main thrust of the invasion, and headed straight for the circle of stones. They were perhaps thirty minutes away, or even less. No time left for thought or planning; only desperation, and one last throw of the dice. The magi clasped each other's hands tightly, and raised their voices in a new song. They called upon the walkers of the Low Road, the road taken by the spirits of the dead as they made their way unseen to Shadows Fall and the Forever Door, and their final rest. Most of the dead could or would not hear them, but the newly dead of Shadows Fall, murdered by the Warriors, stepped aside from their last journey to help protect their town one last time. They sank into the circle of stones, giving all they had left to give: themselves. New power thundered through the magi, coursing round and round as they sought frantically to harness and control it. The hold they finally managed was tentative at best, but for the moment it would serve. They gave it shape and form as geomancy; the magic of the earth and all that moved in it. They sang, their voices hoarse and strained but still true, and the earth heard.

The Warrior platoon was drawing closer. There was time only for one last spell. They could attack the main invasion force, or defend themselves, but not both. To their credit, the magi did not hesitate. They raised their song and called on something that lived deep within the earth; old and awful and magnificent in his power. The main advance stopped again as the Warriors felt his coming. The ground trembled beneath their feet, as though a tube train was barrelling through its tunnel far below. But the trembling grew stronger as something rose through the earth towards them; something huge and potent. The earth cracked open and great vents widened, through which could be seen the enormous white segments of Cromm Cruach, the great Wurm.

The magi watched the Wurm's progress as tanks and

jeeps and soldiers disappeared into great cracks in the earth. They watched as the Wurm burst up out of the ground, scattering tanks and troop transporters like toys. The earth swallowed up screaming soldiers, and shook endlessly with the Wurm's rage. The Warriors opened fire on the great white segments as they appeared through the vents in the earth, but their guns did little damage. He was too big, too vast for their tiny weapons. A giant hole opened up beneath one platoon, swallowing men and vehicles alike, and then the two sides slammed together as Cromm Cruach closed his huge mouth, and the Warriors were gone, as though they had never been.

And still the Wurm raged on, his subterranean path undermining buildings on all sides. A house collapsed suddenly, as though all the strength had gone out of it. Cracks sprang up walls as more buildings shifted, falling slowly in on themselves as the Wurm swept on. Innocent people were crushed in the wreckage, and the air was full of the screaming of the trapped and injured. The magi watched with horror and changed their song, ordering Cromm Cruach back into the depths of the earth, but he fought them with slow, implacable power. For the first time in centuries he was free, and he would not willingly be bound again.

The magi didn't have enough power left to compel him and they knew it. They also knew that the approaching Warrior platoon was almost upon them. They could not bind the Wurm, and they could not protect themselves now that they had been found, so they did the only thing they could. They allowed the Warriors to breach the circle of stones, and made no defence as the soldiers shot them all. They lay in silent, bloody heaps among the stones, but in the few instants left to them they drew upon the magic generated by their own deaths and used it to bind the Wurm and send him back into the depths of the earth. Some weapons are too powerful to use. The ground grew still and buildings settled, and people began to search among the rubble for survivors.

The Warriors urinated on the bodies of the magi, blew up the standing stones with explosives, and went on to the next objective.

Frank Morse, who had been to the town before as an assassin, now walked naked and unarmed through chaos and destruction, and none of it touched him. To every side of him his Warrior brothers shot down the fleeing scum and torched their diseased buildings, but even though the Godforsaken inhabitants sometimes found the desperation to fight back, Frank Morse took no harm at all. He strode happily at the front of the invasion force, singing the praises of the Lord and damning the unbelievers, and a warm glow filled his heart that he had proved worthy of God's protection. Not that he'd ever really doubted it, of course. He was pure and exemplary, and steadfast in his persecution of the ungodly. He looked about him, taking in the smoke and flames of the burning buildings, and the screaming of the townspeople, and laughed out loud. God was in his Heaven, and finally all was right with the world, or soon would be. Soon the Warriors would seize control of the Forever Door from the unworthy, and then they would take their rightful place as rulers of this sinful world. The word of the Lord would be mercilessly enforced, and God help the guilty.

Some of his brother Warriors fell as the townspeople fought back, striking viciously at the soldiers of the Lord like cornered rats. Some of his brothers did not rise again, and Morse said a prayer for their souls. Only a short prayer, since obviously they were unworthy. If their faith had been as pure and holy as his, they would not have fallen to the unbelievers. And then he rounded a corner and all was quiet. He looked quickly about him, but the rest of the invasion force was nowhere to be seen. The street was empty, the buildings untouched by fire or destruction. He must have taken a wrong turning. He hurried back round the corner, but that street was deserted too. Somehow he'd become separated from his brothers, and he was naked and alone in the territory of the enemy. Morse felt a brief twinge of panic and ruthlessly fought it down. He was not alone. The Lord was with him and would protect him. Perhaps this was some kind of test . . .

He heard something moving down at the other end of the street, and looked quickly round. A small dark figure was moving slowly but steadily towards him. His hands twitched, reaching for guns he didn't have. The figure stepped out of the shadows and into the light, and Morse's heart jumped. He knew the creature, and it knew him. The four-foot teddy bear with golden honey fur and dark knowing eyes came to a halt a dozen feet away. He was wearing his usual bright red tunic and trousers and a bright blue scarf, and carrying an automatic rifle. Bandoliers of ammunition crossed his chest, falling almost to his ankles. Morse had never heard of Bruin Bear. His parents had protected him from such trivial and fanciful material when he was a child. There had been no room for magic and imagination in his life, even then. But he remembered the Bear from the churchyard at All Souls. He remembered firing at it and being unable to hit it, and just when he thought he'd escaped up the rope ladder to the helicopter, the unnatural beast had grabbed his ankle in its filthy paw and crushed it. He still had the bruises.

'Demon,' said Morse. 'I do not fear you. The Lord is with me.'

'I remember you too,' said Bruin Bear. 'You shot my friend. You would have shot me too, if you could. But now I've got a gun and you haven't. Any last words, assassin?'

'You cannot harm me. God will strike you down.'

'You shot my friend,' said the Bear, and for the first time a shiver of uncertainty went through Morse. There was something in the Bear's voice, and in his eyes; something cold and implacable. Morse tried to smile. He couldn't take this seriously, a teddy bear with a gun; but the rifle looked very real and very dangerous, and the more he thought about it, so did the Bear. He shuddered suddenly as a cold wind caressed him, and he tried to stand a little straighter so the demon wouldn't think he was shivering out of fear. The Bear raised his gun and took aim, and for a long moment the two of them just stood there, looking at each other.

And then the Bear lowered his gun, looked at it, and sighed quietly. He knelt down and laid his rifle gently on the ground, took off his bandoliers of ammunition, and put them down beside it. He straightened up and looked steadily at Morse.

'No,' he said, quietly but firmly. 'I'm not a killer, and I won't let you make me one. That would be a betrayal of everything I ever stood for in a child's world. I'd say to hell with you, but I think you're already there.'

Bruin Bear turned and walked away, and Morse watched him go. The Bear turned a corner and disappeared, and the paralysis that had held Morse suddenly vanished. He ran forward, grabbed the bandoliers of ammunition and threw them over his shoulder, snatched up the rifle, and ran down the street after the Bear. The little bastard had actually dared to threaten him, dared to make him afraid . . . He rounded the corner, gun at the ready, and then had to stop abruptly as he almost ran straight into his brother Warriors.

'Ah, there you are, Frank,' said the Major in charge of his unit. 'Thought we'd lost you for a minute. Hardly surprising in all this confusion, but do try and stick with us, there's a good chap. Haven't got time for search parties. Found yourself a gun too, I see. That's what I like to see in a man; initiative. I think we can forget the naked and unarmed bit now; you've proved your point. Now come along; we've been tracking a demon this way, and with any luck it'll lead us right to where the others of its kind are hiding.'

He broke off and looked down the street. Morse followed his gaze. A large cartoon dog, some five feet tall and wearing an ill-fitting white suit with spats, was shambling away from the Warriors. It looked old, with white and grey hairs on its face, and its long ears dropped lifelessly.

It looked back, double-taked on seeing the Warriors, and tried to run faster. The Major laughed. 'After him, men! Don't let him out of your sight. I want his ears. Come on, Frank. Keep up. Don't want to miss out on the sport, eh?'

The soldiers ran down the street after the dog, who looked as though he might collapse at any moment but still somehow managed to keep ahead of his pursuers. The Warriors laughed and shouted as they ran, sometimes firing their guns into the air for the fun of seeing the dog cringe and jump and howl piteously. Morse didn't laugh. The dog seemed harmless enough, but he didn't trust anything in this Godforsaken town. Besides, this was duty, not entertainment. Laughter was frivolous, and a distraction.

The dog ran into a narrow alley and the Warriors ran in after it, whooping and laughing. But once inside the alley, there was no sign of the dog anywhere. The soldiers stumbled to a halt and looked about them. The alley was a dead end, and there were no turnings off. There was nowhere for the dog to have gone. Morse felt a sudden cold hand clutch at his heart, and he turned to the Major.

'Get us out of here, now. It's a trap.'

'Steady, Frank. We'll find where it's hiding. Can't just have vanished, after all. Could be there's a secret door here somewhere, that'll lead us right to the rest of them. Nothing to worry about. It's just a dog, after all.'

'No,' said a calm, quiet voice from the shadows. 'Not just a dog. A *cartoon* dog.'

It stepped out into the light again, and the Warriors stirred uneasily. It stood straighter, and its gaze was cold and direct. It didn't look old or harmless any more. It grinned, and its mouth stretched unnaturally, showing large blocky teeth.

'I'm not real,' said the dog. 'And though I live in the real world, I still retain some of the characteristics from the animated world that birthed me. For example, I can be bigger . . .' It shot up twenty feet in height, ballooning in size, and the Warriors fell back, aiming their guns. 'Or

343

smaller.' It shrank to the size of a mouse, and scurried about between the Warriors' feet. They shouted and stamped, but it dodged them easily. The dog resumed its original size and place and stood grinning nastily at the unnerved soldiers. Its teeth had points now, and its paws sprouted vicious-looking claws. 'And just in case that isn't enough, I brought a few friends with me.'

The shadows stirred, growing teeth and eyes, and monsters stepped out into the light of the alleyway. They grew and shrank and changed shape with sickening, fluid ease. They had teeth and claws and huge, impossible muscles. In a cartoon they might have been funny, but in the real world they were awful and hideous, like every bad dream a child ever had. One Warrior suddenly panicked. He put his rifle to his shoulder and opened fire, and in a moment they were all firing. The alley was full of smoke and the crash of guns, firing over and over again. Finally, one by one they stopped, and lowered their weapons. The smoke cleared, and the cartoon monsters were still there, horrid and impossible in their vivid, Technicolor hues. They were riddled with bullet holes, which healed in seconds as the Warriors watched. The monsters' shapes ran and changed with dreadful ease, and one soldier whimpered. The monsters laughed. They didn't look at all funny. The dog was still grinning.

'You can't hurt us. We're cartoons, and anything's possible in a cartoon. Anything at all.'

The monsters ballooned up, filling the alley, and fell on the Warriors with teeth and claws. The alley was full of screams and horrid laughter, and the soft tearing sound of rending flesh. The cartoons tore the soldiers apart and played with the pieces, and never stopped laughing.

Frank Morse turned and ran the moment the monsters moved, and was out of the alley and running for his life by the time he heard the first screams. The bandoliers of ammunition flapped painfully against his bare chest and back as he ran, the rifle all but forgotten in his hands. He forgot all about his friends and brother soldiers, his duty and his faith, and ran full tilt, gasping for breath, expecting at any moment that something awful would grab him from behind, but nothing did. He almost reached the end of the street, and then stumbled to a halt as a single figure stepped out into the light to face him.

Morse just stood there for a moment, his heart hammering and his lungs straining, and then he jerkily brought the rifle to bear on the newcomer, standing only a few yards away. But he didn't shoot. He recognized the figure. Seven feet tall, wrapped in a long trenchcoat, with a large and blocky goat's head, he was carrying a pistol carelessly in one hand. They stood and looked at each other for a while.

'You're dead,' said Morse finally. 'I shot you.'

'Just wounded,' said the Sea Goat. 'You're not as good a shot as you think. I'm glad you remember me, though. I remember you.'

'Demon,' said Morse. 'Hellspawn.'

'That's pretty good, coming from someone who just ran off and left his friends to die. Pretty good, from someone who stood by and watched as his friends murdered innocents and burnt down their homes. But none of that matters now. Now, there's just you and me. You've got a gun, and so do I. Unlike last time. Maybe you'll shoot me, or I'll shoot you. Neither of us is going to miss at this range. I guess you've got to ask yourself; do you feel lucky, punk?'

Morse turned and ran. He'd get away, and then come back and kill the beast. Kill them all. He could feel the ground pounding under his feet, and smelt smoke on the chilly air. He opened his mouth to scream, and the Sea Goat shot him in the back of the head.

Warriors of the Cross dragged the seven Councillors they'd found through the ruins of what had once been their town. Ruined buildings were ablaze to every side, flames leaping up into the night sky from blackened skeletal frames. Rubble and broken glass lay scattered across the deserted street, and the dead and the dying lay everywhere. The Warriors passed them by. They were celebrating. Some were drinking wine and spirits they'd looted from abandoned stores. They laughed and sang and kicked the Councillors to make them walk faster, or just for the fun of it. The seven Councillors kept their heads down, and said nothing. They all showed blood and bruising from severe beatings, and they knew better now than to make any protest or complaint. Three Councillors were already dead; shot down in cold blood because they were surplus to requirements, and to ensure the other Councillors would do as they were told.

Their hands were handcuffed behind their backs, and they each had a noose around their neck, with a Warrior on the other end of the rope to keep them moving. They trudged along, heads bowed through fatigue if not respect, and watched the ground carefully, not wanting to trip or stumble. If they fell, the Warriors just dragged them till they found their feet again. The soldiers thought that was hilarious. The Councillors had given up all thought of escape or rescue. There wasn't even anyone left to see their shame. Those townspeople who had survived the constant shelling and the attentions of the blood-crazed invaders had either gone to ground or run for their lives. As if there was anywhere left to run, in Shadows Fall. The Warriors sang drinking songs mixed with hymns, and dragged the Councillors through the blazing ruins of Hell.

They finally reached the old Georgian house that had served as a formal meeting place for the town Council. It had been shelled like all the others, but the ground floor was still pretty much intact. The soldiers led the Councillors inside, encouraging them on with blows and kicks, and finally seated them around a table in what had once been their main meeting room. That seemed like another world now. The Councillors weren't surprised the Warriors knew so much about them; the soldiers had already boasted of the spies they'd infiltrated into the town. The Lieutenant in charge of the soldiers pulled up a chair, dusted off the

346

seat, and sat down facing the Councillors. He was young, barely out of his twenties, with a receding hairline and a constant, humourless smile. He smoked a thin black cigar and didn't bother to take it out of his mouth when he spoke. The Councillors listened carefully to whatever he said. If they missed something, and the Lieutenant had to repeat himself, they were beaten.

'Well, here we all are,' said the Lieutenant. 'Isn't this cosy? Sit up straight, all of you. I can't abide a man who slouches. Let us now get down to business. Of the fifteen Councillors of Shadows Fall, three are dead, and five are missing, presumed dead. So as far as civil authority goes in this cesspit of a town, you are it; and you are mine, body and soul. We were supposed to accept the town's surrender from you, but I think we can take that as read. There's no real opposition left anywhere, and what there is, is being mopped up even as we speak. Which really leaves us with only one thing we still need to talk about. Can you guess what that is, gentlemen?'

'Time,' muttered one of the Councillors.

'Got it in one. Old Father Time himself. We were hoping to reach him via the Sarcophagus in the park, but apparently our people are encountering difficulties there. So, you gentlemen are going to contact Time, and persuade him to surrender the Galleries of Frost and Bone to us. On the grounds that if he doesn't, we will kill you all, one at a time, and then start executing groups of townspeople gathered at random until he does.'

'It's not that simple,' said the Councillor, and the Lieutenant back-handed him casually across the face. There was unexpected strength in the blow, and the Councillor rocked in his chair. Blood poured in a steady stream from one nostril.

'Speak when you are spoken to,' said the Lieutenant. 'If I want your advice, unlikely as that seems, I'll ask for it. What's your name, Councillor?'

'Marley. Patrick Marley. May I speak?'

'Depends. If I don't like what you have to say, I might

get annoyed with you. And we wouldn't want that, would we?'

'We can't just pick up a phone and talk to Time,' said Marley doggedly. 'We each have a ring that Time gave us. We speak his name to the ring, and if he feels like it he'll acknowledge us. If he doesn't, he won't, which usually means we have to send messengers to the Galleries to find out why.'

'All right,' said the Lieutenant. 'Call him. And for your sake, he'd better answer.'

He gestured to one of his soldiers, who produced a ring of keys and unlocked Marley's handcuffs. He wiped blood from his mouth, massaged his wrists, and then stopped as the soldier put a gun to his head. He lifted a blocky gold signet ring to his mouth, and spoke distinctly.

'Time, this is Councillor Marley. Please respond. I have been told my life and others will be forfeit if you do not.'

There was an uncomfortably long pause, and then there was a sudden silent thump, felt more than heard, like the striking of a mute bell, and Time was standing among them. He stood by the window, with his back to the flames and devastation, but the anger in his face made it plain he was aware of it. He appeared to be a cross between a living man and one of his own metal automatons; a cyborg hybrid of man and machine. Cables and machinery protruded from his dead white flesh, and half his face was painted ceramic. Marley had never seen him this way before, but kept his mouth shut. Presumably Time was showing the Warriors what they consciously or subconsciously expected to see.

'Don't bother to threaten me with your weapons,' said Time flatly. 'I'm not here; this is just an image I've placed in your minds. Relax, Marley. Help is on the way. I would have come sooner, but I've been rather busy. My helpers are spread rather thin at the moment.'

'He called you because I told him to,' said the Lieutenant. 'He'll do anything for me. If he knows what's good for him. I have a proposition to put to you . . .'

348

'I know,' said Time. 'I was listening. The answer's no. The town is more important than its people or its Councillors. But you won't have time to kill many more anyway. The town is awakening, and forces beyond your comprehension are rising against your petty army. Did you really think you could conquer Shadows Fall by force of arms? Fools. There are forces in the world that will not be denied or dictated to. You'll understand soon. For the moment your sorcerer priests are strong enough to keep me from interfering directly, but that will pass. Listen to me, Lieutenant; it's still not too late to stop this madness. Gather your men and leave the town. You won't find what you're looking for here or in my Galleries.'

'Nice try,' said the Lieutenant. 'But if it's not here, why are you so desperate to keep us from it? The executions will begin now, with Marley, followed by another Councillor every five minutes. After that, we'll start dragging people in here and get creative. Feel free to watch.'

'I think you'll find you have other, more pressing matters to worry about,' said Time. 'Why don't you look out of the window?'

He disappeared between one moment and the next, and the Warriors looked at each other uncertainly. Time's voice rang on the air, cool and calm and eerily disturbing.

'I have unleashed my hound, Lieutenant, and soon you will hear him howling for your blood.'

The Lieutenant chuckled quietly, shaking his head admiringly. 'Full of bravado, even to the end. I'll see him kneel and beg for mercy after we've dragged him out of his hole.' He gestured casually at the soldier guarding Marley. 'Take him outside, and hang him from the nearest lamppost.'

And then he broke off, and turned quickly to look out of the window, as from outside came the sudden sounds of shouting and gunfire, followed by horrified, agonized screams.

'Watch the Councillors!' snapped the Lieutenant to his men. 'If they give you any trouble, shoot them.'

349

He looked out of the window again, and had he not had his back to them, his men could have watched the colour drain from his face. Out in the street, Warriors were dying.

The soldiers fired wildly, hitting each other as often as not, but the killer moved smoothly among them, slaughtering everyone he touched. His hands were like razors and a terrible strength moved in his spindly arms. He looked across at the window with his smiling turnip head, and mockingly saluted the Lieutenant. Jack Fetch had come to town.

He tore a bloody path through the demoralized soldiers, tearing men literally limb from limb with his unnatural strength. Bullets slammed into him from all sides, raising puffs of smoke from his ragged clothes, but since he was not alive and never had been, he took no hurt from any of it. He had no blood to lose or bones to break, and the damage the bullets caused to his unliving components healed in seconds, as though drawing new material from the air itself. His gloved hands closed like vices, and his slender form moved with a deadly grace and speed almost too fast to follow.

A tank roared out of a side street and tracked Jack with its gun. He turned to face it and the tank fired. Jack Fetch dodged the shell easily, ran forward and grabbed the right-hand caterpillar track with both hands. It took him only a moment to lift the tank up and turn it on its side, shifting the many tons of steel as though they were weightless. The tank commander crawled out of the turret at the top, wildly waving a handgun. Jack seized the man's head with both hands, and turned it through one hundred and eighty degrees. The sound of the man's neck snapping was too quiet to be heard in the general din.

A soldier threw a grenade at the scarecrow. Jack caught it and threw it back. He was still close enough to feel the effects of the blast, but he stood unmoving and unharmed as the explosion destroyed everything around him. A helicopter gunship came screaming out of the dark, its hammering guns digging trenches in the street. It made two passes over the scarecrow, strafing him with thousands of rounds a minute, but he just stood there and took it. The helicopter banked around to make a third pass. Jack pulled a lamp-post out of the ground and threw it like a javelin. It smashed through the windshield, transfixing the pilot in his seat like a bug on a pin. The helicopter spun out of control and smashed into the side of a burning house. The explosion sent burning fuel out over a wide area. Soldiers ran screaming through the night like blazing torches.

Jack Fetch had stood far enough back not to be affected, and this raised a faint hope in one of the Warriors. He advanced on the scarecrow with a flamethrower, and Jack came to meet him with his unwavering smile. The soldier opened up as soon as he was within range, and liquid fire washed over the scarecrow. He burned with a bright flickering light, but was not consumed. He strode on, an unstoppable, unflinching juggernaut, and the Warrior threw aside his flamethrower and ran, screaming. Jack Fetch stopped and looked about him. The soldiers had fled. All that remained were unmoving bodies and the burning wreckage of the crashed helicopter, further down the street.

The scarecrow turned and walked steadily towards the Council meeting house, leaving a trail of burning footsteps behind him. Flames licked around him like a living cloak. The Lieutenant pushed up the window and opened fire, but the scarecrow barely shuddered under the bullets' impact. The Lieutenant ordered his men to open fire too, and two soldiers moved in beside him with their automatic weapons and added their fire to his. Jack Fetch advanced through the hail of bullets like a man breasting a not particularly heavy tide. Even through the flames, the Warriors could see his turnip head was still smiling.

Jack walked up the steps, pushed open the front door and strode down the hall towards the Council meeting room. Warriors filled the hall before him, firing wildly and backing away as he advanced unhurriedly towards them.

And then silence fell across the scene, as one by one the soldiers ran out of ammunition, or their guns overheated, and in a matter of moments all that could be heard in the hall was the quiet crackling of the flames licking around the scarecrow's body, and the brief rasp of his twiggy feet on the floor. The Warriors backed away into the Council meeting room, and Jack Fetch went in after them. The Lieutenant grabbed Marley, pulled him close and put his gun to the Councillor's head.

'I still have some ammunition left. Get out of here, demon. Get out or I'll kill him.'

Jack nodded his turnip head once, and disappeared. One moment he was there, standing in the doorway wreathed in crackling flames, and then the doorway was empty and the room was completely silent. The Lieutenant gaped, frozen in place for a moment, and Jack Fetch reappeared behind him. The Lieutenant just had time to feel the sudden burst of heat, and then the scarecrow embraced him in his burning arms. The Lieutenant screamed for help, and his men bolted, fighting each other in their need to get out of the room. The scarecrow hugged the Lieutenant to him, and the man's back and neck broke in a series of quiet pops. Jack released his hold and let the dead man fall to the floor, and then set about calmly beating out the flames on his body with his gloved hands. The Councillors looked at each other, slowly realizing they were free again. Marley stooped down and picked up the Lieutenant's gun. Jack Fetch gave him a brief salute, and then disappeared, leaving nothing behind him but the smell of burning rags. Marley looked at the other Councillors.

'I didn't know he could do that. Did you know he could do that?'

Lester Gold, the Mystery Avenger, leaned against a lamp-post and tried to get his breath. He felt old. No, worse than that; he felt old and tired and useless. He pushed himself away from the lamp-post, and wiped his mouth with the back of his hand. Had to keep moving. Standing around could get you shot. He led his people down the deserted street, gun ready in his hand, eyes alert for any sign of movement. They were almost back in the suburbs now. Safe enough. There might be an army of the bastards, but Shadows Fall was a big place, and they couldn't be everywhere at once. They'd been here, though. Several of the houses had been shelled, and two had been gutted by flames. You could still smell the smoke in the air. There was a haphazard, almost absent-minded feel to the damage, as though the invaders had just done it in passing, on their way to somewhere more important. But for the moment the streets were empty and things were quiet. Gold was grateful for that. He needed somewhere to rest and get his second wind. And more than that, he needed to feel there was still somewhere safe to be found in Shadows Fall. Without that, he couldn't go on.

When he'd first heard the news of the invading army, he'd set off to meet them in his old costume, not really knowing what to expect, but still fairly confident he could do something to help defend his adopted town. He'd caught a glimpse of himself in a shop-front window, and nodded crisply to himself in passing. He'd looked smart and fine in his gleaming black body armour with its brave red and blue flashes, and his cape swirled and snapped magnificently as he walked. He still had an old man's face, but he felt young and strong and confident. He found the soldiers as they came howling through the narrow Old Town streets, shooting at everything that moved, and torching buildings at random. There were shouts and screams and thick black smoke billowing up as the invaders swept aside all resistance with almost casual ease. They'd barely even noticed the Mystery Avenger. He was one man, and they were an army, and even a Man of Action couldn't hope to stand against tanks and rocket-launchers.

He'd exchanged a few shots and then been forced to run for his life. He was soon caught up in a crowd of refugees, running this way and that as the soldiers herded them. He finally fought his way clear of the panic, and joined up

with a group of other costumed adventurers and superheroes. Like him, they'd taken costumes and uniforms out
of old closets and put them on again for the first time in
years, somehow convinced that the town needed them.
And like him they'd gone to meet the invaders and found
garish uniforms made them an easy target for soldiers with
modern weaponry. Everyone had stories to tell, of heroes
left bloodied and dying in the streets, or shot out of the air
like clay pigeons.

Heatstroke had been caught in a crossfire. The Double
Danger twins had been buried under a collapsing building
while trying to rescue the tenants. The Living Lightning
had gone down trying to fight a dozen men at once. They
kicked him to death. Someone took his bloodied cowl as a
souvenir. And Ms Fate had tried to take on a helicopter
gunship single-handed. It shot her out of the air with a
smart missile that followed her wherever she flew.

They should have known. The really powerful heroes
never came to Shadows Fall. They were still in print in the
outside world. People still believed in them. Only the
second-raters, the lesser heroes, came to Shadows Fall.
They were still brave and true and magnificent, and they
went uncomplaining to their deaths like so many brightly-
coloured mayflies.

They didn't all die. Some had the sense to run. The
survivors found each other and banded together in small
groups, as much for reassurance as strength. Superheroes
joined up with super-villains, old enmities forgotten. Many
old foes had made their peace on coming to Shadows Fall.
For them the war was over, and it didn't take them long
usually to find they had more in common with each other
than with 'civilians'.

The surviving heroes adapted, and fought a guerrilla
campaign against the invaders, striking from the shadows
and disappearing before they could be caught. They had
some successes, but not enough to do more than slow the
soldiers' relentless advance. Heroes without any special
abilities worked in small groups on the edges of the fray,

rescuing innocent bystanders where they could, and getting them to safety. Or what safety was left in an occupied town.

Gold stopped again, looked about him and listened carefully. Somewhere not too far away a fire was burning, but otherwise there was no sight or sound of the invaders. Either the army had passed this area by as not worth occupying, or they were spread so thinly now they couldn't guard every street. Either way, there were bound to be patrols, and he'd better get his people moving before a patrol turned up and found them out in the open. He breathed hard, trying to force the exhaustion from his body. He was in excellent shape for a man of his age, but seeing so many die as he stood by helplessly had knocked a lot of his strength out of him. He felt his age now. But he couldn't let that stop him. Not while people still depended on him.

He looked back at his people, to find they were looking back at him with what little hope remained in them. Twenty-three men and women, the only survivors from an entire block targeted by the soldiers for destruction. They'd lost everything they ever owned or cared for, and now they were relying on him and his three fellow adventurers to save the day at the last possible moment, and get them to safety. Just like they always did in the stories. Gold knew better, but he didn't say anything to disillusion them. It would have been cruel.

He looked at his fellow heroes, and smiled slightly. Not the companions he would have chosen, but needs must when the devil drives. The Bloodred Claw had been an oriental villain, back when such things had been fashionable. He had to be in his nineties now, and looked older than God, but he could still fire a poisoned dart with the best of them. The soldiers' savagery hadn't touched him, but their casual destruction had raised an anger in him he hadn't felt for decades. He'd put on his ceremonial armour, left his restaurant, armed only with his old trademark dart gun, had gone out alone to stop the invaders.

Then there was Ms Retaliator. She had had a brief career in the late seventies, when they were trying practically anything, but she never caught on. Ms Retaliator was actually a transvestite; a man who dressed up as a super-heroine to fight crime. That wasn't actually common knowledge, but you can't keep secrets for long in a place like Shadows Fall. She was a good and brave fighter at close quarters, but not much use against tanks and automatic weapons.

The only one who seemed at all in his element was Captain Nam; a patriotic super-hero created to put a more positive face on the Vietnam war. He'd never really been popular, and was a merchandising disaster. He was coping well with the invasion; for him it was like coming home. At the moment he was sulking because Gold had hit him for saying he loved the smell of napalm in the evening.

Gold looked up and down the street. Time to get moving, while it was still quiet. Not for the first time, he wondered who exactly it was he was hiding from. He had a name, the Warriors, but he was no wiser after Father Callahan's explanation than before. The invaders didn't seem to belong to any particular race or country. They had no flags and no particular uniforms. Just soldiers, with guns. They'd made no attempt to explain who they were, or what they wanted. They just moved in, took over, and shot anyone who complained. Sometimes they hanged protesters from lamp-posts, and left them dangling as a warning to others. But whoever or whatever they were, they were professional soldiers, and so far Shadows Fall had been unable to find anything with which to stop them.

Somebody screamed, in the next street. Gold gestured quickly for his people to stay put, padded silently forward, and eased his head round the corner of the street. Two soldiers had cornered a teenage girl in a doorway, and were laughing as they pulled at her clothes. She was crying and pleading with them, but they found that even funnier. Gold thought briefly that he ought to ignore this and take his people some other way. He had a responsibility to protect them, not go charging off to be a hero one more time. But he couldn't turn his back on a cry for help. He protected the innocent and punished the guilty. That was who he was. He was the Man of Action, the Mystery Avenger, and that had to mean something.

Besides, there were only two of the bastards. He could take them out, rescue the girl, and be gone before anyone even noticed he'd been there. He eased round the corner, moved silently down the street, and was upon the soldiers in a moment. He couldn't use his gun; too noisy. One of them heard something, and started to turn. Gold hit him just above the ear, with all his strength behind it. The soldier's head whipped round, and he was unconscious before he hit the ground. Nothing like brass knuckles under your glove to give you an edge. The other soldier started to bring his gun to bear, and Gold kicked it out of his hands. He winced despite himself as he recovered his balance; he wasn't as supple as he used to be. The soldier lashed out with a karate kick, and he blocked it instinctively. Nice to know the old reflexes were still there.

He closed with the soldier and coolly proceeded to beat the living crap out of him. His hands were hard and sure, and he had years of training and experience the soldier couldn't hope to match. And the soldier didn't have Gold's anger; his ice-cold rage. Blood flew on the air, and none of it was Gold's. It felt good to finally get his hands on one of the faceless enemy who had come to destroy his town, and he only stopped when he decided he was enjoying it too much. He let the unconscious soldier slump to the pavement, and moved forward to comfort the sobbing girl. She clung to him like a child, reassured by his costume. Children trusted heroes.

He heard the soldiers coming before he saw them, and gave the girl a push to start her down the street towards his people. The girl didn't want to leave him, and he had to push her again, harder. Then she heard the approaching jeep too, and turned and ran. Gold stood his ground. He couldn't hope to outrun a jeep, but he should be able to hold it off long enough for the girl to reach his people and escape. They'd get her to safety. He'd catch up with them later. He drew his gun from the holster on his hip. It was old-fashioned now, not nearly as powerful as some modern handguns, but they'd been together for too many years to think about changing. It was accurate and reliable, and that was all he'd ever asked of any gun.

The jeep came roaring round the corner at speed, practically on two wheels. One of the soldiers in it saw Gold, pointed at him and shouted something. It didn't sound friendly. Gold took careful aim and blew the man right out the back of the jeep. It screeched to a halt, turning sideways to block the street. Gold aimed again and shot the driver while he was still in his seat. The other two soldiers bailed out and crouched down behind the jeep, bringing their own guns to bear. Gold moved quickly off the street to take cover in a doorway. It didn't look too bad. There were only two of them. He could take care of them and catch up with his people later.

And then another jeep roared round the corner into the street, followed by more soldiers hurrying on foot behind it. One of the trapped soldiers must have radioed for reinforcements. Gold counted fourteen before a sputter of gunfire drove him back into the doorway. Not good odds, but he'd faced worse. He ran a quick check through his pockets. One grenade, a smoke bomb well overdue for testing, and a handful of spare ammunition. He'd used up all his other tricks and pieces to get this far. More gunfire raked his position, some of it ricocheting off his body armour. He swore feelingly. The bullets weren't powerful enough to penetrate, but the impact hurt like shit. He was going to be a mass of bruises tomorrow.

One of the jeeps started to edge down the street, providing cover for the soldiers behind it. Gold leaned out of the doorway just long enough to blow out one of its tyres. He couldn't let them get past him. His people needed time to get away. Bullets hammered all around him, chipping away at the brickwork. He could always try and shoot out the door's lock and retreat into the house, but there'd be time for that later, when things got really desperate. They weren't good now, but he could handle it. He grinned nastily. Strangely enough, he felt younger and more alert now than he had in ages. Fighting alone against overwhelming odds, to protect the innocent; that was what being a hero was all about.

He leaned out of the doorway, snapped off two quick shots, and ducked back again, laughing breathlessly as he heard the soldiers shouting and cursing and scrabbling for cover. He'd play with them a little longer, until he'd bought enough time for his people, and then he'd make his usual last-minute, death-defying escape. He felt young again. He was the Mystery Avenger, the Man of Action, and he was going to show these people what that meant.

He never saw the soldier with the sniper's rifle, in a second-floor window at the house opposite. Never saw the soldier put his eye to the telescopic sight, take careful aim and pull the trigger. The bullet hit Gold squarely through the left eye, slamming his head back against the closed door. Lester Gold slumped bonelessly to the ground, leaving a thick smear of blood and brains on the door.

The soldiers took it in turns to kick his body, and then set off down the street after the ones who'd got away.

The two Warrior officers looked round Doctor Mirren's study with the same considered contempt they'd shown him. Dealing with traitors was a dirty business, their gaze implied, and not one they undertook by choice. They'd come to see Doctor Mirren because they'd been ordered to, but they didn't have to like it. Mirren was studiously polite, and offered the officers a chair and a brandy, both of which the Warriors declined.

The Colonel looked to be in his mid-fifties, with a lined face and iron grey hair cropped brutally short. Deep scowl and thin lips. Mirren knew the sort. Heavily into cold showers and healthy exercise. Prides himself on never losing his temper, and drinks glasses of milk in private to placate his ulcers. Well into heart-attack territory. His aide was young and faceless and pathetically eager to look good in his Colonel's eyes. Early twenties, immaculately turned out, no sense of humour. They both looked at Mirren as though they'd just caught him scooping money out of the local church's poor box.

'We have very little time to spare, Doctor,' said the Colonel brusquely. 'Let us get to the purpose of this visit. The information you provided on the town's defences has proved useful, but we need more. We are facing increasing and unexpected opposition, and the town . . . is not quite what we expected.'

'Shadows Fall rarely is,' Mirren said calmly. 'This is a special place, quite unique in the world. In this town, you can find what you need. Not what you want, necessarily, but what you *need*. You can find judgement, redemption, long-lost friends or a second chance. A toy you lost in your childhood, or vengeance on the man who did you wrong. You can find anything here; anything at all. But you have to be careful. You might not know what you need, till you get it.'

'Is it possible to get a straight answer from anyone in this cursed town?' snapped the Colonel. 'When I ask a simple question, I expect a simple answer, not a long rambling speech stuffed with hippie mysticism. I expected better from you, Doctor. You were supposed to be a man of science. Now tell me about the town's defences. What more can we expect to encounter as we press further into the town? How big is the town? And who's in charge of defence and counter-attack?'

'Three simple questions, three simple answers. First: expect the unexpected. Second: the town is as big as it needs to be. And third: no one's in charge here, except sometimes possibly Time. Anything more than that is going to cost you. Shall we discuss my terms?'

'You know, I could make you talk sense,' said the aide.

Mirren smiled at him. 'I doubt that.'

There was something in the Doctor's voice and in his

eyes that kept the aide from replying. He looked to the Colonel for support and reassurance, but he too seemed lost for words. Mirren leaned back in his chair by the fire, and looked calmly up at the Warriors. They'd thought remaining standing while he was seated would give them a psychological advantage, but it wasn't working, and they all knew it. The scene was not a military interrogation; rather, it was more that of two errant schoolboys called before their headmaster. Mirren ignored the aide, and fixed his gaze on the Colonel.

'It's been almost a year now since I stumbled over one of your spies here in Shadows Fall. He'd been killed in a traffic accident, and they couldn't find anything on him to identify him. So they brought him to me, and I raised his spirit and asked him questions. Imagine my surprise at the answers I got. But it turned out to be a fortuitous accident, for both of us. Even then I was experiencing . . . difficulties in my research, and I saw in you a chance for much needed extra financing, and a measure of protection from the enemies I was making. So I contacted your people and made a deal. I'd give you the information you needed on how to locate and break into Shadows Fall, and you'd give me what I needed. I've done my part; I'm waiting for you to do yours.'

'First, you must release the Warrior spirit you called up,' said the Colonel.

'Him? He's long gone. It takes a lot of power to keep a spirit on this plane; I let him go as soon as I'd got all I needed from him.'

'Then I see no reason to stay here any longer.' The Colonel smiled thinly. 'We don't need you any more, Doctor. We can overcome our difficulties with a little effort and application. And with our man's spirit safe from you, you no longer have any hold over us. You were promised money, but you'll have to wait for it. You'll have your seven pieces of silver when the town is fully secure, and not before. As to your demand for protection; we need every man we have to press our attack. We don't have a man to spare, and won't for some time. I suggest you make other arrangements.'

'The money doesn't matter,' said Mirren evenly, 'but my enemies are getting closer with every hour. I must have protection now, or it'll be too late. You're an officer; these things can be arranged. It might be possible for you to keep the money I'm owed. No one would ever have to know.'

'Are you offering us a bribe?' said the aide. Mirren didn't look at him.

'Not to you, boy. You don't have anything I need. But your Colonel looks like a man who understands the realities of this world.'

'If I had time,' said the Colonel calmly, 'I'd have my men drag you out of this house, and flog you within an inch of your miserable life. Perhaps I will anyway, once the town is secured. I am a soldier of the Lord, and beyond temptation.'

'You all claim to serve the Lord,' said Mirren, 'but I don't think you know his real name. I don't think you know who your superiors are really bowing to. I have talked with the dead, and they see much that is denied the living. You serve the Lord of Flies, Colonel. You'd better wise up soon, or you're in for one hell of a shock later on.'

The aide lifted his hand as though to strike Mirren, but the Colonel stopped him with a gesture. 'Blasphemy. I should have expected as much. Congratulations, Doctor. You've convinced me you are worth taking the time to discipline. I have men under my command who understand everything there is to know about pain. After a short time in their company, you'll tell us everything you know about this town and its defences.'

And then he broke off and stepped back a pace, and the aide fell back with him. There was a shotgun in Mirren's hands that hadn't been there a moment before. Mirren rose up out of his chair, and the Warriors backed away until they bumped up against the wall behind them.

'Get out of my house,' said Mirren. 'I can't trust you to

362

protect me, so you're no use to me any more. Leave. Now.'

'We'll be back,' said the Colonel.

'I doubt that,' said Mirren.

He escorted them out of the study, down the hall and out of the front door. He stood in his doorway, the gun covering both the Warriors, and watched as they strode off into the overgrown excesses of his garden. Branches stirred, though no wind blew, and the ivy pulsed like veins. The dark green masses of the garden heaved with life, and the Warriors stopped and looked uncertainly about them. *Now*, breathed Mirren, and the garden fell hungrily upon the Warriors. Creepers lashed out to ensnare the two men, and ivy sank into their flesh with little mewling sounds. Greenery tore the bodies apart like paper, and scattered the largesse about the garden. Flowers chewed on flesh, and roots sucked up the blood where it fell.

Mirren nodded composedly. If the Warriors would not help him, he was forced to fall back on his own defences. Whoever fell in his garden would rise again in spirit to serve him, no matter where their loyalties might have lain before. When the dead finally came looking for him, he'd have an army of his own dead to defend him. He walked unhurriedly down the path, and the whispering greenery drew back to let him pass. He stopped and knelt down as something on the path caught his eye. It was a walkie-talkie. One of the Warriors must have dropped it. A thought came to him, and he smiled. He raised it to his mouth, and contacted the Warrior headquarters.

'This is Doctor Mirren. Please send me more soldiers.'

For a long time, there was only silence. And then, in the darkness under the rubble that was all that remained of the Cavern club, someone stirred. He wasn't sure who he was, but he hurt all over. Something heavy was lying across him, and he wriggled slowly out from under it. It felt like a body, disturbingly limp and unresponsive. Soft creaking and groaning sounds surrounded him in the darkness. He reached out cautiously with both hands and felt only space around him. He got his feet under him and stood up slowly, expecting to bang his head on something at any moment, and then reached upwards with his hands. His fingertips brushed against a mass of compacted rubble and jutting stone. It seemed secure enough under his fingers, even firm. Hart shrugged. There wasn't much he could do about it if it wasn't.

He froze where he was as identity trickled back into his mind. James Hart, in the Cavern club, in Shadows Fall. Polly . . . He crouched down and felt around him in the darkness, and his hands found the heavy weight that had been lying across him. It was a body, soft and yielding and utterly still. He found the face, and a murmur of breath moved against his fingers. For the first time in a long time, Hart wished he hadn't given up smoking. He would have killed for his old lighter right then. He crouched where he was, paralysed by an overwhelming sense of helplessness, and then someone moaned and protested feebly in a blurred, uncertain voice. The body stirred under his hands, and Hart carefully helped it sit up.

'Polly? Is that you? Are you all right? Are you hurt?' He realized he was babbling, and shut up to let her answer.

'I don't know,' said Polly's voice. 'It's too dark to tell. Everything seems to be attached that should be, but I've got a killer of a headache. What the hell happened?'

'Beats the hell out of me. I think I remember an explosion, but that's all.' His groping hand found hers, and he squeezed it reassuringly. It trembled constantly, like the heart of a captured bird. 'I don't suppose you've got a lighter on you? Or matches?'

'No. Are we where I think we are? Underneath a whole lot of collapsed building?'

'I'm afraid so. Don't worry. We're in an air pocket of some kind, and the roof seems solid enough. Someone'll be here soon to dig us out. Try and stay calm.' He didn't mention that the air was probably limited, and the less

364

they moved around, using it up, the better. He didn't think she was ready for that. He wasn't sure he was.

'Maybe they think everyone's dead,' said Polly finally. 'Maybe they've given up on us, and left. There could be tons of rubble above us.'

'There can't be that much, or the ceiling would have collapsed by now. We'll wait a while. If no one comes, we'll just have to dig our way out.'

He did his best to sound calm and casual, though his nerves were yammering at the unrelieved darkness. A sudden feeling of claustrophobia hit him, bringing a cold sheen of perspiration to his face. He lurched to his feet and tested the roof again. A stone block moved slightly as he applied pressure, and ominous creaks and groans sounded all around him. He snatched his hand away, but the sounds didn't stop. Hart grinned harshly in the darkness. In for a penny, in for a pound . . . He pushed harder, and the stone slipped sideways and fell away, landing by his feet. A grey shaft of light fell down, pushing back the darkness. It wasn't much, but at least he could make out shapes now. Polly turned her face into the light, and Hart fought to keep the concern out of his face. She was a mass of cuts and bruises, and shaking uncontrollably. And then he looked past her, as something else stirred in the gloom. There were two other people in the air pocket with them, lying crumpled together. One was trying to sit up. Hart scooted over to crouch beside them, and Polly gave a gasp of recognition as her eyes adjusted to the sparse light.

'It's Suzanne . . . and Sean Morrison. What are they doing here? Their table couldn'ti have been anywhere near ours . . .'

'Never question good luck,' said Hart. 'It might turn on you. See if you can get them up and moving, while I very carefully make us a bigger hole in the roof. I think we're not far from the surface.'

He worked slowly and cautiously, enlarging the hole piece by piece, waiting every now and again as the mass of rubble shifted to new positions. He hadn't a clue what was holding it up, but he had to take some chances. Finally he decided the hole was big enough, and he helped Polly and the other two clamber up out of the gloom and into the light. Hart was the last out, and then they moved quickly away across the sea of broken stone and metal to safer ground. Morrison kept shaking his head to clear it, and Suzanne was nursing what was very probably a broken arm, but otherwise they seemed to have come out of it reasonably intact. Polly was still trembling, and Hart put an arm round her shoulders. And then, finally, they looked around them; and wherever they looked there was devastation and bodies lying still in pools of blood. Here and there houses were burning, the flames leaping up unchallenged into the evening sky.

'How long were we down there?' said Hart slowly. 'It was barely getting dark when I arrived here.' He looked at his watch. 'Three hours? That can't be right. Can't be. How can so much have happened in three hours?'

'Do you think anyone else made it out of the club?' said Suzanne, grimacing as she tried to find a more comfortable way of supporting her injured arm.

'Not from the look of it,' said Morrison. 'It's a wonder we got out alive. A miracle. What the hell happened to the town while we were buried? It looks like a war zone . . . There must be dozens of bodies. Dozens . . .' He pulled a handkerchief from his pocket, and rubbed gingerly at his face. Blood had poured down from a long cut on his forehead, sealing his left eye shut when it dried. He worked doggedly to get the eye open, as though convinced the scene would change if he could only see it with both eyes. 'Something bad must have happened here. Something really bad.'

They moved out on to the deserted street, keeping close together for mutual support. Most of the street lights had been smashed, but there was a full moon and the light from the burning buildings. The smell of smoke was thick on the air. There were bodies and pieces of bodies everywhere. Most of the blood had dried, but some of it was still

366

wet to the touch. Morrison tested it once, but only once. Some of the dead wore military uniforms.

'We've been invaded,' said Suzanne. 'Terrorists, or something.'

'No,' said a sharp voice. 'Not terrorists. Soldiers of the Lord. Stand still where you are, and raise your hands above your heads.'

They all turned cautiously round, raising their hands. A single figure in a military uniform was covering them with an automatic rifle. He looked surprisingly young, but his face was set and grim, and the rifle was perfectly steady in his hands. He looked confident and professional, and quite ready to use the gun if he felt it necessary. The soldier looked coldly at Suzanne, who had raised only one hand.

'I said, everyone raise their hands.'

'She can't,' said Polly. 'She's got a broken arm.'

'Raise it anyway,' said the soldier. He smiled slightly as he watched Suzanne struggle to raise her other arm more than a few inches. Sweat ran down her face from the pain and effort. Hart scowled, but fought to control his anger. Trying to jump the soldier would just get him killed. There would be other times, other chances. The soldier finally tired of his game, and gestured to Suzanne to forget it.

'We're supposed to take prisoners, when the opportunity presents itself,' he said easily. 'Never know when you'll need a few hostages to keep the population quiet. Unfortunately, the rest of my squad have gone on and left me behind. The Sergeant didn't think this pile of rubble rated more than one guard. But now you've turned up. Four sinners who've crawled up out of what should have been their grave. The only survivors of that decadent club.'

'Decadent?' said Morrison. 'You must not get out much.'

'Shut up,' said the soldier calmly. 'You four are complications. I don't like complications. I can't stand guard over you, and I've no one to hand you over to for safe keeping. So, the only sensible thing to do is shoot the lot of you. Nothing personal, you understand.'

Before any of them could even start to say anything, the soldier aimed his rifle at Hart, and pulled the trigger. There was a quiet click, and nothing happened. The soldier looked down, confused, and Morrison stepped forward and punched him in the mouth. The soldier fell back a step, but didn't fall down or drop his gun. Morrison took careful aim, and kicked the soldier solidly in the groin. The colour dropped out of his face, and he dropped to his knees. Morrison took the rifle away from him, and hit him on the side of the head with the butt. The soldier fell forward and lay still. Morrison grinned at him savagely.

'Next time I hit you, fall down, shithead.'

'I think we should all get the hell out of here,' said Hart, 'before some of shithead's friends come looking for him.'

They set off slowly down the deserted street, unsure which direction to choose for the best. The street had the unnatural quiet of a bad dream. There was only the crackling of the flames, and their own footsteps. Everywhere they looked there was more devastation, more bodies. Men, women and children lying in awkward poses, watching their homes burn with empty eyes. Hart tried to think of something comforting to say to Polly, who was still trembling uncontrollably, but the words wouldn't come. It was all too big, too overwhelming, to be reduced to some simple phrase or platitude. He'd seen any number of wars and rebellions on television, but none of them had prepared him for the reality of broken bodies, and the thick sooty smell of burning buildings. It was as though some angry god had reached down and destroyed the street in a fit of childish pique, punishing it for being too independent, too safe and unconcerned. As though its happy everyday reality had somehow offended a vindictive world.

They all looked round sharply at the sound of an approaching vehicle. Hart led the way into the shadows of the nearest alleyway, and they watched in silence as a convoy of jeeps roared past, packed with armed soldiers. None of them paid any attention to the devastation they passed through, as though they'd seen so much of it that it no longer had any power to move them, one way or the other. The last jeep finally rounded the corner and was gone, and quiet returned to the scene.

'We've got to get off the street,' said Morrison. 'Stay out in the open, and those troops are bound to spot us eventually.'

'Suzanne can't go far,' said Polly. 'She needs a doctor.'

'Here's as good a place as any to hole up,' said Hart, indicating the building next to them. 'It looks like a shell or something hit the roof, but fire never got a hold, and the ground floor looks safe enough. There doesn't seem to be anyone home. You'll be safe here while I go and look for some help. Assuming there is some still to be found in Shadows Fall.'

'You can't go,' said Polly. 'It isn't safe.'

'I lead a charmed life,' said Hart. 'And someone has to go, if only to find Suzanne a doctor. I won't be long. Look after the women, Sean. Make yourselves comfortable, but keep your heads down. I'll be back with help before you know it.'

He flashed them all a quick grin, and hurried off down the street. The shadows swallowed him up, and he was gone. Polly shook her head dazedly.

'We shouldn't have let him go. He'll be killed.'

'Not necessarily,' said Morrison. 'I've been checking the gun I took away from that soldier. There's nothing wrong with it. Full clip of ammo. No reason in the world why it shouldn't have worked when the soldier turned it on Hart. Maybe he does have a charmed life, after all. It could be why we all survived the wreck of the Cavern; because we were close to him.'

'It just goes to show how tired I am that that actually seems to make sense,' said Suzanne. 'Now can we please get off the street before I puke and pass out? Hopefully in that order.'

Father Callahan sat alone in his study, and worried. There was nothing to worry about; he'd been promised that everything would go smoothly. But still he sat in his study and listened sickly to a woman screaming outside in the street. The screams broke off suddenly, and the silence that followed was somehow worse. Callahan looked out of his window, and watched smoke rise from burning buildings. His hands clenched into fists as he tried again to tell himself it was all for the best. He'd always known that letting in the Warriors would inevitably result in conflict, but the end justified the means. The Forever Door had to be brought under the control of a Christian authority. It was far too important, too powerful, to be left in the hands of a pagan creature like Time, answerable only to himself. If the Door truly was access to the Godhead itself . . . Control of the Door inevitably meant control of the town too, but only temporarily. Peace would return once the Warriors had overcome all opposition, and then buildings could be rebuilt, and the innocent comforted. The invasion was a necessary evil, to bring about a greater good.

Everything would work out all right, in the end. They'd promised.

But it was still hard to sit in his study and do nothing while people suffered. Right from the beginning of the invasion, he'd wanted to go out and help, but the Warriors wouldn't allow it. They insisted he stay put, and even put a guard at his door, to protect him in the event his collaboration with the Warriors became known. He hadn't liked the use of the word collaborator, but he'd nodded and agreed. There were those who wouldn't understand.

For a time people had phoned him, begging for help, and he'd offered what comfort he could, but then the phone stopped ringing, and when he lifted the receiver there was only silence. He didn't know whether that was part of a general problem, or simply that the Warriors didn't want him talking to anyone. It had been hours now, since the phone went dead. The Warriors had assured him the invasion would be over quickly, with a minimum of force, that the element of surprise gave them all the advantage they needed to overwhelm the town's defences. And with the defences down, there should have been nothing to stop the Warriors roaring right through the town to the Sarcophagus, and via that, Time himself. He'd tried contacting the Warriors on his special phone. He could hear it ringing at the other end, but no one answered. They must be busy. They wouldn't just ignore him.

There was a loud knock at his front door, and he jumped in his chair. He flushed guiltily, and for a moment didn't want to answer the door, in case the Warriors had come to punish him for harbouring doubts. But he pushed the thought aside, and got to his feet. Undoubtedly someone had been sent to explain to him what the problem was, and why things were taking so long. How thoughtful. They didn't want him to be concerned. He composed himself, and went unhurriedly to answer his front door. The soldier on guard nodded casually to Callahan, and presented him with a large hat-box. Callahan took it automatically, and was surprised by its weight.

'The Imperial Leader sends you a present,' said the soldier. 'He says it's for your collection.'

Callahan tried to thank the soldier, but he just turned away and resumed his guard duties. Callahan blinked at the soldier's unresponsive back for a moment, and then stepped back into his hall and shut the door. His collection? He had talked briefly with Royce about his interest in pulp magazines and memorabilia, but the Leader hadn't seemed particularly interested. And why send him such a gift now? To keep his mind off things perhaps, to stop him worrying? He hefted the hat-box, and something moved heavily inside it. The lid had been sealed shut with masking tape. Perhaps there was a note inside; in any event, it'd be a damn sight more sensible to take the thing into his study and open it, than stand around in his hall wondering what it was.

He took the heavy box into his study, dumped it on his desk, and went looking for some scissors. As always, they turned up in the last place he thought of looking. He briskly cut the tape, lifted off the lid, and then stopped as

371

the smell hit him. It was thick and unpleasant, and vaguely familiar, though he couldn't place it. He put the lid down beside the box, lifted out a wad of paper that had been used as packaging, and looked at what Royce had sent him. It was Lester Gold's severed head. One eye had been shot out, and the back of the head was a ragged crimson mess. The mouth gaped slackly, the chin crusted with dried blood, and the single eye looked up at Callahan accusingly.

Something for your collection . . .

Callahan was too shocked to feel ill or angry or even regretful. There was only room in him for a raging sense of betrayal. They promised him the invasion would be a civilized affair, with only the barest minimum of force used.

They lied.

He had to get out of the house. Go out into the town and see what the Warriors were really doing. If the Warriors had lied to him about the use of force, what else had they lied about? Dear God, what had he let loose in Shadows Fall? He bit his lip hard, breathing deeply as he fought for control. He had to think this through. Obviously Royce didn't expect him to be any threat to the Warriors' plans, or he wouldn't have sent the head. It was meant to intimidate him; make sure he wouldn't interfere. Royce thought he was weak. He'd have to prove the Warrior Leader wrong.

Getting out of the house shouldn't be too difficult. There was a guard at the front door, and probably someone watching the back, but he doubted there was anyone watching the patio doors. After all, they only led into a walled garden with no exit. Except for the low door the previous occupant had put in for his dog. Callahan hadn't seen a need for it, and had allowed it to become overgrown. Now you couldn't even see it, unless you knew it was there. It would be a tight squeeze, but he'd make it. He had to. He put the lid back on the hat-box, patted it once as though apologizing, and then left by the patio doors before he could start thinking of reasons not to go.

It was easy. No one saw him, and no one tried to stop him. His car was out in the street where he'd left it. He opened the door and got in, half expecting a shout or even a bullet at any moment, but all was quiet. He started up the engine, murmured a brief prayer, and drove down the street, into the town. Into hell.

In every street there were buildings that had been shelled or torched. Fires were still burning, and no one came to put them out. Men and women had been shot, and left impaled on railings as examples to others. Here and there some had been crucified, nailed to stone walls with heavy iron stakes through their arms. A few were still alive. There were signs and slogans everywhere, painted on walls. *Repent, Sinner. The Guilty Will Be Punished. This is the Day of the Lord.* Bodies lay sprawled in the street, in pools of their own blood, left to lie where they fell. Flies were gathering. Callahan had to slow down to drive around the bodies. There were more houses burning as he drew nearer the centre of the town, flames leaping up on all sides. *This is the day of the Lord of Hell,* thought Callahan. *And I made it possible.*

He stopped at the end of a street to check his way, and saw a group of soldiers having fun with Derek and Clive Manderville, his church handymen. The soldiers had formed a circle, and were taking it in turns to knock Clive back and forth within the circle, hitting him just a little harder each time. Already there was blood on his face, and his legs were weakening. He was too dazed to defend himself. The Sergeant was standing outside the circle, laughing, and keeping Derek back at gunpoint. Derek was talking desperately, no doubt using all his persuasive skills, trying to make a deal. The Sergeant didn't look as though he was listening.

Callahan looked away. He couldn't interfere. He couldn't risk being stopped and captured. He was responsible for what was happening in Shadows Fall, so it was up to him to put a stop to it. He thought he knew a way. There was one man who might be able to stop the Warrior invasion and turn it back. One man, with the faith and the power. Saint Augustine.

Father Callahan laughed aloud, and it was not a cheerful sound. Together, he and Augustine would show the Warriors the true meaning of the wrath of God.

The elves came howling out of the land beneath the hill, materialized in the town of Shadows Fall, and fell upon the Warriors like wolves upon their prey. Thousands of elves appeared in a moment, clad in their ancient armour, with all their awful weapons. They rode on elvensteeds of gleaming brass and copper, and swept through the skies on gossamer machines of spun silver. Kobolds rode on magnificent motorbikes whose fuel was human blood, and Spriggans came in shapes that were so inhuman they were barely recognizable as life. The Warriors stopped in their tracks, angered and bewildered by the new enemy. The officers quickly named them demons and devils, Satan-spawn from the Pit itself, and tried to ward them off with raised crucifixes, but the elves just laughed. They were older than any human religion. They ripped through the massed soldiers with heartstopping speed, and bodies fell to all sides in a welter of blood. Swords flashed and guns roared, and energy weapons blazed in the evening gloom.

The battle raged all across the town, with scattered elves taking on isolated Warriors. One elf threw himself upon an armoured tank as it lumbered out of a sidestreet. His long claws ripped through the steel plating with ease, opening it up like a tin can to get at the goodies within. The soldiers screamed, and the elf clung to the side of the tank like a rider on a steed as it rocked and roared, trying to throw him off. He laughed breathlessly, squirmed through the opening he'd made and leapt on the terrified soldiers. They were trapped in the cramped confines of the tank, without room to fight or retreat. The elf ripped off their heads and drank their blood as it spouted from their necks. Piercing screams resounded briefly inside the tank, and the elf ripped and tore and was content. He saved the driver till last, tore out his heart, and ate it while it was still beating. Then he left the tank, singing an old song in a forgotten language, and went in search of new prey to assuage his awakening hunger.

Out in the streets and squares, the Warriors met the elves with a withering crossfire of spraying bullets. The elves were slowed but not stopped. It took a lot to kill an elf, and cold iron was just a myth man made up to comfort himself. Sometimes a group of soldiers trapped an isolated elf and raked him with bullets over and over, to watch him squirm and scream. But inevitably they stopped, or ran out of bullets, and then the soldiers watched in horror as the elf healed in seconds and fell upon them with undiminished fury. Rocket shells and grenades tore elves to pieces and scattered them across the streets, but even these would slowly crawl together and reform, given time. The Faerie could not shapechange and still wield weapons, thus making themselves more vulnerable, but the damage those weapons could do far outweighed the drawbacks. They met rockets and explosives with particle beams and high energy lasers, and death and destruction ran riot.

Up in the skies, dragons went one on one with helicopter gunships. The helicopters had armour plating and devastating firepower, but the dragons were faster and more manoeuvrable, and they breathed fire. They launched themselves upon the helicopters from impossible angles, and burning machines fell out of the sky like crumpled handkerchiefs. The wreckage landed upon soldiers and elves alike, but only the elves walked away.

Tremble all the worlds that be. The elves go to war once more.

Oberon rode his elvensteed of gleaming bones into the heart of the chaos, and the Spear of Light flew from his hands again and again. The Spear could not be stopped or evaded, and could pick out one man among thousands, wherever he might hide. It drove through houses and punched through steel to find its victims, and then returned to Oberon's hand like a hound to its master. Warrior officers died one after another, sometimes carried away transfixed on the glistening length of the Spear. Oberon kept their heads and tied them to his saddle.

Titania strode through the heart of the fighting wrapped in an armour of thorns, the ancient long sword Bone Ripper in her hand. It cut through flesh and bone and metal alike, and none could stand before it. She hefted the great length of metal as though it was weightless, and the sword cut a wide path through the battle.

And Puck, withered Puck, Weaponmaster Puck, hobbled through the fighting, giving orders and planning strategies, and laughed to see men die. He wore the Diadem of Chaos, and ill luck walked with him, touching all he passed.

Some weapons clattered unmanned through the press of bodies, obeying the Faerie will to destruction in their own, private rages. The Howling Tide swayed this way and that, trampling soldiers underfoot, and could not be stopped. The Shatterer of Dreams could not be looked upon, and destroyed hope and faith wherever its burning gaze fell. Warriors lost all they had believed in, and ran sobbing from the field. The Spirit Thief ripped the senses out of soldiers, and left them giggling and shrieking. And everywhere the Warriors fell their bodies were seized and borne back to the Cauldron of the Night, from which they emerged as hollow-eyed undead, to fight on in the service of Faerie. Soldiers screamed as they went down beneath the weapons of their friends, seeing in their empty gaze their own inevitable fate.

There were thousands of Warriors and thousands of elves, but the soldiers died so easily, and the Faerie did not die. But still the battle raged this way and that as first one side and then the other seized the advantage. The Warriors produced their own sorcerer priests, to turn aside the magics and enchantments of the Faerie. They tore the possessing spirits out of the undead, so that they fell lifeless once again, and threw the magic weapons into confusion, so that they struck at friend and foe alike.

Grenade and mortar attacks scattered the elves and kept them from advancing.

Neither side cared about the destruction they wrought upon the town, or the townspeople who died, caught up in the furious engagements. A creature of howling winds stalked through the streets, so cold it froze all it touched or looked upon. The Warriors retaliated by dynamiting buildings so that they fell on the elves, burying them alive. The Warriors and the elves fought on, blind to everything but the dark joys of battle, until finally, by some unspoken agreement, they disengaged and fell back, retreating to their separate grounds, to nurse their wounds and plan anew.

A slow silence fell across what remained of Shadows Fall, and the smoke and the flames rose up everywhere.

9

Interlude

Night.

The town was quiet, tending its wounds. Both sides had fallen back from battle, having encountered unexpected casualties, and for the moment were content to dig in and get their breath back before the next assault. The soldiers and the defenders had left the streets, and the dragons and helicopters had left the skies, leaving behind a wounded, fragile silence. No one and nothing moved in the empty streets, the only sound the quiet crackle of flames in smouldering buildings. Their dim crimson glow showed fitfully against the night, like so many guttering candles. Like a city in Hell. Somewhere in the night a door was banging over and over, with no one to shut it. The gusting wind tossed a scrap of paper down the street, till it wrapped itself around an unmoving outstretched leg. There were bodies lying everywhere in the street outside the house where Sean Morrison was hiding. They lay still and broken, in pools of drying blood, as though the battle had moved on and forgotten them. Morrison kept expecting someone to show up and take the bodies away, but no one did.

He sat in a chair by a window on the ground floor of a house that had been shelled, staring out into the night. The upper floor had been devastated by the explosions, and there were sudden ticking and groaning noises from the ground floor ceiling as the wreckage above constantly changed position, as though trying to find one that was comfortable. By some miracle the fire had failed to take hold, and the ground floor was almost untouched, if you ignored the cracked and broken windows. The heating and the light were both out, but the room was full of moonlight, reflecting off the ice covering the canal that ran by the side of the house. Morrison sat watching the deserted street through a cracked window, looking for some sign of James Hart. He'd been gone almost two hours, and there was no sign of him or the help he'd promised to bring back.

It was cold in the room, and getting colder. Morrison could see his breath steaming on the air before him. He pulled his blanket more tightly about him, but it didn't help much. He'd found the blankets on the next floor; one of the few things that had been worth salvaging. He was beginning to wish he'd looked a little harder, but the upper floor had groaned ominously with every step he took, and he hadn't felt like pushing his luck. He looked across the room at Suzanne Dubois and Polly Cousins, sleeping the sleep of the exhausted on the single wide couch. They were curled together under the rest of the blankets, sharing their warmth. Their sleep was deep but fitful, as though disturbed by dreams. They'd both shown surprising reserves of strength and calm since they dug their way out from what remained of the Cavern club, and Morrison envied them that, but in the end sleep had taken them but rejected him. So he sat watch alone, as usual. The two women had drawn strength and comfort from each other, but in a way that excluded him. He didn't think it was deliberate. It was just that they were old and close friends, and he'd never really been close to anyone. He'd always gone his own way, and sometimes that meant leaving people behind and going on alone.

Only this time he'd been left alone. Suzanne and Polly had escaped into sleep, so it was up to him to stand guard. He didn't want to sleep anyway. After spending so long trapped in the darkness under the Cavern wreckage, he didn't think he'd ever want to sleep again. The moonlight in the room was a comfort to him, calm and consistent,

380

bright and shimmering on every edge and angle. In a strange way it was almost like being underwater, too far away to be touched by anything on the surface. One of the women murmured in her sleep, and he got up from the chair and went over to the couch to make sure everything was all right. Polly's face was as quiet and empty as a child's, but Suzanne was frowning in her sleep, as though she disapproved of her dreams. A stray curl of hair had fallen across her face, and Morrison gently brushed it back out of the way. Suzanne murmured something and sank deeper into sleep with a sigh.

Morrison crouched down beside her, thinking unfamiliar thoughts. He'd always liked Suzanne; given a little encouragement he might even have loved her. But it had never happened. She was always busy caring for someone else, for one of her stray ducks or walking wounded, and he always had another song to sing and a glass to drain, and usually both. And now it was too late. Things had changed, the world had moved on, and if he did what he was planning to do, he'd never have the chance to find out whether he might have loved her.

He got up and went back to his chair by the window. He felt tired and drained and just a little old. No longer young, anyway. He'd lost track of how long he'd been in Shadows Fall, particularly when he spent so much time with the Faerie, but it had to be quite a few years since he'd died so young in Paris, and become a legend. The legend hadn't lasted long; only a few years later the same people who'd encouraged him to live fast, die young and leave a good-looking corpse had found some other legend to believe in. And he ended up in Shadows Fall. He smiled slightly, remembering the life he'd led. The songs, the poetry, the drink and drugs and eager women, but always the music. He hadn't treated his friends particularly well, but he'd left them a few songs that mattered.

He pulled his chair up to the desk in front of him. He'd been writing a song most of the time he'd been sitting there, and he wanted to get it right before he left. He didn't think he had much time left. The town didn't have much time left. The two sides had forgotten what they were supposed to be fighting over, so taken up in their need to defeat the enemy that they seemed ready to destroy the town rather than see it fall into the hands of the opposition. Morrison hadn't forgotten. The town had to survive. It mattered to too many people. He even had an idea on how to save it. It was a good plan; one that would defeat the Warriors and save Shadows Fall from further destruction. If it worked. His last plan, to bring the Faerie out from under the hill, could only be described as a qualified success, but this time he was sure his plan would work. The only problem was, it would quite probably get him killed.

He scowled out of the window at the empty street. He wasn't ready to die yet. He still had so much left to do. The Forever Door had called to him ever since he arrived in Shadows Fall, but he'd refused to listen to it. Things were different now. He looked back at the couch, and sighed quietly. There wasn't much he'd miss, but he'd definitely miss Suzanne. He wished he'd known her before she came to Shadows Fall, when they were both still real, and had yet to be misunderstood as legends.

But it seemed to him now that he'd done all the things that really mattered. Someone else could sing the songs and be a bad example to the town. There was only one thing that needed doing now, and that was to save the town that had given him a second chance. He smiled suddenly. Who'd ever have thought he'd turn out to be the hero? He sat for a while, looking at nothing in particular. He was scared, but it wouldn't stop him. The town mattered more than he did. He'd always known that.

He looked at the sheet of paper on the desk before him. The last song he'd ever write, perhaps. Not one of his best, but good enough to go out on. He only wrote it to say goodbye, because he doubted he'd get a chance to say it in person. He'd leave it there, on the desk, when he left; and it would be there for Suzanne and Polly when they woke up. He had thought about waking them before he left, but decided against it. They'd only try and talk him out of what he meant to do, and he was just weak enough that he might listen.

He stood up, and moved quietly over to the couch. He took the blanket from around his shoulders, and draped it carefully over the two sleeping forms. He looked around him, enjoying the silver shimmer of the moonlight, and sighed once. He left the room, closing the door quietly behind him, walked down the hallway, and out of the house. The street was cold and empty. There was no one around to disturb Suzanne and Polly's rest, but he made sure the front door was locked securely, just in case. He walked off down the street, humming the tune of his new song to the rhythm of the frost crunching under his feet. The air was sharp and very clear, and the moon was like a spotlight.

10

Second Strike

Everyone waited for the dawn, but it never came. Hours passed, and the night dragged on. The moon shone brightly, but no stars came out to join it. All across the town of Shadows Fall, fires gradually died out and blood dried on the sidewalks. Soldiers dug in and built gun emplacements, while defenders barricaded streets and gathered what weapons they could find. Tension grew as both sides prepared for the battle to enter the next phase, knowing that this time the killing and destruction would not stop until one side or the other had victory. Total victory. There were no peace negotiations, no attempts at diplomacy. This battle was for the heart and soul of Shadows Fall, and neither side had any interest in compromise.

William Royce, Imperial Leader of the Warriors of the Cross, sat in his office in his mobile trailer, currently parked on the fringes of town. Despite all his army had achieved, it still wasn't considered safe for him to advance any further into the town. Even the occupied areas could not be trusted. Royce looked at the papers piled before him on his desk, and fought to keep control of his temper. Nothing had gone to plan. All the advance work his agents had done in and around the town had proved worthless once the fighting had begun. The whole town had risen against his army, often in completely unanticipated ways. The defenders should have been easy meat, without the faith and dedication that gave the Warriors their strength, but the townspeople had fought back with a ferocity and determination that had slowed the Warrior advance to a crawl.

On top of that, the main force of the attack had been broken apart and splintered by the very nature of the town. The soldiers had bogged down on a hundred fronts, fighting battles and skirmishes in a hundred different locations and time zones, often against unfamiliar forces and weaponry. Communications were a mess. The Warriors had anticipated some of the difficulties, but not nearly enough. For all their advance intelligence work, they had failed to appreciate the sheer complexity of the town. Royce's frown deepened. He had failed. He hadn't understood. His carefully trained army had achieved some successes, and its sheer size and weaponry gave it an overall advantage, but he couldn't find a single main front to use it against.

And on top of all that, there were the elves. Royce slammed a fist down on the pile of reports. His intelligence people had been convinced that the Faerie had no plans to leave their land beneath the hill, let alone come forth to defend the town. There had even been some indications that the elves were planning to cut themselves off entirely from the world of man. Royce had planned on that, even depended on it to some extent, and he'd been wrong. Something must have happened to change things, but what? There was nothing in his reports to explain it.

The elves symbolized everything that had gone wrong with the invasion. Their very presence upset his troops. The soldiers were having trouble coming to terms with the fact that their faith and their crucifixes weren't enough to give them automatic victory over 'demons from Hell'. This wasn't what they'd been taught, what they'd been led to expect. Doubt undermined faith, and without faith there could be no discipline.

According to the reports, the elves were unstoppable and unkillable. Their presence was often enough to swing a battle in favour of the defenders. Royce cleared the reports from his desk with one sweep of his hand, and let them flutter to the floor. There had to be some secret to the town's resistance, something his intelligence people hadn't told him about. He turned in his chair to face the television set standing in its blue chalk pentacle, and the blank screen stared back mockingly. He reached for the remote control, and then froze as the television turned itself on. His hand was still several inches away from the control, but the screen was already lighting up. The image quickly cleared to show Royce himself, sitting on a golden throne in a sea of flames. Goat's horns burst out of his brow, and curled up above his head. His feet were cloven hooves. The image smiled at Royce, and winked.

'William, sweet William; I've been expecting your call.'

'You broke the agreement,' said Royce stonily. 'You must not come except when I call you. That was the compact we entered into.'

The figure shrugged. 'Such arrangements have always been flexible. We're growing closer, you and I. Soon nothing will be able to keep us apart.'

'Liar and Prince of lies.' Royce fought to keep control and maintain a calm front. It wouldn't do to let the demon think it could rattle him. It wouldn't be safe. 'Talk to me, hellspawn. My invasion has ground to a halt, because of the cursed elves. Why didn't you warn me they would interfere?'

'At the time you asked, they had no such plans. And you didn't ask again. Tut, tut, William; a lapse. A definite lapse. Still, it doesn't really matter. You can still defeat the Faerie with your sorcerer priests.'

'You're very free with suggestions now, demon. How can I trust you?'

It smiled widely, revealing filthy, pointed teeth. 'You are my son, William, in whom I am well pleased.'

The image disappeared from the screen, and the television turned itself off. Royce looked at the remote control, and then at his hands, which were shaking slightly. The intercom buzzed suddenly, and he jumped in his chair. He waited a moment, so as not to give the impression he'd been waiting for a call, and then pressed the switch.

'I said I wasn't to be disturbed.'

'I'm sorry, sir,' said his secretary, 'But your inner Council is here. They insist on seeing you.'

Royce's eyebrows rose slightly at the word *insist*, but when he spoke his voice was calm and even. 'They've saved me the trouble of sending for them. Tell my Council I'll be with them in a moment.'

He cut off the intercom before his secretary could respond, and stared determinedly at his hands until they stopped shaking. It wouldn't do to let his people think they could rattle him. It wouldn't be safe. He got to his feet, brushed at himself here and there to be sure he looked his best, and then left his office to meet his Council.

The ten Generals were standing grouped together before the banks of flickering monitor screens, showing varying views of the town. Few of the scenes were particularly encouraging. There was much destruction, and bodies beyond counting, but far too many of them were Warriors. Royce coughed briskly to get his Council's attention, and quietly noted which of the Generals sprang to attention, and which did not. Martyn Casey, his Second in Command, did not. He nodded briefly to Royce, as to an equal, and then looked back at the screens.

'We've been talking, Royce, in your absence. Given how precarious our present position is, and the serious mistakes you made in putting together this invasion, I'm afraid we've been forced to decide that the invasion must be called off. We can't hope to beat the elves and their weaponry, not with things as they are.'

'Demons,' muttered one of the Generals. 'Imps from Hell.'

'Quite, General,' said Martyn Casey. He turned to look at Royce, and his face was calm and unmerciful. 'We will withdraw our people, and wait for a more propitious time. After we've determined how to deal with the elves. In the meantime, I'm afraid we have also decided, regretfully, that it would be in everyone's best interests if you were to step down as Imperial Leader. Immediately. I will take charge, temporarily, to superintend the withdrawal.'

Royce drew the gun on his hip and shot Casey in the throat. The Warrior Second in Command was thrown back against the monitors, and one of the Generals cried out in shock. Casey sank to his knees, blood gushing from his mouth. He tried to say something past the blood, and Royce shot him again. The bullet punched through Casey's head and smashed the monitor screen behind him. Blood sprayed from the exit wound in a misty haze across the other screens, so that they looked like snapshots from Hell. Casey fell forward and lay still. Royce kicked the man's outstretched arm, but there was no response. He nodded, satisfied, and looked at the Generals, who looked back with wide, shocked eyes. Royce smiled pleasantly at his inner Council.

'Anyone else think we ought to withdraw? Anyone still think I should step down as Imperial Leader of the War-riors? No? I am pleased. But do feel free to come to me if you have any other problems with the way I'm running things.' The smile suddenly disappeared, and Royce's voice became as flat and cold as his gaze. 'We do the Lord's work here, and defiance of my authority is treason against God's will. I will brook no more treachery, gentlemen. Your rank is no protection when you turn against God and me. We are here to carry out God's will, and we will not leave until victory is ours. No matter what the cost.

'So; what do we do next?' His voice was calm and easy again, and he holstered his gun without looking at it. Several of the Generals sighed in relief, but none of them relaxed much. Royce studied the monitor screens, his lips pursed thoughtfully. He pulled a handkerchief from his pocket and wiped some of the blood from the monitors where it obscured his view.

'I know what you're thinking, gentlemen, and you're wrong. We have encountered difficulties, but none that can't be overcome through force of arms and a little lateral thinking. We can't afford to just sit here, waiting for the town to make the next move. They don't realize how badly they've hurt us, but once they do, you can be sure the elves won't hesitate to press the advantage. And against their infernal weaponry, we're nothing more than sitting ducks. We also can't allow ourselves to remain as scattered as we've become. It dissipates our strength, and makes us vulnerable to attack by larger forces. Of which there seem to be many in this cursed town. So; we can't retreat, and we can't press on. Therefore, we must do the unexpected.'

He looked at the bloody handkerchief still in his hand, handed it briskly to one of his Generals, and then looked at his secretary, still sitting frozen behind her desk. 'Have the sorcerer priests been assembled as I ordered?'

'Yes, Leader. They're waiting outside for your instructions.'

'Just a little impatiently, I suspect. Come, gentlemen; you are about to meet the real strength behind our forces. I could have sent them in with the first wave, as some of you suggested, but I wanted to wait and see what hidden strengths the town had. Now we know their strengths, but they do not know ours. The sorcerer priests are our secret weapon, our ace in the hole, and they will give us victory.'

'Of course, Leader,' said one of the Generals quickly. 'It is our destiny.'

Royce gave him a hard look, and the General fell back a step instinctively. The other Generals nearest him stepped unobtrusively away, so as not to be contaminated by his presence. And so that whatever happened to him wouldn't happen to them. Royce sniffed disdainfully. 'Destiny, General? If I thought for a moment you really meant that, I'd be seriously worried about you. Blind obedience is all right and proper for the rank and file, but I don't expect to hear it from my officer class. God expects us to make our own destiny, through faith and hard work, and slaughtering the unbelievers. Now come with me, gentlemen. I want you to meet my sorcerer priests. You might learn something useful.' He broke off and looked down at the crumpled figure of Martyn Casey, lying in his own blood with a confused look on his face. Royce sniffed again, and glanced at his secretary. 'Have the garbage removed, and then get some people in here to clean up the mess. I'm expecting company later.'

His secretary nodded quickly, and reached for the phone on her desk. Royce strode briskly out of the trailer, leaving the Generals to hurry after him. Outside the trailer, one hundred Warrior priests stood waiting at parade rest in ranks of ten. The moment Royce emerged from the trailer, they crashed to attention and stared straight ahead, waiting for orders. They wore robes of purest white, gleaming in the gloom like so many ghosts. Royce snapped his fingers, and the trailer's exterior lights came on. The sudden glare must have been blinding for the priests, but none of them so much as blinked. Royce smiled at them fondly. They'd been his idea, right from the beginning. The finest soldiers, the most devout Warriors, drilled to the peak of physical perfection, and then trained in all the mystic arts, to better serve the glory of the Lord. And the Warriors, of course. Trained to use the enemy's own weapons against him. Royce nodded to them briskly, and they all bowed to him, light flashing briefly from their tonsured heads.

'My friends,' said Royce, his voice perfectly clear in the quiet of the night, 'your time has come. I know it's been hard for you, waiting on the sidelines while your brothers were being cut down by the enemy, but you are my main strength, and I couldn't afford to squander you by acting too soon. No more waiting, my friends. You have your orders; carry them out. Make me proud.'

The hundred priests bowed as one, and then sat down cross-legged on the bare concrete, arranging themselves comfortably. They paid no attention to the watching Generals, or to each other; their gaze was already turning inwards, where their true power lay. Royce put a finger to his lips, and gestured for the Generals to follow him back into the trailer. They did so, and the sorcerer priests were left alone in the night. Their minds eased slowly out from their relaxing bodies, and joined together in a single thrust of pure force. It moved out over the unsuspecting town, gathering above it like an invisible thunderstorm.

Royce gave the Generals one last pep talk, mixed with a few jovial threats, and then sent them on their way. He didn't think they posed much of a threat to his authority any more, and besides, he was sick of the sight of them. He stood uncertainly before the monitor screens, and realized he didn't want to look at them for a while either. He discovered without much surprise that he was feeling restless, and wanted just to get away from things for a while. And why shouldn't he? There was nothing more he could do until the sorcerer priests had completed their work, and there was no telling how long that would take. So he nodded a brisk goodbye to his secretary, pulled a trenchcoat over his uniform, and was gone and out of the door before she could raise any objections. He had a bleeper for emergencies, but for her sake she'd better not use it for anything less than a real emergency.

He glanced briefly at the motionless priests, and then walked unhurriedly away into the camp. There were twenty more trailers, parked in neat rows, packed to bursting with surveillance equipment, computers, and hard-working men. He had no doubt that by now Martyn Casey's fate was common knowledge among his people, and they were all doing their best to look extremely busy, and competent, just in case he decided to drop in on them. Royce snorted. They'd been overdue a reminder of who was really in charge here. He should have killed Casey months ago, when he first showed signs of ambition, but the man had been an efficient Second in Command for all his faults, and they were hard to find. He hadn't a clue who he was going to replace him with. But that could wait.

He walked on, through the endless row of tents, gleaming palely in the night, where his soldiers were snatching a few hours sleep before his orders sent them out to fight again. No one was abroad, save for a few sentries out on the perimeter, to back up the surveillance equipment, and he didn't feel like walking that far. He felt mildly disappointed. He would have liked to walk among his men, spreading calm and assurance with a few well-chosen words, and the sheer strength of his personality. Fight on, because the Lord is with you. Take no prisoners; send the demons back to Hell where they came from. That sort of thing. A little touch of King Harry in the night.

But there was no one there to share the night with him. He was alone. Just as he always was, no matter how many people he surrounded himself with. He had followers beyond counting, any number of whom would have willingly laid down their life for him, but not a single friend he could talk to, as one man to another. He had power, but no one to show it off to. He shrugged, and headed back to his trailer. His life belonged to God, and he would walk the path that had been appointed for him. He would lead the Warriors to victory over the Devil's spawn infesting Shadows Fall, and maybe then, when it was all over and evil had been vanquished, he would be allowed to approach the Forever Door and ask a few simple questions of his own.

Back at his office in his trailer, more reports had appeared in his absence, all but covering his desk. Royce sat down and leafed through them listlessly. He already knew what they were going to say. His people had spread death and destruction throughout Shadows Fall, but not enough to break the town's spirit. His first wave had been stopped in its tracks, breaking against the inhuman power of the elves. He scowled. Either his sorcerer priests would give him the edge he needed to defeat the Faerie, or he and the rest of the Warriors might as well pack up and go home. He smiled briefly. The elves were so arrogant in their power, so sure in their tactics, but his priests would teach them a lesson they'd remember for what little remained of their lives. Unnatural creatures. He'd show them. He'd show them all.

Outside, the sorcerer priests sat still and empty, their minds elsewhere. Their power grew, gathering like storm-clouds, and they sent it sweeping out over the town. Sleepers stirred in their beds as their dreams turned dark and foul. Children woke crying in the night, and would not be comforted. Dogs barked and cats howled and everyone with the slightest trace of magic in them looked nervously up at the sky, and knew not why. Only the elves did not react, because the sorcerer priests had hidden themselves from the denizens of Faerie. So when the priests finally fell on the elves like wolves on unsuspecting sheep, the elves had no warning at all. The priests' magic came down like a hammer, and in that moment the priests imposed shape and order on the elves, trapping them in a single form, with all its frailties and vulnerabilities. They still had their advanced weaponry, but no longer could they wield it with impunity. From this moment on, the elves could be hurt. The elves could die. There was much panic and shouting among the elves, but the priests did not hear it. They were already planning what to do next. They had so much power, and a whole town to use it on . . .

The Warrior soldiers burst out of their positions and fell upon the town's defenders again. Revitalized by a few hours' rest, and their own fanatical faith, they surged through the narrow streets, their guns filling the night with fire and noise. The elves rose up to meet them, but there wasn't enough room to use their energy weapons, and the fighting quickly deteriorated into hand-to-hand, and swords clashed with bayonets. The town's defenders watched almost in shock as the first elves died, shrieking in horror as much as in pain, and then men and women poured out from their safe hiding places to support the elves. The Shining Folk had many friends and admirers in Shadows Fall. Blood flowed in the gutters, and the streets were soon blocked with struggling, shouting crowds, surging this way and that as first one side and then the other briefly gained the advantage.

The battle was so fierce, and pressed on so many fronts, that the defenders completely overlooked one small force of Warriors that bypassed the fighting, slipping quietly between battles, heading always for the centre of town. Royce led them himself, wearing only standard fatigues, with nothing to betray his exalted rank. He saw his men bleed and die, but did not turn aside to help. They were dying to buy him time, time to reach the town park, and the Sarcophagus of Time.

They reached it easily enough, and found the gates already open. A small force of soldiers snapped to attention and saluted Royce as he led his people into the park. He returned their salutes and raised an eyebrow at the officer in command. The officer grinned.

'We had a chance to get here first, Leader, so we thought we'd better take it, if only to make sure no unfriendly types got to the Sarcophagus before you did. Just as well we did; turns out the park becomes suddenly infested with dinosaurs once it gets dark. Big, nasty-looking brutes. Our main force is keeping them busy with mortar attacks and rocket launchers. They're ugly, but by God they're stupid. Easiest big game shoot I was ever on. We've had some trouble with Time's automatons, but they disappeared a while back. You do what you have to, Leader; no one's going to interrupt.'

'Thank you, my son,' said Royce, clapping him on the shoulder. 'The Lord is pleased with you, and so am I. Who are those two?'

The officer looked across at the two young men standing sullenly to one side. They were handcuffed, and they'd both recently been on the wrong end of a bad beating.

'Just a couple of locals, Leader. After a little persuading they told us all about the dinosaurs, and how to get to the Sarcophagus safely. I thought I'd better hang on to them in case it turned out they knew anything else useful.'

'Very thoughtful of you, Lieutenant, but I don't think we'll be needing them any more. Dispose of them.'

The Lieutenant nodded briefly, and gestured to the soldiers guarding the two prisoners. Knives flashed briefly before sinking into flesh, and Derek and Clive Manderville fell to the ground and lay still as the breath went out of them. Blood pooled around their bodies.

Royce had eyes only for the Sarcophagus; the massive block of grey stone standing on a raised dais. It showed no signs of age or weathering, though it had stood in the park for centuries beyond counting. It looked solid, but it wasn't. According to some reports, it was a single moment taken out of Time; the exact moment when Shadows Fall was created, frozen in material form to hide and protect it. And now it was all that stood between the Templars and the Galleries of Frost and Bone, Old Father Time, and the Forever Door itself. Royce turned to the single sorcerer priest he'd brought with him, calm and silent in his white robe.

'You're still in touch with your fellow priests, aren't you? Good, good. Open this stone for me. Open it now.'

The priest bowed to him respectfully, and opened himself to his brothers. The full force of their magic flowed into and through him to break open the Sarcophagus. The priest's body burst into cold flames, and his flesh ran like wax down a candle as the magic that roared through him burned him up. A single crack appeared in the stone of the Sarcophagus, and in that moment Royce and his people disappeared, transported elsewhere. All that remained before the breached Sarcophagus were the bodies of two young gravediggers, and the burnt-out corpse of a dead priest.

Rhea Frazier slowed the car to a halt, and she and Leonard Ash stared at the crucified man in silence. They both knew him by sight, if not to talk to; Tim Hendry, one of Erikson's Deputies. He'd been nailed to the wall with long metal spikes through his arms and ankles, and his eyes had been put out. Blood had poured down his cheeks and splashed on his chest. It wasn't the first crucifixion Rhea and Ash had seen; the soldiers had left them all over town as signs to show where they'd been, like a dog marking its territory. But this was the first victim they'd known, and that somehow made it worse. More real. Rhea revved the engine up again, ready to move off, and Hendry lifted his bloodied head an inch.

'He's alive! He's still alive!' Rhea shut off the engine, opened the door, and scrambled out of the car to stand before Hendry. Ash came round to join her. She looked at him pleadingly. 'We've got to get him down, get him to a hospital . . .'

'It's not going to be easy,' said Ash quietly. 'Those spikes are going to be hard to move, and it'll hurt him like crazy. It might actually be kinder to leave him there till we can find a doctor and the right equipment . . .'

'If we leave him, he'll die!' snapped Rhea. 'There's a crowbar in the back of the car; use that.' Ash nodded, and went to look for it. Rhea stared up into Hendry's bloody face. 'Tim; can you hear me, Tim?'

There was no response. Ash came back with the crowbar, looked at Hendry almost dispassionately, then eased the end of the crowbar under Hendry's left arm and applied a steady pressure. The arm jerked an inch away from the wall, sliding along the metal spike, and Hendry raised his head and screamed. Rhea stepped back involuntarily, as though driven back by the sound of so much pain. Ash applied more pressure to the crowbar, and the arm jerked a little further away from the wall. Hendry screamed again. It was such a raw, harsh sound it had to be hurting his throat, but then, Rhea thought, he probably doesn't notice that compared to everything else he's suffering. Ash eased the crowbar out from under Hendry's arm, and looked at Rhea.

'This isn't going to work,' he said flatly. 'In his weakened state, this much pain and shock will kill him long before I can get all these spikes out.'

'But if we leave him, he'll die anyway. Please, Leonard; can't we at least save one? There must be something we can do.'

'Yes,' said Ash. 'There is something.' He reached out

with his empty hand and placed the palm flat against Hendry's forehead. 'Go in peace, Tim.'

Hendry let out his breath in a long sigh, and didn't take it back in again. His muscles relaxed as much as the spikes would allow, and his chin dropped on to his chest. It took Rhea a moment to realize he was dead.

'It was the only kindness we could do for him,' said Ash. 'To put a stop to his pain.'

Rhea looked at him expressionlessly. 'You killed him. You touched him, and he died.'

'Yes.'

'I didn't know you could do that.'

'There are a lot of things you don't know about me, Rhea.' Ash looked around the deserted street. 'We'd better get moving again. I don't like standing around like this. It makes us more obvious, and we can't afford to be noticed. Let's go.'

They got back in the car, and Rhea drove off down the street. The car's engine sounded very loud in the quiet. It had once been a residential area, but now there were ruins and burnt-out shells to every side. Most of the street lights had been smashed, but the street was full of shimmering moonlight. It was like driving along on the bottom of the sea.

They'd been driving for some time, turning this way and that to avoid road blocks. Ash could sense them, and any other concentrations of soldiers, long before he could see them, and that gave them an edge. Other people weren't so lucky in avoiding the soldiers. Rhea and Ash had seen their bodies everywhere, hanging or crucified or just left to lie in the street with bloody holes in them. At first Rhea thought she was going to be sick, but there were so many of them she quickly grew numb. She couldn't even think about them. It was as though her head was full of novocaine. Ash didn't say anything, but he didn't look away either. Presumably death didn't have the power to disturb him that it once had. Rhea didn't ask.

She wasn't really sure where they were going. She'd

started out with some idea of contacting Sheriff Erikson or the rest of the town Council, but she couldn't get an answer from any of them on her car phone. She stopped to try public phones a few times, but it was no good. Most of the time it didn't even ring through, and on the few times it did, no one ever answered. Which had to mean the Council were either dead, or arrested by the soldiers. So now she was heading for the centre of town, and the Sarcophagus in the park, hoping against hope that if she could just get to Old Father Time, he would put everything right again. If the town could ever be made whole again, after everything that had happened to it. Her mouth set into a firm line. Everything would be put right again. She had to believe that, or she'd go mad. She didn't say it aloud, though. Partly because she didn't want to hear Ash's answer, but mostly because of a crazy feeling that to say it aloud might draw Fate's attention. She drove on, steering the car this way and that to avoid the bodies in the road.

They'll have to be picked up soon, she thought, surprisingly calmly. *This many bodies will mean flies and rats and disease.*

Things got worse the further into town they went. More death, more destruction, blood and bodies everywhere. It was as though everything Rhea had ever cared for had been ruined or defiled by the soldiers. Occasional streams of refugees passed by the car, heading for the supposed safety of the town's limits. They didn't know that Time had isolated the town, and Rhea didn't have the heart to tell them. They carried their most precious belongings with them, like people from some Third World country caught up in the middle of a civil war. Rhea needed to see the refugees. Partly to reassure herself that there were still some people left alive in Shadows Fall, but also because they made her feel angry, and as long as she was angry, there wasn't room in her to be afraid too. Ash didn't seem afraid of anything, but then, he wouldn't be. Rhea found herself smiling. It seemed there were some advantages to being dead.

'Why isn't Time protecting us?' she said suddenly. 'Things like this aren't supposed to be possible here.'

'Maybe something's happened to him,' said Ash. 'Maybe he's dead. Or been captured.'

Rhea shook her head. 'All my life I've heard how powerful Time is, and how safe Shadows Fall is, compared to the rest of the world. Now we've a serial killer on the loose, the town is a war zone, and Time isn't doing a thing to help us. I don't know what to believe any more.'

'Believe in me,' said Ash. 'I'll never let you down.'

Rhea smiled at him, but didn't answer. She saw the traffic light up ahead turn to red, and brought the car to a halt at the junction. There was no other traffic in any other direction. Rhea drove on without waiting for the light to change. She asked Ash to try the car phone again, but there was still no reply. They drove for a long while without saying anything, deeper and deeper into the nightmare, and then Ash suddenly told her to stop the car. She did so, and looked around her, but the street seemed deserted. Ash's frown deepened into a scowl.

'There are soldiers up ahead. Just round that corner. I think they've caught someone. Drive on slowly.'

Rhea's first impulse was to turn the car around and take a different route. It wasn't as if there was anything they could do. She could smell smoke on the air, and not that far away someone was firing a gun. Nothing new in that, but she had a bad feeling about it. She crushed the thought ruthlessly. They had to try. If she just gave up, then the soldiers had won. She eased the car forward and round the next corner, and then hit the brakes. Half-way down the street, a group of soldiers had set fire to a house and were shooting the occupants as they ran out into the street to escape the flames. The soldiers were laughing and making wagers. A man staggered out of the front door with his clothes on fire. The flames leapt up as he hit the fresh air, and his hair caught alight too. He didn't scream. One of the soldiers shot him in the leg, and then they watched the man scrabble helplessly on the ground, burning up, and they all laughed like it was the funniest thing they'd ever seen. Rhea turned to Ash.

'We've got to do something. Use your spook power to make them run away.'

'It doesn't always work out that way,' said Ash. 'I can't guarantee what the results will be.'

'Try,' said Rhea. 'I can't just stand by and let this happen.'

'No,' said Ash. 'Neither can I. Stay in the car. Whatever happens, stay in the car.'

He opened his door and got out, and then gestured for Rhea to lock the door behind him. She did, and he smiled at her briefly beforeng down the street towards the soldiers. One of them saw him coming, and alerted the others. They raised their guns, and yelled for him to stop. Ash raised his hands to show they were empty, but kept on going. One soldier fired a shot between his feet. Ash didn't even flinch. He was almost upon them now. The burning figure on the ground had stopped moving, though the flames still leapt and danced. The soldier aimed his rifle at Ash, and he stopped and drew his death around him like a cloak.

The soldier paled and swallowed hard. The rifle trembled in his hands as though it had suddenly become very heavy. He lowered the gun, and fell back a step. The other soldiers fell back with him, panic rising among them, and then one of them raised his rifle in a sudden desperate movement, and shot Ash in the chest. The impact sent him staggering backwards. Rhea screamed. Either the bullet or the scream broke Ash's spell, and all the soldiers opened fire on him. A row of bullets stitched across his chest, and burst out of his back. He kept staggering backwards, jerking this way and that as the bullets hit him, until finally he tripped and fell. The soldiers stopped shooting.

And Ash sat up. The soldiers didn't move. Ash got slowly to his feet, and absent-mindedly brushed the dust from him. His shirt and jacket were riddled with bullet holes, the back almost completely torn away, but there was no sign of any blood. Ash was dead, and bullets couldn't hurt him. He ran forward, impossibly quickly, and was among the shocked soldiers in a moment. He grabbed the nearest man, lifted him off the ground with one hand, and threw him a dozen feet down the street. The soldier hit hard, and lay still. Ash grabbed another soldier, and slammed him face first into the nearest wall. He let go and the soldier collapsed, clutching at his ruined face. Blood poured between his fingers. Another soldier stepped forward, and shot Ash between the eyes. His head whipped back, but no blood spilled, and there was no exit wound. Ash coughed once, and spat the flattened bullet out into his palm.

The soldier turned to run, and Ash caught him from behind. The soldier screamed helplessly. Ash broke the man's neck with one quick twist, and let him fall. He stepped over the body, and was among the remaining soldiers before they could turn to run. He threw them about the street as though they were dolls, and the soldiers screamed as they died. Ash didn't care. All he had to do was look at the burning man, and he didn't care at all. Eventually he ran out of soldiers, and stood among the bodies, looking calmly about him. He wasn't even breathing hard. And then the bullet tore his shoulder apart.

His arm flailed uselessly as he turned unsteadily to see more soldiers spilling into the far end of the street. They saw the dead soldiers and opened fire with their automatic weapons. The repeated impacts sent Ash staggering backwards, shaking and shuddering as the bullets tore at him. He lost half his head and one hand, but still he wouldn't fall. The bullets hit him again and again, chipping away at him, whittling him down. He tried to get to the soldiers, but the sheer pressure of the gunfire kept him back. And then one of the soldiers produced a rocket launcher. Ash looked back at the car, and tried to shout something to Rhea. She couldn't hear him above the roar of the guns, but she knew what he was saying.

Stay in the car. Whatever happens, stay in the car.

He turned to face the gunfire again, and managed one step, then another, moving against the hammering bullets like breasting a tide. And then the rocket hit him, and he disappeared in a cloud of smoke and fire. The soldiers stopped shooting. When the smoke cleared, Ash was lying still on the ground. His head and shoulders had been torn away from his body, and one arm lay detached in the gutter, hand held out in supplication.

Rhea got out of the car and ran over to Ash. She stood over him, unable to scream or cry or do anything but stare down at him. Ash's mouth moved slightly. Rhea started crying in great sobbing gulps, and fought the soldiers fiercely when they came to drag her away. Her last glimpse of Ash was of the soldiers gathering up his body and throwing the pieces into the flames of the burning house.

Peter Caulder slipped away from his fellow Warriors when no one was looking, and disappeared into the shadows of a back alley. He walked a way without thinking of where he was going, and then he stopped and sank down on a doorstep, and hugged his knees to his chest. He could still hear the screams of the man Colonel Ferris was interrogating. Caulder shook his head slowly back and forth, a young man with old eyes and someone else's blood on his sleeves. This couldn't be right. It couldn't. This was supposed to be a glorious Crusade, to punish the sinners who had stolen a powerful relic of the Lord and selfishly kept it for themselves. He'd been told the town was overrun with demons and unnatural creatures, and that some fighting might be necessary. That was why they'd trained so hard, with all kinds of weapons. He'd never thought he'd be expected to turn his gun on civilians. On unarmed men and women. On innocents.

He'd believed in the Warriors with all his heart and all his soul. He'd needed something to believe in back then, the way a drowning man needs a lifebelt, and the Warriors had fitted the bill perfectly. He'd lost his job to the recession, and then his apartment, when he couldn't pay the rent any more. He lost everything else in the months that followed, and when the Warriors found him he'd been living on the streets and eating out of dumpsters for three weeks. They took him in and gave him a purpose. Gave him back his pride and promised him a cause to fight for. A chance to be a hero, fighting against the darkness. He'd promised to honour and defend the Warriors with his life, and he'd meant it back then, but since the invasion of Shadows Fall he'd seen nothing but death and destruction, and it sickened him.

He'd seen men and women shot for talking back or just being in the way. Seen their houses torched, and men dragged away bloodied and broken for further questioning. He hadn't seen anything that even looked like a demon. These people didn't deserve such treatment, even if they were sinners. The soldiers were getting out of hand, shooting at anything that moved. What was supposed to have been a search and find mission with the minimum necessary violence had deteriorated into a bloodbath, and no one was doing anything to stop it. If anything, the officers were encouraging their men to greater and bloodier excesses. Anything was permitted, because the enemy were sinners. Murder, torture, rape. The power and the fighting had gone to the soldiers' heads, and God save him, he'd felt it too. He'd torched buildings, even when he knew there had to be people still inside, and shot running men and women in the back when they wouldn't stop. It had even been fun, until he made the mistake of getting close enough to see their faces. Then they stopped being sinners and started being people, and everything changed for him.

Thank God he hadn't shot any children. Some had, but he hadn't.

He had to get away and think. Just stop everything, and think things through. So he slipped away from his company when they started knocking their latest prisoner about. Just a little casual brutality, to soften him up before the interrogation. Before the pain and the blood. He'd wanted to rescue the prisoner, or at least save him from the beating, but he had no doubt his fellow soldiers in the Lord would turn on him if he tried to cheat them of their fun. Punishing the sinners had given them a taste for blood, and they didn't care where they found it any more. So he'd slipped away to be on his own, even though it was strictly against orders. He didn't dare be away for long. If they thought he was trying to get away from them, they'd shoot him as a deserter. There were a lot of things the Warriors would shoot you for. Questioning orders was another. Warrior officers took their instructions from the Imperial Leader, who got them from God, so questioning of orders was blasphemy. Caulder had believed in the Leader. He believed in William Royce with all his heart and soul. Royce had saved him when there was nothing left of him worth saving. It wasn't that he'd stopped believing; he'd still die for William Royce. He just didn't think he could kill for him any more.

He heard quiet footsteps approaching, and looked up sharply. A short, stocky figure had entered the alleyway and was heading straight for him. Caulder grabbed his rifle and rose quickly to his feet. His training had the gun aimed and on target before he even realized what he was doing. He hesitated, and then the breath went out of him as the small figure stepped out of the shadows and into the light. It was a four-foot-tall teddy bear with golden honey fur, wearing a bright red tunic and trousers, and a long blue scarf. His eyes were dark and knowing, and full of all the compassion and forgiveness in the world. Caulder lowered his rifle.

'But . . . I know you,' he said quietly. 'You're Bruin Bear. I used to read your adventures all the time when I was a kid. What are you doing here?'

'People stopped believing in me,' said the Bear. 'This is the place where dreams end up, and toys come to grow old. What are you doing here?'

'I don't know. I don't know anything any more. The Leader said this place was full of sinners and demons . . .'

'There are no demons here, and not that many sinners.

Only people like me. All the creatures from books that were banned because people didn't believe in fantasy any more. Nothing is ever really lost, not while there are places like this. We're all here, looking for a little peace at the end of our lives.'

'Royce said you'd kill me.'

'You're the one with the rifle.'

Caulder threw the gun away from him, stepped forward hesitantly, and then sank to his knees to embrace the Bear. He buried his face in the thick golden fur, and sobbed for the loss of his childhood and his faith. The Bear hugged him back with short, strong arms, understanding everything, forgiving everything, and for the first time in a long time Peter Caulder felt at peace. After all, if you couldn't trust Bruin Bear, who could you trust?

New footsteps entered the alleyway, and the two of them broke apart. Caulder looked automatically for the rifle he'd thrown away, but it was well out of reach. The Bear stood his ground and looked mildly at the newcomer as he entered the light. Caulder's heart missed a beat as he saw who it was; a tall, gaunt man with surgeon's hands and an officer's uniform. Apparently Colonel Ferris had finished interrogating his prisoner. Caulder moved to stand between the Bear and the Colonel, suddenly afraid Ferris would just shoot the Bear on sight as a demon. Ferris smiled coldly.

'You disappoint me, Caulder. I expected better of you. Allowing yourself to be fooled by a pleasant exterior, after all the warnings you were given. You can't trust anything here, boy. Now stand aside and let me deal with the vermin.'

'You can't shoot him,' said Caulder shakily. 'You can't. He's Bruin Bear. He was my hero when I was a child. He was every child's hero. I won't let you hurt him.'

'Stand aside,' said Ferris. 'There's no room for weakness in the Warriors. We do the Lord's work, and it's not for us to question it. That thing behind you is an abomination. It's everything we swore to sweep from this town with fire and steel. It's not too late, Caulder. You can still return to the bosom of the Lord. But if you stay where you are, I'll shoot through you to get the demon. Move, boy.'

Caulder tried to say no, but he was so scared he couldn't get the word out, so he just shook his head numbly. Colonel Ferris raised his pistol and shot Caulder at point blank range. Caulder cried out, and flung up his arms as though to protect himself. The roar of the gun was still echoing in the narrow alleyway when he realized he was unhurt, and slowly lowered his arms. He looked down at himself, but there was no sign of any blood or bullet hole. The Colonel looked at him stupidly, his arm still extended, smoke still rising from the barrel of his gun. There was no way he could have missed at such short range. Another step forward and the gun would have touched Caulder's chest. Ferris realized his mouth was hanging open and closed it with a snap. He straightened his arm and pulled the trigger again and again. Caulder flinched at the noise, but didn't step away. And when the echoes died down again, Caulder was still standing there unharmed. Bruin Bear stepped out from behind him, and smiled at Ferris.

'You're in my world now, Colonel, and in my world bad things don't happen to good people. Please be good enough to surrender. You really don't have any choice.'

Ferris snarled at him, threw aside his gun and snatched from the top of his boot a sanctified silver dagger. He started towards the Bear, his face ugly with rage and fear. He managed two steps, and then the Sea Goat stepped out of the shadows behind him and hit him very professionally over the head with a long and heavy club. Ferris swayed on his feet, dropped the dagger, but didn't go down. The Sea Goat hit him again, putting some effort into it, and Ferris crashed to the ground and lay still. The Goat kicked him somewhere painful, just to be sure Ferris really was unconscious, and then lowered his club and grinned cheerfully at Caulder.

'You can always spot an officer. They're so thick you have to hit them twice before they notice anything's happened. Hello, son; welcome to the bleeding Resistance. Bring your own gun and ammunition, and you can forget about hazard pay.' He glared at the unconscious Colonel, and then looked hopefully at Bruin Bear. 'Any chance I'll get to kill this one? We've already got half a dozen sodding officers as prisoners.'

'We don't kill,' said the Bear firmly. 'We're the good guys.'

The Sea Goat turned and butted his head against the nearest wall several times. Caulder watched interestedly. 'Does that help?'

'Not as much as it used to,' admitted the Goat. 'All right; let's get the hell out of here before Sleeping Beauty's friends come looking for him.'

He picked up Ferris, draped him casually over one shoulder, and set off down the alley. Caulder and Bruin Bear went after him.

'You said something about the Resistance,' said Caulder. 'Who exactly are the Resistance?'

'Anyone too dumb to know they're beaten,' said the Goat. 'Mostly animals at the moment, but we don't discriminate. Basically, we kick Warrior ass, break up their schemes, embarrass the hell out of them and generally act up cranky.'

'But we don't kill,' said the Bear.

'Why not?' said Caulder.

'Because we don't like what it does to us,' said the Goat quietly.

And so Peter Caulder went with Bruin Bear and the Sea Goat to join the Resistance, where he found many childhood friends and the beginnings of a new cause to believe in.

The Faerie and the Warriors battled themselves to a standstill all across the town, and finally ended up facing each other from opposite sides of Glencannon Square. It wasn't much of a Square, as Squares go, with two rows of shaggy trees and a statue of a man on a horse that looked like it could use a good clean. The Faerie had the superior weaponry, but the Warriors had the numbers. All around them, on every side, lay nothing but destruction. Every building was a ruin, blackened and burnt out as often as not. All the street lights had been smashed, and the approaching streets had all been sealed and barricaded. The dead and the dying were everywhere, left to lie where they had fallen. Both sides had taken massive losses, and were prepared to take more, but for the moment they hesitated. Their strength and their spirit remained unbroken, but they were both beginning to realize that victory could only be won at a terrible price. It would mean using weapons and tactics that would quite probably destroy the whole town; everyone and everything in it. Both sides were considering it, but for the moment, they hesitated.

It was still night. The full moon shone brightly overhead, painting the scene black and white and blue. There were still no stars, or any sign the night would pass soon. Neither side had offered any kind of peace talks. There was no point. It wasn't as if they had any common ground to argue over, never mind agree on, and surrender was not an option. The Warriors' beliefs were built upon the rock of self-sacrifice, and the Faerie had a long tradition of fighting to the death over the smallest of insults. It was only a small step for both sides to plunge into a battle they knew they couldn't win, as long as they could be sure the other side would lose too. And only a small quiet voice murmured in their hearts that it wasn't too late to withdraw with honour, and fight another day.

The Warriors had automatic weapons, tanks and napalm and smart weapons. The Faerie had high energy lasers, plasma beam weapons, magic swords and enchanted devices. And they both had many deaths to avenge. Every now and again one side would stir restlessly and the other would react, but so far it had come to nothing. No one wanted to commit themselves prematurely, but neither could afford to be the last one off the blocks. A growing tremor built among both armies as they reacted to each

409

other, neither backing down. Men stirred, weapons were readied, and everyone prepared themselves for one last charge into the valley of death. And in that moment, when all seemed finally lost, a single voice was heard, singing in the night.

The Warriors and the Faerie stopped and looked about them, and out of the shadows came Sean Morrison, singing like an angel. Behind him walked a once-famous guitarist, adding his music to the song. And behind him, every singer and musician and rock-and-roller who'd ever died too young or been forgotten and ended up in Shadows Fall. The singer shot by his own fan, and the guitarist who overdosed. All the high-flying angels who crashed under the weight of booze and drugs and fame. All the rising stars who died too soon, or the faded stars who made the mistake of outliving their own legend. Everyone who died in plane or car crashes, or drowned in their own swimming pool before they had a chance to find out who they really were. They all came to Shadows Fall when the fans finally stopped believing in them, and found peace at last in a town where legends were two a penny. Now they all came together for one last concert, one last song, one last spit in the eye of fate.

The music grew and grew as more joined in, the music shifting and changing like a living thing. Sometimes rock and sometimes folk, punk and acid and bubblegum all come together in a triumphant whole that was so much greater than the sum of its parts. It filled the night, pushing back the dark, an army of song. And at their head, his voice soaring effortlessly above them all, Sean Morrison, whose name wasn't Sean, who died too soon while he still had songs left to sing.

The music washed over the Warriors and the Faerie, and they stopped to listen. The music touched something in them all, something small but stubborn that had somehow survived all the hate and horror of the killing, and here and there among the soldiers and the elves, some responded. A little touch of awe and wonder and joy, just

410

when the night seemed at its darkest. Soldiers threw aside their guns and elves dropped their swords, and in ones and twos they walked out across the Square to greet each other. Another day they might meet and fight, and another day they might die, but for the moment they drew back from the brink, and the air was suddenly so much sweeter. They gathered in the centre of the Square, more and more of them, spurred on by the song and those who sang it. It was a quiet celebration, with no shouting or rejoicing; only a simple satisfaction that the war was over, and they'd come through it alive.

But not everyone heard the song. For some it was just noise, a distraction from what really mattered. The Warrior officers tried to control their men with shouted orders and threats, and when that didn't work they ordered those men still loyal to them to open fire on the traitors. They did so, and the night was suddenly full of the roar of gunfire. The Faerie responded with their uncanny weapons, strange energies blazing against the dark. But the music rose above it all, strong and stirring and potent, and the weapons on both sides were helpless against it. The song protected those who heard it. Morrison and the others sang and played as though their hearts would burst, filling the night with all the lost strength and broken-off potential of their short lives. They sang the songs they might have sung if death had not cut them short, like wild flowers in a regimented garden. They sang and played and the music hammered in the blood of all who heard it.

The Warriors broke first, and either turned and ran or poured out across the Square to join the milling crowd in the centre. The Faerie laughed and applauded and put aside their weapons. The elves had always had a soft spot for human music, and they cared more for the joy of joining their voices to the song than chasing after a defeated enemy. The singing and the music finally crashed to a halt as though they'd planned it that way, and the audience cheered and applauded till their throats were raw and their hands ached. Morrison grinned and bowed, exhausted and drenched with sweat, but feeling the power of the music still moving within him, as though asking what it should do next. Oberon and Titania and Puck came forward to bow to him, and Morrison wiped the sweat from his face with his sleeve, and grinned at them.

'Do I hear a request for an encore?'

In a deserted house on an empty road, Suzanne Dubois sat alone by the downstairs window, keeping a weary eye on the desolate scene outside. She tried not to move, and breathed as shallowly as she could. Even the smallest movement sent jagged shocks of pain shooting through her broken arm, some bad enough to make her grey out for a moment. She'd thought at first the arm had just been sprained or badly bruised in the collapse of the Cavern club, but as the shock wore off and the pain grew steadily worse, it got harder and harder to believe that. She tried, she really tried, because the thought of a broken arm on top of everything else was just too much to bear, but now even that small comfort was denied her.

The arm itself was hidden by the long sleeve of her dress. The material was torn and ragged and stained with blood, but she hadn't pulled it back to look at her arm. She didn't think she could handle that just yet. She wished Polly would hurry up and come downstairs. She'd gone up to the next floor to see if the extra height would give her a better view out over the town. All you could see from the ground floor were the surrounding shelled and burnt-out houses, the empty canal, and sometimes a column of soldiers streaming past, on their way to devastate some other part of the town. There hadn't been any soldiers for some time now, but Suzanne had no doubt they'd be back eventually. This was just a lull in the storm, and lulls inevitably ended in fresh violence. Pain gnawed at her arm again, and she concentrated on breathing more shallowly, so as not to jog it.

She felt cold and tired and very alone. Polly was still upstairs, and Sean Morrison had disappeared some time during the night, when she and Polly were still asleep. She supposed she shouldn't really have been surprised. Sean had never been reliable. That was part of his charm. But even so, sneaking out like that was a new low, even for him. Not that James Hart had proved any better. He'd promised to come back when he found a safe haven for them, but that was hours ago, and there was still no sign of him. Anything could have happened to him. Anything.

She sighed, and then had to grit her teeth as fresh pain surged through her arm. She was cold, but sweat was pouring down her face. Not a good sign. She felt increasingly dizzy, on the edge of fainting, but she wouldn't give in to it. She couldn't afford to pass out. Anything might happen while she was helpless. She wasn't used to feeling helpless. Usually she was the one that other people came to with their problems, and she would read the Cards, and See what to do. She'd always prided herself on being able to find an answer for every problem, sooner or later. She'd also prided herself on being able to look out for herself; reliant on no one for anything. Now the town she'd helped for so long was torn apart far beyond her ability to put things right, and she was trapped in a deserted house with a broken arm and a rising fever. She wished Polly would hurry up and come down. She felt a little better when Polly was with her. She smiled sourly. For years Polly had leaned on her for help to get through her fractured life, and now here she was, relying on Polly. Funny how the world turns. Funny. What was taking her so long up there? Suzanne felt like calling to her to hurry up, but she didn't. That would be giving in to her fear and her weakness, and she had a strong feeling that if she gave in to them even once, she'd never be able to regain control. But what the hell was Polly doing up there all this time?

On the next floor up, Polly Cousins stood before a jagged hole in the wall, looking out into the night and hugging herself tightly to keep from falling apart. She was miles from the safety and security of her own house, surrounded by threats on all sides, and panic attacks were ripping through her in waves. She wanted to scream or run or do something; but there was nothing she could do, nowhere to run, and she knew if she started screaming she wouldn't be able to stop. She was shaking in every limb, her vision greying in and out, and it was all she could do to keep from passing out. She had to hang on, Suzanne needed her, but that thought only made things worse. It was hard enough trying to cope with her own problems, without knowing that someone else was depending on her. It wasn't fair. She wasn't ready to handle this kind of pressure. Not yet.

She crouched down on the floor, and rocked back and forth on her haunches. She was hugging herself so tightly now she could hardly breathe. Why wasn't James back yet? He'd promised he wouldn't be long. She'd feel stronger if he was there; more able to cope. Morrison leaving while she was asleep hadn't helped either. But she'd always known she couldn't rely on him. She'd thought she could rely on Suzanne and James, but Suzanne couldn't even look after herself, and James hadn't come back. Something must have happened to him; something bad. He wouldn't have just gone off and left her. He wouldn't.

She took one deep breath after another, trying to calm herself, but the extra oxygen just made her feel even more light-headed. She had to get it under control. She couldn't go down again until she had. She couldn't let Suzanne see her like this. Suzanne was depending on her. The thoughts flashed back and forth through her mind, like birds unable to settle on a shaking branch. She made herself stand up straight again, and looked through the gap in the wall in the hope there would be something there to distract her. At the far end of the street, a column of soldiers was heading straight for her. She almost stopped breathing. The soldiers hurried down the street, looking straight ahead, and went past the house without even looking at it. They turned a corner and were gone, and as quickly as that the street was empty again.

Polly looked carefully in all directions, but there was no

sign of any more soldiers. It occurred to her that there hadn't been any for some time now. The war in Shadows Fall seemed to have passed her by. Perhaps it was over. She wondered who'd won, and then shook her head. It didn't matter. All that mattered now was getting some kind of medical help, for Suzanne and herself. She could use a little something, to settle her nerves. She walked round the room in a circle, over and over again. The simple repetition was comforting. She could still feel herself coming apart at the seams, but it was a familiar feeling, and she knew how to cope. She had to keep busy, so busy she didn't have time to think. She walked a little faster. It didn't matter what she did, as long as she was doing something. Her breathing began to slow and her head began to clear. After a while she felt stronger, and went down the stairs to rejoin Suzanne.

She was half-way down the stairs when she heard someone moving about in the hall. She froze where she was, listening. It couldn't be Suzanne; she was too weak and in too much pain to be wandering about. But it couldn't be one of the soldiers either. She'd watched them all pass the house by without even a glance. Unless that was what she was supposed to think. She looked about her for something she could use to defend herself, but there was nothing to hand. She wasn't sure she'd have been able to use it if there was.

Her next thought was to retreat back up the stairs and hide, but she couldn't do that. She couldn't just abandon Suzanne. Suzanne had never abandoned her, through all the bad years. Polly crept down the stairs, one at a time, her hands clenched into fists. She'd decide what to do when she saw who it was. If all else failed, she'd say she was alone in the house, and hope Suzanne had enough sense to stay quiet. She rounded the corner of the stairs, and James Hart grinned up at her.

'Ah, there you are. I thought I heard someone moving about. Get yourself down here. I've got some good news.'

She didn't know whether to hit him or hug him, and in

the end she settled for following him down the hall and into the room where Suzanne was waiting. She looked round as they came in, and Hart shot a quick glance at Polly as he took in Suzanne's deteriorating condition. All the colour had gone from her face, and she looked like death warmed over and allowed to congeal. Hart sat down opposite her and tried to look relaxed and confident.

'There's a church just a few blocks away, acting as a sanctuary. There are people there trying to help. The soldiers are leaving churches alone, for some reason. The place I found has a doctor and some medical supplies. I think we ought to get you to them. How do you feel about travelling, Suzanne?'

'I'll manage,' Suzanne said flatly. 'We can't stay here.'

She got to her feet in a series of small movements, grimacing at the pain but refusing to cry out. Polly hovered at her elbow, ready to help, but knowing Suzanne well enough to stay back until asked. Suzanne didn't like people fussing over her, even when she needed it. She stood stiffly for a moment, holding her broken arm flat against her side, and then nodded curtly to Hart and Polly that she was ready to go. Suzanne didn't believe in being beaten by anything, least of all her own weakness. Hart exchanged another glance with Polly, shrugged slightly, and then led the way slowly out of the room and into the hall. None of them saw the sheet of paper with Morrison's song, which had fallen to the floor out of sight.

'What happened to Sean?' said Hart.

'Made off while we were asleep,' said Polly.

There was enough repressed anger in her voice to keep Hart from pursuing the matter any further. They left the house and stepped cautiously out into the empty street. Hart locked the door behind them. No point in attracting looters. There was the smell of smoke on the air, and the crimson glare of flames in the distance, but the street was eerily quiet. It was easy to imagine they were the only living things left in Shadows Fall. Hart led the way down the street, keeping the pace slow so as not to tire Suzanne out too quickly.

'I have a strong feeling something important has happened,' he said quietly, as much to distract Suzanne's attention as anything. 'The fighting seems to have stopped for the moment, and from what I overheard on a radio at the church, the invaders have run into something that scared the hell out of them. Most of them are just milling about. Some are even retreating, heading for the town boundaries as though half the devils in hell were chasing them. The trouble isn't over by any means, but for the first time I feel like we're in with a fighting chance. Somewhere along the line, the soldiers got their ass kicked in no uncertain manner.'

And then he broke off, and the three of them came to a sudden halt as a dozen soldiers stepped out of the shadows to block their way. Hart looked behind him, but there were soldiers there too. They looked tired and grim, but they held their guns steady. One of the soldiers before him stepped forward. He wasn't an officer, but his attitude made it clear he was in charge. He looked Hart over, and then the two women, taking his time. Finally he sniffed once, and locked eyes with Hart.

'It isn't over yet,' he said coldly. 'We're experiencing a few difficulties, that's all. Nothing we can't handle. We're regrouping, and soon this cesspit of a town will pay for all the trouble it's caused us. None of this was supposed to happen. You were supposed to be an easy target. Civilians, unbelievers. We were just going to walk in and occupy the town. But no, you had to fight back, and now thousands of Warriors are dead. Thousands of good men dead, because of you.' He looked back at his men. 'Shoot them.'

He stepped back out of the way, and as suddenly as that the soldiers were raising their guns and aiming them at Hart and Polly and Suzanne. Hart moved forward to stand between the soldiers and the two women, knowing even as he did so that there was nothing he could do. Polly started some quick speech of apology or appeal, but no one was listening. Suzanne just glared at the soldiers and didn't even flinch away from the guns. And then the rifles all spoke at once, and the street was full of thunder.

Time slowed right down. Everyone was still as a statue, and the air was thick as syrup. The bullets hung on the air like fat ugly insects. Hart felt as though he could reach out and move them around, like beads on an invisible abacus. Power churned in him, filling him to bursting. It was power beyond limits, beyond good and evil, power naked and intense. Time's power. He looked at Polly and Suzanne beside him, frozen in a moment of fear, with death only inches away, and a sudden anger flared up within him. He lashed out, and the bullets and the men who fired them were swept away in a moment.

Time crashed back into motion, and the soldiers blew apart in a cloud of blood and tattered flesh. Polly and Suzanne screamed. Blood and flesh pattered to the ground like a horrid rain, hitting the ground with soft slapping sounds. Hart looked around him, and everywhere was an abattoir. He was surprised how little he cared. The soldiers had tried to kill him and Polly and Suzanne, and now they were dead instead. He realized Polly was looking at him with a shocked, dawning recognition, and he reached out a hand to her, to reassure her. She flinched away from him. Suzanne was looking at him as though he was a stranger. Perhaps he was. He didn't feel much like himself, just at the moment. He nodded to them both, to show he understood, and then set off down the street towards the church. He tried to avoid treading in the blood, but there was too much of it. After a moment, Polly and Suzanne followed him.

Father Callahan drove his car through the silent streets, heading deeper into Hell. He'd known these streets from before the invasion, but he didn't know them now. Everywhere he looked he saw ruined buildings, burnt-out cars, and bodies hanging from street lights or just left to lie where they had fallen. No crucifixions here. The Warriors must have been in a hurry. But still, every time he saw a new victim of the invasion, a part of his mind insisted *You did this. You're responsible.* He drove on, keeping his speed down, partly so he could steer around the bodies in the road, but mostly because he wouldn't allow himself to look away from what he'd brought to Shadows Fall. The town the Church had put in his charge. At first he prayed for the victims, and then he damned the Warriors, and finally he just drove, numbed by the sheer extent of the horror. Only one thing kept him going: the thought that Saint Augustine would know what to do.

And together they would teach the Warriors of the Cross the true meaning of the wrath of God.

He tried the hospital first. You could never tell where Augustine might turn up next, but he'd worked at Manderlay hospital as a doctor before he became a Saint, and he still spent a lot of time there, doing what he could. There's always demand for a miracle worker in a hospital, and with everything that had happened no doubt the hospital needed him now more than ever. Callahan found the place easily enough, but had to stop and park some distance away. Ambulances and cars with hastily painted red crosses were streaming in from all over, and he didn't want to block their path. He strode quickly through Manderlay's crowded grounds, rehearsing in his mind what he was going to say, and then he forgot all that as he took in the new hell of the hospital.

Men and women were pouring in and out of the old-fashioned double doors, some in white coats smeared with other people's blood, some carrying or leading injured friends and relatives. Inside the casualty department Callahan found a bedlam of milling people and deafening noise; a mixture of desperate calls and screams and naked pain that was almost unbearable. There were people on stretchers and trolleys, sitting slumped in chairs or just left to lie on blankets on the floor. There was blood and burns and the stench of too much disinfectant trying to cover something worse. Here and there, friends and relatives sat with the injured, holding their hands and looking lost and helpless. There was just one doctor and three nurses, stepping carefully between the injured, giving each patient a brief examination and a number, according to how urgent the case was. Sometimes all they could do was close the eyes, cover the face with a blanket, and move on.

Callahan kept out of their way. There was nothing he could do to help, except perhaps offer the comfort of the last rites, and he didn't feel qualified to do that at the moment. Not until he had made his peace with God. He made his way slowly through the noise and confusion of the packed hospital corridors, asking quietly but persistently where he might find Saint Augustine. And finally he found him in the main operating theatre, healing the injured by the laying on of hands.

There was no one to help him, no nurse to hand him instruments or mop his brow, only the endless stream of patients brought in and wheeled out by exhausted, grey-faced porters. Callahan stood just inside the theatre doors, watching quietly, out of everyone's way. He watched Augustine place his bare hands on an open wound, and saw the ragged edges crawl together and heal in seconds. Each miracle took a little more out of the Saint, and his face was already painfully gaunt. He'd always been a big man, but now his bloodied hospital gown hung loosely about him, like a shroud. He looked like he'd been on a hunger strike. There were dark smudges under his eyes, and the bones in his face stood out against the taut skin. He looked like an Old Testament prophet fresh in from the desert.

Two porters brought in the next patient and dumped him on the operating table. Augustine pulled back the bloodstained sheet covering him and blood spilled out, running over the edge of the table. The man had been gutted, ripped open from sternum to groin. Augustine plunged his hands into the gaping wound and moved quickly from organ to organ, repairing damage at a touch. His eyes narrowed as he worked, and light flickered briefly over his head, a neon halo come and gone in a moment.

Finally he withdrew his hands, and sealed the wound with a gesture. The porters snatched the man away the moment Augustine finished, and dumped another in his place.

Callahan stood and watched. Patients came and went, and no matter how many the Saint healed, there were always more. The strength was going out of Augustine, slowly but surely, taking years of his life with it. He must have known, but still he carried on. Callahan had been there twenty minutes or more when finally there was a lull. Augustine looked round and smiled at him. On anyone else's face it would have been a death's-head grin, but for him it was a real smile, despite his tiredness.

'Come to help, Nate? Always use for an extra pair of hands here.'

'I've come to you for help, Augustine. The Warriors must be stopped. You have the power of the Lord in you. Come with me, and use it against the Warriors.'

Augustine's smile changed slightly, and he shook his head. 'Did you think that hadn't occurred to me, laddie? It was the first thing I thought of, when I saw what those butchers were doing in the Lord's name. But you can't stop violence with violence. I won't raise my hand against another. It goes against everything I ever believed in.'

'But I need you. The town needs you.'

'I'm needed here.'

'All you're doing here is mopping up other people's messes! You could stop the fighting, stop the killing; stop the flow of wounded at the source.'

'Only by denying everything I ever stood for. Everything the town stands for. Look at these people here, Nate. Some of the wounded are townspeople, some are Warriors. I don't ask which is which. It doesn't matter. I just help, where I can.'

'And how many more will die, because you didn't stop the fighting when you could?'

'Do you think I don't understand the temptations of violence? The attraction of simple action, good guy versus bad guy; the appeal of the easy answer? No, laddie; I'm not a fighting man, and I won't let those butchers make me one.' He smiled at Callahan, with understanding and compassion. 'I know more about what's going on in this town than you do, Nate. Already forces are gathering that will put a stop to the fighting. But if you need to be a part of that, then so be it. I give you the power of God; use it as you see best.'

He reached out and placed his hand on Callahan's head in a blessing, and a powerful shock tore through the priest. His legs buckled and he fell to his knees. Power burned and heaved within him, power beyond hope or sanity. Callahan could hear the minds of everyone in the hospital, crying and screaming and babbling all at once. He got his feet under him and staggered out of the operating theatre, his hands pressed uselessly to his ears. He didn't look back, so he never saw the look of understanding and sorrow on Augustine's face before he turned back to his next patient.

Callahan made his way out of the hospital, barging through the crowds and crying out at the pressure of the power seething within him. He stumbled out into the hospital grounds and the volume of the voices in his head died away a little. He grasped at the sudden sense of control, and forced the voices out of his mind. He stood for a long moment, shuddering helplessly, slowly coming to terms with what had been done to him. He had power now, real power, and unlike Augustine he wouldn't hesitate to use it.

He reached out tentatively with his new augmented senses and found a battle going on half a dozen blocks away. The two sides had fought themselves almost to a standstill, but neither wanted to be the first to back off. Callahan tapped the merest fraction of his new power and rose effortlessly into the air. He soared through the night sky, the cold wind blowing tears from his eyes, and headed towards the gunfire and the screaming.

He stood on emptiness above the two sides, and where he looked guns would not fire and explosives were made harmless. Wounds were healed and the near-dead rose blinking to their feet and looked uncertainly about them. For a long moment it seemed the battle was over, and then a Warrior officer barked an order, and his men filled their hands with knives and bayonets and threw themselves at their enemies. The town's defenders did the same, and in a moment the two sides were at each other's throats again. Callahan smiled grimly.

All right, Augustine. I tried it your way. The Warriors cannot be trusted. Now we do it my way. And may God have mercy on their souls.

He raised his hands above his head, brought them together and then moved them slowly apart. On the ground below the two sides were separated and forced apart by an invisible irresistible compulsion. Callahan looked down upon the Warriors and no mercy moved within him; only a dark and bitter hatred for what they had done in God's name. All the terrible things that he had made possible through his blindness. Power blasted down from him, crushing the Warriors to the ground like ants under a boot. They screamed and pleaded as they struggled helplessly under the unbearable pressure. Blood spilled from their mouths, and one by one they died. And all the suffering Callahan had caused burned in him like all the fires of Hell.

He fell out of the night sky like a wounded bird as the dying thoughts of the Warriors howled through his mind. He hit the ground hard, but took no harm from it. It would take more than that to hurt him now. Callahan lay curled in a ball on the ground as he fought for control, but the pain of the dead was just too much to bear. They hadn't been evil, most of them. Just soldiers doing what their officers and superiors had assured them was the right thing. They had listened to the wrong people, and hadn't questioned enough, but often that was the extent of their guilt. To understand all is to forgive much, and Callahan finally realized what Augustine had meant. You can't fight evil by becoming evil. By showing no mercy to the Warriors he had been just as blind as them.

Vengeance is mine, saith the Lord.

Callahan rose shakily to his feet as the voices gradually died away in his mind. They'd never be completely silent; they were a part of him now, and always would be. The triumphant defenders approached him diffidently to offer thanks, but he waved them away. They would only ask questions he didn't have the answers for yet. He turned and walked away, and the defenders let him go. Living in Shadows Fall you learned to respect power where you found it.

Callahan walked on through the town, stopping the fighting wherever he came across it. He took no vengeance on the Warriors, and stopped any who tried to take it in his place. Let the law handle it. Human law. He walked on, street by street, square by square, and a slow healing calm settled over his part of the town. He knew the power within him was capable of much more, but he refused to be tempted by it. Trying to impose his will on the town by force was what had got him into all this trouble in the first place. He was a man of God, a man of peace, though it had taken Augustine's power to remind him of that. Choosing violence inevitably took you down the Warriors' path, where everyone who disagreed with you was automatically a sinner, and therefore an enemy. In their pursuit of their version of justice, the Warriors had forgotten mercy and compassion. And more than that, they'd forgotten the strength such things could inspire.

Callahan stopped before an open square and looked about him. The place was silent and deserted, though there were signs that a battle of some kind had taken place there quite recently. He reached out with his heightened senses, and found them blunted, masked. There was something in the square with him, something he was being prevented from seeing. Even as he realized that, magic roared around him, consuming him and his surroundings in incandescent flames. Nearby street lamps drooped like dying flowers, and the street cracked open under the impact of the raging heat. Throughout the square the air was scorched away, and paintwork blistered and boiled on even the furthest buildings.

And in the midst of those flames stood Father Callahan, serene and untouched. The magic intensified, boiling the surface of the street around him, and still it couldn't touch him. He was a man of God, and the Lord's power was with him. He reached out with his heightened senses, and quickly located the source of the attack. The Warriors had set their sorcerer priests against him. Their power raged within them, fell and potent, and Callahan knew he couldn't turn away. As long as the circle of sorcerer priests still held, Shadows Fall would never be truly safe. He smothered the flames around him with a thought, and reached out to the priests, and in that moment battle was joined, their faith against his.

The two forces came together, clashing head on. There was no room for subtlety of manoeuvre, for dialogue or compromise. The battle raged this way and that, switching from physical to spiritual and back again. The square was consumed in an inferno, blowing apart the surrounding buildings like rotten fruit. And slowly, step by step, Callahan was driven back. He was still new in his power, and there were so many of them. He drew on greater and greater reserves of power, knowing the toll it was taking on his mortal frame, but helpless to prevent it. Man was not meant to use such power as this, and it was consuming him, body and soul. So he did the only thing he could, the one option left to him. He called up all his power in a single moment, and let it do what it would with him. The power lashed out, driven by every last vestige of his life force, and the sorcerer priests fell back, unable to match his magic; because in the end Callahan was not afraid to die, and they were. The circle disintegrated as each man tried to save himself, and with their power broken and their faith shattered they were no match for the force that swept over them.

The flames died down, guttered, and went out. The temperature dropped quickly back to normal, and all was still and silent in the fire-blackened square. And in the middle of it all lay one dead man, burned to a charred corpse. A man at peace with himself at last.

Rhea Frazier stopped struggling and let the two soldiers drag her where they wanted. She stumbled along, her head swimming, the world passing by in brief impressions of wrecked buildings and running men. One of her eyes was swollen shut, and there was blood on her face and in her mouth from the beating the soldiers had given her when they captured her. They were furious over the men Ash had killed, before they killed him. They'd thrown her back and forth between them, not letting her fall, hitting her again and again. She had no doubt they would have beaten her to death if she hadn't managed to make them understand that she was the Mayor of Shadows Fall. They'd backed off then, reluctantly, and left her to lie shaking and crying on the ground while one of them radioed his superiors for instructions.

The beating had shaken her, destroying her confidence on some basic, instinctive level. They'd taken their time with her, enjoying it, and there had been nothing she could do to stop them. Except out-think them. As long as she was still thinking, planning, they hadn't beaten her. They could break her body, but not her spirit. She stopped crying, forcing it back by sniffing and swallowing, and sat up slowly. Her ribs hurt her with every breath, and her stomach was a single mass of pain. She spat several times, trying to get the taste of blood out of her mouth.

A soldier came back and stood over her, and she shrank back instinctively. He hauled her to her feet without speaking to her, and held her there while another soldier handcuffed her hands behind her back. Then they dragged her over to a nearby jeep, threw her in the back, and drove off. She had no idea where she was going, the passing streets merely an impression of noise and movement, but just the fact that the beating had stopped gave her hope. Somebody still thought she was valuable, that she could be

426

of use to them. With a little luck, she might find a way out of this yet. The jeep finally stopped, and they hauled her out of the back and down the street. Finally she stumbled up some steps and into a building, and it was only then she realized where they'd brought her. The town Library.

It seemed pretty much untouched by the general destruction, and she just had time to wonder why when the two soldiers stopped suddenly and threw her to the floor. Without her arms to protect her she landed hard. The thick carpet cushioned some of the impact, but it was still enough to knock the breath out of her. She lay still, struggling to get her breath back, and they left her alone. For the first time, she allowed herself to think about Ash. She didn't cry, there wasn't enough strength left in her for that, but seeing him die again had hurt her on a level that the soldiers hadn't even come close to touching with their beating. It was as though there was a gap in her now, a hole the shape of Leonard Ash, and all he'd meant to her. She'd lost him again.

She pushed the thought aside. She couldn't think about that now. It would have to wait. She raised her head slowly and looked around her. She was in the midst of the main Library stacks, and soldiers were crossing back and forth before her, carrying arm-loads of books from the shelves and stacking them in neat piles by the reception desk. There was a definite sense of purpose to it, and Rhea turned the thought over in her mind. Surely the soldiers hadn't destroyed half the town just to seize some books from the Library? The town had its fair share of important and forbidden texts, but they were all safely locked away in the Archives at All Hallows Hall, under Time's watchful eye. There was nothing in the Library worth fighting a war over.

She saw someone approaching her, and tried to sit up straight. It was hard to get her balance with her hands handcuffed behind her back, and she moaned despite herself at the pain her efforts caused her. One of the soldiers standing over her grabbed a handful of her hair and jerked her head back so that she was looking up at the newcomer. He was an officer of some kind. Mid-forties, stocky, but little of it fat, back straight as a poker and hair cropped right back to the skull. His face was cold, his eyes impersonal. Just from looking at him, Rhea knew that he was sharp, intelligent, controlled. He saw her pain, but took no pleasure from it, just noted that it would make her questioning that much easier. Rhea struggled to clear her mind. This man was dangerous. He listened calmly as the soldier holding her hair described Ash's attack and death, and her capture. The officer thought for a moment, and then turned his attention to Rhea. When he spoke, his voice was slow and calm.

'I've been an army man all my adult life. Seen a fair amount of combat, here and there. Got my hands dirty on occasion, and never once gave up on a mission until it was completed. I've seen some strange things in my time, and none of them threw me for more than a moment or two. But this town of yours is pushing me to my limits. From what I've seen, I'd say it's infested with demons, witches and unbelievers. Which are you?'

Rhea swallowed hard. She wanted to be sure her voice was clear and calm and steady when she answered. 'I'm Rhea Frazier, Mayor of Shadows Fall.' Her lips split open again as she spoke, and she tasted fresh blood in her mouth. Some of her teeth felt uncomfortably loose too, but she could cope with that. She did her best to look coldly at the officer. 'I speak for this town and its defenders. Is there anyone among your people with two brain cells to rub together that I could talk to?'

The soldier with his hand in her hair shook her head roughly. Tears ran down her face, as much from weakness as pain. The officer waited for her to regain her composure.

'Mind your manners,' he said finally. 'I am Major Williams of the Warriors of the Cross, and I speak for God, in the absence of a superior officer. We are all warriors of God, and an insult to us is an insult to him.'

'What are you doing here?' said Rhea flatly. She knew

428

it was important not to seem cowed before this man. He respected strength. 'Why are your men taking those books?'

'We have come to bring the word and will of God to this sink of iniquity. The guilty shall be punished. Blasphemers will be punished. The word of God shall reign supreme here. As for the books; we're sorting the wheat from the chaff. We're removing all books of a fantastic nature. Fantasies are unhealthy. People must learn to live in the real world. Besides, many of these books deal with magic, and the word of the Lord is clear. Thou shalt not suffer a witch to live.

'We are also removing all books that contain information that the common people are not ready to cope with. A little knowledge is a dangerous thing, and is best left to those who have been trained in the proper ways of interpreting it. And finally, we are removing all books which in any way contradict God's word. Blasphemy is not permitted. As soon as this town is secured, we'll have a communal book-burning. Sit around the fire, toast marshmallows, sing a few songs. I like a good book-burning. Helps bring a community together.'

His voice never rose and his face remained calm all the time he was talking. There was little point in trying to reason with the man. Rhea knew a fanatic when she saw one. But she had to try; the town was depending on her. She couldn't lose that as well as Ash. A sudden rush of grief swept through her, catching her by surprise. Ash was dead. She'd only just got him back and now he was gone again. *I can't have lost you again, Leonard. I couldn't bear it.* She forced the thought away. She'd grieve for him later, when she had the time. The town needed her now.

'I'm the Mayor of Shadows Fall,' she said again, doggedly. 'As representative of the town's civil authority, I'm prepared to discuss surrender terms.'

'Terms?' said Williams, his mouth twitching in something that might have been a smile. 'You're in no position to dictate terms. The town will surrender or it will be destroyed. Your fellow town Councillors also tried to dictate terms. They are now dead, executed in the name of the Lord.'

He watched the realization of what that meant sink into her, and smiled inwardly. She had no way of knowing he was lying, and the damned Councillors had actually escaped for the moment. It was true enough anyway; the Leader had given orders they were all to be shot on sight. The Mayor also had no way of knowing that portions of the Warrior forces were currently getting their ass kicked in no uncertain manner. If she could be persuaded to surrender the town, the enemy forces would have to stand down, without ever knowing how close to victory they'd come. Might as well try her with a few pertinent questions, while she was still off balance.

'What do you know about the Imperial Leader's present whereabouts?' he said casually. 'We haven't heard from him since he went to visit the Sarcophagus in the town park. What could have happened to him there?'

Rhea shrugged dully. 'Anything. The park's a dangerous place at night. There are dinosaurs. Maybe they got him. Or Time.'

'Old Father Time,' said Williams distastefully. 'He may hide behind a child's name here, but we know who he is. Who he has to be. The Fallen One, the Lord of Flies; the Great Enemy himself. No doubt he was responsible for the death of our sorcerer priests.'

He stopped suddenly, realizing that he'd miscalculated. He'd thought the Frazier woman had broken under her treatment, but she was looking at him now in a calm, thoughtful way that showed she understood the implications of what he was saying. The Warriors' Leader was missing, and one of their most powerful forces had been neutralized. He'd underestimated her. He wouldn't do that again. For the moment, it was important he regain control of the situation. He gestured to the soldier holding her hair.

'Release her from the handcuffs.' He waited patiently

while the soldier did so. 'Now stretch out her left hand before her, and hold it steady on the floor.' Rhea began to struggle then, but she was no match for the soldier in her weakened state. Williams waited till the hand was positioned where he wanted it, and then smiled coldly at Rhea. 'What's going to happen now is very simple, Mayor Frazier. I am going to ask you questions about the town's strengths and weaknesses, and you are going to answer me fully and truthfully. If you lie to me, I'll cut off one of your fingers. If you run out of fingers on the left hand, we'll move to the right. If you run out of fingers entirely, I'll get inventive. And just to prove that you should take me very seriously, I think we'll remove the little finger on your left hand now. Hold her steady.'

He leant down to reach for her hand, and Rhea lunged forward. The suddenness of the move caught them all by surprise, and her head slammed into his face. She felt as much as heard his nose break under the impact, and then all of them were sprawling on the floor. She scrambled to her feet, kicked away the soldier as he grabbed for her, and then turned to the other soldier who'd brought her in and punched him in the throat. He sank to the floor making horrid coughing noises, and Rhea ran for the door. Behind her she could hear Williams calling for someone to stop her. She tried to hurry, but her balance was still uncertain, and she crashed into a pile of books. She fell over them, landed heavily, and was still trying to find the strength to get to her feet when hands grabbed her from behind and pulled her back from the door.

And then suddenly, everything stopped. The hands holding her fell away, and she was left on her knees, facing the door. Someone was standing there, and it took Rhea a long moment to recognize the ragged figure in his shabby clothes. Jack Fetch grinned down at her with his fixed smile, and then stalked past her on twiggy feet. There was a brief pause as the Templars grabbed for the guns they'd put aside to carry books, and then everyone opened up at once on the advancing scarecrow. Bullets pounded him from every direction, knocking him this way and that and raising puffs of smoke from his torn rags, but he was not alive and never had been and didn't give a damn for their bullets. He leapt forward into the midst of the Warriors, and his hands closed remorselessly on living flesh. He raged through the Library, overturning the stacks on soldiers and throwing bloodied men about him like broken dolls. Some Warriors broke and ran, while others fired blindly, not caring if they shot their own men in their desperation to stop Jack Fetch.

Rhea watched from the doorway, but didn't move until Major Williams emerged out of the chaos and pointed a gun at her. There was blood on his face, and he was shouting something, but it was drowned out in the bedlam. It didn't matter anyway; the gun in his hand was clear enough. She tried to get up, but her legs weren't strong enough yet. She backed away on her ass, and Williams came after her. And then suddenly, someone was standing between her and the Warrior. Williams fired anyway, but the newcomer just laughed softly and snatched the bullet out of mid-air. He hefted it casually in his hand and then threw it calmly aside as Williams gaped incredulously. Rhea looked up at the newcomer, and he turned back to smile down at her.

'Don't worry, love,' said Leonard Ash. 'Everything's going to be all right.'

Williams threw the gun at Ash and turned to run. Ash caught him inside half a dozen steps, picked him up with one hand and threw him face first into the nearest wall. The plaster cracked raggedly under the impact. Williams slid slowly to the floor and lay there, twitching. Ash came back and helped Rhea to her feet, and she clung to him with all her remaining strength, as though afraid he might disappear again if she lost hold of him. He murmured soothingly to her, and her breathing finally slowed back to normal.

'You really shouldn't have worried,' Ash said finally. 'I'm dead, remember? You can't kill a man who's already dead. I was brought back for a purpose, and until I find out what it is, I can't rest. It took me a while to get myself together and then track you down, but I got here as soon as I could. Let's get out of here. Jack seems to have everything nicely under control. He's much better at fighting than I am. I go all to pieces.'

Rhea hit him in the chest. There wasn't much strength behind the blow, but he grunted obligingly anyway.

'Go and fetch Williams,' she said, pushing herself away from Ash. 'I have to talk to him. Maybe now he'll listen to reason.'

Ash shrugged, went over and picked up Williams, and brought him back. The Major was unsteady on his feet, and blood was dripping from his broken nose, but his eyes were clear.

'We have to stop the fighting,' said Rhea shortly. 'Too many have died already. I speak for the town, you can speak for the Warriors. As Mayor of Shadows Fall, I am prepared to discuss terms for your surrender.'

Williams laughed breathlessly. 'Your town is an abomination, a breeding ground of sinners and unnatural creatures. I'll see it burned to the ground and everyone in it slaughtered before I call off my men. Your very existence is an offence. To Hell with you.'

He produced a knife from somewhere, and Ash moved quickly to step between Williams and Rhea, but the Major turned the knife on himself, and thrust it unflinchingly into his own heart. He slumped over sideways, and lay still. Ash stirred the body with his foot, but there was no response.

'Fanatic,' said Ash. 'We can't deal with these people, Rhea. It's us or them. Us or them.'

The Warriors came running through the town like panicked cattle, pursued by an enemy they couldn't face. They ran blindly, paying no attention to where they were or where they were going, knowing only that the music which still roared in their heads and in their hearts had undone them. They ran, and behind them came Sean Morrison and his fellow musicians, and all the ranks of Faerie. The Warriors didn't look back; they didn't dare. All that mattered to them now was their desperate need to get out of this terrible town that wasn't at all what they'd expected. They threw away their guns and ammunition as they ran; useless to them now and too heavy to carry far. Harpies and lamia had torn their helicopters from the skies, and the tanks and troop transporters had disappeared into the gaping maw of Cromm Cruach, the Great Wurm. The Warriors ran shouting and sobbing and screaming through the devastated and fire-blackened streets, and the music drove them on like a whip. There was magic and power in the music, and the Warriors' vain, self-satisfied faith wasn't enough in the face of real glory.

In another street, in another part of the town, more Warriors were running, pursued by Jack Fetch, Leonard Ash and Rhea Frazier. Not many soldiers, perhaps a hundred or so, but all of them so demoralized by what they'd seen the ghost and the scarecrow do that there was room for nothing in their hearts but flight. They ran till their legs ached and their lungs laboured, and behind them came a ragged figure with a carved smile, that never grew tired. Ash and Rhea followed behind in a Warrior jeep, happy in each other's company. The Warriors ran, and the three Furies of vengeance followed close behind, snapping at their heels.

And down another street came more Warriors, the last fleeing remnants of what had once been a great army. They cast aside their weapons in their panic, for behind them came the Devil himself, or so they thought. But it was just a man, coming at last into his awesome power. James Hart, the man of prophesy, and in him ran all the power of the town, and of Time. He floated on the air, swept above and along by his magic, and some distance behind, following as best they could, came Polly Cousins and Suzanne Dubois. Their injuries no longer bothered them, for he had healed them all at a touch, but even so

434

they were hard put to keep up with the chase. Hart had forgotten they were there, dazzled by the light of his own glory. The two women struggled on after him, not wanting to be left behind, but scared to get too close. This wasn't the man they'd known, or thought they'd known. This James Hart was someone new, someone different and very dangerous.

And finally, almost as though the town had planned it that way, the three streams of fleeing soldiers all came together in one place, in the vast open prospect of Gorky Square. They slowed to a halt as they became a milling, confused crowd, and looked around to see where their flight had brought them. The Square was a great open space in the heart of the city, bounded on all sides by huge towering buildings of ancient stone, brooding over the Square like so many grey mountains. The soldiers looked for a way out, but all the routes were blocked. Suddenly, everything was quiet.

Down one avenue stood the Faerie, with Morrison and his musicians at their head, silent at last. Down another stood Jack Fetch with blood on his hands, and with him Ash and Rhea, gazing in silent wonder at the trapped and demoralized army before them. In the third approach stood James Hart, wrapped in his glory, standing at the edge of the Square in silent judgement. The last avenue slowly filled with light, showing itself open and empty. A quiet murmur ran through the soldiers, only to stop abruptly as the ground suddenly split open and apart, forming a great chasm through which could be seen the sickly white flesh of the Great Wurm.

The murmuring began again as the soldiers realized they were trapped and surrounded. The watching forces readied themselves. Nothing fights more viciously than a cornered rat. Officers raised their voices here and there among the Warriors, demanding the soldiers fight to the last man, with their bare hands if need be. God's name was invoked many times, as a spur and a threat. The soldiers looked at each other, and then at the forces surrounding them, who stared impassively back. An officer raised his voice threateningly, and a shot rang out. The officer fell dead to the ground, the soldiers around him backing away, and it was a long tense moment before everyone realized the shot had come from inside the crowd. A ripple ran through the packed crowd as both soldiers and officers became aware which way most guns were facing. And then an officer made his way out of the crowd, followed by a soldier pressing a gun into his back, and they slowly approached Rhea Frazier. She went forward to meet him, with Ash a watchful presence at her side.

The officer bowed, just a little sardonically. 'You are the Mayor of this town, I believe. Apparently, we wish to surrender.'

'I think that would be best,' said Rhea steadily. 'No conditions, but rest assured you'll be treated better by us than we would have been by you.'

'We never stood a chance,' said the officer, not bothering to keep the bitterness from his voice. 'We've lost contact with our Leader, the sorcerer priests are dead, and our transport is lost or destroyed. God has made his will known. He has turned away from us.'

'Besides,' said the soldier behind him, 'they lied to us. This town isn't what we were told it was. They told us we'd be fighting demons and witches and unnatural creatures, for the greater glory of God. No one said anything about women and children and childhood heroes. We came to rescue and avenge the innocent, and found ourselves slaughtering them instead. We've seen things here; strange things, marvellous things . . . the town isn't what they said it was.'

'No,' said the soldier Peter Caulder, stepping forward from the ranks of Faerie with Bruin Bear at his side. 'It's much more. This is a place of dreams and wonders, and we ran amok here like spiteful children in a cathedral, destroying what we could not understand or appreciate. No more fighting. No more killing. We've done enough damage here. This is the place where our dreams live. We couldn't have destroyed it, without destroying ourselves as well.'

And then, one by one throughout the great dispirited crowd, the soldiers dropped their remaining weapons, and raised their hands above their heads. The general tension slowly began to relax, as everyone in and outside the Square realized that the fighting was over. The war for Shadows Fall had come to its end, and they'd come through it alive. Men turned to each other and smiled and laughed and embraced each other, relief washing through them like a blessing. Ash draped a companionable arm round Rhea's shoulders.

'So, madam Mayor, what do we do now? We won, but the town's a ruin. And what are we to do with our prisoners of war? We haven't the facilities to lock them up or guard them, but we can't just let them go. Not after everything that's happened here. The townspeople would never stand for it. I'm not sure I would either.'

'The officers will stand trial,' said Rhea. 'As will anyone responsible for an atrocity that can be identified. The rest . . . were just soldiers, doing what they believed was right. They were lied to, and they know better now. They will stay here and become part of the town. They'll want to make atonement, and this way they can. They can start by burying the dead from both sides, and then they can set about rebuilding all the places they destroyed. By the time that's finished years will have passed, long enough for forgiveness from both sides.'

Ash nodded, and for a time they stood in silence, lost in their own thoughts. Finally, Ash stirred. 'I wonder what did happen to their Imperial Leader?'

Rhea shrugged. 'I don't know. Probably we'll never know. Maybe he just ran out of Time.'

Royce's men heaved and strained to close the heavy door against the pressure of the raging blizzard outside. Thick bursts of snow blew past them, spilling into the Hall. There were twelve of them altogether, and it still took their combined strength to force the door closed, inch by inch. Finally they got it shut, slammed home the heavy bolts, and then leaned limply against the door while they got their breath back. A few stray specks of snow still floated on the air, driven into All Hallows Hall by the unrelenting pressure of the storm outside. Royce and his people beat snow from their hair and clothes and looked around them. They'd come a long hard way to reach this place, and it rewarded them by being just as huge and impressive as they'd imagined it to be. The ceiling disappeared into the darkness high above, and the Hall was wide enough to drive a troop carrier through. It was also very quiet, the storm outside not even a murmur, for all its fury.

William Royce, Imperial Leader of the Warriors of the Cross, allowed himself to feel a small glow of satisfaction. He had sworn to come to this place, despite whatever obstacles Fate placed in his path, and he had done it. From here it was only a short walk to the Gallery of Frost and the Forever Door. He stood quietly, savouring the moment, while his men formed a defensive perimeter around him. They were good men, good soldiers. He'd picked and trained them personally down the years to be his élite guard. He trusted them with his life; perhaps the only ones he did trust. They weren't going to like being told to stay behind here while he went on into the Hall alone. But this was his moment, his destiny, and he would not share what lay ahead with anyone. He was finally near his goal, only moments away from opening the Forever Door and asking the question he'd waited a lifetime to ask. To know the answer at last . . .

He raised his voice, and the twelve men snapped to attention. Royce looked them over, allowing them to see a little of his jubilation, and then told them his intention. He was right, they didn't like it, but none of them questioned him or his plan. He'd taught them well. They were his, body and soul, and they would no more have questioned him than the God they both served. Royce ordered them to stand guard by the entrance to the Hall, and see to it that no one got the chance to follow him. Anyone they encountered was to be killed on sight, no exceptions, and they were to hold this position till he returned, no matter how long that might be. They nodded silently, and saluted him. He saluted them back, smiled briefly, and then set off into the gloom of the Hall.

The guards watched him go until he'd disappeared into the dark, and then spread out to cover the entrance to the Hall. They knew what to do. Royce had rehearsed them enough times. Even so, the sheer size of the Hall made them nervous. Every sound echoed endlessly on the quiet, and shadows seemed to move at the corners of their eyes. The soldiers hefted their guns professionally, and kept a watchful eye on the door. Which was at least partly why they never saw the girl named Mad creeping up behind them till it was far too late.

Madeleine Kresh slipped silently through the shadows, her dark leathers blending seamlessly into the gloom. She'd removed all her usual chains and ornaments, so they wouldn't give her away with any betraying gleam or sound. She eased up behind the nearest guard, scowling with concentration. The flick-knife was a comforting weight in her hand, ready for use. She'd changed her usual black and white makeup for a more neutral grey that would hide her face in the shadows, and greased down her mohawk haircut so that its movement wouldn't give her away. Mad was the last defender between Time and these people, and she was determined not to let him down. Whatever it took.

She took a deep breath, slid smoothly out of the shadows and took the guard from behind with brutal simplicity. A hand over his mouth to stifle any outcry, the knife between his ribs, and then all she had to do was drag his body back into the shadows before anyone had a chance to notice anything. She let the limp body drop quietly to the floor, and checked quickly about her. Everything was quiet. It had all been over in a moment. Mad stuck the knife neatly through one of the guard's eyes, just to be sure, and then readied herself for her next target. She grinned broadly. She was doing what she'd been born to do, and it felt great. She'd waited a long time to repay Time's kindness, but even though she fully intended to get through this as quickly as possible so that she could get back to Time's side, she wasn't going to hurry this. She was enjoying herself. She'd seen what had happened to the town in the Gallery's portraits, and it was payback time. She might not live in the town, but it was still her town. Mad's loyalties were few and uncomplicated, and she liked it that way. She peeked out of the shadows at her next target, and deliberately made a brief scuffing noise with her foot. The guard looked round, frowning, certain he'd heard something but not sure what. Mad made the sound again, and the guard headed towards her. Madeleine Kresh smiled, and readied her knife.

William Royce stalked through the Gallery of Bone, staring straight ahead. The portraits on the walls were full of sound and fury, and sometimes people or creatures raged inside the polished wooden frames, trying desperately to break free. Royce paid them no attention. He had a purpose and a destiny to fulfil, and the wonders of the Gallery were nothing to him. He realized he was responsible for most of the scenes of destruction and suffering, but he felt no guilt. He had done what was necessary to bring him to this place, at this time. Nothing else mattered. He'd been here before many times, in his dreams. He'd dreamed of the Gallery since he was a child, though it was a long time before he was able to discover what the place was. The size and extent had frightened him as a child, but it held no terrors for him now. This was just a place he had to walk through on his way to the Forever Door, and direct access to the Godhead itself. His pulse jumped, and he quickened his pace in spite of himself. He was almost there. Soon he would stand before the Door, open it and ask his question, the question he'd waited a lifetime to ask.

He made his way unhesitatingly through the corridors

his dreams had revealed to him, and finally they ended and he came to the Gallery of Frost. He stopped at the entrance to the Gallery, and gazed in awe at a sight he'd always been denied in his dreams. For all his discipline and single-mindedness, he still stopped to look and wonder, for there were some things almost too beautiful for human eyes to bear. The Gallery of Frost had been constructed from delicate traceries of curling ice and strands of shimmering moonlight. It was a vast dome of frosty spiderwebs, intricate beyond measure, towering high above him. Royce took a deep breath and stepped out on to the floor of shining glass. There was a feeling to the Gallery of immense, subtle tension, as though the whole giant structure was balanced so exactly that were even one key thread to break, that would be enough to bring the whole place down. Without knowing why, Royce knew beyond doubt that the Gallery of Frost was barely real, only just tangible, and even he hesitated a moment before striding out across the floor of glass.

He didn't know how long he walked under the delicate shimmering strands of ice, but finally he came to the heart of the web, and the Forever Door. The sight of it stopped him in his tracks. It was just a door. An ordinary, everyday door, standing upright and alone. Royce stared at it speechlessly. He'd done so much, sacrificed so much, and come all this way just for this? He'd never seen the Forever Door in his dreams, but he'd imagined . . . everything but this. Disappointment came close to crushing him, and then anger thrust it away. He was used to anger. He could deal with that. It never occurred to him to doubt that this really was the Forever Door; he knew, on some basic level that could not be questioned. It was one of the true Great Wonders of the World, and he stood before it.

'I know what you're thinking,' said a quiet voice beside him. 'You thought it would be bigger, more impressive. Everyone does.'

Royce spun round, startled; he hadn't heard anyone approach him. Standing beside him, close enough to touch, was a tall, dignified figure in a spotlessly white suit, carrying a large and ornate Bible. But though the gaunt, forbidding face was familiar to him, the eyes were older, much older, and Royce had no doubt who he was really looking at.

'Old Father Time, I assume. I've come a long way to meet you. Why do you look like my foster-father?'

Time shrugged. 'Don't ask me; it's your subconscious. Everyone sees me differently. You see me as an authority figure, which is fair enough; your unconscious mind supplies the details. The Forever Door and I are of the same unique nature, shaped by the viewer. The Door takes its shape from a real door in your past; one that was important or significant to you at some vital moment of your life. Do you recognize it?'

Royce looked at the Forever Door for a long time, and then nodded slowly. He did know it. He hadn't seen or thought of it in years, but he remembered it. It was the front door of the house he'd been taken to live in as a child, after his parents died in the car crash, and his foster-parents took him in. There hadn't been much love, but his foster-father had set him firmly on the path of the Lord, so Royce tried to think kindly of him. When he thought of him at all. He remembered this door. When he'd walked through it, his life had changed for ever.

'I remember it,' he said finally. 'Interesting symbolism. Open it.'

'I'm afraid it's not that simple,' said Time. 'There's someone else here who's been waiting for you.'

There was a sudden blast of heat from Royce's other side, and he flinched away from it instinctively. The stench of brimstone and burning meat was suddenly heavy on the air, and even before he turned to look, Royce knew who it was; who it had to be. The demon he'd struck a bargain with so many years ago had finally come to stake its claim. He lifted his chin and turned unhurriedly round to study his enemy. It took all his courage and resolution not to fall back a step. Eight feet tall, and radiating heat almost beyond bearing, the demon had come as a patchwork figure of sliding metal plates, in roughly human form; a steel construction that only mimicked humanity in order to mock it. The steel plates slipped and slid as it moved, glowing red with heat, and metal spikes protruded from its brow like horns, above two deepset eyes of molten crimson.

'You are mine,' it said, its voice like rusty steel bars grating together. 'The dreams I sent brought you here, and me, to the place I could not come uncalled. Now you will open the Door for me, and I shall have my long-awaited revenge on He who cast me down.'

'Sorry,' said Time. 'As long as Shadows Fall still stands, you have no power over the Door. That's the way it is. And despite this gentleman's best efforts, the town still stands.'

The demon looked at Royce. 'It was worth a try. Something still is left to me. All wards are forfeit here, and you have no protection from me. I granted you power in return for the many deaths you promised me in Shadows Fall, but you must have known there'd be a further price to pay. By your actions are you damned, and I shall take you to your damnation. We're going to have such fun together, you and I.'

'Not necessarily,' said Time. 'You know the rules.'

The demon hissed at Time, but fell silent, and Royce realized that the demon was afraid of Time. He filed the thought away. It might prove useful. He stared commandingly at Old Father Time, who looked calmly back at him, unmoved.

'This Door leads to God,' said Royce. 'I have come here to open the Forever Door, and nothing you can say or do will stop me. You're powerful, but I have power too, more than you'd imagine. I have men standing guard to see that we won't be disturbed.'

'I'm afraid not,' said Time. 'The men you left in my entrance Hall are dead, unfortunately.'

Royce stared at Time. It never occurred to him to doubt Time's word. If he said they were dead, then they were.

The casualness of it shook him, but he held it in, controlled it. This was no place to appear weak. Time nodded understandingly.

'I wouldn't dream of trying to stop you, William. The Forever Door is here for everyone. If you're really determined to speak with God, all you have to do is open that Door and walk through. Of course if you do, you can't come back. Don't look at me like that, William. I don't make the rules. I just work here.'

'What lies beyond the Door?' said Royce. His mouth was dry but he kept his voice steady.

'I don't know,' said Time. 'It's the only place in Shadows Fall I can't see. It's the last great mystery, the final answer to all the questions you ever had. And isn't that why you came here? To ask a question?'

'Yes,' said Royce. 'A question. Quite a simple one really, but it's driven me all my life. Is there really a God?'

The demon hissed, but didn't move. Time smiled.

'I have to *know*,' said Royce. 'I built my whole life around God and his word. Gave up every chance of a normal life, all hope of earthly love and family, to dedicate myself to the Lord. I trained as a Warrior, built my army and brought it here, because in the end faith isn't enough. Not as long as proof exists. If God exists, then everything I've done, and I've done terrible things, can be justified. If not, then my life has been a lie, and it was all for nothing. All the deaths, all the suffering . . . everything I gave up to be Leader.

'Ironic, isn't it; an army of Christian fanatics who never doubted, led by a man who lost his faith.

'I've dreamed of this place for so long. Of the Forever Door, beyond which all truths can be found, all questions answered. I had to come here, whatever the price, to *know*, beyond all shadow of doubt. To know.'

He stepped forward and opened the Forever Door. Light spilled out, bright and warm and comforting. He strode unhesitatingly into the glow, and the Door closed behind him, cutting off the light. The world was a darker place without it. Old Father Time looked at the steel demon.

'Some day there may come a time when no one believes in you any more. What will you do then?'

'It's not time yet,' said the demon, in its voice like grating rust. 'And many things may happen before then.'

It vanished, leaving behind only a fleeting stench of sulphur, and two flaming footsteps where it had been standing. Time stamped them out. He looked at the closed Door, and sighed quietly. It wasn't his time to go through either, but one day even he would have to pass through and see what lay on the other side. He was quite looking forward to it. He turned away from the Forever Door and walked back through the Gallery of Frost. Hopefully by now Mad would have finished her work and tidied up the mess. He hoped so. He felt very much that he could use a good strong cup of tea, and he hated having to make it for himself.

Time walked away through the shimmering traceries of ice, and the Door waited patiently behind him for all those yet to come.

11

Endgame

Rhea Frazier drove the Warrior jeep through the empty streets at more than sufficient speed to make Ash grab surreptitiously at his seatbelt. He might be dead, but there was no point in taking chances. Rhea had found the jeep abandoned by retreating Warriors outside the Library, and commandeered it on the spot. Ash wasn't entirely sure she had the authority to do that, but knew better than to raise the point. Rhea was not in the mood to listen to details. The Warriors turned out to have been inconsiderate enough not to leave the keys in the ignition, but Ash gave the motor a stern look and it obligingly coughed into life. Rhea drove the jeep through the devastated streets at increasing speed, staring grimly straight ahead. It was as though she couldn't bear to see what had been done to her town, and thought that if she could just get through it fast enough, she'd break through into a part of town that had somehow survived undamaged. But no matter how fast she drove, there was always more destruction, more smouldering fires, more bodies lying in the street. The Warriors had come to Shadows Fall, and it would never be the same again.

The jeep roared on and the town passed by, and it was the things that were missing that bothered Ash the most. No one walked the streets or came to mourn the dead. The few survivors watched nervously from behind barricaded windows. There was no traffic on the roads apart from the jeep. The traffic lights all showed red, but Rhea paid them no attention. The Warriors had been defeated, but the town still felt under siege, as though the hostilities had only ended for a moment, and the uneasy peace was just a pause before the next onslaught. Ash scowled. He had a bad feeling himself, though he couldn't put a finger on anything specific. He thrust the feeling away and looked again at Rhea. Her face was bruised, and some bastard had split her lower lip, but she looked as tough and uncompromising as ever. And that worried Ash most of all. It couldn't be healthy to be so rigid, so controlled. Sooner or later she was going to have to stop and mourn all the things she'd lost in the invasion, and the longer she left it, the harder it was going to be for her. That was why she was keeping herself so busy; so she wouldn't have time to stop and think. But the town was still there, no matter how fast she drove through it. Ash rocked in his seat as the jeep took a corner at speed, and looked about him. Presumably Rhea had some destination in mind, but Ash hadn't a clue what it might be. He wasn't even that sure where he was. One shelled and burnt-out street looked much like another.

'Where exactly are we going?' he said finally, raising his voice to be heard above the roar of the engine, and then tried not to wince as Rhea steered the jeep through a series of potholes without slowing.

'To see Richard Erikson,' said Rhea shortly. 'Hopefully we'll find him at his office. The town's going to need a centre of communications and authority if we're going to start putting things back together again. There's so much to do . . . we have to find out what our resources are now, and how best to put them to work. People, skills, supplies . . . We can't ask the outside world for help, so everything we need is going to have to come from us. The Councillors are all dead, so we have to do something to recreate authority, and the chain of command. Otherwise everyone will just be dashing around, getting in everyone's way and overlooking the things that really need doing. We've got to get organized, Leonard, and for that we need the Sheriff and his people.'

She slowed the jeep a little, and looked around as though noticing for the first time just what she was driving through. Everywhere had taken some kind of damage, and here and there smoke still rose into the early morning sky. There were overturned and burnt-out cars, smashed windows and shattered street lights, and bodies everywhere. They lay carelessly, in grotesque positions, as though they didn't have to care any more. Rhea sighed, and concentrated on the road ahead. For the first time she looked tired, beaten down, as though the long night's events were finally catching up with her.

'The Warriors must have been the size of a regular army to have done so much damage,' she said finally. 'I keep thinking there must be some part of town they didn't reach, some piece still untouched, but no . . . No matter what we do, the town will never be the same again. Shadows Fall was supposed to be a sanctuary from the world, a place where even dreams and legends could come to find peace and comfort before passing on. But the world found us anyway. I keep coming up with plans for rebuilding, for putting things back together again, and then I look around me and think, what's the point? With so many dead, so much destroyed; maybe it would be kinder just to leave, and let the town die in peace.'

'No,' said Ash. 'We have to rebuild Shadows Fall and make it work again. Or the Warriors will have won after all.'

Rhea sniffed once, and then concentrated on her driving, for which Ash was grateful. Rhea had never taken advice easily, even when he'd been alive. But she'd never talked about giving up before, either. The invasion had changed everyone. They drove on in silence, until finally they reached the Sheriff's centre of operations. The building was part of a civil service block, and looked pretty much unscathed by the fighting. Rhea eased the jeep to a halt, and then sat there for a while, frowning. The Warriors had to have known the location of the Sheriff's office, and taking out someone of his authority should have been one of their first objectives. She shrugged, but the thought wouldn't go away, and she was still scowling as she parked the jeep in a space marked Reserved, and jumped out of the jeep while the engine was still turning itself off.

She hurried up the steps of the building with Ash right behind her, feeling the pressure build almost unbearably within her, only to find there was no one there to take it out on. The place was empty, and eerily quiet. There should have been Deputies and office staff bustling back and forth, answering queries and dealing with problems, but the corridors were deserted, and unoccupied offices stood with open doors whichever way they looked. Rhea and Ash walked on, their footsteps echoing loudly in the quiet, and no one came to stop them. Finally they came to the Sheriff's inner offices, and there they found two Deputies, sitting slumped in easy chairs, drinking coffee. They looked up as Rhea and Ash strode in, and then rose to their feet as they recognized Rhea. One of the Deputies was blond, and the other was dark, but they were both pretty much of a type; tall, muscular and running a little wide in the beam from spending too much time sitting in cars. They both looked tired, and they both had blood on their uniforms that didn't seem to be theirs. They both glanced briefly at the closed door of the Sheriff's inner office, but neither said anything.

'All right,' said Rhea coldly, 'what the hell is going on here? There had better be a good answer, because I am really not in the mood for a bad one. I have had a really bad day and yours could be about to get a hell of a lot worse. Talk to me.'

The two Deputies looked at each other. 'I'm Collins,' said the one with the blond hair. 'This is Lewis. For the moment, we're the law in Shadows Fall. Which only goes to show how desperate things have got. The rest of us are either dead, or missing, presumed dead, and the Sheriff is . . . incommunicado. The radio system's out. No one left to operate it. Apparently the Warriors got here early on, marched everyone out at gunpoint, stood them in a line

450

against a wall at the back of the station, and shot them all. The bodies are still there, if you want to take a look. The Warriors probably meant to take this place over and run it themselves, but there was no one here when Lewis and I got back. We've been up all night, dashing here and there like mad things, helping where we could. Now we're tired, and we're taking a break. And if that doesn't suit you, madam Mayor; tough. We're all used up.'

Rhea surprised Ash by answering in a calm, reasonable tone of voice. 'We're all tired, but we can't stop to rest yet. The invasion has been stopped, but there are still things left to be done. The dead have to be collected and buried, or soon we'll have epidemics sweeping through the town. Then the living have to be found food and drink and shelter. We'll rest later, when there's time. Richard's in his office, I take it?'

The Deputies looked again at the closed door, and Collins nodded reluctantly. 'He's there, but you can't see him. He isn't seeing anyone at the moment.'

'He'll see me,' said Rhea. 'I pay his wages.' She marched over to the door and rattled the handle. It was locked. Rhea glared at the door and raised her voice carryingly. 'Richard, this is Rhea. Open the door. We have to talk.'

There was no reply. Rhea rattled the door handle again, and then stepped back and gestured to Ash. He gave the lock a firm look and it clicked open. Rhea sailed into Erikson's office with a scathing remark on her lips, and then swallowed it as she saw Richard Erikson sitting in his chair, sprawled across his desk, fast asleep. There were scorch marks on his clothes, as though he'd got too close to a fire at some stage. At first Ash thought the man was just exhausted, but then he saw the empty whisky bottle lying on its side on the floor by the desk, and the open bottle not far from Erikson's outstretched hand. Rhea let out her breath in a long slow sigh.

'Oh Richard . . . not now. Not *now*.'

She moved over to him, and shook him by the shoulder. He stirred and muttered something, but that was all. Rhea gestured to Ash, and between them they got Erikson sitting more or less upright in his chair. Rhea checked his pulse against her watch, wrinkling her nose at the smell of stale booze on him.

'Is he . . . okay?' said Ash.

'Dead drunk, but still with us.' Rhea let the Sheriff's hand fall limply back on to the desk. It landed with a solid-sounding thud, and Ash winced in sympathy. Rhea looked back at the door, and the two Deputies looking in. 'Lewis, Collins; get in here. How long has he been like this?'

The two Deputies shrugged, almost in unison. 'He was like that when we got here, an hour ago,' said Collins. 'He must have been out when the staff were killed. We kept trying to raise him all during the invasion, but there was never any reply. Now we know why. I gather from your look, madam Mayor, that you're not entirely surprised.'

'Not really, no,' said Rhea. 'He was always fond of a drink, in a crisis. First thing is to wake him up, then sober him up. We need him up and about. The Sheriff's a symbol; people will listen to him when they might not listen to me. I presume there are some showers in this place? Good. Take him there, strip him, put him under one and run it cold. I'll make some coffee. One way or another I want him awake and able to function in under an hour. Why are you still standing there?'

Collins looked at Lewis. 'And we always thought he was exaggerating about her. You take one arm, I'll take the other. If he looks like puking, drop him. I'm not messing up my clothes any more.'

They got him to the door, and then Collins looked back. 'You might want to take a look at the papers on his desk. We put them there for him to read, when he was feeling himself again.'

Rhea picked up the papers from the desk and studied them intently as the two Deputies hauled the Sheriff out of his office. Ash started to say something diplomatic about Erikson, and then stopped as he saw the expression on her face. She looked suddenly tired and beaten, as though what

452

she'd found in the reports had been one last straw too many.

'What is it?' said Ash.

'It would seem our troubles aren't over,' said Rhea. 'According to these reports, there's growing evidence of a series of killings unconnected to the Warriors that took place during the invasion. Some in areas the Warriors barely touched. From the MO, it's clear our resident serial murderer used the invasion as a cover to go on a killing spree. As usual, there are no witnesses and no clues; just bodies.'

They stood for a while in silence. Rhea dropped the papers on the desk, and sat in the Sheriff's chair.

'What are we going to do?' said Ash.

'First we sober up Richard,' said Rhea. 'And then . . . we're going to set a trap.'

Mad was dragging the last dead Warrior down a corridor in the Gallery of Bone when Time contacted her. The dead man was the heaviest of the lot, and she'd deliberately left him till last. Six foot six, and two hundred and fifty pounds if he was an ounce. She'd wistfully considered having him stuffed and mounted and placed somewhere prominent in the Gallery to discourage visitors, but she knew she'd never get Time to go along with it. The man had no sense of style. She stopped for another breather and stretched her aching back. It had been hard work disposing of the twelve Warriors she'd killed, but for the most part she hummed and whistled cheerfully as she worked. Twelve professional fighting men, armed to the teeth and dripping with testosterone, and not one of them had known what was coming till she'd rammed it between their ribs.

She'd dropped the previous eleven into a portrait that looked out over a bottomless pit. At least, she assumed it was bottomless. Certainly nothing she'd dropped into it had ever come back to complain. The twelfth body, as well as being the largest and heaviest, had also been the furthest from the portrait, but even so she'd made good time dragging it through the corridors. She'd go back and clean up the bloody trail later. Well, actually she'd probably get an automaton to do it, when they were working again. Mad wasn't particularly domestic.

She heaved the chest of the body over the edge of the portrait, and then set about persuading the rest of the body to follow it. She heaved and strained till her eyes bulged and sweat ran down her face, and the damn thing didn't budge an inch. She stood back and kicked it a few times, just on general principles, and then grabbed a leg and tried levering the body over the edge. She put her back into it, and finally got the body balanced just right. One last heave, and over it would go. And that, of course, was the exact moment when Old Father Time's voice sounded loudly in her mind.

Madeleine. Come to me. I need you.

'Can this wait a while?' said Mad, just a little breathlessly. 'I've got my hands full at the moment.'

Come. Come now.

'It's at times like this,' said Mad, 'That I feel our relationship would profit greatly from some professional counselling. Or, to put it another way, if you don't say please, and sound like you mean it, not only am I not going to come and join you till Hell installs sunbeds, but I might actually decide to stand here and hold my breath till I turn blue.'

Please come. I need your help.

'That's better,' said Mad grudgingly. 'I'll be with you in a minute, if I don't throw my back out first. Break out the liniment bottles and plump up some cushions till I get there.'

She took a firm hold on the dead Warrior's leg, and threw herself into the task with renewed vigour. The body teetered on the edge, there was a brief argument as to which one of them was in charge, and then the body gave up, slipped gracefully over the edge and disappeared into the darkness. Mad spat after it, wiped the sweat from her face with her sleeve, and set off through the Gallery of

Bone. Time had sounded urgent, and had given in far too easily, which wasn't like him. If there was one thing Old Father Time had plenty of, it was time. Being immortal tended to give you a leisurely view of things. But Time had said he needed her. Mad walked a little faster. Whatever was wrong, he wasn't far. He never was, no matter where she started from. It was that sort of place.

She rounded a corner, and without warning found herself in his inner sanctum. As always, she saw the great Hall of a Medieval Castle, complete with blazing torches and hanging tapestries. To one side stood a great sword, thrust through an anvil on a stone. She didn't need to read the name on the crosspiece. She knew the sword was Excalibur, and this was Camelot. Or at least, one of them. There had been a great many versions down the years, and only a few of them were still believed in with any real conviction. Mad strode confidently forward, and tried hard to keep the frown from her face as she took in the state of the Hall. There were cobwebs everywhere, and the tapestries were stained and faded. The torches had burned down to nubs, and dust hung thickly on the golden air.

Old Father Time was sitting slumped on a great iron throne, on a raised dais of blue-veined marble. He wore a magician's dark gown, covered with obscure mystical symbols. Sometimes an owl sat on his shoulder, but there was no sign of it now. Mad stopped before the throne, saluted briskly, and then fought off a sense of shock as she got her first look at Time's face. He looked incredibly old and frail, far too old for this stage of his life cycle. His skin was so pale as to be almost translucent, and above his jutting cheekbones his eyes had sunk deep into his face. His gaze was firm, but his mouth trembled. He'd aged a hundred years since she last saw him, less than an hour ago. Mad did her best not to react. Presumably dealing with the Warrior invasion had taken a lot out of him.

'All right, I'm here,' she said briskly. 'What do you want?'

'We have to talk,' said Time, and his voice shocked her
again. It was low and quiet, little more than a murmur.

'It's all right,' Mad said quickly. 'No need to thank me.
Just doing my job.'

'What?' Time looked at her blankly. 'What are you
talking about, child?'

'Taking care of the Warriors. No problem. There were
only twelve of them.'

Time shook his head slowly. 'That's not why you're
here, Madeleine. Now pay attention, please. I only have
the time and the energy to go through this once.'

He stopped to get his breath, and Mad pouted. She was
proud of taking out twelve Warrior soldiers without even
a scratch to show for it, but she should have known Time
wouldn't approve. For a man of his position and authority,
he could be surprisingly squeamish on occasion. And he
never did appreciate the things she did for him. Time
began to speak again, slowly and with effort, and she paid
attention.

'I closed the Forever Door to protect it from the Warriors. But when the Imperial Leader appeared on his own,
I opened it again, just for him. It seemed the simplest
solution. But once he'd gone through, everything changed.
The call of the Door was suddenly stronger, much stronger.
The silent voice that summons all who have not yet passed
through the Door was suddenly overpowering.

'It grew increasingly powerful, despite everything I
could do to temper it. I tried closing the Door again, and I
couldn't. The power has been taken away from me. The
Forever Door stands open, calling in a voice that will not
be denied. The psychic pressure on those in the town must
be unbearable. I think we must expect a stream of visitors.
Most will find their own way to the Door, and pass through
unattended, but some will need personal attention. You're
going to have to deal with them, Madeleine. Do whatever
you have to, to keep order. I intend to invest some of my
power in you; I trust you to use it responsibly. Jack Fetch
will obey your orders, within certain limits. I know you

two don't get along, but you'll have to learn to work together.'

'Why?' said Mad. 'What's happened? Are you going somewhere?'

'In a manner of speaking,' said Time. 'Now pay attention. Something bad is coming. Something terrible.'

'Worse than the Warriors?'

'Oh yes. Much worse. The time of the Wild Childe is upon us. Soon it will sweep through the town, and there's nothing I can do to stop it. Something has triggered my death and reincarnation early. Some outside force is tampering with the flow of events, and I appear to be helpless to stand against it.'

'How long have we got?' said Mad. 'Before you die again?'

'Maybe an hour. I'm holding it off as best I can, but the pressure is becoming unbearable. I'll be dead soon, and then Time will be a baby again, for a while. Shadows Fall will have to get along without me for a few days, until I'm able to take charge of matters again. Normally that isn't a problem, but right now there are all kinds of forces poised to take advantage of the situation. Madeleine; you see the sword over there? Of course you do; do you know what it is?'

'Yes,' said Mad. 'It's Excalibur. King Arthur's sword.'

'And now it's yours. Pull the sword from the stone, Madeleine.'

She looked at him for a long moment, and then looked at the sword. What she could see of the blade seemed to glow a little brighter under her gaze. She walked slowly over to stand before the anvil on its stone. The crosspiece was burnished silver, but the hilt was wrapped in ancient leather, darkened here and there by age and old sweat. Excalibur. She took hold of the hilt, and it fitted into her hand as though it belonged there. She drew the sword from the anvil and the stone with one easy pull, and held it up before her. Light radiated from the blade, filling the Hall like the dawn of a new sun. It weighed hardly anything despite its size, but Mad had no doubt of its strength and power. She could feel it deep within her, like a song wrapped around her soul. She turned and walked back to Time on his throne as though she was leading a parade. He had a scabbard and belt in his hands, and she took them from him, sheathed the sword and buckled it about her waist. She felt like she could do anything; anything at all.

'So,' she said lightly. 'Does this mean I'm Queen of England now?'

Time smiled slightly. 'I'm afraid not. That offer was only good once. But you could say you're Queen of Shadows Fall, if you like. My power is in the sword; draw on it as you need it. Perhaps I'm just being paranoid, and you'll never have to draw it in anger; but if you have to draw Excalibur, do what's necessary. Whatever that might be.'

He paused for a moment, his eyes almost shut, and Mad wondered if he'd fallen asleep, but he stirred himself suddenly, as though fighting against the tides of sleep, and smiled at Mad again.

'Madeleine; this may be the last chance we'll have to talk. There are so many things I wish I'd said to you, and never did. No doubt the Time who replaces me will have access to all my memories, but I wanted to say this to you now, while I'm still me. I have always cared for you, Madeleine. I couldn't have loved you more if you'd been my own daughter. I wish . . . we'd had more time together.'

He leaned back in his chair and closed his eyes. Mad sniffed a couple of times, to keep the threatening tears from her eyes. She waited, but he said nothing more. She climbed up on the dais beside the throne and leaned over him. His face was deeply wrinkled, like a mummy's, and his hands were little more than bones wrapped in shrivelled skin. She said his name, but there was no response. His breathing was slow, and disturbingly shallow. Mad sat down beside his throne, to wait.

'I never wanted to be your daughter,' she said quietly. 'Not your *daughter*.'

Sean Morrison returned to the land beneath the hill with a song on his lips and a great weight lifted from his heart. The town had survived the Warrior invasion, more or less, and he'd seen the Faerie go to war again in all their glory. And on top of all that, the music had moved within him the way it used to, before he died and came to Shadows Fall. He'd sung with his friends, wild and raw and overpowering, and for a while his legend had lived again. He strode through the earth tunnels, grinning broadly and singing an old song, and it was a great day to be alive.

The tunnels were all empty, and after a while he realized his voice was the only sound on the still air. He broke off from his song, and stopped to listen. Nothing moved in the tunnels, and for the first time he became aware he was moving in a pale circle of light like a spotlight in the darkness. He frowned, and looked about him. Even the will-o'-the-wisps that should have lighted his way were missing. He started off again, and the light moved with him. His frown deepened. He should have encountered some kind of life by now, even if it was just a kobold passing through, or worms curling in the earth walls, but there was nothing, nothing at all. He began to walk a little faster.

He came to the Watcher, the great snarling head that blocked the tunnel, filling it from floor to ceiling. The pale grey stone was cracked and faded, as though all its long years had finally caught up with it. The jaws were open, its eyes staring sightlessly over Morrison's head, and he knew on some deep, primal level that it was only stone, and nothing more. The Watcher was gone. He walked through the gaping jaws, and suddenly he was running, arms pumping at his sides, not from anything in the tunnel but towards a possibility that filled his heart with fear. He ran faster and faster, as though he could outrun the doubts and fears that milled within him, and finally he burst out of the tunnels and into the great earth cavern that held the Court of Faerie.

The courtyard stretched away before him, still and silent. He took a deep breath, and the smell of decay filled his head. He walked slowly forward through the tall gates of rusting black iron, and shivered suddenly. The air should have been uncomfortably warm and humid, but it was cold, cold as a grave. The jungle of vegetation before him was dead and rotting, as though the processes of decay had been running wild for weeks. The scattered sculptures of weird creatures and heroic elves lay toppled on their sides, brought down by the weight of rotten ivy engulfing them. The remains of small bodies lay everywhere, all that was left of the little creatures that had lived in the jungle. Morrison examined a few gingerly, but there was nothing to show what they'd died from.

He walked on, and found two elves standing face to face, wrapped in faded roses whose thorns had pierced the elves' colourless flesh. Their eyes were closed, and their chests did not move. Morrison touched one of them hesitantly, and the two elves fell stiffly to the ground, wrapped in dead roses like a brittle shroud. He knelt down beside them, but again there was no trace of any cause of death. Their flesh was cold and horribly yielding to the touch. Morrison got to his feet again, breathing harshly and shaking his head in denial. He broke into a run again, forcing his way through the decaying vegetation. He shouted for help, for someone to come, for someone to answer him, but there was no reply and nobody came. His voice was the only sound in the all-pervasive quiet. It seemed to take him ages to cross the vast courtyard, but finally he came to the tall, narrow gate in the far wall. The gate hung open, as though there was no longer any need for it to remain closed.

He passed through and into Caer Dhu, the last Castle of the Faerie. He hurried through the great stone corridors, still calling out at intervals, but no one answered him. From time to time he passed elves engulfed in the stone walls. They were all dead. Finally he came to the Unseeli Court itself, the Gathering of Faerie, and he stopped before the vast double doors. They stood slightly ajar, as though daring him to push them open and see what they hid. Part of him didn't want to, wanted instead to turn and run back through the courtyard, rather than face a truth he already suspected. But he couldn't do that. He had to know. He pushed the doors, and they swung smoothly open before him.

And so at last Sean Morrison came to the Unseeli Court, the final resting place of the elves of Caer Dhu, and found them waiting for him, stretched out on the floor in their gorgeous robes like so many dead birds of paradise. There were hundreds of them, hundreds beyond counting, lying gracefully together as though they had all just laid down where they stood and fell into a sleep from which there would be no awakening. Morrison stepped slowly over them, making his way carefully forward, looking about him with increasing desperation for any sign of life. But there was none, in the Court of the elves.

And at last he came to the twin thrones on their raised dais at the end of the great Hall. On them sat King Oberon and Queen Titania, marvellous beyond measure, beautiful beyond hope, both of them quite dead. They were holding hands. Beside them Puck, the only imperfect elf, hung from a makeshift gallows, turning slowly this way and that, as though moved by some unfelt breeze. The thick rope had dug deeply into his throat, but his face was calm and peaceful. Morrison climbed up on to the dais, and hesitantly touched Oberon and Titania's linked hands. Their flesh was heartbreakingly cold. He turned away and looked at Puck, and the elf opened his eyes and winked at him.

Morrison shouted in surprise, jumped backwards and sat down suddenly. His heart was racing and there was sweat on his face. Puck chuckled softly, still hanging from his gallows. Morrison scrambled to his feet again.

'You bastard,' he said finally. 'I thought you were dead.
I thought you were all dead.'

'Oh we are,' said Puck easily. 'Or they are, and I soon
will be. I only held on to say a last farewell to you, little
human, little bard. The day of the elves has finally reached
its end, and only I remain to tell you why. I always had a
fondness for you, and the breath of fresh air you brought
to the Court, with your human wonder and your human
songs. You've no idea how boring immortality can become.
So I waited just a little, to say fare you well and thank you
for what you gave us, your last great gift.'

'I don't understand,' said Morrison numbly. 'What
happened here?'

'We decided to die,' said Puck. 'We'd forgotten how
much we had declined from the days of our prime. We
were glorious then, wise and wonderful, and unbeatable on
the field of battle. We fought all the races there were, and
many that no longer exist, and none could stand against
us. Eventually we reached a point where the only foe
worthy of our attention would have been ourselves. But
by that time we'd developed weapons and devices of such
fell power that to turn them on ourselves would have
inevitably destroyed us all. So we turned our face away
from the dark joys of battle, locked our weapons away
where we could not easily reclaim them, and turned our
thoughts inward.

'You saw what that did to us. We declined from our
glory, and fell so far we no longer even remembered what
we had once been. And then you came, little bard, and
helped us to remember. And having remembered, we knew
we could not go back to what we had become.

'It was a wonderful last battle that you brought us to.
Many the men and creatures of all sorts who fell beneath
our sciences and our steel, never to rise again save in our
service. Marvellous the destruction, glorious the thrill of
battle. All that was missing was the wanton destruction
and the looting, but we forgave you that in return for the
sport you provided us. We relearned old thrills, old

pleasures, and gloried in our martial strength. But having rediscovered the joys of being wolves, we could not, would not, go back to being sheep again. So we decided to take our leave of life in a dignified manner, and go out on a high note, at the peak of our history. We knew there would never be a better day than this. So we came home, said our goodbyes, laid ourselves down and died.'

Morrison wanted to say something, anything, but the words wouldn't come. Tears burned in his eyes.

'One last word,' said Puck, not unkindly. 'One last warning, to show our gratitude. The time of the Wild Childe is almost upon you, when friend shall turn on friend, brother on brother. We saw its coming long ago, but said nothing, out of kindness. There was nothing we could do to stop it, or save you from the darkness to come. Perhaps, in the end, that was also why we decided to die. Because we would have missed you humans so much. Goodbye, Sean. Sing a last song for us, if you would.'

He closed his eyes and the breath went out of him. Puck the Weaponmaster, the only elf who was not perfect, hung limp and dead at the end of his rope. Morrison reached out and touched Puck on the shoulder. There was no response. He pushed a little harder, and the body turned slowly, the rope creaking quietly. And Sean Morrison, the only human bard to sing in the last Court of Faerie, turned and walked slowly out of the Hall of death, head held high, not crying, not yet. Crying would come later. Instead he raised his voice and sang one last song for those who could no longer hear it. He sang, heartbroken, and the sound of his voice echoed through the empty Court and all the empty corridors of Caer Dhu.

Rhea Frazier and Leonard Ash found Suzanne Dubois at her shack down by the river. It was early in the morning, and the rising sun shed golden light all across the world. Somewhere birds were singing, sharp and insistent, and on the river a single swan floated majestically past the stone statue of a mermaid, half immersed in the dark green water. Rhea looked at it thoughtfully. She was sure the statue hadn't been there the last time she'd come to call on Suzanne. But then, that was Shadows Fall for you. She checked Ash over quickly to make sure he looked respectable, and then knocked on the front door of the shack. The door opened the moment she'd finished knocking, almost as though Suzanne had been expecting visitors. And who was to say she hadn't? Rhea hid her surprise behind a pleasant smile. The lady who lived by the river knew many things; that was, after all, why they'd come to see her.

Suzanne stepped back for her visitors to enter, and then looked suspiciously at Ash. He smiled at her charmingly, and she sniffed and turned pointedly away. Rhea looked at Ash, and he shrugged. They realized then that Suzanne already had visitors, getting to their feet and smiling and nodding to Rhea and Ash. Rhea slipped into social politeness mode, and took the opportunity to look unobtrusively about her. The place still looked as though a bomb had hit it. Her fingers itched for a duster, a dustpan and brush, and just maybe a shovel. Suzanne had been known to refer to her preferred living conditions as a comfortable clutter, which was a little like describing the Warriors of the Cross as over-enthusiastic tourists.

'And I'm James Hart,' said a voice nearby, and Rhea's attention slammed back into the here and now. The man before her was an average-looking guy, perhaps a little too old for the clothes and pigtail he affected. He also looked like he could afford to lose a few pounds. None of which detracted from her easy smile and friendly manner. The man was a voter. Rhea automatically shook the hand he held out to her.

'So you're James Hart,' she found herself saying. 'I always thought you'd be taller.'

Hart laughed politely. 'A lot of people tell me that.'

The woman at his side introduced herself as Polly Cousins, and Rhea had to fight from doing a double-take. Everyone in Shadows Fall had heard of the woman trapped in her house by her own memories. Something drastic must have happened to change her circumstances, but Rhea hadn't heard a word about it. Which just went to show how out of touch she was getting. She shook Polly's hand and flashed a standard politician's smile. Questions would have to wait for another time. She had work to do here. She turned to Suzanne.

'I'm afraid this is a professional visit, my dear. We need your skill with the Cards.'

'Let me guess,' said Suzanne. 'You want me to use my Cards to discover who the killer's next victim will be, and possibly provide a few clues as to the killer's identity while I'm at it. Right? You needn't look so surprised. I knew you were coming, and why. The Cards told me. They've been full of possibilities today. My friends here had the same idea, but I thought we'd better wait for you before we started. I don't fancy going through this twice. Take a seat round the table please, everybody.'

A small circular table stood in the exact centre of the room. The wood was dull and chipped and clearly hadn't seen a coat of polish in years. A pack of cards sat on the table like an unexploded bomb. They seemed ordinary enough, but just looking at them made Rhea shiver. There was something about them; a sense of potential . . . She realized the others had already seated themselves, and were waiting for her. She pulled back the one remaining chair and sat down next to Ash. She felt very much that she would have liked to take hold of his hand, for comfort, but she couldn't do that. She couldn't afford to appear weak.

Suzanne shuffled the Cards, while the others sat and watched. She did it for some time, and Rhea's thoughts began to drift again. She glanced round the dishevelled room, and her thoughts took her back to the last time she'd visited Suzanne. She and Richard Erikson had found the first murder victim here, lying in his own blood on Suzanne's floor. This was where it had all started, and perhaps it was only right that she should come here looking for the end of the story. Suzanne finished shuffling, and began slapping the Cards down on the table with what

Rhea considered to be quite unnecessary force. The sounds seemed impossibly loud and penetrating, and Rhea winced in spite of herself. She was glad she was sitting down. She still felt weak and fragile after the beating she'd taken from the Warriors, and had a tendency to start trembling if she was kept on her feet too long.

She'd heard Suzanne had been badly injured during the invasion, but she seemed well and whole now. Presumably she'd found a magical healer. Ash had taken Rhea to one of the town's hospitals, but the place had been packed with people, most of them much worse than her, so Rhea had insisted they leave. She had work to do, and she was damned if she'd be stopped or even slowed by her own weakness. The town needed her. Ash leaned in close beside her, murmuring questions as to how she felt, and she made herself smile and shake her head dismissively. He worried too much. Besides, she didn't want to think about how bad she felt. If she didn't think about it, she could pretend it wasn't happening. She made herself concentrate on Suzanne, who was laying out her Cards in patterns that meant something only to her. She finally finished, or ran out of Cards, and sat back to study the pattern she'd made. Everyone waited respectfully. Things were coming to a head. They could all feel it. Suzanne scowled at Ash.

'Everything's clouded, obscure. It's hard to See details even under the best conditions, and having a dead man sitting at the table isn't helping.'

'Would you like me to leave?' said Ash politely.

'Unfortunately, you can't. You're part of the pattern; you're supposed to be here, like the others, but don't ask me why. You shouldn't be here at all, revenant. You should have passed through the Door long ago.'

'I can't,' said Ash. 'I'm needed here.'

'Why? What for?'

'I don't know.'

Suzanne sniffed. 'Convenient.'

Hart saw thunderstorms forming on Rhea's face, and hastily intervened. 'Look, we can insult each other's lifestyles later; for the moment, let's stick to the Cards. Can you See anything at all, Suzanne?'

Suzanne scowled reluctantly at the Cards before her, trying to lose herself in her usual trance, but the world clung stubbornly to her senses, anchoring her firmly in the here and now. She started to say something about trying again later when Hart, sitting beside her, reached out and took her hand in his. She slammed back in her chair, her back arching, as uncontrollable power surged through her. She gasped for breath, her hand clamping down on Hart's. The power was harsh, inhuman, beyond anything she'd ever felt before, and for a moment it blotted out her mind, concentrating only on the Cards and what they held. She began speaking, or something spoke through her, and she could only sit helplessly and listen with the others to what her voice said.

'The call of the Forever Door is stronger now. It's calling all its lost souls home.'

'She's right,' said Ash quietly. 'I can feel it.'

Suzanne ignored him, her eyes somewhere else. 'The Wild Childe is coming into his power. It is his time, come round at last.'

'Can you identify the next victim?' said Hart gently.

'Yes. It's Sean Morrison. He wants to die, and the Wild Childe can sense that. But if you prevent his death, worse will follow. Something monstrous lies in the future, waiting to be born.'

'What, again?' said Ash. Rhea shushed him.

'Something monstrous, but something wonderful too. Everything will change in Shadows Fall, and it will never be the same again. The world will end and be transformed, and all things shall be made new again.'

Hart jerked his hand away from hers, and Suzanne fell forward across the table as the strength went out of her. Her face hit the table painfully hard, but she was too weak to move, her thoughts whirling wildly as she trembled in every limb. Polly was quickly there with her, helping her to sit up and then leading her away from the table. Hart sat very still, his face pale. Polly helped Suzanne stretch out on her bed, and sat beside her, holding her hand. Ash looked at Hart, and then at Rhea.

'What the hell was that all about? The end of the world? Did somebody raise the stakes while we weren't looking?'

'Presumably it's a metaphor,' said Rhea. 'Prophecies are usually symbolic.'

'Not necessarily,' said Hart. 'The prophecy concerning me is quite clear; I will bring an end to Shadows Fall. It can't be just a coincidence.'

'Let's put that comforting thought to one side, shall we?' said Rhea. 'Till we're all feeling a little calmer. I think it would be very dangerous just now to start jumping to conclusions without any real evidence.'

'All right,' said Ash. 'What do you think we should do?'

'First, contact the Sheriff's office. We have to locate and protect Sean Morrison.'

'Last I heard, the Sheriff was missing,' said Polly, from Suzanne's side.

'He's back, but he's . . . indisposed,' said Rhea. 'It doesn't matter. There are a couple of Deputies there who can help. They've got the resources to help us find Sean.'

'Hold on a minute,' said Ash. 'Let's think about this. Suzanne said if we prevent his death, worse will follow.'

'So we just let him die?' said Rhea. 'Is that what you're suggesting?'

'I don't know,' said Ash. 'But it seems to me we need to think this through very thoroughly, before we set anything into motion that we might not be able to stop.'

'I don't think we've got that much time to spare,' said Hart. 'According to Suzanne, Morrison wants to die. If we don't get to him soon, the whole thing might become moot, and we'll have lost our chance to set a trap for the killer. The Wild Childe, whatever the hell that is.'

'Sean is my friend, and Suzanne's,' said Polly, growing anger giving weight to her words. 'If he's in trouble, we have to help him. Everything else can wait.'

'She's right,' said Rhea. 'We've all lost too many friends

in these last hours to lose one more because we didn't act fast enough. I know Sean; if I can get to him, he'll listen to me. He never could say no to me.'

'I never knew that,' said Ash. 'Where did you know Sean from?'

'Polly can stay here with Suzanne,' said Rhea, ignoring him. 'The rest of us will head for the Sheriff's office. We can keep Sean there, under protective custody. He'll be safe there. Then all we have to do is wait for the Wild Childe to come and get him.'

'Then we close the trap, and he's ours,' said Hart. 'And maybe then, finally, we'll get some answers.'

And as easily as that, it was settled. A telephone call to Collins and Lewis at the Sheriff's office set things up, and they tracked down Morrison inside an hour. He was found wandering at the edge of town, dazed and incoherent. A doctor at the Sheriff's office diagnosed shock from the invasion. There was a lot of that, in Shadows Fall. They let him lie down in a cell, and he was asleep in minutes. People took it in turn to stand guard.

There weren't many at the Sheriff's office. The Sheriff had been sent home, to sleep off his drunk, and so far Lewis and Collins were the only Deputies to report in. There were others, but they were busy overseeing relief and restoration work. There was a lot of that in Shadows Fall too. Rhea and Ash and Hart found places to conceal themselves not far from Morrison's cell, and then they all sat back, and waited.

Time passed, slowly. Collins and Lewis at least had work to keep them busy. Ash and Rhea talked quietly, catching up on their years of separation. Hart just sat and stared at the wall, turning over in his mind all the things that had happened since he came home to Shadows Fall. He wished Friend was with him. Two hours passed, and all was quiet. Hart was actually half dozing when Ash's urgent voice woke him up. Footsteps were approaching, quiet and unhurried. Hart got silently to his feet, and readied himself. What the hell had happened to the two Deputies?

They were supposed to provide a warning if anyone wanted to come back this way. Surely the killer couldn't have taken them both out already . . . Hart clenched and unclenched his hands.

Theoretically, as Time's grandson he had enough sheer power in him to deep-fry a dozen killers, but he was still learning how to use it, and didn't feel at all ready to rely on it in an emergency. He might blow up the whole building trying to get the killer . . . He wished now he'd asked the Deputies for a gun of some kind. Not that he'd have known how to use it if they had . . . He realized he was rambling, and concentrated on the approaching footsteps. He was hidden from sight behind the closed door of a storeroom just off from the cells. The footsteps passed by his door, heading for the cells, and then they stopped. Hart tensed, listening. They'd locked Morrison's cell door, just in case, but there was no guarantee that would be enough to keep the killer out. There was a pause, and then a familiar voice spoke quietly in the corridor.

'Time to die, Sean. The Wild Childe demands it.'

There was a sudden squeal of straining metal as the killer bent apart the bars of the cell door. Hart wrenched open his door, charged out into the corridor and threw himself on to the hulking figure by Morrison's cell. The killer threw him off easily. Hart hit the floor hard, but was back on his feet in a second, fuelled by rage and adrenalin. And then he stopped and stared at the figure before him, holding his nightstick like a club. The killer. The Wild Childe. Sheriff Richard Erikson. Ash and Rhea appeared in the corridor behind him, and the Sheriff turned to look at them. Rhea shook her head dazedly. Ash looked at Erikson sadly.

'Not you, Richard. Not you.'

'He has to die,' said Erikson reasonably. 'It is necessary.'

Without warning, he lashed out with his nightstick. Hart ducked under it at the last moment, and the stick cracked the plaster on the wall where he had been standing. Ash jumped Erikson from behind, and tried to pin his arms to his sides. Erikson threw him off without even trying. Hart threw a punch. Erikson sidestepped impossibly quickly, and Hart staggered forward, caught off balance. The Sheriff brought his stick down hard. Hart caught some of it on an upraised arm, but the force of the blow was enough to send him to the floor. And then the temperature plummeted as Ash imposed his presence on the corridor. Dazed as he was, Hart tried to back away from the dead man. Erikson didn't even turn to look at him. Calm and unhurried, he raised his stick for the blow that would crush Hart's skull as it had so many others. Hart tried to get up, but knew he wasn't going to make it in time. The stick started down, and then a dark clinging mass fell across Erikson's head and shoulders, blinding him. The Sheriff staggered back and forth, fighting for air. He dropped his nightstick to claw at the black stuff, but couldn't find a hold on it. He dropped to his knees as his air ran out, and then he was lying on the floor, unconscious. Hart's Friend flowed away from him, jumped up on to Hart's shoulders and nuzzled him like a cat.

'Can't I leave you alone for five minutes without you getting into trouble? I don't know what you'd do without me.'

'Friend,' said Hart, 'neither do I. How long have you been here?'

'Not long. I sensed you needed me, so I came straight away. I can do that. I can do other things too . . .'

'I'm sure you can,' said Hart, 'But first, we have a killer to deal with.'

Between them, Hart and Ash carried the unconscious Sheriff upstairs to his private office. Collins and Lewis were suitably shocked. Of course they'd let Erikson go down to the cells without alerting the others. They were his cells. They helped Hart sit the Sheriff in his chair in his private office, and provided a pair of handcuffs to hold his arms behind his back. They also drew their guns and kept them trained on Erikson. No one felt like taking any

chances until they'd got some kind of answer as to what
the hell was going on.

'It explains a lot,' said Rhea. 'He could go anywhere,
any time, and no one would challenge him. He had
complete access to the murder investigation. Who knows
how many false trails he sent his people down?'

'I still can't believe this,' said Collins. 'I know Richard.
I've known him for years. He's not a killer. What motive
would he have, to kill all those people?'

'It's not just him,' Ash said suddenly. 'There's something inside him; something dark. I can sense it.'

'You mean he's possessed?' said Rhea. 'Like DeFrenz?'

'Maybe. I don't know. But something's working through
him.'

'The Wild Childe,' said Hart.

Ash shrugged. 'Presumably. We'd better work out what
we're going to do about him. Whatever's inside him is
waking up.'

The Sheriff lifted his head suddenly and looked about
him. He seemed calm and composed, but his face didn't
look like Erikson's. Behind the calm, steady gaze something else was looking out. They could all feel it, like
another presence in the office.

'Who are you?' said Rhea.

'You know,' said Erikson. 'You were warned about me.
I'm the Wild Childe. I do what must be done.'

'You kill people,' said Rhea.

'I send through the Forever Door those who should have
gone willingly. I am necessary. There are forces that
cannot be denied. You think you have me, but you don't.
I am everywhere. This is my time, come round at last.'

The Sheriff shuddered suddenly, and then was still.
Something went out of him in that moment, and his face
was his own again.

'Richard?' said Rhea.

'Yes. I'm back. I knew it was there from the moment it
first arrived, but it kept making me forget. It used everything I knew to plan its murders, and then carry them out.

It used me.' His face was slack and grey, like someone recovering from a long illness. 'I'm tired. So tired . . .'

Collins and Lewis released him from the handcuffs, after Ash had quietly verified that the possessing spirit was gone, and took him away to one of the cells, to lie down. They didn't lock the door, for which he was almost pathetically grateful. The others sat and looked at each other.

'What do we do now?' said Ash. 'We caught our killer, but he's gone. He could be anywhere. Or anyone.'

'Suzanne found him once,' said Rhea.

'With my help,' said Hart. 'I only lent her a little of my power, but that was enough to blow all her fuses. I don't know if she could survive a second attempt.'

'What power?' said Rhea, staring at him intently. 'Who are you, really? What are you doing here in Shadows Fall?'

'I came home,' said Hart.

Rhea waited, and then realized he'd said all he was going to. She turned to Ash. 'Leonard; what can you sense about Hart?'

'Nothing,' said Ash. 'He's shielded. I've been trying to get in ever since he supercharged Suzanne back at her place, but I keep being pushed out. It's not his shield. He doesn't even realize he's doing it.'

'Could he be the Wild Childe?' said Rhea. 'The source of the possessing spirit?'

'No,' said Ash. 'That's gone from here.'

'Please believe me,' said Hart carefully, 'I'm not connected with the Wild Childe in any way. I want to stop these murders just as much as you do. I'm just someone who came home, looking for answers.'

Rhea looked at him for a long moment, and then looked away. 'There's something you're not telling us, but that's par for the course in this town. Whatever it is, it'll have to wait till we've dealt with our current problem. We have to find the Wild Childe before he kills again.'

'If we can,' said Ash. 'He said some interesting things. He said he only killed people who should have gone

473

through the Forever Door, but there are thousands of people like that in Shadows Fall. Why did he only choose some, and not others?'

Rhea shrugged. 'He was only one man, and there was a limit to what he could do without being suspected and caught.'

'Now he doesn't have to worry about that any more,' said Hart. 'Still, whatever body he chooses, I can find him. Eventually.'

'He said he was necessary,' said Ash. 'What did he mean by that?'

'Probably just trying to confuse us,' said Rhea. 'We have to warn people. Find the bastard before he kills again.'

The door burst open and Collins rushed in. 'We have a problem. There are radio reports coming in from all over town. There are killings everywhere, more than a hundred, all of them following the Wild Childe's MO. Only they can't all be him; these murders are taking place simultaneously all across the town. You'll have to look after yourselves from now on; Lewis and I are going out.'

And with that, he was gone. Ash and Hart and Rhea looked at each other.

'He isn't trying to hide any more,' said Ash. 'And it seems he's no longer limited to possessing just one person. You could say he's . . . swarming.'

'We have to talk to Old Father Time,' said Hart. 'He's the only one with enough power to stop all this.'

'He isn't seeing anyone,' said Rhea.

'He'll see me,' said Hart.

The Wild Childe, let loose at last, ran through the streets of Shadows Fall in a thousand bodies. Their hands were claws and their eyes were dark, and they laughed and howled as they ran, slaughtering all in their path who were not also possessed. They killed as easily and as naturally as they breathed, for that was their function and their purpose. Crowds of panicked townspeople ran before them in the streets, pursued by the Wild Childe in all his many identities. No one was safe, no one could be trusted. Friend turned on friend, wife on husband, father on son. The dead were everywhere, lying battered and broken in pools of their own blood. Some of the possessed broke down barricaded doors with their unnatural strength, to get at those hiding within. The Wild Childe could not be stopped, deterred, reasoned with or warned off; there was no room in them for compassion or caution, only the endless urge to kill. They ravaged through the town, in all its many times and places, killing with their bare hands, or any weapon that came to hand.

Most of the town's survivors were in shock from the Warrior invasion, but still many fought back against the new enemy, using weapons they'd taken from dead or captured Warriors. Some even fancied themselves hardened fighters, only to find that was no help at all when they found themselves fighting killers with familiar faces. All too many stood helplessly and died, unable to raise a hand against their loved ones.

Doctor Mirren watched it all from the fortress he'd made of his house. He'd barricaded all the doors and windows, and sat in his study with his shotgun on his lap, watching the growing horror through his most powerful scrying glass. He begrudged the power that took from him, but he had to know. Mystical wards surrounded the house, put together and maintained by his power over many years, and they ought to be strong enough to keep anything out, but he wasn't as sure of his power as he once was. Too much had changed in Shadows Fall; nothing could be counted on any more. He sat in his study, hands clenched on his shotgun, and watched helplessly as the scrying glass showed him scene after scene of the Wild Childe running mad in the streets. The scenes frightened him in a way the Warriors never had. He had made many promises in return for his power and his knowledge, promises he'd never thought he'd really have to make good, and now it seemed he'd risked his life and his soul for nothing. Fear yammered at the barriers of his self-control. He couldn't afford to die. The dead were waiting for him.

The Wild Childe gathered around his house in crowds, pressing against his mystic wards in growing numbers, watching and waiting; a hundred faces with the same expression, the same dark smile. They prowled outside the walls of his grounds, testing the wards again and again, until finally the sheer weight of numbers was too great to be borne, the wards came down, and the possessed spilled into his garden like starving wolves. Mirren reached out with his power, and sent his dead Warriors to meet them. All the soldiers he'd summoned and tricked into his grounds and then killed with his deadly garden rose again to defend him.

The dead fought with the possessed, and for a moment the forces seemed equal, but the dead were slow and awkward, motivated only by Mirren's will, and he quickly realized he'd spread himself too thin. The Wild Childe pushed past the dead and swarmed through his garden. Mirren reached out again, and the deadly plants and vines of his garden fell upon the possessed, weighing them down and tearing them apart. But still some escaped the greenery, and flocked around his house to hammer on the closed doors and shuttered windows.

Mirren knew he should stay in his study, where he was safest, but he couldn't just sit and watch and do nothing. He rose jerkily to his feet and hurried out of the study to check the state of his defences. He ran from room to room, and everywhere the possessed were tearing away the shutters and forcing their way past the barricades. The front door shook under a thunderous hammering. He ran back to his study, his thoughts whirling, still gripping his shotgun fiercely, though he'd lost all faith in its ability to save him. He would have liked to just stop, put the barrels to his head and pull the trigger, but he couldn't do that. The dead were waiting for him. There had to be a way out of this. There had to be.

He reached his study unmolested, dived inside and

slammed the door shut behind him. And only then realized that the Wild Childe had got there first. Three of them, two men and a woman, with the same smile and the same darkness in their eyes. He got the woman with his shotgun, and then the two men took it away from him and threw him to the floor. He huddled into a ball, cringing away from the expected follow-up, but nothing happened. He uncurled slowly and cautiously and looked up to see the two possessed just standing there, as though waiting for something. Or someone. The answer came to Mirren almost immediately, and his heart jumped in his chest. The air was suddenly full of the stench of brimstone, and a new figure appeared in the room. He was naked, slim and delicately formed, inhumanly beautiful, and he sweated drops of blood that ran down his colourless flesh to stain the study carpet. Flies buzzed in the room, circling the figure's head like moths round a lantern. The figure snatched one out of the air and ate it, and then turned to face Mirren, and his smile was the same the possessed wore.

'Dear Doctor, I have so enjoyed looking forward to this moment. We have so much to discuss.' The demon stretched languorously, like a cat before a fire. 'The deaths of the Warriors and the townspeople have made me very strong, Doctor. The Wild Childe murders will make me stronger still.' Flames leapt up around the figure, and Mirren flinched away from the raging heat. The demon continued, as though nothing was happening. 'I have used my new power to take control of the Wild Childe for my own purposes. I brought him into existence long before he would normally have appeared, and now he does my will in all things. The possessed townspeople will kill and kill until no one is left alive but them, and then they will kill each other. And the power that slaughter will provide will enable me to tap the power of the town itself, and the Galleries of Frost and Bone, and finally the Forever Door itself.' The blazing flames had reduced the figure to a charred and blackened husk, but its voice never wavered.

Flies swarmed about it more thickly than ever, and the smell of burnt meat was sickening in the confined space. Mirren had backed away from the burning man till he'd slammed up against the wall behind him, and now he had nowhere left to go. He was dimly aware that he'd wet himself. He didn't realize he was making little moaning, entreating sounds. The demon chuckled softly.

'Power over the Forever Door will give me power over Life and Death. And with that, I'll change the world till no one can recognize what it used to be. There will be an infinity of suffering and corruption, and I shall be Lord over all. Why reign only in Hell when the world's pickings are so much sweeter?

'And you helped to make it all possible, Doctor. You betrayed the town's defences and let the Warriors in, but more than that, it was your questioning into areas you had no business in that let me find my first toehold in this town. You are responsible for everything that has happened here, dear Doctor, and I have come to give you your reward. You wanted so very much to know about death and what comes after; allow me to show you.'

Mirren screamed for a long time, and then he died. And then the screaming began again.

Outside in the streets, the Wild Childe was everywhere, and blood and death and darkness covered the town of Shadows Fall.

Rhea, Ash, Hart and Morrison dived into the plastic snowscene and clawed their way down through the raging blizzard to drop unceremoniously on to the snowy waste below. They landed hard, but the snow was deep enough to soften the impact. They got to their feet and set off through the knee-deep snow, holding hands to keep from being separated by the fury of the storm. One direction looked much like any other, but Hart could sense the right direction, like a compass that knows its way home. It was just the latest in a series of things he seemed to know because he needed to. After an endless time they finally

478

came to the great hulking shape of All Hallows Hall, only to find more evidence that all was not as it should be. The Hall was dark, with no lights showing at any of the windows.

Hart pushed open the front door, and herded the others in out of the blinding snow. He slammed the door shut after them, and for a long moment they all stood together, getting their breath back. Everything was dark, and silent. Hart called upon the power within him, and a pool of light formed around the group. He frowned. Things like that were getting easier and more natural all the time. He had a feeling he could do other things too, astounding things, but he backed away from the temptation. More than ever he wanted, needed, to feel human, ordinary; safe.

They stamped the snow from their boots, rubbed their hands together to get the blood flowing again, and then Hart led the way through the broad, intersecting corridors of the Gallery of Bone. He knew the right way instinctively, as though he belonged there. Everywhere they went was still and silent, and nothing moved in the darkness but them. The portraits on the walls were dark and empty, with nothing left of the scenes they were supposed to show. Which, as far as Hart was concerned, raised an interesting question; where were the people and creatures some of those portraits were supposed to be guarding? Were they still somehow held in place, or were they running loose in the Gallery; hiding in the dark beyond his light? It was an interesting question, but not one Hart felt like sharing with his companions. They were concerned enough as it was; the last thing they needed was something else to worry about. He pressed on, paying just a little more attention to his surroundings. He was pretty sure he'd be able to tell if something was lurking nearby, just as he knew other things, but it was all too new for him to be able to really trust it yet.

They walked on, none of them saying anything, and the tension in the group was thick enough to cut with a knife. The Gallery wasn't supposed to be like this, ever, and they all knew it. And what that implied about Time's condition was increasingly worrying. Old Father Time was supposed to be immortal, and powerful beyond belief, with mastery over Time and Space and anything that hung around the edges. The thought of anyone, or anything, powerful enough to affect Time was disturbing on a very basic level. They walked on, and the darkness pressed in close around them. Every now and again they'd come across one of Time's metal automatons, the gleaming clockwork figures standing motionless, frozen in mid-movement, as though the force that motivated them had been cut off suddenly, without warning.

They headed for Time's inner sanctum, feeling more jumpy all the time, ready to start at any suspected sound or movement. But there was never anything except the dark. The only sound was the soft slap of their feet on the polished wooden floor, quickly swallowed up by the quiet before it even had time to echo. It was like walking at the bottom of the sea, with light and sound and freedom far from reach. Hart stopped suddenly, and the others stopped with him. There was a sound not far ahead, quiet and muffled. It took Hart a long moment to realize it was the sound of someone crying. He started forward again, rounded a corner that hadn't been there a moment before, and found Mad sitting slumped before the door of Time's inner sanctum. She was crying quietly, openly, with the slow jerky tears of someone who knows that hope is gone, and only the inevitable remains. The tears shook her with every breath, and had made thick runnels through the grey makeup on her face. She looked like a young girl dressed up in an older sister's clothes. Hart knelt before her.

'What is it, Mad? What's happened here?'

It took Mad a moment to get control of her voice. 'Time's dying, but it's far too early. He ought to have months left in him yet, but something's eating him up from the inside. He's going to die, and I don't know if he's going to come back this time. You've got to do something.'

'We'll do what we can,' said Hart. He didn't want to lie

to her, not now. He helped Mad to her feet, and she sniffed and knuckled her eyes as he pushed open the door and led the others in. The room was large, but not uncomfortably so, though there were no fittings and furnishings, save for a plain, functional bed in the middle of the room. And lying on that bed, under rumpled blankets, Old Father Time.

The varying details of his appearance and surroundings had been put aside, as though he no longer had the time or energy to bother with such fripperies. He was just an old man lying in a bed, breathing noisily through his open mouth. He seemed a thousand years old, a small wrinkled mummy of a man for whom each breath was an effort. He looked only seconds away from death, as though it might claim him at any moment. Hart stood at the bedside, looking down at the dying man with a mixture of compassion and annoyance. If he hadn't known better, he'd have sworn Time was doing this just to get out of answering questions. The others crowded behind him, but didn't approach the bed, as though they were too awed or too nervous to get any closer.

'I don't get this,' murmured Ash, at Hart's shoulder. 'So what if he's dying? He'll just come back again as a baby.'

'You're right, you don't get it,' said Morrison, not bothering to lower his voice. 'Time's life cycle may be continuous, but it's regimented to the second, so that it ties in with the needs and cycles of the town. Something's sucked the remaining months of his life and power right out of him. Which means he's helpless to do anything about what's happening in the town until he's died, been born again and matured out of childhood. And that could take days. Anything could happen in that time. Anything.'

'Cheerful sort, isn't he?' Ash said to Rhea. She shushed him without taking her eyes off the old man in the bed.

'Who would have the power to do something like this to Time?' she said finally.

'Good question,' said Morrison. 'If you come up with an

answer that won't loosen our bowels too much, feel free to share it with us.'

They moved a little closer, none of them sure what to do next. Mad sat on one side of the bed, sniffing occasionally and holding one of Time's wrinkled hands in both of hers. She looked at the others, and her face said *Do something*. And then Time opened his eyes, and began to speak in a low, breathy whisper.

'I suppose you're wondering why I've called you all here today. You're here because it's time you knew what's really been going on in Shadows Fall. Listen carefully; I doubt very much if I'll have the time or the strength to go through this twice. The Wild Childe is a physical manifestation of entropy; a living reminder that all things must pass, whether they want to or not. It's supposed to be spontaneously created by the unconscious mass mind of the town, when the population becomes dangerously large. It's a safeguard built into the system, for when I am incapable or unwilling to do my job. There are forces in the universe that will not be denied.

'There are always some who are supposed to go through the Forever Door, and don't. The system allows for that. They settle in the town, become real, live out a normal lifespan and die. Only sometimes, they don't. They find a way to hang on to life long after they should have passed on. Too many of them, and the town becomes too big, too unwieldy. Things start to break down. The Wild Childe is supposed to manifest at this point, and persuade the trouble-makers to pass through the Door. He's an archetype, called up from the collective unconsciousness of the town, which means he has incredible power to draw on, if he should find it necessary to send someone through the Forever Door by force. But he was never supposed to be a killer.'

Time broke off, and for a moment all he could do was gasp for air like a drowning man. Mad squeezed his hand hard, and finally he was back in control again. He resumed his lecture, and his voice actually seemed a little stronger.

482

'The town's population is nowhere near large enough to have given rise to the Wild Childe spontaneously. Something, some outside force, has brought it into being early, and corrupted its purpose. That's why it's been possessing others instead of creating a form for itself. Now it's running loose in a thousand bodies, dancing to someone else's tune, and it won't stop until every living creature in Shadows Fall has been sent through the Forever Door, one way or another.'

There was a long pause before they realized he'd said all he had to say.

'All right,' said Hart, 'who's behind it? Why does he want to kill everyone? What can we do to stop him?'

'You can't,' said Time.

His eyes closed and he stopped breathing, and it was some time before they realized he was dead.

It was the day of the Wild Childe, and they were everywhere. Throughout the beleaguered town of Shadows Fall, thousands of men and women with the same grinning face ran rabid through the streets, killing anyone who was not them, and gathering in crowds around the few remaining pockets of resistance. Blood ran in the gutters, and sometimes the possessed would stop to kneel and lap at it like dogs. Inside the Sheriff's office, the Deputies Collins and Lewis nailed boards across the windows while Suzanne and Polly barricaded the doors. Outside, the screaming was deafening, and there was a constant thunder of hammering fists on the other sides of the doors. The Wild Childe wanted in, and deep down the defenders knew that eventually he would find a way.

Collins and Lewis poked their guns between the nailed-up boards and fired off a few shots every now and again, whenever the press of surrounding bodies seemed too great, but they had to make each shot count. Ammunition was limited. They'd never had to rely on guns before to keep the peace in Shadows Fall. The Wild Childe had guns they'd taken from dead Warriors, but luckily there was even less ammunition for those. The two Deputies shot to kill, even when they thought they recognized the face before them. They had to, because the Wild Childe would not be stopped by anything less. There was nothing human left in them; nothing that could be reasoned with or appealed to.

Suzanne and Polly had guns the Deputies had given them, but so far they hadn't found the courage or the desperation to use them. They sat together at a table, and Polly watched as Suzanne laid out a pack of playing cards she'd found in a drawer. Some of Hart's power still moved within her, and she saw things in the patterns the cards made. She saw the mob running loose in the streets, drunk on blood and suffering, and she saw its name, Wild Childe, though it meant nothing to her. She was trying to see a safe way out of the Sheriff's office, and then out of the town, but wherever she looked, the Wild Childe looked back. There was no way out. No way past the Wild Childe, and the madness he'd brought to town.

The two Deputies suddenly opened up with a fusillade of shots, and Suzanne and Polly looked round quickly, their hands going to their guns lying before them on the table. Collins moved away from the window, and hurried out of the room. The two women jumped to their feet, guns at the ready.

'What is it?' said Suzanne. 'Are they in the building?'

'No,' said Lewis, picking off his targets with cold efficiency. 'The mob's chasing some of their victims this way. There's only a few of them, one human and three anthropomorphics, but they're all armed, and they're holding the killers back. Collins has gone down to open a side door for them. If they get that far.' He stopped firing, and looked puzzled, craning his neck this way and that to get a better view between the boards. 'The mob must really want these people; they've forgotten all about us to concentrate on the poor bastards outside.'

'What can we do to help them?' said Polly.

'Not much,' said Lewis. 'Collins will stand by to open

the side door if he gets a chance, but he won't put us at risk to rescue them. It's all down to the poor bastards outside. They'll have to make their own luck.'

Outside in the street, Scottie the Wee Terror threw himself at the grinning man before him and tore out his throat with a practised snap of his jaws. He wasn't a particularly big dog, but he had a lot of teeth. He hit the ground feet first and looked quickly about him for a new victim. His studded leather jacket was torn and bloodied, some of the blood his, and someone had torn the safety pin from his nose, though he couldn't remember when. Peter Caulder fought at his side, firing his two machine pistols in practised bursts. The ex-Warrior was dog tired and bone weary, but his aim never wavered. He had vowed to protect the Underworld of the Subnatural with his life, and though his faith had been proved false, his word was still good.

Bruin Bear and the Sea Goat stood back to back, their guns uncomfortably warm in their paws from too much use. There had been a time, not all that long ago, that the Bear had thought himself incapable of killing. Time and circumstance had proved him wrong. With the Wild Childe it was kill or be killed, and the Bear wasn't ready to die. Not yet. Many of the Underworld of the Subnatural had refused to kill, for many reasons, and Bruin Bear had watched them die till he couldn't stand it any more. He picked up a gun, and was surprised how easy it was to use.

The Sea Goat had a gun in one hand and a bottle of vodka in the other. He laughed and roared insults as he fired, in his element at last. The Bear tried not to listen to him. He concentrated on the matter at hand, cutting down any of the manic horde who got too close, and felt a little of himself die every time he pulled the trigger.

The mob pressed forward on all sides, and the three animals and one human ran before it, this way and that, maintaining a respectful distance from the horde with their guns. None of the manic faces before them seemed at all afraid to die, but they showed a certain primitive caution, as though not wanting to throw away their life for no purpose. Caulder stopped suddenly as a wall loomed up before him, and a brief surge of panic flared up as he realized there was nowhere left to go. He put his back to the wall, and Scottie crouched panting at his feet, his eyes just a little wild. Bruin Bear and the Sea Goat were quickly there beside them, and without having to say anything, they all knew they'd got as far as they were going to go. There was no room left in them for despair, only determination. They lifted their guns one last time, and then a door opened beside them, and an arm reached out to drag them in.

They threw themselves into the opening, and someone slammed the door shut behind them in the face of the howling mob. They lay in a heap on the floor, happy for the moment just to lie there and get their breath back as the mob hammered futilely on the locked door. The Sea Goat was the first back on his feet, gun in hand, still somehow clinging to his bottle of vodka. He glared at the figure before him, and sniffed loudly.

'Took you long enough to let us in. Any longer and those assholes would have walked right over us. Who the hell are you, and is there another way out of this place?'

'You must excuse the Goat,' said Bruin Bear tiredly. 'I used to know why, but I've forgotten.'

'I'm Collins,' said the Deputy. 'And there's no way out for any of us. Come and meet the others.'

'Are they all as cheerful as you?' growled Scottie.

They quickly joined the others, found vantage points from which to fire at the mob outside, and took it in turns to tell their story. They were all depressingly similar.

'We've tried radioing for help,' said Suzanne, 'But there's never any answer. The phones are dead. I think the wires have been cut. For all we know, we could be the only ones left alive in Shadows Fall.'

Polly shivered briefly. 'Don't. I can't believe that. There has to be someone else out there. If we can just hold out long enough, they'll come to rescue us.'

'I wouldn't count on it,' said Scottie, scratching his ear

with his back paw. Specks of dried blood fell to the floor. 'The crazy people are all over the place. We're all that's left of the Underworld of the Subnatural.'

There was a sudden crash from the floor below, and a roar of triumphant voices. Everyone looked automatically at the door. Beyond it lay an open corridor, with two lifts and a stairway giving access to the floor below. The sound of broken glass and furniture being thrown about was clear and distinct, even above the animal growls and screams of the Wild Childe.

'Damn,' said Collins tonelessly. 'They're in the building.'

The Sea Goat took a quick drink from his bottle, and bared his blocky teeth. 'I'm still waiting to hear if there's another way out of this death trap, though I have a sneaking suspicion I already know the answer. Don't all speak at once.'

'There's no way out,' said Lewis. He turned away from the window, ejected a spent clip from his gun and slipped in a new one. 'If there was a way out, we'd have used it. We're not going anywhere.'

'It's at times like this,' said Scottie, 'that I wish my creator had stuck to paperback thrillers. I didn't ask to be created.'

'We can't just stand here and wait for the mob to come and get us!' snapped Suzanne. 'If you want to give up, take a walk downstairs and get it over with. I am going to set up more barricades, at least partly because I'd feel such an idiot if I just gave up, and help arrived a few minutes later.'

'She's got a point,' said the Sea Goat.

It took only a few minutes to disable both the elevators, throw furniture down the stairway, retreat back into the reception area and jam the heaviest desk up against the only door. They reloaded their guns, took up defensive positions behind overturned tables, and waited. The uproar from below showed no signs of abating, though there couldn't have been much left to smash. Bruin Bear hugged

487

his gun to his furry chest, and felt more sad than anything else. He'd done many things he knew his creator would never have approved of, in the interests of survival, and now he wondered if he'd made the right choice after all. He was less than he once was, he knew that. He'd been special before. Guns wouldn't work near him, and bad things didn't happen to him and his friends, because . . . because he was Bruin Bear. But being special hadn't been enough to save his fellow creatures from the curse of the Wild Childe, so he'd taken up the gun, to try and force the world to be the way it should be. He'd cast aside what made him unique, and little good it had done him. He was still going to die, and his friends with him. A door opened behind him, and he spun round, his thick finger on the trigger. Sheriff Erikson blinked at all the guns pointing at him, and raised his hands. Everyone let their breath out again, and lowered their guns a little.

'Sorry, Sheriff,' said Collins. 'With everything that's happened, I'd forgotten you were still . . . sleeping it off. How are you feeling?'

'Fine,' said Erikson. 'I feel fine. I know I was . . . out of control there, for a while, but I'm better now. Really, I'm feeling just fine now, and I'd like to help. If you'll give me my gun back.'

'I don't think that would be a good idea, Sheriff,' said Lewis carefully. 'You go back and get some more rest. We'll take care of things here.'

Erikson nodded, and then turned and went back into his inner sanctum, shutting the door behind him. They didn't trust him. He didn't blame them. He'd been the Wild Childe once, and presumably could be again, though his mind felt clearer now than it had been for months. He remembered the murders he'd committed as a series of murky dreams, where he was just a silent, helpless observer. They still didn't seem real to him, though he had no doubt he'd done the things they said he had. He was the murderer he'd tried so hard to find.

He sat down behind his desk, and knew what he had to

do. He felt calm and sure and not at all frightened. Whatever happened, he couldn't let the Wild Childe take hold of him again. It wasn't going to be easy, without a gun. He looked about him, and his eye fell on the letter spike. Yes; that would do. He picked it up and placed it carefully before him, and removed the letters. He didn't look to see what they were. They didn't matter any more. The metal spike was eight or nine inches long. Long enough. He placed his hands flat on the desk on either side of the letter spike, and bent forward so that he was looking down at it. He wasn't scared at all.

I'm sorry. I'm really sorry.

He slammed his face down on to the spike with all his strength. The last thing he saw was the metal point flying up to fill his left eye.

Out in the reception office, the defenders listened to the Wild Childe clambering up the stairs, throwing aside the blocking furniture as though it was weightless. It wasn't long before they were banging on the door till it shuddered in its frame. The Sea Goat fired a shot through the door, but it didn't seem to bother them. Collins and Lewis stood together, guns trained on the door. Their breathing was fast and hurried, but their hands were steady. Bruin Bear and the Sea Goat took it in turns to drink from the vodka bottle. It was almost empty. Peter Caulder sat quietly behind them, thinking about the many strange changes his life had taken recently, and smiled as he realized he wouldn't have changed any of them. Scottie glared at the shuddering door, and growled deep in his throat. Suzanne and Polly held hands, and tried to hold their guns professionally.

The door burst open, and the Wild Childe swarmed in, sweeping aside the heavy desk as though it was nothing. The defenders opened up with a withering fire, and the possessed men and women were thrown aside like dolls. The thunder of the guns was deafening in the confined space, but the Wild Childe only laughed and pressed forward, scrambling over the bodies of the fallen to get at the defenders. More of the possessed appeared through the doorway, and some of them had guns too. Blood splashed the walls and pooled on the floor, but the Wild Childe just kept coming.

Scottie was the first to die. A burst of machine pistol fire picked him up and threw him aside like a toy. He died still trying to snap at the ankles of those treading around him. Collins and Lewis went down under a crowd of the possessed, still firing their guns. The Wild Childe tore them apart with its unnatural strength. Peter Caulder tried to rescue them, and a slim young woman with mad eyes and a wide smile stuck a knife in his throat before he even knew she was there. He fell to his knees, his mouth suddenly full of blood.

Bruin Bear was quickly at his side, trying to pull him back to cover. A bullet hit him square in the forehead, and he was thrown backwards to lie helpless on the floor, blood filling his eyes as his life ebbed away. The Sea Goat screamed with fury and loss, threw his empty bottle into the face of the crowd, and jumped out to stand over his two friends. He fired his gun till it ran out of ammunition, and then he fought with his hands and his horns, until finally they dragged him down.

Suzanne shot Polly in the back of the head, one last act of friendship, and then put the gun in her own mouth and pulled the trigger. They died still holding hands, and the Wild Childe screamed in thwarted rage.

In a back room in the Gallery of Bone, they stood around Time's bed, watching numbly, as though expecting him to start breathing again at any moment, or sit up and laugh and say he was just fooling. But Old Father Time lay motionless in his bed, a withered, shrunken mummy of a man. He looked like he'd been dead for centuries, only recently disinterred from some ancient pyramid. All around them, the room was dark and quiet. There were no walls or ceiling any more, the only light a pale golden glow from an old-fashioned lamp on the bed's high headboard.

Outside the pool of light there was a feeling of emptiness, as though they were afloat in a sea of darkness.

Rhea and Ash stood together at the foot of the bed, holding hands and drawing what comfort they could from each other. Time's death struck at the heart of everything they believed in. He was the single constant in a changing world, the glue that held Shadows Fall together; with him gone, there was no way the town could survive. Ash looked at the wizened body and felt a twinge of mortality. If even Time could die, and pass through the Door from which no one returns, then he had to accept his almost-life must have an end too. He'd always known that, but it had never really bothered him before. He'd had no right to a second chance at life. Only now Rhea loved him again, and he had so much to lose he couldn't bear it. He smiled briefly. That's love for you.

Ash's hand tightened on Rhea's and she squeezed it comfortingly in return. Her own thoughts were racing wildly, searching desperately for some way out of the corner they'd been backed into. They couldn't have come through so much, survived so much, only to fail now. It wasn't fair. They'd beaten the Warriors without Time's help, but the Wild Childe was different. His origin and power lay in the subtle magics that made Shadows Fall, and only Old Father Time had the power to understand and manipulate those forces. Without his help, there was no way to stop the Wild Childe running amok until no living thing remained in the town . . . and without Time to oversee Shadows Fall, the town itself would cease to exist. The end of everything. Rhea's hand tightened on Ash's. There had to be a way out of this. There had to be.

Sean Morrison sat on the end of the bed, his feet dangling, staring at nothing. He tried to think of something he could play, some song to sing to mark Time's passing, but the music wouldn't come. Music had died for him along with the Faerie. Without them the world had lost its flavour, life had lost its purpose. The Faerie had embodied everything he'd ever believed in. Now they were

491

gone, the splendour and the majesty, the laughter in the woods, dead by their own hand. How could there be music, in such a world?

Madeleine Kresh, Mad to most, sat on the edge of the bed and held Time's dead hand in both of hers. He'd been her world, her love, her meaning for existence. He'd cared for her when no one else had, protected her when no one else could. He let her stay, though he didn't need her, let her love him, though he knew nothing could ever come of it. She would have given her life for him, but he'd gone on without her, and now her life had no meaning or purpose. She'd dedicated her life to looking after Time, and she'd failed. She wanted to end her own life in some suitably dramatic way, and follow wherever he had gone, but she knew he wouldn't have wanted that. He believed in life, and hope and possibilities. Mad didn't know what she believed in any more. All she knew for sure was that she was alone again.

And James Hart stood at the foot of the bed, staring exasperatedly at his dead grandfather, and wondered what the hell he was supposed to do now. Old Father Time had been the only one with all the answers, and now he was gone, leaving his poor confused grandson to muddle on alone and unadvised. He was the one on the spot now, the one everyone would be looking to for answers, and he hadn't a clue what he was going to tell them. He'd have to think of something. There was nowhere left to run to, nowhere left to hide. Either he found an answer to the Wild Childe, or he and his friends and the whole damned town of Shadows Fall were dead.

The answer was in him somewhere. He could feel his grandfather's power bubbling and simmering within him, pressing and probing and looking for a way out. He didn't understand the power yet, its possibilities and limitations, and he wasn't sure he trusted it either. He felt there were all kinds of things he could do, that the power wanted him to do, but caution held him back. He had a strong feeling the power had its own agenda, that might or might not have anything to do with what he wanted or needed.

But the temptation nagged at him always, like a quiet insistent voice he couldn't ignore.

He glared at the withered remains of his grandfather, and his hands curled into fists. If the man hadn't been already dead, he'd have killed the infuriating old bastard for landing him in such a mess. And then he stopped and looked again, certain he couldn't have seen what he thought he had. He leaned forward over the bed to get a better look. Time was definitely dead, no breath of air moving through his slack mouth, but his chest was moving. Not the steady movement of heartbeat or regular breathing, but sudden jerky movements, as though something within was trying to break out. He stepped back instinctively, his imagination supplying nightmare images of some horrid parasite that had somehow worked its way into Time's immortal body and killed it.

Everyone looked round at his sudden movement, and then followed his gaze. Mad cried out in shock and surprise, dropping Time's hand, and then leant over to press her ear against Time's twitching chest. She laughed suddenly and straightened up, grinning all over her face. Her flick-knife was suddenly in her hand, the blade snapping out with a flat, functional sound. She slid it carefully into Time's gut, just under the breastbone, and then jerked it up sharply. The chest split open, cracking apart like a nutshell. Dust sprayed from the crack, and in the narrow gap they could all just make out something pale, moving feebly. Mad put her knife away, and eased both her hands into the opening. She took a firm hold and jerked the two sides apart, and the chest opened like a book, filling the air with sharp cracking sounds. And in the chest cavity, small and pink and perfect, lay a new-born baby, staring calmly up at Mad. She reached in and carefully lifted him out, cradling him in her arms.

'Time is dead,' she said softly. 'Long live Time.'

The others crowded round Mad as she hugged the baby

to her in a surprisingly maternal way. It looked much like any other baby, tiny and harmless, but it didn't take them long to realize that one, he didn't have a navel, and two, his eyes were clear and calm. He waved a chubby hand at them, and then yawned widely.

Morrison looked at Mad reproachfully. 'You might have told us what you were doing. I nearly had a coronary.'

Mad shrugged. 'I wasn't sure. He usually goes off on his own and takes care of this himself. I only ever saw him after a couple of days had passed, and he was old enough to take charge again. Cute little thing, isn't he?'

She made cootchie-coo noises at the baby, who looked back at her with knowing eyes.

Ash looked at Rhea. 'You're the Mayor. Didn't you know about this?'

'I don't think anybody did,' said Rhea. 'Time was a very private person. I never pushed.'

Morrison sniffed. 'I suppose we should be grateful she didn't try and open him up with that bloody big sword she's got hanging from her hip. Where did that come from, anyway?'

'Time gave it to me,' said Mad, and then pointedly gave all her attention to the baby.

'He must be very weak now,' Rhea said thoughtfully. 'I never saw him this young. I don't think anyone did. Presumably his powers don't kick in till he's old enough to think and talk coherently.'

'And how long's that going to take?' said Hart.

Rhea shrugged. 'Like Mad said, a couple of days. Normally that wouldn't affect the town or the Galleries; their own momentum would be enough to keep things going till Time was ready to take control again. But now, after everything that's happened . . . I don't know.'

'We can't wait two days,' said Hart. 'We don't have that long. The town doesn't have that long. The Wild Childe will have killed everyone by then.'

'If you've another suggestion, I'm sure we'd all be happy to hear it,' snapped Rhea. 'I don't like the idea of him being this helpless. Jack Fetch should be here to protect him. Why isn't he here?'

'Oh please,' said Morrison. 'Things are complicated enough without turnip-head interfering.'

Hart frowned. 'Time thought some outside force was interfering with the proper flow of events,' he said slowly. 'Maybe it deliberately brought on Time's death early, so that his younger self would be helpless and open to attack.'

'Cootchie, cootchie-coo,' said Mad. 'Who's a special little baby, then?'

'I didn't think anybody could interfere with Jack Fetch,' said Ash diffidently. 'If he was meant to be here, I think he'd be here by now.'

'You know,' said Hart. 'This really doesn't make sense, when you think about it. I mean, why would someone as important and powerful as Time have such a vulnerable spot in his life cycle?'

Rhea shrugged. 'Maybe . . . in case he ever got out of control, and had to be stopped or replaced.'

'Who could replace Time?' said Morrison.

'Oh, very deep,' said Rhea.

'Something's coming,' said Ash suddenly. Everyone looked at him. His gaze was far away, as though fixed on something only he could see.

'What is it, Leonard?' said Rhea, putting a hand on his arm. He didn't react.

'Something's coming. Something bad.'

'Form a circle round the bed,' snapped Mad, laying the baby carefully on the rumpled blankets. She drew the sword on her hip, and it settled into her hand as though it belonged there. The others made a ring around the bed, glaring out at the impenetrable gloom beyond the lamplight. For a long moment there was only silence and the dark.

'Who's coming?' said Hart finally. 'And from where? I can't see a damn thing.'

'It's close now,' said Ash. 'Very close. It's almost here.'

There was a sudden drop in temperature, as though

someone had opened a door to the cold outside, and then Jack Fetch was suddenly in the room with them. Everyone relaxed a little, and let out the breath they'd been holding. Jack stood quietly before them, smiling his turnip smile.

'About time you got here,' growled Rhea, stepping out of his way as he started towards the bed.

But there was something in the way the scarecrow moved, something in the way he held himself, that set off alarm bells in Hart's head. He reached out and grabbed the scarecrow by the arm, his hand closing easily around the heavy stick that was all that filled the scarecrow's sleeve. Fetch threw him off violently, without even looking round, and his gloved hands reached out to take the baby from the bed.

'Get the baby away from him!' said Hart. 'Something's wrong; I can feel it.'

Rhea snatched up the baby and backed away from the bed. Jack Fetch went after her. Ash stepped between them and pulled his death around him like a shield. The others paled and fell back, but the scarecrow didn't even slow his advance. He had never been born, and so had no fear of death. Rhea kept backing away, holding the baby protectively. Ash grabbed the scarecrow's arms with all his unnatural strength. For a moment they stood face to face, the dead man struggling with something that had never lived, and then Fetch threw Ash to one side. Morrison called his guitar out of nowhere and began a song, but his voice was uncertain, and the scarecrow might have been deaf for all the attention it paid him.

Mad jumped forward and cut at Fetch with her sword, the blade seeming to guide her hand. Excalibur had been wielded by many great swordsmen, and the sword remembered. It punched through Fetch's shirt front and out his back, stopping him short. He looked down, grabbed the blade with his gloved hands, and pulled it out of his body inch by inch, despite everything Mad could do to keep it there. She stepped back and jerked the blade out of the scarecrow's hands, slicing open the gloves as she did so.

Fetch reached out to grab the blade again, and Mad swept the sword across in a savage cut that sliced clean through the bundle of twigs that made up the scarecrow's wrist. The gloved hand fell to the floor. The fingers twitched and scrabbled on the floor like a huge leathery spider. Mad kicked out at it, and it jumped up, avoiding her foot, and reattached itself to Jack Fetch's wrist. Mad blinked, and then cut at the scarecrow again and again. Sawdust flew from his chest as the blade ripped open his shirt, but still he advanced on her, and she was forced to back away step by step. Rhea stayed behind her, holding the baby almost painfully tightly, though he never once made a sound.

Mad's arms grew tired as she swung the heavy blade. No matter what she did she couldn't hurt Jack Fetch; when all was said and done he was only a collection of wood and twigs and old clothes, topped by a turnip head. And even as she whittled him away, piece by piece, the magic that made him Jack Fetch put him back together again. In the end the sword grew too heavy or she grew too tired, and one wild stroke missed the scarecrow completely. Fetch seized her arm while she was off balance, and threw her to the ground. Her elbow hit the floor hard, and the sword flew from her hand. Jack Fetch bent over her, his gloved hands reaching for her remorselessly.

'No,' said Hart. 'Stop that.'

The scarecrow hesitated, and then turned his turnip head to look at Hart. The tension within him was almost palpable, as he struggled between the power of what drove him and the authority in Hart's voice. The tension grew, an almost physical presence in the room, and then the scarecrow turned its head away as it stepped over Mad and reached for the baby in Rhea's arms. Hart reached inside himself, and let loose his grandfather's power. It was very close to the surface in him now, and at his acceptance it leapt free like an unchained beast. Power surged through him, wild and awful and very potent. He lashed out with it, and the scarecrow exploded.

The others cried out as they were hit by flying pieces.

Bits of twig and tatters of cloth fell to the floor like ugly snowflakes, and Hart began to relax again. He'd done it. The threat was over. And he'd finally let the power run loose within him, and it hadn't been so bad after all. He smiled at the others, preparing a few modest remarks for when they thanked him, and then realized they weren't looking at him. He looked behind him, and there in mid-air, the thousands of pieces of Jack Fetch were knitting themselves together again. The scarecrow rebuilt himself in a matter of moments, whole and intact once more. His turnip mouth grinned mockingly, and Hart's temper snapped. He dug deep into his power, called it all up in a moment, and used it to rip the life force right out of the scarecrow. All the old and subtle magics that made Jack Fetch what he was were cancelled in an instant, and everything that made him unique and individual was sucked out of him and channelled into Hart. It felt good going down, like a fiery brandy, warm and tingling, and it was only when the empty husk of the scarecrow fell stiff and lifeless to the floor that he realized what he'd done.

No one had ever had a good word for Jack Fetch, protector of Time and of the town, but he had fought well and nobly against the Warriors of the Cross, and would have fought the Wild Childe, if he could. He deserved a better ending.

'Is that it?' Rhea said finally. 'Can my heart start beating now, or is he likely to get up again?'

'No,' said Hart, fighting to keep the sickness out of his voice. 'He won't be coming back. Ever.'

'First good news I've had all day,' said Rhea, putting the baby back on the bed. 'At least we can relax a little now.'

'No we can't,' said Ash. 'Something's coming. It's still coming. It's very bad and it's very close and it isn't Jack Fetch.'

By then they could all feel it; something great and malignant, too large to be easily understood, drawing nearer every moment like a runaway train. They would all have liked to run and hide, but there was nowhere they could go, and they knew it. They turned away from the bed, looking out into the gloom that filled the bedchamber, but the feeling came from everywhere at once, and they didn't know where to look. And then suddenly he was there in the room with them, tall and striking and altogether horrible, and they flinched away from the twisted figure as they would from a blazing fire. He'd come as an angel, ten feet tall with perfect alabaster skin and flaring wings, but his bones were too large, and his form was hunched as though by the weight of his sins. His face was beautiful but very cold, and on his brow were two raised nubs that might have been horns, like the thorns on a rose.

Of them all, only Ash didn't flinch or fall back, or turn his face away, perhaps because being dead he had less to lose, but even so he had to try a few times before he could speak.

'Who are you?' he said flatly. 'What do you want here?'

'Who am I?' said the corrupt angel, in calm, almost cultured tones. 'How soon they forget. I have many names, but one nature. Call me Prometheus, if you like. The old jokes are always the best. As to what I'm doing here; this is my time, come round at last, and I can no longer be denied. I'm here to tear down the Galleries of Frost and Bone, undo Time, and break the lock on the Forever Door. Their time is over, their functions now irrelevant. My word shall be the Law, Life and Death will be what I choose to make of them, and yesterday and tomorrow will disappear in the hideous and unrelenting now. I have broken the doors of Hell, and I will not be put back again.'

'Run that past me again,' said Ash. 'I think I fell off at the corner.'

'A sense of humour,' said the fallen angel. 'Good. You're going to need that where you're going, you presumptuous shade. Please; make yourself comfortable, all of you. I'm here to kill Time, but there's no hurry. The long war is finally over, I hold all the trump cards, and there's nothing you can do to stop me. The oldest prophecy in Shadows

Fall says that once the town has fallen, no man, living or dead, can hope to stand against me in my moment of triumph. So pardon me if I feel the need to preen a little. I've always been at my best before an audience, but then, ego was always one of my problems.

'I'm behind everything that's been happening; every unexpected turn and unfortunate choice. I'm the one who took control of the Wild Childe, and sent it out into Shadows Fall to kill and be killed. But I'm getting ahead of myself. In the beginning, I made myself known to Royce and his Warriors of the Cross, and offered them the power they thought they needed to take Shadows Fall for themselves. My price for that power was the many deaths they'd cause in taking the town. That's why the Warrior officers encouraged their men to hate you so much, so there'd be deaths aplenty for me to feed on. Then there was dear Doctor Mirren. A simple, frightened man whose search for the answers behind Life and Death took him into unfortunate areas, and made him ever so vulnerable to my offers and seductions. Through him I discovered and negated the town's defences.

'I brought forth the Wild Childe early, placed it unknown and unsuspected in the perfect host, and had him kill the archangel Michael when he came to warn you. Dear Michael. So pure and honest and delightfully single-minded. Once he'd been thrown out of his host, it was child's play for the Warrior sorcerers to keep him from coming back again. Once I'd manifested the Wild Childe, I had no choice but to let him kill every now and again; that was his function, after all, and if I didn't indulge him he'd just fade away. There were clues to his identity, but you never worked it out; I kept you too busy and too distracted with other matters. Like dear Polly and her father.

'I've been behind so many things. That's my nature in this world, to be the worm in the apple, the smiler in the shadows, pulling the strings that make the world go round. I had the Warriors kill James's parents, so that he would return to the town and reactivate the old prophecy. I like to think I cover all the angles. But I don't need to hide in the shadows any more. All the deaths and suffering in the destruction of Shadows Fall have made me mightier than you can imagine, powerful beyond hope. It's my turn now, to strut the stage and crack the whip. You are the last hope of the living, and all of you are powerless against me. But do feel free to try. I'd be disappointed if you didn't try.'

They all looked at each other, but none of them moved. The sheer presence of the fallen angel was enough to strike them dumb. He had the impact of a force of nature, like an earthquake or a cyclone or a thunderstorm, too huge and overwhelming for mere men to stand against.

And then Sean Morrison struck an angry chord on his guitar and raised his voice in song. Of them all, he had something of the arrogance of the enemy they faced, perhaps because there had always been an undertone of darkness in rock-and-roll; the Devil's music. It was a simple song, one of his old standards, setting his music defiantly against the surrounding gloom like a lighthouse in a storm. But even as he called up all the strength and potency of his music, he knew he was wasting his time. The angel just stood there, smiling, unaffected, and Morrison broke off in mid song. The angel applauded politely.

'It's been said the Devil has all the best tunes, but actually I'm tone deaf. It's always been just noise to me. The opposition always got more out of music than I ever did.'

A sudden thunder of shots filled the bedchamber as Rhea produced a handgun she'd taken from a dead Warrior and blazed away at the fallen angel. She pulled the trigger again and again until the gun was empty, and then she stopped, and slowly lowered it again. The echoes died quickly away. The angel hadn't even blinked.

'Well, really. I'm almost insulted. Bullets, against such as I? You hadn't even carved a cross on them. Not that it would have made any difference at this stage, but I'm a great one for tradition.'

'You want to talk about tradition,' said Mad, hefting her

sword, 'Let's talk about tradition, scumbag. This is the sword Excalibur, and it remembers you.'

She threw herself at the angel, the long blade flashing bright as day as she brought it round in a wide arc. The angel caught the blade effortlessly with one hand in the middle of its swing, and snatched it out of Mad's grasp. She stumbled forward, caught off balance, and the angel ran her through with her own sword. The blade slammed into her belly and punched out of her back in a spray of blood. Mad sank to her knees, and the angel jerked the sword out of her. She shuddered as the steel left her body, and blood spilled from her mouth. Morrison was quickly there, kneeling beside her, and she clutched at him with desperate strength. She tried to tell him something, but she couldn't force the words past the pain and the blood. She died in his arms.

'Nasty little toy,' said the angel, holding up Excalibur like a slug found in a salad. He snapped the blade neatly over his knee, and threw the pieces aside. 'This has all been very amusing, but I think it's time we moved on. I have so much to do. Beginning with Time's death. Anyone want to say a few last words?'

He stepped towards the baby lying on the bed, and Hart's shadow leapt up off the floor and wrapped itself around the angel's head like a blanket. He tore at the black stuff with his clawed hands, but it just oozed thickly between his fingers.

'You're going to have to stop him, Jimmy,' said Hart's Friend desperately. 'I can't hold him for long.'

The angel sank his fingers into the shadow and pulled Friend away from his face like sticky toffee. The shadow writhed and struggled in the angel's hands, and then howled soundlessly as it was torn apart. The angel let the pieces fall to the ground, and grinned at Hart.

'You can't stop me. No one can stop me now. Time is helpless, and the Galleries are unprotected. I'll set the Gallery of Bone on fire, and let the heat from the flames melt the Gallery of Frost. Shadows Fall is dead. Not a

502

single living soul remains amid the ruins. The Wild Childe killed them all, and then they killed each other. You are the only survivors. I allowed you to get this far; I wanted someone here as witnesses to my triumph. In a moment I will kill Time, and then there will be no past, no present, no future; only an endless now, cut off from God, to do with as I choose for all eternity. And all the world will suffer as it never has before.'

And then the Forever Door was suddenly in the room with them, and everything changed. The angel's mood of despair was swept aside as though by a cool, refreshing breeze, and the room was suddenly alive with prospects and possibilities. The Door stood alone, unsupported, an enigmatic blank slate waiting to be written on. The angel stared at the Forever Door, struck dumb by an event he had neither planned for nor anticipated, and then he whirled and glared at the others.

'I didn't bring that here. Who dares bring that here? Send it away!'

James Hart looked at the Forever Door, and it spoke to him on a level he'd never known before; speaking directly to the part of him that was descended from Time, and finally he understood what he had to do, what he'd been brought back to Shadows Fall to do. His purpose, his destiny, and the town's.

'It's not your time come round,' he said to the fallen angel, almost casually. 'This is my time. Time for me to do what I was born to do. You never did understand what the Forever Door really is. The Warriors almost had it right. They thought it was access to God. It is, in a way, but it's more than that. Much more. The Forever Door existed so that the living might have access to what lies beyond life, but that was only part of its intent. I'm the last component in a centuries-long equation; I'm going to open the Door all the way and keep it open, so that all those who have left the world and passed on can come back through the Door, to rejoin the living. Death shall no longer have any hold over the living, nor any victory.

Don't look so surprised. A door, by its very nature, has always been an entrance as well as an exit.'

'No,' said the angel. 'No; I won't let you! You can't stop me. Neither the living nor the dead can have power over me. I was promised this!'

'Should have read the small print,' said Hart.

'I'll stop you! I'll kill you!'

The fallen angel started towards Hart, and Ash stepped forward to block his way. 'I don't think so. To get to him, you've got to get past me. And since, technically speaking, I'm neither living nor dead, I have a feeling you are in deep trouble. In the material world, you're bound by material rules. Which means, I'm going to kick your ass. That's what I came back for.'

The angel laughed harshly, and threw himself at Ash, who fell back a pace and then wrestled with the angel, calling up all his unnatural strength. They stamped back and forth, surging this way and that, and then the angel broke free and knocked Ash to the ground. He kicked the angel's feet out from under him, and the two of them struggled together on the floor. The angel pinned Ash on his back, knelt on his chest, took a firm hold with both hands and ripped Ash's head from his shoulders. Rhea screamed. The angel laughed, and tossed the head to her so that it rolled to a halt by her feet. The eyes glared unblinkingly at the corrupt angel, who started to get up, and then stopped abruptly as Ash's headless body wrapped its arms tightly around him.

Hart put them both out of his mind, and concentrated on what the Forever Door was saying to him. He could open the Door, but it was going to take every bit of power he had. He smiled wryly. He'd never wanted it anyway. He reached inside himself, and it was the simplest thing in the world to release all his power in one great outpouring. The fallen angel cried out in rage and dismay, but it was too late. Ash had distracted him just long enough. The Forever Door swung slowly open, and a brilliant light spilled out into the room. The angel shrank back, turning his face away from the light. And through the Door, striding confidently and freely, came Madeleine Kresh, not Mad any longer. She walked up to Morrison and smiled at him. He looked numbly back at her, wanting so much to believe in her, but not daring to touch her. She laughed and crushed him to her in her muscular arms.

The Door swung wide open, and the light flared up, pushing the dark boundaries of the room further and further back until it seemed they were all standing on a vast open plain. Jack Fetch walked through the Door, bowed deeply to Hart, and then crossed over to bow and kneel to a suddenly adult Time, who clapped the scarecrow forgivingly on the shoulder. And behind him came Sheriff Richard Erikson, with his Deputies Lewis and Collins. They went to join Rhea and Ash, now fully restored by the light. They all knew without having to be told that he was no longer a revenant, but alive once more.

Suzanne Dubois and Polly Cousins tripped through the Door together, giggling at the expressions on everyone's faces. Polly went to Hart, and they hugged each other silently for a long moment, Friend wrapped around both their shoulders. Doctor Mirren came next, along with the Warrior Leader William Royce, both shaking their heads ruefully at how wrong they'd been. Lester Gold, the Mystery Avenger, young again, walked arm in arm with a revitalized Father Callahan. Derek and Clive Manderville walked in together, slapping each other's shoulders and exchanging cheerful insults. And behind them came Bruin Bear and the Sea Goat and Peter Caulder and Scottie the Wee Terror, and behind them came Oberon and Titania and Puck, perfect at last. The dead were alive again, all hurts healed, all souls soothed, ready for whatever their strange new world might offer.

The hosts of Faerie strode through the widening Door, followed by all the townspeople of Shadows Fall and all the Warriors of the Cross, and still people came streaming through the Door and out on to the limitless plain of light. James Hart found his mother and father again, and Time

505

found his lost love. Parents were reunited with lost children, lovers with sweethearts, friends with enemies, all old scores forgotten and forgiven.

Angels were everywhere, blazing bright in the unending dawn, their song filling all the world. No one noticed the fallen angel shrinking slowly smaller and smaller, made insignificant by the glory of the light, until only a tiny shadow remained, to be picked up and comforted by the archangel Michael.

And still they came surging through the Door, in numbers beyond counting. All the dead of all the world, spilling out on to a plain without end. All who had ever died returned now from that undiscovered country, to walk with all the living in a new world, where all that was old would be made new again, where death would be but a memory, and where things would be very different, this time. Someone cleared His throat, and everyone turned to look.

The shadows had fallen, all prophecies fulfilled, and the light was everywhere.